FANGS

ALSO EDITED BY OTTO PENZLER

The Black Lizard Big Book of Pulps

The Vampire Archives

Agents of Treachery

Bloodsuckers

FANGS

◆◆◆

The Vampire Archives

VOLUME 2

EDITED AND WITH AN INTRODUCTION BY

OTTO PENZLER

VINTAGE CRIME BLACK LIZARD
VINTAGE BOOKS
A Division of Random House, Inc.
New York

A VINTAGE CRIME/BLACK LIZARD ORIGINAL, AUGUST 2010

The Library of Congress has cataloged *The Vampire Archives* as follows:
The vampire archives / edited by Otto Penzler.
p. cm.
1. Vampires—Fiction. 2. Horror tales, American. I. Penzler, Otto.
PS648.V35V25 2009
813'.0873808375—dc22
2009008864

ISBN: 978-0-307-74185-1

Book design by Debbie Glasserman

www.vintagebooks.com

Printed in the United States of America
10 9 8 7 6 5 4 3 2 1

Contents

Introduction

♦♦♦

OTTO PENZLER

While Bram Stoker's outstanding Victorian novel *Dracula* is certainly the most famous vampire story, it is not the first, having been preceded by John Polidori's *The Vampyre* (1816). This story was invented in perhaps the most significant single moment in the history of supernatural literature. As Gordon Lord Byron read "Christabel," Samuel Taylor Coleridge's vampire poem, to his friend Percy Bysshe Shelley, his wife, Mary Wollstonecraft Shelley, and their physician, Dr. Polidori, he challenged the group to come up with an equally frightening story. Mary Shelley conceived the story of *Frankenstein* that night, and Polidori, clearly an untalented hack, was inspired to write the first English-language vampire story which is, alas, far too tedious to include in this collection.

None of these works to any significant degree inspired Stoker to write *Dracula*, an honor that fell to the great author of macabre fiction, Sheridan Le Fanu, whose novelette *Carmilla* (1870) featured a lesbian vampire with the ability to transform herself into a gigantic cat, scandalizing Victorian readers.

The great gothic tradition of ruined castles and abbeys whose rooms and crypts serve as resting places for vampires is well represented in this volume. There are numerous spires, clouds passing in front of full moons, handsome men in full evening dress coming to bite the necks of beautiful and innocent young women in the dead of night, and coffin lids being raised to reveal their horrible residents.

But vampires come in many guises, and they are here, too. Some that look pretty much like the rest of us, some who have frustrating, even occasionally humorous difficulties, and some who are not interested in blood at all, merely wanting to suck the life out of their victims in a metaphorical way. There are stories here by men and women, from every literary era of the past century and a half, right up to the most talented writers of the present day. There are familiar classic stories here, and a few that you are unlikely to have encountered previously.

No matter whether you decide to approach the reading of this tome in small bites or as a gigantic feast, I hope it provides you with a bloody good read.

FANGS

◆◆◆

DOWN AMONG THE DEAD MEN

◆◆◆

GARDNER DOZOIS AND JACK DANN

Bruckman first discovered that Wernecke was a vampire when they went to the quarry that morning.

He was bending down to pick up a large rock when he thought he heard something in the gully nearby. He looked around and saw Wernecke huddled over a *Musselmänn,* one of the walking dead, a new man who had not been able to wake up to the terrible reality of the camp.

"Do you need any help?" Bruckman asked Wernecke in a low voice.

Wernecke looked up, startled, and covered his mouth with his hand, as if he were signing to Bruckman to be quiet.

But Bruckman was certain that he had glimpsed blood smeared on Wernecke's mouth. "The Musselmänn, is he alive?" Wernecke had often risked his own life to save one or another of the men in his barracks. But to risk one's life for a Musselmänn? "What's wrong?"

"Get away."

All right, Bruckman thought. Best to leave him alone. He looked pale, perhaps it was typhus. The guards were working him hard enough, and Wernecke was older than the rest of the men in the work gang. Let him sit for a moment and rest. But what about that blood? . . .

"Hey, you, what are you doing?" one of the young SS guards shouted to Bruckman.

Bruckman picked up the rock and, as if he had not heard the guard, began to walk away from the gully, toward the rusty brown cart on the tracks that led back to the barbed-wire fence of the camp. He would try to draw the guard's attention away from Wernecke.

But the guard shouted at him to halt. "Were you taking a little rest, is that it?" he asked, and Bruckman tensed, ready for a beating. This guard was new, neatly and cleanly dressed—and an unknown quantity. He walked over to the gully and, seeing Wernecke and the Musselmänn, said, "Aha, so your friend is taking care of the sick." He motioned Bruckman to follow him into the gully.

Bruckman had done the unpardonable—he had brought it on Wernecke. He swore at himself. He had been in this camp long enough to know to keep his mouth shut.

The guard kicked Wernecke sharply in the ribs. "I want you to put the Musselmänn in the cart. Now!" He kicked Wernecke again, as if as an afterthought. Wernecke groaned, but got to his feet. "Help him put the Musselmänn in the cart," the guard said to Bruckman; then he smiled and drew a circle in the air—the sign of smoke, the smoke which rose from the tall gray chimneys behind them. This Musselmänn would be in the oven within an hour, his ashes soon to be floating in the hot, stale air, as if they were the very particles of his soul.

Wernecke kicked the Musselmänn, and the guard chuckled, waved to another guard who had been watching, and stepped back a few feet. He stood with his hands on his hips. "Come on, dead man, get up or you're going to die in the oven," Wernecke whispered as he tried to pull the man to his feet. Bruckman supported the unsteady Musselmänn, who began to wail softly. Wernecke slapped him hard. "Do you want to live, Musselmänn? Do you want to see your family again, feel the touch of a woman, smell grass after it's been mowed? Then *move.*" The Musselmänn shambled forward between Wernecke and Bruckman. "You're dead, aren't you, Musselmänn," goaded Wernecke. "As dead as your father and mother, as dead as your sweet wife, if you ever had one, aren't you? Dead!"

The Musselmänn groaned, shook his head, and whispered, "Not dead, my wife . . ."

"Ah, it talks," Wernecke said, loud enough so the guard walking a step behind them could hear. "Do you have a name, corpse?"

"Josef, and I'm not a Musselmänn."

"The corpse says he's alive," Wernecke said, again loud enough for the SS guard to hear. Then in a whisper, he said, "Josef, if you're not a Musselmänn, then you must work now, do you understand?" Josef tripped, and Bruckman caught him. "Let him be," said Wernecke. "Let him walk to the cart himself."

"Not the cart," Josef mumbled. "Not to die, not—"

"Then get down and pick up stones, show the fart-eating guard you can work."

"Can't. I'm sick, I'm . . ."

"Musselmänn!"

Josef bent down, fell to his knees, but took hold of a stone and stood up.

"You see," Wernecke said to the guard, "it's not dead yet. It can still work."

"I told you to carry him to the cart, didn't I," the guard said petulantly.

"Show him you can work," Wernecke said to Josef, "or you'll surely be smoke."

And Josef stumbled away from Wernecke and Bruckman, leaning forward, as if following the rock he was carrying.

"Bring him *back*!" shouted the guard, but his attention was distracted from Josef by some other prisoners, who, sensing the trouble, began to mill about. One of the other guards began to shout and kick at the men on the periphery, and the new guard joined him. For the moment, he had forgotten about Josef.

"Let's get to work, lest they notice us again," Wernecke said.

"I'm sorry that I—"

Wernecke laughed and made a fluttering gesture with his hand—smoke rising. "It's all hazard, my friend. All luck." Again the laugh. "It was a venial sin," and his face seemed to darken. "Never do it again, though, lest I think of you as bad luck."

"Carl, are you all right?" Bruckman asked. "I noticed some blood when—"

"Do the sores on your feet bleed in the morning?" Wernecke countered angrily. Bruckman nodded, feeling foolish and embarrassed. "And so it is with my gums. Now go away, unlucky one, and let me live."

At dusk, the guards broke the hypnosis of lifting and grunting and sweating and formed the prisoners into ranks. They marched back to the camp through the fields, beside the railroad tracks, the electrified wire, conical towers, and into the main gate of the camp.

Josef walked beside them, but he kept stumbling, as he was once again slipping back into death, becoming a Musselmänn. Wernecke helped him walk, pushed him along. "We should let this man become dead," Wernecke said to Bruckman.

Bruckman only nodded, but he felt a chill sweep over

his sweating back. He was seeing Wernecke's face again as it was for that instant in the morning. Smeared with blood.

Yes, Bruckman thought, we should let the Musselmänn become dead. We should all be dead. . . .

Wernecke served up the lukewarm water with bits of spoiled turnip floating on the top, what passed as soup for the prisoners. Everyone sat or kneeled on the rough-planked floor, as there were no chairs.

Bruckman ate his portion, counting the sips and bites, forcing himself to take his time. Later, he would take a very small bite of the bread he had in his pocket. He always saved a small morsel of food for later—in the endless world of the camp, he had learned to give himself things to look forward to. Better to dream of bread than to get lost in the present. That was the fate of the Musselmänner.

But he always dreamed of food. Hunger was with him every moment of the day and night. Those times when he actually ate were in a way the most difficult, for there was never enough to satisfy him. There was the taste of softness in his mouth, and then in an instant it was gone. The emptiness took the form of pain—it *hurt* to eat. For bread, he thought, he would have killed his father, or his wife. God forgive me, and he watched Wernecke—Wernecke, who had shared his bread with him, who had died a little so he could live. He's a better man than I, Bruckman thought.

It was dim inside the barracks. A bare light bulb hung from the ceiling and cast sharp shadows across the cavernous room. Two tiers of five-foot-deep shelves ran around the room on three sides, bare wooden shelves where the men slept without blankets or mattresses. Set high in the northern wall was a slatted window, which let in the stark white light of the kliegs. Outside, the lights turned the grounds into a deathly imitation of day; only inside the barracks was it night.

"Do you know what tonight is, my friends?" Wernecke asked. He sat in the far corner of the room with Josef, who, hour by hour, was reverting back into a Musselmänn. Wernecke's face looked hollow and drawn in the light from the window and the light bulb; his eyes were deep-set and his face was long with deep creases running from his nose to the corners of his thin mouth. His hair was black, and even since Bruckman had known him, quite a bit of it had fallen out. He was a very tall man, almost six feet four, and that made him stand out in a crowd, which was dangerous in a death camp. But Wernecke had his own secret ways of blending with the crowd, of making himself invisible.

"No, tell us what tonight is," crazy old Bohme said. That men such as Bohme could survive was a miracle—or, as Bruckman thought—a testament to men such as Wernecke who somehow found the strength to help the others live.

"It's Passover," Wernecke said.

"How does he know that?" someone mumbled, but it didn't matter how Wernecke knew because he *knew*—even if it really wasn't Passover by the calendar. In this dimly lit barrack, it *was* Passover, the feast of freedom, the time of thanksgiving.

"But how can we have Passover without a *seder*?" asked Bohme. "We don't even have any *matzoh*," he whined.

"Nor do we have candles, or a silver cup for Elijah, or the shankbone, or *haroset*—nor would I make a *seder* over the *traif* the Nazis are so generous in giving us," replied Wernecke with a smile. "But we can pray, can't we? And when we all get out of here, when we're in our own homes in the coming year with God's help, then we'll have twice as much food—two *afikomens*, a bottle of wine for Elijah, and the *haggadahs* that our fathers and our fathers' fathers used."

It *was* Passover.

"Isadore, do you remember the four questions?" Wernecke asked Bruckman.

And Bruckman heard himself speaking. He was twelve years old again at the long table beside his father, who sat in the seat of honor. To sit next to him was itself an honor. "How does this night differ from all other nights? On all other nights we eat bread and *matzoh*; why on this night do we eat only *matzoh*?

"M'a nisht' ana halylah hazeah. . . ."

Sleep would not come to Bruckman that night, although he was so tired that he felt as if the marrow of his bones had been sucked away and replaced with lead.

He lay there in the semidarkness, feeling his muscles ache, feeling the acid biting of his hunger. Usually he was numb enough with exhaustion that he could empty his mind, close himself down, and fall rapidly into oblivion, but not tonight. Tonight he was noticing things again, his surroundings were getting through to him again, in a way that they had not since he had been new in camp. It was smotheringly hot, and the air was filled with the stinks of death and sweat and fever, of stale urine and drying blood. The sleepers thrashed and turned, as though they fought with sleep, and as they slept, many of them talked or muttered or screamed aloud; they lived other lives in their dreams, intensely compressed lives dreamed quickly, for soon it would be dawn, and once more they would be thrust into hell. Cramped in the midst of them, sleepers squeezed in all around him, it suddenly seemed to Bruckman that these pallid white bodies were already dead, that he was sleeping in a graveyard. Suddenly it was the boxcar again. And his wife Miriam was dead again, dead and rotting unburied. . . .

Resolutely, Bruckman emptied his mind. He felt feverish and shaky, and wondered if the typhus were coming back, but he couldn't afford to worry about it. Those who couldn't sleep couldn't survive. Regulate your breathing, force your muscles to relax, don't think. Don't think.

For some reason, after he had managed to banish even the memory of his dead wife, he couldn't shake the image of the blood on Wernecke's mouth.

There were other images mixed in with it: Wernecke's uplifted arms and upturned face as he led them in prayer; the pale strained face of the stumbling Musselmänn; Wernecke looking up, startled, as he crouched over Josef . . . but it was the blood to which Bruckman's feverish thoughts returned, and he pictured it again and again as he lay in the rustling, fart-smelling darkness, the watery sheen of blood over Wernecke's lips, the tarry trickle of blood in the corner of his mouth, like a tiny scarlet worm. . . .

Just then a shadow crossed in front of the window, silhouetted blackly for an instant against the harsh white glare, and Bruckman knew from the shadow's height and its curious forward stoop that it was Wernecke.

Where could he be going? Sometimes a prisoner would be unable to wait until morning, when the Germans would let them out to visit the slit-trench latrine again, and would slink shamefacedly into a far corner to piss against a wall, but surely Wernecke was too much of an old hand for that. . . . Most of the prisoners slept on the sleeping platforms, especially during the cold nights when they would huddle together for warmth, but sometimes during the hot weather, people would drift away and sleep on the floor instead; Bruckman had been thinking of doing that, as the jostling bodies of the sleepers around him helped to keep him from sleep. Perhaps Wernecke, who always had trouble fitting into the cramped sleeping niches, was merely looking for a place where he could lie down and stretch his legs. . . .

Then Bruckman remembered that Josef had fallen asleep in the corner of the room where Wernecke had sat and prayed, and that they had left him there alone.

Without knowing why, Bruckman found himself on his feet. As silently as the ghost he sometimes felt he was becoming, he walked across the room in the direction Wernecke had gone, not understanding what he was doing nor why he was doing it. The face of the Musselmänn, Josef, seemed to float behind his eyes. Bruckman's feet hurt, and he knew, without looking, that they were bleeding, leaving faint tracks behind him. It was dimmer here in the far corner, away from the window, but Bruckman knew that he must be near the wall by now, and he stopped to let his eyes readjust.

When his eyes had adapted to the dimmer light, he saw Josef sitting on the floor, propped up against the wall. Wernecke was hunched over the Musselmänn. Kissing him. One of Josef's hands was tangled in Wernecke's thinning hair.

Before Bruckman could react—such things had been known to happen once or twice before, although it shocked him deeply that *Wernecke* would be involved in such filth—Josef released his grip on Wernecke's hair. Josef's upraised arm fell limply to the side, his hand hitting the floor with a muffled but solid impact that should have been painful—but Josef made no sound.

Wernecke straightened up and turned around. Stronger light from the high window caught him as he straightened to his full height, momentarily illuminating his face.

Wernecke's mouth was smeared with blood.

"My God," Bruckman cried.

Startled, Wernecke flinched, then took two quick steps forward and seized Bruckman by the arm. "Quiet!" Wernecke hissed. His fingers were cold and hard.

At that moment, as though Wernecke's sudden movement were a cue, Josef began to slip down sideways along the wall. As Wernecke and Bruckman watched, both momentarily riveted by the sight, Josef toppled over to the floor, his head striking against the floorboards with a sound such as a dropped melon might make. He had made no attempt to break his fall or cushion his head, and lay now unmoving.

"My *God,*" Bruckman said again.

"Quiet, I'll explain," Wernecke said, his lips still glazed with the Musselmänn blood. "Do you want to ruin us all? For the love of God, be *quiet.*"

But Bruckman had shaken free of Wernecke's grip and crossed to kneel by Josef, leaning over him as Wernecke had done, placing a hand flat on Josef's chest for a moment, then touching the side of Josef's neck. Bruckman looked slowly up at Wernecke. "He's dead," Bruckman said, more quietly.

Wernecke squatted on the other side of Josef's body, and the rest of their conversation was carried out in whispers over Josef's chest, like friends conversing at the sickbed of another friend who has finally fallen into a fitful doze.

"Yes, he's dead," Wernecke said. "He was dead yesterday, wasn't he? Today he had just stopped walking." His eyes were hidden here, in the deeper shadow nearer to the floor, but there was still enough light for Bruckman to see that Wernecke had wiped his lips clean. Or licked them clean, Bruckman thought, and felt a spasm of nausea go through him.

"But *you,*" Bruckman said, haltingly. "You were . . ."

"Drinking his blood?" Wernecke said. "Yes, I was drinking his blood."

Bruckman's mind was numb. He couldn't deal with this, he couldn't understand it at all. "But *why,* Eduard? Why?"

"To live, of course. Why do any of us do anything here? If I am to live, I must have blood. Without it, I'd face a death even more certain than that doled out by the Nazis."

Bruckman opened and closed his mouth, but no sound came out, as if the words he wished to speak were too jagged to fit through his throat. At last he managed to croak, "A vampire? You're a vampire? Like in the old stories?"

Wernecke said calmly, "Men would call me that." He paused, then nodded. "Yes, that's what men would call me. . . . As though they can understand something simply by giving it a name."

"But Eduard," Bruckman said weakly, almost petulantly. "The Musselmänn . . ."

"Remember that he *was* a Musselmänn," Wernecke said, leaning forward and speaking more fiercely. "His strength was going, he was sinking. He would have been dead by morning anyway. I took from him something that he no longer needed, but that I needed in order to live. Does it matter? Starving men in lifeboats have eaten the bodies of their dead companions in order to live. Is what I've done any worse than that?"

"But he didn't just die. You *killed* him. . . ."

Wernecke was silent for a moment, and then said, quietly, "What better thing could I have done for him? I won't apologize for what I do, Isadore; I do what I have to do to live. Usually I take only a little blood from a number of men, just enough to survive. And that's fair, isn't it? Haven't I given food to others, to help them survive? To you, Isadore? Only very rarely do I take more than a minimum from any one man, although I'm weak and hungry all the time, believe me. And never have I drained the life from someone who wished to live. Instead I've helped them fight for survival in every way I can, you know that."

He reached out as though to touch Bruckman, then thought better of it and put his hand back on his own knee. He shook his head. "But these Musselmänner, the ones who have given up on life, the walking dead—it is a favor to them to take them, to give them the solace of death. Can you honestly say it is not, *here*? That it is better for them to walk around while they are dead, being beaten and abused by the Nazis until their bodies cannot go on, and then to be thrown into the ovens and burned like trash? Can you say that? Would *they* say that, if they knew what was going on? Or would they thank me?"

Wernecke suddenly stood up, and Bruckman stood up with him. As Wernecke's face came again into the stronger light, Bruckman could see that his eyes had filled with tears. "You have lived under the Nazis," Wernecke said. "Can you really call me a monster? Aren't I still a Jew, whatever else I might be? Aren't I *here*, in a death camp? Aren't I being persecuted, too, as much as any other? Aren't I in as much danger as anyone else? If I'm not a Jew, then tell the Nazis—they seem to think so." He paused for a moment, and then smiled wryly. "And forget your superstitious boogey tales. I'm no night spirit. If I could turn myself into a bat and fly away from here, I would have done it long before now, believe me."

Bruckman smiled reflectively, then grimaced. The two men avoided each other's eyes, Bruckman looking at the floor, and there was an uneasy silence, punctured only by the sighing and moaning of the sleepers on the other side of the cabin. Then, without looking up, in tacit surrender, Bruckman said, "What about *him*? The Nazis will find the body and cause trouble. . . ."

"Don't worry," Wernecke said. "There are no obvious marks. And nobody performs autopsies in a death camp. To the Nazis, he'll be just another Jew who had died of the heat, or from starvation or sickness, or from a broken heart."

Bruckman raised his head then and they stared eye to eye for a moment. Even knowing what he knew, Bruckman found it hard to see Wernecke as anything other than what he appeared to be: an aging, balding Jew, stooping and thin, with sad eyes and a tired, compassionate face.

"Well, then, Isadore," Wernecke said at last, matter-of-factly. "My life is in your hands. I will not be indelicate enough to remind you of how many times your life has been in mine."

Then he was gone, walking back toward the sleeping platforms, a shadow soon lost among other shadows.

Bruckman stood by himself in the gloom for a long time, and then followed him. It took all of his will not to look back over his shoulder at the corner where Josef lay, and even so Bruckman imagined that he could feel Josef's dead eyes watching him, watching reproachfully as he walked away abandoning Josef to the cold and isolated company of the dead.

Bruckman got no more sleep that night, and in the

morning, when the Nazis shattered the gray predawn stillness by bursting into the shack with shouts and shrill whistles and barking police dogs, he felt as if he were a thousand years old.

They were formed into two lines, shivering in the raw morning air, and marched off to the quarry. The clammy dawn mist had yet to burn off, and marching through it, through a white shadowless void, with only the back of the man in front of him dimly visible, Bruckman felt more than ever like a ghost, suspended bodyless in some limbo between Heaven and Earth. Only the bite of pebbles and cinders into his raw, bleeding feet kept him anchored to the world, and he clung to the pain as a lifeline, fighting to shake off a feeling of numbness and unreality. However strange, however outré, the events of the previous night had *happened*. To doubt it, to wonder now if it had all been a feverish dream brought on by starvation and exhaustion, was to take the first step on the road to becoming a Musselmänn.

Wernecke is a vampire, he told himself. That was the harsh, unyielding reality that, like the reality of the camp itself, must be faced. Was it any more surreal, any more impossible than the nightmare around them? He must forget the tales that his grandmother had told him as a boy, "boogey tales" as Wernecke himself had called them, half-remembered tales that turned his knees to water whenever he thought of the blood smeared on Wernecke's mouth, whenever he thought of Wernecke's eyes watching him in the dark. . . .

"Wake up, Jew!" the guard alongside him snarled, whacking him lightly on the arm with his rifle butt. Bruckman stumbled, managed to stay upright and keep going. Yes, he thought, wake up. Wake up to the reality of this, just as you once had to wake up to the reality of the camp. It was just one more unpleasant fact he would have to adapt to, learn to deal with. . . .

Deal with how? he thought, and shivered.

By the time they reached the quarry, the mist had burned off, swirling past them in rags and tatters, and it was already beginning to get hot. There was Wernecke, his balding head gleaming dully in the harsh morning light. He didn't dissolve in the sunlight—there was one boogey tale disproved. . . .

They set to work, like golems, like ragtag clockwork automatons.

Lack of sleep had drained what small reserves of strength Bruckman had, and the work was very hard for him that day. He had learned long ago all the tricks of timing and misdirection, the safe way to snatch short moments of rest, the ways to do a minimum of work with the maximum display of effort, the ways to keep the guards from noticing you, to fade into the faceless crowd of prisoners and not be singled out, but today his head was muzzy and slow, and none of the tricks seemed to work.

His body felt like a sheet of glass, fragile, ready to shatter into dust, and the painful, arthritic slowness of his movements got him first shouted at, and then knocked down. The guard kicked him twice for good measure before he could get up.

When Bruckman had climbed back to his feet again, he saw that Wernecke was watching him, face blank, eyes expressionless, a look that could have meant anything at all.

Bruckman felt the blood trickling from the corner of his mouth and thought, *the blood . . . he's watching the blood* . . . and once again he shivered.

Somehow, Bruckman forced himself to work faster,

and although his muscles blazed with pain, he wasn't hit again, and the day passed.

When they formed up to go back to camp, Bruckman, almost unconsciously, made sure that he was in a different line than Wernecke.

That night in the cabin, Bruckman watched as Wernecke talked with the other men, here trying to help a new man named Melnick—no more than a boy—adjust to the dreadful reality of the camp, there exhorting someone who was slipping into despair to live and spite his tormentors, joking with old hands in the flat, black, bitter way that passed for humor among them, eliciting a wan smile or occasionally even a laugh from them, finally leading them all in prayer again, his strong, calm voice raised in the ancient words, giving meaning to those words again. . . .

He keeps us together, Bruckman thought, he keeps us going. Without him, we wouldn't last a week. Surely that's worth a little blood, a bit from each man, not even enough to hurt. . . . Surely they wouldn't even begrudge him it, if they knew and really understood. . . . No, he is a good man, better than the rest of us, in spite of his terrible affliction.

Bruckman had been avoiding Wernecke's eyes, hadn't spoken to him at all that day, and suddenly felt a wave of shame go through him at the thought of how shabbily he had been treating his friend. Yes, his friend, regardless, the man who had saved his life. . . . Deliberately, he caught Wernecke's eyes, and nodded, and then somewhat sheepishly, smiled. After a moment, Wernecke smiled back, and Bruckman felt a spreading warmth and relief uncoil his guts. Everything was going to be all right, as all right as it could be, here. . . .

Nevertheless, as soon as the inside lights clicked off

that night, and Bruckman found himself lying alone in the darkness, his flesh began to crawl.

He had been unable to keep his eyes open a moment before, but now, in the sudden darkness, he found himself tensely and tickingly awake. Where was Wernecke? What was he doing, whom was he visiting tonight? Was he out there in the darkness even now, creeping closer, creeping nearer? . . . Stop it, Bruckman told himself uneasily, forget the boogey tales. This is your friend, a good man, not a monster. . . . But he couldn't control the fear that made the small hairs on his arms stand bristlingly erect, couldn't stop the grisly images from coming. . . .

Wernecke's eyes, gleaming in the darkness . . . was the blood already glistening on Wernecke's lips, as he drank? . . . The thought of the blood staining Wernecke's yellowing teeth made Bruckman cold and nauseous, but the image that he couldn't get out of his mind tonight was an image of Josef toppling over in that sinister boneless way, striking his head against the floor. . . . Bruckman had seen people die in many more gruesome ways during this time at the camp, seen people shot, beaten to death, seen them die in convulsions from high fevers or cough their lungs up in bloody tatters from pneumonia, seen them hanging like charred-black scarecrows from the electrified fences, seen them torn apart by dogs . . . but somehow it was Josef's soft, passive, almost restful slumping into death that bothered him. That, and the obscene limpness of Josef's limbs as he sprawled there like a discarded rag doll, his pale and haggard face gleaming reproachfully in the dark. . . .

When Bruckman could stand it no longer, he got shakily to his feet and moved off through the shadows, once again not knowing where he was going or what he was going to do, but drawn forward by some obscure instinct he himself did not understand. This time he went cautiously, feeling his way and trying to be silent, expecting every second to see Wernecke's coal-black shadow rise up before him.

He paused, a faint noise scratching at his ears, then went on again, even more cautiously, crouching low, almost crawling across the grimy floor.

Whatever instinct had guided him—sounds heard and interpreted subliminally, perhaps?—it had timed his arrival well. Wernecke had someone down on the floor there, perhaps someone he seized and dragged away from the huddled mass of sleepers on one of the sleeping platforms, someone from the outer edge of bodies whose presence would not be missed, or perhaps someone who had gone to sleep on the floor, seeking solitude or greater comfort.

Whoever he was, he struggled in Wernecke's grip, but Wernecke handled him easily, almost negligently, in a manner that spoke of great physical power. Bruckman could hear the man trying to scream, but Wernecke had one hand on his throat, half-throttling him, and all that would come out was a sort of whistling gasp. The man thrashed in Wernecke's hands like a kite in a child's hands flapping in the wind, and, moving deliberately, Wernecke smoothed him out like a kite, pressing him slowly flat on the floor.

Then Wernecke bent over him, and lowered his mouth to his throat.

Bruckman watched in horror, knowing that he should shout, scream, try to rouse the other prisoners, but somehow unable to move, unable to make his mouth open, his lungs pump. He was paralyzed by fear, like a rabbit in the presence of a predator, a terror sharper and more intense than any he'd ever known.

The man's struggles were growing weaker, and Wernecke must have eased up some on the throttling pressure of his hand, because the man moaned "Don't . . . please don't . . ." in a weaker, slurred voice. The man had been drumming his fists against Wernecke's back and sides, but now the tempo of the drumming slowed, slowed, and then stopped, the man's arms falling laxly to the floor. "Don't . . ." the man whispered; he groaned and muttered incomprehensively for a moment or two longer, then became silent. The silence stretched out for a minute, two, three, and Wernecke still crouched over his victim, who was now not moving at all. . . .

Wernecke stirred, a kind of shudder going through him, like a cat stretching. He stood up. His face became visible as he straightened up into the full light from the window, and there was blood on it, glistening black under the harsh glare of the kliegs. As Bruckman watched, Wernecke began to lick his lips clean, his tongue, also black in this light, sliding like some sort of sinuous ebony snake around the rim of his mouth, darting and probing for the last lingering drops. . . .

How smug he looks, Bruckman thought, like a cat who has found the cream, and the anger that flashed through him at the thought enabled him to move and speak again. "Wernecke," he said harshly.

Wernecke glanced casually in his direction. "You again, Isadore?" Wernecke said. "Don't you ever sleep?" Wernecke spoke lazily, quizzically, without surprise, and Bruckman wondered if Wernecke had known all along that he was there. "Or do you just enjoy watching me?"

"Lies," Bruckman said. "You told me nothing but lies. Why did you bother?"

"You were excited," Wernecke said. "You had surprised me. It seemed best to tell you what you wanted to hear.

If it satisfied you, then that was an easy solution to the problem."

"Never have I drained the life from someone who wanted to live," Bruckman said bitterly, mimicking Wernecke. "Only a little from each man! My God—and I believed you! I even felt sorry for you!"

Wernecke shrugged. "Most of it was true. Usually I only take a little from each man, softly and carefully, so that they never know, so that in the morning they are only a little weaker than they would have been anyway. . . ."

"Like Josef?" Bruckman said angrily. "Like the poor devil you killed tonight?"

Wernecke shrugged again. "I have been careless the last few nights, I admit. But I need to build up my strength again." His eyes gleamed in the darkness. "Events are coming to a head here. Can't you feel it, Isadore, can't you sense it? Soon the war will be over, everyone knows that. Before then, this camp will be shut down, and the Nazis will move us back into the interior—either that, or kill us. I have grown weak here, and I will soon need all my strength to survive, to take whatever opportunity presents itself to escape. I *must* be ready. And so I have let myself drink deeply again, drink my fill for the first time in months. . . ." Wernecke licked his lips again, perhaps unconsciously, then smiled bleakly at Bruckman. "You don't appreciate my restraint, Isadore. You don't understand how hard it has been for me to hold back, to take only a little each night. You don't understand how much that restraint has cost me. . . ."

"You are gracious," Bruckman sneered.

Wernecke laughed. "No, but I am a rational man; I pride myself on that. You other prisoners were my only source of food, and I have had to be very careful to make sure that you would last. I have no access to the Nazis, after all. I am trapped here, a prisoner just like you, whatever else you may believe—and I have not only had to find ways to survive here in the camp, I have had to procure my own food as well! No shepherd has ever watched over his flock more tenderly than I."

"Is that all we are to you—sheep? Animals to be slaughtered?"

Wernecke smiled. "Precisely."

When he could control his voice enough to speak, Bruckman said, "You're worse than the Nazis."

"I hardly think so," Wernecke said quietly, and for a moment he looked tired, as though something unimaginably old and unutterably weary had looked out through his eyes. "This camp was built by the Nazis—it wasn't my doing. The Nazis sent you here—not I. The Nazis have tried to kill you every day since, in one way or another—and I have tried to keep you alive, even at some risk to myself. No one has more of a vested interest in the survival of his livestock than the farmer, after all, even if he does occasionally slaughter an inferior animal. I have given you food—"

"Food you had no use for yourself! You sacrificed nothing!"

"That's true, of course. But *you* needed it, remember that. Whatever my motives, I have helped you to survive here—you and many others. By doing so I also acted in my own self-interest, of course, but can you have experienced this camp and still believe in things like altruism? What difference does it make what my reason for helping was—I still helped you, didn't I?"

"Sophistries!" Bruckman said. "Rationalizations! You twist words to justify yourself, but you can't disguise what you really are—a monster!"

Wernecke smiled gently, as though Bruckman's words

amused him, and made as if to pass by, but Bruckman raised an arm to bar his way. They did not touch each other, but Wernecke stopped short, and a new quivering kind of tension sprung into existence in the air between them.

"I'll stop you," Bruckman said. "Somehow I'll stop you, I'll keep you from doing this terrible thing—"

"You'll do nothing," Wernecke said. His voice was hard and cold and flat, like a rock speaking. "What can you do? Tell the other prisoners? Who would believe you? They'd think you'd gone insane. Tell the *Nazis*, then?" Wernecke laughed harshly. "They'd think you'd gone crazy, too, and they'd take you to the hospital—and I don't have to tell you what your chances of getting out of there alive are, do I? No, you'll do *nothing*."

Wernecke took a step forward; his eyes were shiny and black and hard, like ice, like the pitiless eyes of a predatory bird, and Bruckman felt a sick rush of fear cut through his anger. Bruckman gave way, stepping backward involuntarily, and Wernecke pushed past him, seeming to brush him aside without touching him.

Once past, Wernecke turned to stare at Bruckman, and Bruckman had to summon up all the defiance that remained in him not to look uneasily away from Wernecke's agate-hard eyes. "You are the strongest and cleverest of all the other animals, Isadore," Wernecke said in a calm, conversational voice. "You have been useful to me. Every shepherd needs a good sheepdog. I still need you, to help me manage the others, and to help me keep them going long enough to serve my needs. This is the reason why I have taken so much time with you, instead of just killing you outright." He shrugged. "So let us both be rational about this—you leave me alone, Isadore, and I will leave you alone also. We will stay away from each other and look after our own affairs. Yes?"

"The others . . ." Bruckman said weakly.

"They must look after themselves," Wernecke said. He smiled, a thin and almost invisible motion of his lips. "What did I teach you, Isadore? Here everyone must look after themselves. What difference does it make what happens to the others? In a few weeks almost all of them will be dead anyway."

"You *are* a monster," Bruckman said.

"I'm not much different from you, Isadore. The strong survive, whatever the cost."

"I am *nothing* like you," Bruckman said, with loathing.

"No?" Wernecke asked, ironically, and moved away; within a few paces he was hobbling and stooping, vanishing into the shadows, once more the harmless old Jew.

Bruckman stood motionless for a moment, and then, moving slowly and reluctantly, he stepped across to where Wernecke's victim lay.

It was one of the new men Wernecke had been talking to earlier in the evening, and, of course, he was quite dead.

Shame and guilt took Bruckman then, emotions he thought he had forgotten—black and strong and bitter, they shook him by the throat the way Wernecke had shaken the new man.

Bruckman couldn't remember returning across the room to his sleeping platform, but suddenly he was there, lying on his back and staring into the stifling darkness, surrounded by the moaning, thrashing, stinking mass of sleepers. His hands were clasped protectively over his throat, although he couldn't remember putting them there, and he was shivering convulsively. How many mornings had he awoken with a dull ache in his neck, thinking it was no more than the habitual bodyaches and strained muscles they had all learned to take for granted? How many nights had Wernecke fed on *him*?

Every time Bruckman closed his eyes he would see Wernecke's face floating there in the luminous darkness behind his eyelids . . . Wernecke with his eyes half-closed, his face vulpine and cruel and satiated . . .Wernecke's face moving closer and closer to him, his eyes opening like black pits, his lips smiling back from his teeth . . . Wernecke's lips, sticky and red with blood . . . and then Bruckman would seem to feel the wet touch of Wernecke's lips on *his* throat, feel Wernecke's teeth biting into *his* flesh, and Bruckman's eyes would fly open again. Staring into the darkness. Nothing there. Nothing there *yet. . . .*

Dawn was a dirty gray imminence against the cabin window before Bruckman could force himself to lower his shielding arms from his throat, and once again he had not slept at all.

That day's work was a nightmare of pain and exhaustion for Bruckman, harder than anything he had known since his first few days at the camp. Somehow he forced himself to get up, somehow he stumbled outside and up the path to the quarry, seeming to float along high off the ground, his head a bloated balloon, his feet a thousand miles away at the end of boneless beanstalk legs he could barely control at all. Twice he fell, and was kicked several times before he could drag himself back to his feet and lurch forward again. The sun was coming up in front of them, a hard red disk in a sickly yellow sky, and to Bruckman it seemed to be a glazed and lidless eye staring dispassionately into the world to watch them flail and struggle and die, like the eye of a scientist peering into a laboratory maze.

He watched the disk of the sun as he stumbled towards it; it seemed to bob and shimmer with every painful step, expanding, swelling, and bloating until it swallowed the sky. . . .

Then he was picking up a rock, moaning with the effort, feeling the rough stone tear his hands. . . .

Reality began to slide away from Bruckman. There were long periods when the world was blank, and he would come slowly back to himself as if from a great distance, and hear his own voice speaking words that he could not understand, or keening mindlessly, or grunting in a hoarse, animalistic way, and he would find that his body was working mechanically, stooping and lifting and carrying, all without volition. . . .

A Musselmänn, Bruckman thought, I'm becoming a Musselmänn . . . and felt a chill of fear sweep through him. He fought to hold onto the world, afraid that the next time he slipped away from himself he would not come back, deliberately banging his hands into the rocks, cutting himself, clearing his head with pain.

The world steadied around him. A guard shouted a hoarse admonishment at him and slapped his rifle butt, and Bruckman forced himself to work faster, although he could not keep himself from weeping silently with the pain his movements cost him.

He discovered that Wernecke was watching him, and stared back defiantly, the bitter tears still runneling his dirty cheeks, thinking, *I won't become a Musselmänn for you, I won't make it easy for you, I won't provide another helpless victim for you. . . .* Wernecke met Bruckman's gaze for a moment, and then shrugged and turned away.

Bruckman bent for another stone, feeling the muscles in his back crack and the pain drive in like knives. What had Wernecke been thinking behind the blankness of his expressionless face? Had Wernecke, sensing weakness, marked Bruckman for his next victim? Had Wernecke been disappointed or dismayed by the strength of Bruckman's will to survive? Would Wernecke now settle upon someone else?

The morning passed, and Bruckman grew feverish again. He could feel the fever in his face, making his eyes feel sandy and hot, pulling the skin taut over his cheekbones, and he wondered how long he could manage to stay on his feet. To falter, to grow weak and insensible, was certain death; if the Nazis didn't kill him, Wernecke would. . . . Wernecke was out of sight now, on the other side of the quarry, but it seemed to Bruckman that Wernecke's hard and flinty eyes were everywhere, floating in the air around him, looking out momentarily from the back of a Nazi soldier's head, watching him from the dulled iron side of a quarry cart, peering at him from a dozen different angles. He bent ponderously for another rock, and when he had pried it up from the earth he found Wernecke's eyes beneath it, staring unblinkingly up at him from the damp and pallid soil. . . .

That afternoon there were great flashes of light on the eastern horizon, out across the endless flat expanse of the steppe, flares in rapid sequence that lit up the sullen gray sky, all without sound. The Nazi guards had gathered in a group, looking to the east and talking in subdued voices, ignoring the prisoners for the moment. For the first time Bruckman noticed how disheveled and unshaven the guards had become in the last few days, as though they had given up, as though they no longer cared. Their faces were strained and tight, and more than one of them seemed to be fascinated by the leaping fires on the distant edge of the world.

Melnick said that it was only a thunderstorm, but old Bohme said that it was an artillery battle being fought, and that that meant that the Russians were coming, that soon they would all be liberated.

Bohme grew so excited at the thought that he began shouting, "The Russians! It's the Russians! The Russians are coming to free us!" Dichstein, another one of the new prisoners, and Melnick tried to hush him, but Bohme continued to caper and shout—doing a grotesque kind of jig while he yelled and flapped his arms—until he had attracted the attention of the guards. Infuriated, two of the guards fell upon Bohme and beat him severely, striking him with their rifle butts with more than usual force, knocking him to the ground, continuing to flail at him and kick him while he was down, Bohme writhing like an injured worm under their stamping boots. They probably would have beaten Bohme to death on the spot, but Wernecke organized a distraction among some of the other prisoners, and when the guards moved away to deal with it, Wernecke helped Bohme to stand up and hobble away to the other side of the quarry, where the rest of the prisoners shielded him from sight with their bodies as best they could for the rest of the afternoon.

Something about the way Wernecke urged Bohme to his feet and helped him to limp and lurch away, something about the protective, possessive curve of Wernecke's arm around Bohme's shoulders, told Bruckman that Wernecke had selected his next victim.

That night Bruckman vomited up the meager and rancid meal that they were allowed, his stomach convulsing uncontrollably after the first few bites. Trembling with hunger and exhaustion and fever, he leaned against the wall and watched as Wernecke fussed over Bohme, nursing him as a man might nurse a sick child, talking gently to him, wiping away some of the blood that still oozed from the corner of Bohme's mouth, coaxing Bohme to drink a few sips of soup, finally arranging that Bohme should stretch out on the floor away from the sleeping platforms, where he would not be jostled by the others. . . .

As soon as the interior lights went out that night, Bruckman got up, crossed the floor quickly and unhesitantly, and lay down in the shadows near the spot where Bohme muttered and twitched and groaned.

Shivering, Bruckman lay in the darkness, the strong smell of the earth in his nostrils, waiting for Wernecke to come. . . .

In Bruckman's hand, held close to his chest, was a spoon that had been sharpened to a jagged needle point, a spoon he had stolen and begun to sharpen while he was still in a civilian prison in Cologne, so long ago that he almost couldn't remember, scraping it back and forth against the stone wall of his cell every night for hours, managing to keep it hidden on his person during the nightmarish ride in the sweltering boxcar, the first few terrible days at the camp, telling no one about it, not even Wernecke during the months when he'd thought of Wernecke as a kind of saint, keeping it hidden long after the possibility of escape had become too remote even to fantasize about, retaining it then more as a tangible link with the daydream country of his past than as a tool he ever actually hoped to employ, cherishing it almost as a holy relic, as a remnant of a vanished world that he otherwise might almost believe had never existed at all. . . .

And now that it was time to use it at last, he was almost reluctant to do so, to soil it with another man's blood. . . .

He fingered the spoon compulsively, turning it over and over; it was hard and smooth and cold, and he clenched it as tightly as he could, trying to ignore the fine tremoring of his hands.

He had to kill Wernecke. . . .

Nausea and an odd feeling of panic flashed through Bruckman at the thought, but there was no other choice, there was no other way. . . . He couldn't go on like this, his strength was failing; Wernecke was killing him, as surely as he had killed the others, just by keeping him from sleeping. . . . And as long as Wernecke lived, he would never be safe: Always there would be the chance that Wernecke would come for him, that Wernecke would strike as soon as his guard was down. . . . Would Wernecke scruple for a second to kill *him*, after all, if he thought that he could do it safely? . . . No, of course not. . . . Given the chance, Wernecke would kill him without a moment's further thought. . . . No, he must strike *first*. . . .

Bruckman licked his lips uneasily. Tonight. He had to kill Wernecke *tonight*. . . .

There was a stirring, a rustling: Someone was getting up, working his way free from the mass of sleepers on one of the platforms. A shadowy figure crossed the room toward Bruckman, and Bruckman tensed, reflexively running his thumb along the jagged end of the spoon, readying himself to rise, to strike—but at the last second, the figure veered aside and stumbled toward another corner. There was a sound like rain drumming on cloth; the man swayed there for a moment, mumbling, and then slowly returned to his pallet, dragging his feet, as if he had pissed his very life away against the wall. It was not Wernecke.

Bruckman eased himself back down to the floor, his heart seeming to shake his wasted body back and forth with the force of its beating. His hand was damp with sweat. He wiped it against his tattered pants, and then clutched the spoon again. . . .

Time seemed to stop. Bruckman waited, stretched out along the hard floorboards, the raw wood rasping his skin, dust clogging his mouth and nose, feeling as though he were already dead, a corpse laid out in the rough pine coffin, feeling eternity pile up on his chest like heavy clots of wet black earth. . . . Outside the hut, the kliegs blazed, banishing night, abolishing it, but here inside the hut it was night, here night survived, perhaps the only pocket of night remaining on a klieg-lit planet, the shafts of light that came in through the slatted windows only serving to accentuate the surrounding darkness, to make it greater and more puissant by comparison. . . . Here in the darkness, nothing ever changed . . . there was only the smothering heat, and the weight of eternal darkness, and the changeless moments that could not pass because there was nothing to differentiate them one from the other. . . .

Many times as he waited Bruckman's eyes would grow heavy and slowly close, but each time his eyes would spring open again at once, and he would find himself staring into the shadows for Wernecke. Sleep would no longer have him, it was a kingdom closed to him now; it spat him out each time he tried to enter it, just as his stomach now spat out the food he placed in it. . . .

The thought of food brought Bruckman to a sharper awareness, and there in the darkness he huddled around his hunger, momentarily forgetting everything else. Never had he been so hungry. . . . He thought of the food he had wasted earlier in the evening, and only the last few shreds of his self-control kept him from moaning aloud.

Bohme did moan aloud then, as though unease were contagious. As Bruckman glanced at him, Bohme said,

"Anya," in a clear calm voice; he mumbled a little, and then, a bit more loudly, said, "Tseitel, have you set the table yet?" and Bruckman realized that Bohme was no longer in the camp, that Bohme was back in Düsseldorf in the tiny apartment with his fat wife and his four healthy children, and Bruckman felt a pang of envy go through him, for Bohme, who had escaped.

It was at that moment that Bruckman realized that Wernecke was standing there, just beyond Bohme.

There had been no movement that Bruckman had seen. Wernecke had seemed to slowly materialize from the darkness, atom by atom, bit by incremental bit, until at some point he had been solid enough for his presence to register on Bruckman's consciousness, so that what had been only a shadow a moment before was now unmistakably Wernecke as well, however much a shadow it remained.

Bruckman's mouth went dry with terror, and it almost seemed that he could hear the voice of his dead grandmother whispering in his ears. Boogey tales . . . Wernecke had said *I'm no night spirit.* Remember that he had said that. . . .

Wernecke was almost close enough to touch. He was staring down at Bohme; his face, lit by a dusty shaft of light from the window, was cold and remote, only the total lack of expression hinting at the passion that strained and quivered behind the mask. Slowly, lingeringly, Wernecke stooped over Bohme. "Anya," Bohme said again, caressingly, and then Wernecke's mouth was on his throat.

Let him feed, said a cold remorseless voice in Bruckman's mind. It will be easier to take him when he's nearly sated, when he's fully preoccupied and growing lethargic and logy . . . growing *full.* . . .

Slowly, with infinite caution, Bruckman gathered himself to spring, watching in horror and fascination as

Wernecke fed. He could hear Wernecke sucking the juice out of Bohme, as if there were not enough blood in the foolish old man to satiate him, as if there were not enough blood in the whole camp . . . or perhaps, the whole world. . . . And now Bohme was ceasing his feeble struggling, was becoming still. . . .

Bruckman flung himself upon Wernecke, stabbing him twice in the back before his weight bowled them both over. There was a moment of confusion as they rolled and struggled together, all without sound, and then Bruckman found himself sitting atop Wernecke, Wernecke's white face turned up to him. Bruckman drove his weapon into Wernecke again, the shock of the blow jarring Bruckman's arm to the shoulder. Wernecke made no outcry; his eyes were already glazing, but they looked at Bruckman with recognition, with cold anger, with bitter irony and, oddly, with what might have been resignation or relief, with what might almost have been pity. . . .

Bruckman stabbed again and again, driving the blows home with hysterical strength, panting, rocking atop his victim, feeling Wernecke's blood spatter against his face, wrapped in the heat and steam that rose from Wernecke's torn-open body like a smothering black cloud, coughing and choking on it for a moment, feeling the steam seep in through his pores and sink deep into the marrow of his bones, feeling the world seem to pulse and shimmer and change around him, as though he were suddenly seeing through new eyes, as though something had been born anew inside him, and then abruptly he was *smelling* Wernecke's blood, the hot organic reek of it, leaning closer to drink in that sudden overpowering smell, better than the smell of freshly baked bread, better than anything he could remember, rich and heady and strong beyond imagining.

There was a moment of revulsion and horror, and he tried to wonder how long the ancient contamination had been passing from man to man to man, how far into the past the chain of lives stretched, how Wernecke himself had been trapped, and then his parched lips touched wetness, and he was drinking, drinking deeply and greedily, and his mouth was filled with the strong clean taste of copper.

The following night, after Bruckman led the memorial prayers for Wernecke and Bohme, Melnick came to him. Melnick's eyes were bright with tears. "How can we go on without Eduard? He was everything to us. What will we do now? . . ."

"It will be all right, Moishe," Bruckman said. "I promise you, everything will be all right." He put his arm around Melnick for a moment to comfort him, and at the touch sensed the hot blood that pumped through the intricate network of the boy's veins, just under the skin, rich and warm and nourishing, waiting there inviolate for him to set it free.

DRINK MY RED BLOOD

✦✦✦

RICHARD MATHESON

The people on the block decided definitely that Jules was crazy when they heard about his composition. There had been suspicions for a long time. He made people shiver with his blank stare. His coarse, guttural tongue sounded unnatural in his frail body. The paleness of his skin upset many children. It seemed to hang loose around his flesh. He hated sunlight.

And, his ideas were a little out of place for the people who lived on the block.

Jules wanted to be a vampire.

People declared it common knowledge that he was born on a night when winds uprooted trees. They said he was born with three teeth. They said he'd used them to fasten himself on his mother's breast, drawing blood with the milk.

They said he used to cackle and bark in his crib after dark. They said he walked at two months and sat staring at the moon whenever it shone.

Those were things that people said.

His parents were always worried about him. An only child, they noticed his flaws quickly.

They thought he was blind until the doctor told them it was just a vacuous stare. He told them that Jules, with his large head, might be a genius or an idiot. It turned out he was an idiot.

He never spoke a word until he was five. Then one

night, coming up to supper, he sat down at the table and said, "Death."

His parents were torn between delight and disgust. They finally settled for a place in-between the two feelings. They decided that Jules couldn't have realized what the word meant.

But Jules did.

From that night on, he built up such a large vocabulary that everyone who knew him was astonished. He not only acquired every word spoken to him, words from signs, magazines, books; he made up his own words.

Like, nighttouch. Or, killove. They were really several words that melted into each other. They said things Jules felt but couldn't explain with other words.

He used to sit on the porch while the other children played hopscotch, stickball, and other games. He sat there and stared at the sidewalk, and made up words.

Until he was twelve, Jules kept pretty much out of trouble. Of course, there was the time they found him undressing Olive Jones in an alley. And another time he was discovered dissecting a kitten on his bed.

But there were many years in-between. Those scandals were forgotten.

In general, he went through childhood merely disgusting people.

He went to school, but never studied. He spent about two or three years in each grade. The teachers all knew him by his first name. In some subjects, like reading and writing, he was almost brilliant.

In others, he was hopeless.

One Saturday when he was twelve, Jules went to the movies. He saw *Dracula*.

When the show was over he walked, a throbbing nerve mass, through the little-girl and -boy ranks.

He went home and locked himself in the bathroom for two hours.

His parents pounded on the door and threatened but he wouldn't come out.

Finally, he unlocked the door and sat down at the supper table. He had a bandage on his thumb and a satisfied look on his face.

The morning after, he went to the library. It was Sunday. He sat on the steps all day, waiting for it to open. Finally he went home.

The next day he came back instead of going to school.

He found *Dracula* on the shelves. He couldn't borrow it because he wasn't a member and to be a member, he had to bring in one of his parents.

So he stuck the book down his pants and left the library and never brought it back.

He went to the park and sat down and read the book through. It was late evening before he finished.

He started at the beginning again, reading as he ran from streetlight to streetlight, all the way home.

He didn't hear a word of the scolding he got for missing lunch and supper. He ate, went in his room, and read the book to the finish. They asked him where he got the book. He said he found it.

As the days passed, Jules read the story over and over. He never went to school.

Late at night, when he had fallen into an exhausted slumber, his mother used to take the book into the living room and show it to her husband.

One night they noticed that Jules had underlined certain sentences with dark, shaky pencil lines.

Like: "The lips were crimson with fresh blood and the stream had trickled over her chin and stained the purity of her lawn death-robe."

Or: "When the blood began to spurt out, he took my hands in one of his, holding them tight, and with the other seized my neck and pressed my mouth to the wound . . ."

When his mother saw this, she threw the book down the garbage chute.

The next morning when Jules found the book missing he screamed and twisted his mother's arm until she told him where the book was.

Then he ran down to the basement and dug in the piles of garbage until he found the book.

Coffee grounds and egg yolk on his hands and wrists, he went to the park and read it again.

For a month, he read the book avidly. Then he knew it so well he threw it away and just thought about it.

Absence notes were coming from school. His mother yelled. Jules decided to go back for a while.

He wanted to write a composition.

One day he wrote it in class. When everyone was finished writing, the teacher asked if anyone wanted to read their composition to the class.

Jules raised his hand.

The teacher was surprised. But she felt charity. She wanted to encourage him. She drew in her tiny jab of a chin and smiled.

"All right," she said, "pay attention, children. Jules is going to read us his composition."

Jules stood up. He was excited. The paper shook in his hands.

"My Ambition, by . . ."

"Come to the front of the class, Jules, dear."

Jules went to the front of the class. The teacher smiled lovingly. Jules started again.

"My Ambition, by Jules Dracula."

The smile sagged.

"When I grow up, I want to be a vampire."

The teacher's smiling lips jerked down and out. Her eyes popped wide.

"I want to live forever and get even with everybody and make all the girls vampires. I want to smell of death."

"Jules!"

"I want to have a foul breath that stinks of dead earth crypts and sweet coffins."

The teacher shuddered. Her hands twitched on her green blotter. She couldn't believe her ears. She looked at the children. They were gaping. Some of them were giggling. But not the girls.

"I want to be all cold and have rotten flesh with stolen blood in the veins."

"That will . . . hrrumph!"

The teacher cleared her throat mightily.

"That will be all, Jules," she said.

Jules talked louder and desperately.

"I want to sink my terrible white teeth in my victims' necks. I want them to . . ."

"Jules! Go to your seat this instant!"

"I want them to slide like razors in the flesh and into the veins," read Jules ferociously.

The teacher jolted to her feet. Children were shivering. None of them were giggling.

"Then I want to draw my teeth out and let the blood flow easy in my mouth and run hot in my throat and . . ."

The teacher grabbed his arm. Jules tore away and ran to a corner. Barricaded behind a stool, he yelled:

"And drip off my tongue and run out of my lips down my victims' throats! I want to drink girls' blood!"

The teacher lunged for him. She dragged him out of the corner. He clawed at her and screamed all the way to the door and the principal's office.

"That is my ambition! That is my ambition! That is my ambition!"

It was grim.

Jules was locked in his room. The teacher and the principal sat with Jules' parents. They were talking in sepulchral voices.

They were recounting the scene.

All along the block, parents were discussing it. Most of them didn't believe it at first. They thought their children made it up.

Then they thought what horrible children they'd raised if the children could make up such things.

So they believed it.

After that, everyone watched Jules like a hawk. People avoided his touch and look. Parents pulled their children off the street when he approached. Everyone whispered tales of him.

There were more absence notes.

Jules told his mother he wasn't going to school any more. Nothing would change his mind. He never went again.

When an attendance officer came to the apartment, Jules would run over the roofs until he was far away from there.

A year wasted by.

Jules wandered the streets searching for something; he didn't know what. He looked in alleys. He looked in garbage cans. He looked in lots. He looked on the east side and the west side and in the middle.

He couldn't find what he wanted.

He rarely slept. He never spoke. He stared down all the time. He forgot his special words.

Then.

One day in the park, Jules strolled through the zoo.

An electric shock passed through him when he saw the vampire bat.

His eyes grew wide and his discolored teeth shone dully in a wide smile.

From that day on, Jules went daily to the zoo and looked at the bat. He spoke to it and called it the Count. He felt in his heart it was really a man who had changed.

A rebirth of culture struck him.

He stole another book from the library. It told all about wildlife.

He found the page on the vampire bat. He tore it out and threw the book away.

He learned the section by heart.

He knew how the bat made its wound. How it lapped up the blood like a kitten drinking cream. How it walked on folded wing stalks and hind legs like a black furry spider. Why it took no nourishment but blood.

Month after month, Jules stared at the bat and talked to it. It became the one comfort in his life. The one symbol of dreams come true.

One day Jules noticed that the bottom of the wire covering the cage had become loose.

He looked around, his black eyes shifting. He didn't see anyone looking. It was a cloudy day. Not many people were there.

Jules tugged at the wire.

It moved a little.

Then he saw a man come out of the monkey house. So he pulled back his hand and strolled away, whistling a song he had just made up.

Late at night, when he was supposed to be asleep, he would walk barefoot past his parents' room. He would hear his father and mother snoring. He would hurry out, put on his shoes, and run to the zoo.

Every time the watchman was not around, Jules would tug at the wiring.

He kept on pulling it loose.

When he had finished and had to run home, he pushed the wire in again. Then no one could tell.

All day Jules would stand in front of the cage and look at the Count and chuckle and tell him he'd soon be free again.

He told the Count all the things he knew. He told the Count he was going to practice climbing down walls headfirst.

He told the Count not to worry. He'd soon be out. Then, together, they could go all around and drink girls' blood. One night Jules pulled the wire out and crawled under it into the cage.

It was very dark.

He crept on his knees to the little wooden house. He listened to see if he could hear the Count squeaking.

He stuck his arm in the black doorway. He kept whispering.

He jumped when he felt a needle jab in his finger.

With a look of great pleasure on his thin face, Jules drew the fluttering hairy bat to him.

He climbed down from the cage with it and ran out of the zoo; out of the park. He ran down the silent streets.

It was getting late in the morning. Light touched the dark skies with gray. He couldn't go home. He had to have a place.

He went down an alley and climbed over a fence. He held tight to the bat. It lapped at the dribble of blood from his finger.

He went across a yard into a little deserted shack.

It was dark inside and damp. It was full of rubble and tin cans and soggy cardboard and excrement.

Jules made sure there was no way the bat could escape. Then he pulled the door tight and put a stick through the metal loop.

He felt his heart beating hard and his limbs trembling.

He let go of the bat. It flew to a dark corner and hung on the wood.

Jules feverishly tore off his shirt. His lips shook. He smiled a crazy smile.

He reached down into his pants' pocket and took out a little pocketknife he had stolen from his mother.

He opened it and ran a finger over the blade. It sliced through the flesh.

With shaking fingers he jabbed at his throat. He hacked. The blood ran through his fingers.

"Count! Count!" he cried in frenzied joy. "Drink my red blood! Drink me! Drink me!"

He stumbled over the tin cans and slipped and felt for the bat. It sprang from the wood and soared across the shack and fastened itself on the outer side.

Tears ran down Jules' cheeks.

He gritted his teeth. The blood ran across his shoulders and across his thin, hairless chest.

His body shook in fever. He staggered back toward the other side. He tripped and felt his side torn open on the sharp edge of a tin can.

His hands went out. They clutched the bat. He placed it against his throat. He sank on his back on the cool wet earth. He sighed.

He started to moan and clutch at his chest. His stomach heaved. The black bat on his neck silently lapped his blood.

Jules felt his life seeping away.

He thought of all the years past. The waiting. His parents. School. Dracula. Dreams. For this. This sudden glory.

Jules' eyes flickered open.

The side of the reeking shack swam around him.

It was hard to breathe. He opened his mouth to gasp in the air. He sucked it in. It was foul. It made him cough. His skinny body lurched on the cold ground.

Mists crept away in his brain.

One by one like drawn veils.

Suddenly his mind was filled with terrible clarity.

He knew he was lying half-naked on garbage and letting a flying bat drink his blood.

With a strangled cry, he reached up and tore away the furry throbbing bat. He flung it away from him. It came back, fanning his face with its vibrating wings.

Jules staggered to his feet.

He felt for the door. He could hardly see. He tried to stop his throat from bleeding so.

He managed to get the door open.

Then, lurching into the dark yard, he fell on his face in the long grass blades.

He tried to call out for help.

But no sounds, save a bubbling mockery of words, came from his lips.

He heard the fluttering wings.

Then, suddenly, they were gone.

Strong fingers lifted him gently. Through dying eyes, Jules saw a tall, dark man whose eyes shone like rubies.

"My son," the man said.

THE HOUND

♦♦♦

H. P. LOVECRAFT

In my tortured ears there sounds unceasingly a nightmare whirring and flapping, and a faint, distant baying as of some gigantic hound. It is not dream—it is not, I fear, even madness—for too much has already happened to give me these merciful doubts.

St. John is a mangled corpse; I alone know why, and such is my knowledge that I am about to blow out my brains for fear I shall be mangled in the same way. Down unlit and illimitable corridors of eldritch phantasy sweeps the black, shapeless Nemesis that drives me to self-annihilation.

May heaven forgive the folly and morbidity which led us both to so monstrous a fate! Wearied with the commonplaces of a prosaic world, where even the joys of romance and adventure soon grow stale, St. John and I had followed enthusiastically every aesthetic and intellectual movement which promised respite from our devastating ennui. The enigmas of the symbolists and the ecstasies of the pre-Raphaelites all were ours in their time, but each new moon was drained too soon of its diverting novelty and appeal.

Only the sombre philosophy of the decadents could help us, and this we found potent only by increasing gradually the depth and diabolism of our penetrations. Baudelaire and Huysmans were soon exhausted of thrills, till finally there remained for us only the more direct stimuli of unnatural personal experiences and adventures. It was this frightful emotional need which led us eventually to that detestable course which even in my present fear I mention with shame and timidity—that hideous extremity of human outrage, the abhorred practice of grave-robbing.

I cannot reveal the details of our shocking expedition, or catalogue even partly the worst of the trophies adorning the nameless museum we prepared in the great stone house where we jointly dwelt, alone and servantless. Our museum was a blasphemous, unthinkable place, where with the satanic taste of neurotic virtuosi we had assembled a universe of terror and decay to excite our jaded sensibilities. It was a secret room, far, far, underground; where huge winged daemons carven of basalt and onyx vomited from wide grinning mouths weird green and orange light, and hidden pneumatic pipes ruffled into kaleidoscopic dances of death the lines of red charnel things hand in hand woven in voluminous black hangings. Through these pipes came at will the odours our moods most craved; sometimes the scent of pale funereal lilies, sometimes the narcotic incense of imagined Eastern shrines of the kingly dead, and sometimes—how I shudder to recall it!—the frightful, soul-upheaving stenches of the uncovered grave.

Around the walls of this repellent chamber were cases of antique mummies alternating with comely, lifelike bodies perfectly stuffed and cured by the taxidermist's art, and with head-stones snatched from the oldest churchyards of the world. Niches here and there contained skulls of all shapes, and heads preserved in various stages of dissolution. There one might find the rotting bald pates of famous noblemen, and the fresh and radiantly golden heads of new-buried children.

Statues and paintings there were, all of fiendish subjects and some executed by St. John and myself. A locked portfolio, bound in tanned human skin, held certain unknown and unnameable drawings which it was rumoured Goya had perpetrated but dared not acknowledge. There were nauseous musical instruments, stringed, brass, and woodwind, on which St. John and I sometimes produced dissonances of exquisite morbidity and cacodaemoniacal ghastliness; whilst in a multitude of inlaid ebony cabinets reposed the most incredible and unimaginable variety of tomb-loot ever assembled by human madness and perversity. It is of this loot in particular that I must not speak—thank God I had the courage to destroy it long before I thought of destroying myself!

The predatory excursions on which we collected our unmentionable treasures were always artistically memorable events. We were no vulgar ghouls, but worked only under certain conditions of mood, landscape, environment, weather, season, and moonlight. These pastimes were to us the most exquisite form of aesthetic expression, and we gave their details a fastidious technical care. An inappropriate hour, a jarring lighting effect, or a clumsy manipulation of the damp sod, would almost totally destroy for us that titillation which followed the exhumation of some ominous, grinning secret of the earth. Our quest for novel scenes and piquant conditions was feverish and insatiate—St. John was always the leader, and he it was who led the way to that mocking, accursed spot which brought us our hideous and inevitable doom.

By what malign fatality were we lured to that terrible Holland churchyard? I think it was the dark rumour and legendry, the tales of one buried for five centuries, who had himself been a ghoul in his time and had stolen a potent thing from a mighty sepulchre. I can recall the scene in these final moments—the pale autumnal moon over the graves, casting long horrible shadows; the grotesque trees, dropping sullenly to meet the neglected grass and the crumbling slabs; the vast legions of strangely colossal bats that flew against the moon; the antique ivied church pointing a huge spectral finger at the livid sky; the phosphorescent insects that danced like death-fires under the yews in a distant corner—the odours of mould, vegetation, and less explicable things that mingled feebly with the night wind from over far swamps and seas; and, worst of all, the faint deep-toned baying of some gigantic hound which we could neither see nor definitely place. As we heard this suggestion of baying we shuddered, remembering the tales of the peasantry; for he whom we sought had centuries before been found in this self-same spot, torn and mangled by the claws and teeth of some unspeakable beast.

I remember how we delved in the ghoul's grave with our spades, and how we thrilled at the picture of ourselves, the grave, the pale watching moon, the horrible shadows, the grotesque trees, the titanic bats, the antique church, the dancing death-fires, the sickening odours, the gentle moaning night wind, and the strange, half-heard directionless baying of whose objective existence we could scarcely be sure.

Then we struck a substance harder than the damp mould, and beheld a rotting oblong box crusted with mineral deposits from the long undisturbed ground. It was incredibly tough and thick, but so old that we finally pried it open and feasted our eyes on what it held.

Much—amazingly much—was left of the object despite the lapse of five hundred years. The skeleton, though crushed in places by the jaws of the thing that had killed it, held together with surprising firmness, and we gloated over the clean white skull and its long, firm teeth and its eyeless sockets that once had glowed with a charnel fever like our own. In the coffin lay an amulet of curious and exotic design, which had apparently been worn around the sleeper's neck. It was the oddly conventionalized figure of a crouching winged hound, or sphinx with a semi-canine face, and was exquisitely carved in antique Oriental fashion from a small piece of green jade. The expression of its features was repellent in the extreme, savouring at once of death, bestiality, and malevolence. Around the base was an inscription in characters which neither St. John nor I could identify; and on the bottom, like a maker's seal, was given a grotesque and formidable skull.

Immediately upon beholding this amulet we knew that we must possess it; that this treasure alone was our logical pelt from the centuried grave. Even had its outlines been unfamiliar we would have desired it, but as we looked more closely we saw that it was not wholly unfamiliar. Alien it indeed was to all art and literature which sane and balanced readers know, but we recognized it as the thing hinted at in the forbidden *Necronomicon* of the mad Arab Abdul Alhazred; the ghastly soul-symbol of the corpse-eating cult of inaccessible Leng, in Central Asia. All too well did we trace the sinister lineaments described by the old Arab daemonologist; lineaments, he wrote, drawn from some obscure supernatural manifestation of the souls of those who vexed and gnawed at the dead.

Seizing the green jade object, we gave a last glance at the bleached and cavern-eyed face of its owner and closed up the grave as we found it. As we hastened from the abhorrent spot, the stolen amulet in St. John's pocket, we thought we saw the bats descend in a body to the earth we had so lately rifled, as if seeking for some cursed and unholy nourishment. But the autumn moon shone weak and pale, and we could not be sure.

So, too, as we sailed the next day away from Holland to our home, we thought we heard the faint distant baying of some gigantic hound in the background. But the autumn wind moaned sad and wan, and we could not be sure.

Less than a week after our return to England, strange things began to happen. We lived as recluses; devoid of friends, alone, and without servants in a few rooms of an ancient manorhouse on a bleak and unfrequented moor; so that our doors were seldom disturbed by the knock of the visitor.

Now, however, we were troubled by what seemed to be a frequent fumbling in the night, not only around the doors but around the windows also, upper as well as lower. Once we fancied that a large opaque body darkened the library window when the moon was shining against it, and another time we thought we heard a whirring or flapping sound not far off. On each occasion investigation revealed nothing, and we began to ascribe the occurrences to imagination which still prolonged in our ears the faint far baying we thought we had heard in the Holland churchyard. The jade amulet now reposed in a niche in our museum, and sometimes we burned a strangely scented candle before it. We read much in Alhazred's *Necronomicon* about its properties, and about the relation of ghosts' souls to the objects it symbolized; and were disturbed by what we read.

Then terror came.

On the night of 24 September 19—, I heard a knock at my chamber door. Fancying it St. John's, I bade the knocker enter, but was answered only by a shrill laugh. There was no one in the corridor. When I aroused St. John from his sleep, he professed entire ignorance of the event, and became as worried as I. It was the night that the faint, distant baying over the moor became to us a certain and dreaded reality.

Four days later, whilst we were both in the hidden museum, there came a low, cautious scratching at the single door which led to the secret library staircase. Our alarm was now divided, for, besides our fear of the unknown, we had always entertained a dread that our grisly collection might be discovered. Extinguishing all lights, we proceeded to the door and threw it suddenly open; whereupon we felt an unaccountable rush of air, and heard, as if receding far away, a queer combination of rustling, tittering, and inarticulate chatter. Whether we were mad, dreaming, or in our senses, we did not try to determine. We only realized, with the blackest of apprehensions, that the apparently disembodied chatter was beyond a doubt in the Dutch language.

After that we lived in growing horror and fascination. Mostly we held to the theory that we were jointly going mad from our life of unnatural excitements, but sometimes it pleased us more to dramatize ourselves as the victims of some creeping and appalling doom. Bizarre manifestations were now too frequent to count. Our lonely house was seemingly alive with the presence of some malign being whose nature we could not guess, and every night that daemoniac baying rolled over the windswept moor, always louder and louder. On 29 October we found in the soft earth underneath the library window a series of footprints utterly impossible to describe. They were as baffling as the hordes of great bats which haunted the old manorhouse in unprecedented and increasing numbers.

The horror reached a culmination on 18 November, when St. John, walking home after dark from the dismal railway station, was seized by some frightful carnivorous thing and torn to ribbons. His screams had reached the house, and I had hastened to the terrible scene in time to hear a whirr of wings and see a vague black cloudy thing silhouetted against the rising moon.

My friend was dying when I spoke to him, and he could not answer coherently. All he could do was to whisper, "The amulet—that damned thing—"

Then he collapsed, an inert mass of mangled flesh.

I buried him the next midnight in one of our neglected gardens, and mumbled over his body one of the devilish rituals he had loved in life. And as I pronounced the last daemoniac sentence I heard afar on the moor the faint baying of some gigantic hound. The moon was up, but I dared not look at it. And when I saw on the dim-lighted moor a wide nebulous shadow sweeping from mound to mound, I shut my eyes and threw myself face down upon the ground. When I arose, trembling, I know not how much later, I staggered into the house and made shocking obeisances before the enshrined amulet of green jade.

Being now afraid to live alone in the ancient house on the moor, I departed on the following day for London, taking with me the amulet after destroying by fire and burial the rest of the impious collection in the museum. But after three nights I heard the baying again, and before a week was over felt strange eyes upon me whenever it was dark. One evening as I strolled on Victoria Embankment for some needed air, I saw a black shape obscure one of the reflections of the lamps in the water. A wind, stronger than the night wind, rushed by, and I knew that what had befallen St. John must soon befall me.

The next day I carefully wrapped the green jade amulet and sailed for Holland. What mercy I might gain by returning the thing to its silent, sleeping owner I knew not;

but I felt that I must try any step conceivably logical. What the hound was, and why it had pursued me, were questions still vague; but I had first heard the baying in that ancient churchyard, and every subsequent event including St. John's dying whisper had served to connect the curse with the stealing of the amulet. Accordingly I sank into the nethermost abysses of despair when, at an inn in Rotterdam, I discovered that thieves had despoiled me of this sole means of salvation.

The baying was loud that evening, and in the morning I read of a nameless deed in the vilest quarter of the city. The rabble were in terror, for upon an evil tenement had fallen a red death beyond the foulest previous crime of the neighbourhood. In a squalid thieves' den an entire family had been torn to shreds by an unknown thing which left no trace, and those around had heard all night a faint, deep, insistent note as of a gigantic hound.

So at last I stood again in the unwholesome churchyard where a pale winter moon cast hideous shadows, and leafless trees dropped sullenly to meet the withered, frosty grass and cracking slabs, and the ivied church pointed a jeering finger at the unfriendly sky, and the night wind howled maniacally from over frozen swamps and frigid seas. The baying was very faint now, and it ceased altogether as I approached the ancient grave I had once violated, and frightened away an abnormally large horde of bats which had been hovering curiously around it.

I know not why I went thither unless to pray, or gibber out insane pleas and apologies to the calm white thing that lay within; but, whatever my reason, I attacked the half-frozen sod with a desperation partly mine and partly that of a dominating will outside myself. Excavation was much easier than I expected, though at one point I encountered a queer interruption; when a lean vulture darted down out of the cold sky and pecked frantically at the grave-earth until I killed him with a blow of my spade. Finally I reached the rotting oblong box and removed the damp nitrous cover. This is the last rational act I ever performed.

For crouched within that centuried coffin, embraced by a close-packed nightmare retinue of high, sinewy, sleeping bats, was the bony thing my friend and I had robbed; not clean and placid as we had seen it then, but covered with caked blood and shreds of alien flesh and hair, and leering sentiently at me with phosphorescent sockets and sharp ensanguined fangs yawning twistedly in mockery of my inevitable doom. And when it gave from those grinning jaws a deep, sardonic bay as of some gigantic hound, and I saw that it held in its gory filthy claw the lost and fateful amulet of green jade, I merely screamed and ran away idiotically, my screams soon dissolving into peals of hysterical laughter.

Madness rides the star-wind . . . claws and teeth sharpened on centuries of corpses . . . dripping death astride a bacchanal of bats from night-black ruins of buried temples of Belial . . . Now, as the baying of that dead fleshless monstrosity grows louder and louder, and the stealthy whirring and flapping of those accursed web-wings circles closer and closer, I shall seek with my revolver the oblivion which is my only refuge from the unnamed and unnameable.

THE PARASITE

◆◆◆

ARTHUR CONAN DOYLE

I

March 24. The spring is fairly with us now. Outside my laboratory window the great chestnut-tree is all covered with the big, glutinous, gummy buds, some of which have already begun to break into little green shuttlecocks. As you walk down the lanes you are conscious of the rich, silent forces of nature working all around you. The wet earth smells fruitful and luscious. Green shoots are peeping out everywhere. The twigs are stiff with their sap; and the moist, heavy English air is laden with a faintly resinous perfume. Buds in the hedges, lambs beneath them—everywhere the work of reproduction going forward!

I can see it without, and I can feel it within. We also have our spring when the little arterioles dilate, the lymph flows in a brisker stream, the glands work harder, winnowing and straining. Every year nature readjusts the whole machine. I can feel the ferment in my blood at this very moment, and as the cool sunshine pours through my window I could dance about in it like a gnat. So I should, only that Charles Sadler would rush upstairs to know what was the matter. Besides, I must remember that I am Professor Gilroy. An old professor may afford to be natural, but when fortune has given one of the first chairs in the university to a man of four-and-thirty he must try and act the part consistently.

What a fellow Wilson is! If I could only throw the same enthusiasm into physiology that he does into psychology, I should become a Claude Bernard at the least. His whole life and soul and energy work to one end. He drops to sleep collating his results of the past day, and he wakes to plan his researches for the coming one. And yet, outside the narrow circle who follow his proceedings, he gets so little credit for it. Physiology is a recognized science. If I add even a brick to the edifice, every one sees and applauds it. But Wilson is trying to dig the foundations for a science of the future. His work is underground and does not show. Yet he goes on uncomplainingly, corresponding with a hundred semi-maniacs in the hope of finding one reliable witness, sifting a hundred lies on the chance of gaining one little speck of truth, collating old books, devouring new ones, experimenting, lecturing, trying to light up in others the fiery interest which is consuming him. I am filled with wonder and admiration when I think of him, and yet, when he asks me to associate myself with his researches, I am compelled to tell him that, in their present state, they offer little attraction to a man who is devoted to exact science. If he could show me something positive and objective, I might then be tempted to approach the question from its physiological side. So long as half his subjects are tainted with charlatanry and the other half with hysteria we physiologists must content ourselves with the body and leave the mind to our descendants.

No doubt I am a materialist. Agatha says that I am a rank one. I tell her that is an excellent reason for shortening our engagement, since I am in such urgent need of her spirituality. And yet I may claim to be a curious example of the effect of education upon temperament, for by nature I am, unless I deceive myself, a highly psychic man. I was a nervous, sensitive boy, a dreamer, a somnambulist, full of impressions and intuitions. My black hair, my dark eyes, my thin, olive face, my tapering fingers, are all characteristic of my real temperament, and cause experts like Wilson to claim me as their own. But my brain is soaked with exact knowledge. I have trained myself to deal only with fact and with proof. Surmise and fancy have no place in my scheme of thought. Show me what I can see with my microscope, cut with my scalpel, weigh in my balance, and I will devote a lifetime to its investigation. But when you ask me to study feelings, impressions, suggestions, you ask me to do what is distasteful and even demoralizing. A departure from pure reason affects me like an evil smell or a musical discord.

Which is a very sufficient reason why I am a little loath to go to Professor Wilson's tonight. Still I feel that I could hardly get out of the invitation without positive rudeness, and, now that Mrs. Marden and Agatha are going, of course I would not if I could. But I had rather meet them anywhere else. I know that Wilson would draw me into this nebulous semi-science of his if he could. In his enthusiasm he is perfectly impervious to hints or remonstrances. Nothing short of a positive quarrel will make him realize my aversion to the whole business. I have no doubt that he has some new mesmerist or clairvoyant or medium or trickster of some sort whom he is going to exhibit to us, for even his entertainments bear upon his hobby. Well, it will be a treat for Agatha, at any rate. She is interested in it, as woman usually is in whatever is vague and mystical and indefinite.

10:50 p.m. This diary-keeping of mine is, I fancy, the outcome of that scientific habit of mind about which I wrote this morning. I like to register impressions while they are fresh. Once a day at least I endeavour to define my own mental position. It is a useful piece of self-analysis, and has, I fancy, a steadying effect upon the character. Frankly, I must confess that my own needs what stiffening I can give it. I fear that, after all, much of my neurotic temperament survives, and that I am far from that cool, calm precision which characterizes Murdoch or Pratt-Haldane. Otherwise, why should the tomfoolery which I have witnessed this evening have set my nerves thrilling so that even now I am all unstrung? My only comfort is that neither Wilson nor Miss Penelosa nor even Agatha could have possibly known my weakness.

And what in the world was there to excite me? Nothing, or so little that it will seem ludicrous when I set it down.

The Mardens got to Wilson's before me. In fact, I was one of the last to arrive and found the room crowded. I had hardly time to say a word to Mrs. Marden and to Agatha, who was looking charming in white and pink, with glittering wheat-ears in her hair, when Wilson came twitching at my sleeve.

"You want something positive, Gilroy," said he, drawing me apart into a corner. "My dear fellow, I have a phenomenon—a phenomenon!"

I should have been more impressed had I not heard the same before. His sanguine spirit turns every firefly into a star.

"No possible question about the *bona fides* this time," said he, in answer, perhaps, to some little gleam of amusement in my eyes. "My wife has known her for many years. They both come from Trinidad, you know. Miss Penelosa has only been in England a month or two and knows no one outside the university circle, but I assure you that the things she has told us suffice in themselves to establish clairvoyance upon an absolutely scientific basis. There is nothing like her, amateur or professional. Come and be introduced!"

I like none of these mystery-mongers, but the amateur least of all. With the paid performer you may pounce upon him and expose him the instant that you have seen through his trick. He is there to deceive you, and you are there to find him out. But what are you to do with the friend of your host's wife? Are you to turn on a light suddenly and expose her slapping a surreptitious banjo? Or are you to hurl cochineal over her evening frock when she steals round with her phosphorus bottle and her supernatural platitude? There would be a scene, and you would be looked upon as a brute. So you have your choice of being that or a dupe. I was in no very good humour as I followed Wilson to the lady.

Any one less like my idea of a West Indian could not be imagined. She was a small, frail creature, well over forty, I should say, with a pale, peaky face, and hair of a very light shade of chestnut. Her presence was insignificant and her manner retiring. In any group of ten women she would have been the last whom one would have picked out. Her eyes were perhaps her most remarkable, and also, I am compelled to say, her least pleasant, feature. They were grey in colour—grey with a shade of green—and their expression struck me as being decidedly furtive. I wonder if furtive is the word, or should I have said fierce? On second thoughts, feline would have expressed it better. A crutch leaning against the wall told me what was painfully evident when she rose: that one of her legs was crippled.

So I was introduced to Miss Penelosa, and it did not escape me that as my name was mentioned she glanced across at Agatha. Wilson had evidently been talking. And presently, no doubt, thought I, she will inform me by occult means that I am engaged to a young lady with wheat-ears in her hair. I wondered how much more Wilson had been telling her about me.

"Professor Gilroy is a terrible sceptic," said he. "I hope, Miss Penelosa, that you will be able to convert him."

She looked keenly up at me.

"Professor Gilroy is quite right to be sceptical if he has not seen anything convincing," said she. "I should have thought," she added, "that you would yourself have been an excellent subject."

"For what, may I ask?" said I.

"Well, for mesmerism, for example."

"My experience has been that mesmerists go for their subjects to those who are mentally unsound. All their results are vitiated, as it seems to me, by the fact that they are dealing with abnormal organisms."

"Which of these ladies would you say possessed a normal organism?" she asked. "I should like you to select the one who seems to you to have the best balanced mind. Should we say the girl in pink and white?—Miss Agatha Marden, I think the name is?"

"Yes, I should attach weight to any results from her."

"I have never tried how far she is impressionable. Of course some people respond much more rapidly than others. May I ask how far your scepticism extends? I suppose that you admit the mesmeric sleep and the power of suggestion."

"I admit nothing, Miss Penelosa."

"Dear me, I thought science had got further than that. Of course I know nothing about the scientific side of it. I only know what I can do. You see the girl in red, for example, over near the Japanese jar. I shall will that she come across to us."

She bent forward as she spoke and dropped her fan

upon the floor. The girl whisked round and came straight toward us, with an enquiring look upon her face, as if some one had called her.

"What do you think of that, Gilroy?" cried Wilson, in a kind of ecstasy.

I did not dare to tell him what I thought of it. To me it was the most barefaced, shameless piece of imposture that I had ever witnessed. The collusion and the signal had really been too obvious.

"Professor Gilroy is not satisfied," said she, glancing up at me with her strange little eyes. "My poor fan is to get the credit of that experiment. Well, we must try something else. Miss Marden, would you have any objection to my putting you off?"

"Oh, I should love it!" cried Agatha.

By this time all the company had gathered round us in a circle, the shirt-fronted men, and the white-throated women, some awed, some critical, as though it were something between a religious ceremony and a conjurer's entertainment. A red velvet armchair had been pushed into the centre, and Agatha lay back in it, a little flushed and trembling slightly from excitement. I could see it from the vibration of the wheat-ears. Miss Penelosa rose from her seat and stood over her, leaning upon her crutch.

And there was a change in the woman. She no longer seemed small or insignificant. Twenty years were gone from her age. Her eyes were shining, a tinge of colour had come into her sallow cheeks, her whole figure had expanded. So I have seen a dull-eyed, listless lad change in an instant into briskness and life when given a task of which he felt himself master. She looked down at Agatha with an expression which I resented from the bottom of my soul—the expression with which a Roman empress might have looked at her kneeling slave. Then with a quick, commanding gesture she tossed up her arms and swept them slowly down in front of her.

I was watching Agatha narrowly. During three passes she seemed to be simply amused. At the fourth I observed a slight glazing of her eyes, accompanied by some dilation of her pupils. At the sixth there was a momentary rigor. At the seventh her lids began to droop. At the tenth her eyes were closed, and her breathing was slower and fuller than usual. I tried as I watched to preserve my scientific calm, but a foolish, causeless agitation convulsed me. I trust that I hid it, but I felt as a child feels in the dark. I could not have believed that I was still open to such weakness.

"She is in the trance," said Miss Penelosa.

"She is sleeping!" I cried.

"Wake her, then!"

I pulled her by the arm and shouted in her ear. She might have been dead for all the impression that I could make. Her body was there on the velvet chair. Her organs were acting—her heart, her lungs. But her soul! It had slipped from beyond our ken. Whither had it gone? What power had dispossessed it? I was puzzled and disconcerted.

"So much for the mesmeric sleep," said Miss Penelosa. "As regards suggestion, whatever I may suggest Miss Marden will infallibly do, whether it be now or after she has awakened from her trance. Do you demand proof of it?"

"Certainly," said I.

"You shall have it." I saw a smile pass over her face, as though an amusing thought had struck her. She stooped and whispered earnestly into her subject's ear. Agatha, who had been so deaf to me, nodded her head as she listened.

"Awake!" cried Miss Penelosa, with a sharp tap of her

crutch upon the floor. The eyes opened, the glazing cleared slowly away, and the soul looked out once more after its strange eclipse.

We went away early. Agatha was none the worse for her strange excursion, but I was nervous and unstrung, unable to listen to or answer the stream of comments which Wilson was pouring out for my benefit. As I bade her goodnight Miss Penelosa slipped a piece of paper into my hand.

"Pray forgive me," said she, "if I take means to overcome your scepticism. Open this note at ten o'clock tomorrow morning. It is a little private test."

I can't imagine what she means, but there is the note, and it shall be opened as she directs. My head is aching, and I have written enough for tonight. Tomorrow I dare say that what seems so inexplicable will take quite another complexion. I shall not surrender my convictions without a struggle.

March 25. I am amazed, confounded. It is clear that I must reconsider my opinion upon this matter. But first let me place on record what has occurred.

I had finished breakfast, and was looking over some diagrams with which my lecture is to be illustrated, when my housekeeper entered to tell me that Agatha was in my study and wished to see me immediately. I glanced at the clock and saw with surprise that it was only half-past nine.

When I entered the room, she was standing on the hearth-rug facing me. Something in her pose chilled me and checked the words which were rising to my lips. Her veil was half down, but I could see that she was pale and that her expression was constrained.

"Austin," she said, "I have come to tell you that our engagement is at an end."

I staggered. I believe that I literally did stagger. I know that I found myself leaning against the bookcase for support.

"But—but—" I stammered. "This is very sudden, Agatha."

"Yes, Austin, I have come here to tell you that our engagement is at an end."

"But surely," I cried, "you will give me some reason! This is unlike you, Agatha. Tell me how I have been unfortunate enough to offend you."

"It is all over, Austin."

"But why? You must be under some delusion, Agatha. Perhaps you have been told some falsehood about me. Or you may have misunderstood something that I have said to you. Only let me know what it is, and a word may set it all right."

"We must consider it all at an end."

"But you left me last night without a hint at any disagreement. What could have occurred in the interval to change you so? It must have been something that happened last night. You have been thinking it over and you have disapproved of my conduct. Was it the mesmerism? Did you blame me for letting that woman exercise her power over you? You know that at the least sign I should have interfered."

"It is useless, Austin. All is over."

Her voice was cold and measured; her manner strangely formal and hard. It seemed to me that she was absolutely resolved not to be drawn into any argument or explanation. As for me, I was shaking with agitation, and I turned my face aside, so ashamed was I that she should see my want of control.

"You must know what this means to me!" I cried. "It is the blasting of all my hopes and the ruin of my life! You surely will not inflict such a punishment upon me unheard. You will let me know what is the matter. Consider how impossible it would be for me, under any circumstances, to treat you so. For God's sake, Agatha, let me know what I have done!"

She walked past me without a word and opened the door.

"It is quite useless, Austin," said she. "You must consider our engagement at an end." An instant later she was gone, and, before I could recover myself sufficiently to follow her, I heard the hall door close behind her.

I rushed into my room to change my coat, with the idea of hurrying round to Mrs. Marden's to learn from her what the cause of my misfortune might be. So shaken was I that I could hardly lace my boots. Never shall I forget those horrible ten minutes. I had just pulled on my overcoat when the clock upon the mantelpiece struck ten.

Ten! I associated the idea with Miss Penelosa's note. It was lying before me on the table, and I tore it open. It was scribbled in pencil in a peculiarly angular handwriting.

> *My dear Professor Gilroy* [it said]: *Pray excuse the personal nature of the test which I am giving you. Professor Wilson happened to mention the relations between you and my subject of this evening, and it struck me that nothing could be more convincing to you than if I were to suggest to Miss Marden that she should call upon you at half-past nine tomorrow morning and suspend your engagement for half an hour or so. Science is so exacting that it is difficult to give a satisfying test, but I am convinced that this at least will be an action which she would be most unlikely to do of her own free will. Forget anything that she may have said, as she has really noth-*

ing whatever to do with it, and will certainly not recollect anything about it. I write this note to shorten your anxiety, and to beg you to forgive me for the momentary unhappiness which my suggestion must have caused you.

Yours faithfully,
Helen Penelosa

Really, when I had read the note, I was too relieved to be angry. It was a liberty. Certainly it was a very great liberty indeed on the part of a lady whom I had only met once. But, after all, I had challenged her by my scepticism. It may have been, as she said, a little difficult to devise a test which would satisfy me.

And she had done that. There could be no question at all upon the point. For me hypnotic suggestion was finally established. It took its place from now onward as one of the facts of life. That Agatha, who of all women of my acquaintance has the best balanced mind, had been reduced to a condition of automatism appeared to be certain. A person at a distance had worked her as an engineer on the shore might guide a Brennan torpedo. A second soul had stepped in, as it were, had pushed her own aside, and had seized her nervous mechanism, saying: "I will work this for half an hour." And Agatha must have been unconscious as she came and as she returned. Could she make her way in safety through the streets in such a state? I put on my hat and hurried round to see if all was well with her.

Yes. She was at home. I was shown into the drawing-room and found her sitting with a book upon her lap.

"You are an early visitor, Austin," said she, smiling.

"And you have been an even earlier one," I answered.

She looked puzzled. "What do you mean?" she asked.

"You have not been out today?"

"No, certainly not."

"Agatha," said I seriously, "would you mind telling me exactly what you have done this morning?"

She laughed at my earnestness.

"You've got on your professional look, Austin. See what becomes of being engaged to a man of science. However, I will tell you, though I can't imagine what you want to know for. I got up at eight. I breakfasted at half-past. I came into this room at ten minutes past nine and began to read the 'Memoirs of Mme de Remusat.' In a few minutes I did the French lady the bad compliment of dropping to sleep over her pages, and I did you, sir, the very flattering one of dreaming about you. It is only a few minutes since I woke up."

"And found yourself where you had been before?"

"Why, where else should I find myself?"

"Would you mind telling me, Agatha, what it was that you dreamed about me? It really is not mere curiosity on my part."

"I merely had a vague impression that you came into it. I cannot recall anything definite."

"If you have not been out today, Agatha, how is it that your shoes are dusty?"

A pained look came over her face.

"Really, Austin, I do not know what is the matter with you this morning. One would almost think that you doubted my word. If my boots are dusty, it must be, of course, that I have put on a pair which the maid has not cleaned."

It was perfectly evident that she knew nothing whatever about the matter, and I reflected that, after all, perhaps it was better that I should not enlighten her. It might frighten her, and could serve no good purpose that I could see. I said no more about it, therefore, and left shortly afterward to give my lecture.

But I am immensely impressed. My horizon of scientific possibilities has suddenly been enormously extended. I no longer wonder at Wilson's demonic energy and enthusiasm. Who would not work hard who had a vast virgin field ready to his hand? Why, I have known the novel shape of a nucleolus, or a trifling peculiarity of striped muscular fibre seen under a 300 diameter lens, to fill me with exultation. How petty do such researches seem when compared with this one which strikes at the very roots of life and the nature of the soul! I had always looked upon spirit as a product of matter. The brain, I thought, secreted the mind, as the liver does the bile. But how can this be when I see mind working from a distance and playing upon matter as a musician might upon a violin? The body does not give rise to the soul, then, but is rather the rough instrument by which the spirit manifests itself. The windmill does not give rise to the wind, but only indicates it. It was opposed to my whole habit of thought, and yet it was undeniably possible and worthy of investigation.

And why should I not investigate it? I see that under yesterday's date I said: "If I could see something positive and objective, I might be tempted to approach it from the physiological aspect." Well, I have got my test. I shall be as good as my word. The investigation would, I am sure, be of immense interest. Some of my colleagues might look askance at it, for science is full of unreasoning prejudices, but if Wilson has the courage of his convictions, I can afford to have it also. I shall go to him tomorrow morning—to him and to Miss Penelosa. If she can show us so much, it is probable that she can show us more.

II

March 26. Wilson was, as I had anticipated, very exultant over my conversion, and Miss Penelosa was also demurely pleased at the result of her experiment. Strange what a silent, colourless creature she is save only when she exercises her power! Even talking about it gives her colour and life. She seems to take a singular interest in me. I cannot help observing how her eyes follow me about the room.

We had the most interesting conversation about her own powers. It is just as well to put her views on record, though they cannot, of course, claim any scientific weight.

"You are on the very fringe of the subject," said she, when I had expressed wonder at the remarkable instance of suggestion which she had shown me. "I had no direct influence upon Miss Marden when she came round to you. I was not even thinking of her that morning. What I did was to set her mind as I might set the alarm of a clock so that at the hour named it would go off of its own accord. If six months instead of twelve hours had been suggested, it would have been the same."

"And if the suggestion had been to assassinate me?"

"She would most inevitably have done so."

"But this is a terrible power!" I cried.

"It is, as you say, a terrible power," she answered gravely, "and the more you know of it the more terrible will it seem to you."

"May I ask," said I, "what you meant when you said that this matter of suggestion is only at the fringe of it? What do you consider the essential?"

"I had rather not tell you."

I was surprised at the decision of her answer.

"You understand," said I, "that it is not out of curiosity

I ask, but in the hope that I may find some scientific explanation for the facts with which you furnish me."

"Frankly, Professor Gilroy," said she, "I am not at all interested in science, nor do I care whether it can or cannot classify these powers."

"But I was hoping—"

"Ah, that is quite another thing. If you make it a personal matter," said she, with the pleasantest of smiles, "I shall be only too happy to tell you anything you wish to know. Let me see; what was it you asked me? Oh, about the further powers. Professor Wilson won't believe in them, but they are quite true all the same. For example, it is possible for an operator to gain complete command over his subject—presuming that the latter is a good one. Without any previous suggestion he may make him do whatever he likes."

"Without the subject's knowledge?"

"That depends. If the force were strongly exerted, he would know no more about it than Miss Marden did when she came round and frightened you so. Or, if the influence was less powerful, he might be conscious of what he was doing, but be quite unable to prevent himself from doing it."

"Would he have lost his own will power, then?"

"It would be over-ridden by another stronger one."

"Have you ever exercised this power yourself?"

"Several times."

"Is your own will so strong, then?"

"Well, it does not entirely depend upon that. Many have strong wills which are not detachable from themselves. The thing is to have the gift of projecting it into another person and superseding his own. I find that the power varies with my own strength and health."

"Practically, you send your soul into another person's body."

"Well, you might put it that way."

"And what does your own body do?"

"It merely feels lethargic."

"Well, but is there no danger to your own health?" I asked.

"There might be a little. You have to be careful never to let your own consciousness absolutely go; otherwise, you might experience some difficulty in finding your way back again. You must always preserve the connection, as it were. I am afraid I express myself very badly, Professor Gilroy, but of course I don't know how to put these things in a scientific way. I am just giving you my own experiences and my own explanations."

Well, I read this over now at my leisure, and I marvel at myself! Is this Austin Gilroy, the man who has won his way to the front by his hard reasoning power and by his devotion to fact? Here I am gravely retailing the gossip of a woman who tells me how her soul may be projected from her body, and how, while she lies in a lethargy, she can control the actions of people at a distance. Do I accept it? Certainly not. She must prove and re-prove before I yield a point. But if I am still a sceptic, I have at least ceased to be a scoffer. We are to have a sitting this evening, and she is to try if she can produce any mesmeric effect upon me. If she can, it will make an excellent starting point for our investigation. No one can accuse *me*, at any rate, of complicity. If she cannot, we must try and find some subject who will be like Caesar's wife. Wilson is perfectly impervious.

10 p.m. I believe that I am on the threshold of an epoch-making investigation. To have the power of examining these phenomena from inside—to have an organism

which will respond, and at the same time a brain which will appreciate and criticize—that is surely a unique advantage. I am quite sure that Wilson would give five years of his life to be as susceptible as I have proved myself to be.

There was no one present except Wilson and his wife. I was seated with my head leaning back, and Miss Penelosa, standing in front and a little to the left, used the same long, sweeping strokes as with Agatha. At each of them a warm current of air seemed to strike me, and to suffuse a thrill and glow all through me from head to foot. My eyes were fixed upon Miss Penelosa's face, but as I gazed the features seemed to blur and to fade away. I was conscious only of her own eyes looking down at me, grey, deep, inscrutable. Larger they grew and larger, until they changed suddenly into two mountain lakes toward which I seemed to be falling with horrible rapidity. I shuddered, and as I did so some deeper stratum of thought told me that the shudder represented the rigor which I had observed in Agatha. An instant later I struck the surface of the lakes, now joined into one, and down I went beneath the water with a fullness in my head and a buzzing in my ears. Down I went, down, down, and then with a swoop up again until I could see the light streaming brightly through the green water. I was almost at the surface when the word "Awake!" rang through my head, and, with a start, I found myself back in the armchair, with Miss Penelosa leaning on her crutch, and Wilson, his notebook in his hand, peeping over her shoulder. No heaviness or weariness was left behind. On the contrary, though it is only an hour or so since the experiment, I feel so wakeful that I am more inclined for my study than my bedroom. I see quite a vista of interesting experiments extending before us, and am all impatience to begin upon them.

March 27. A blank day, as Miss Penelosa goes with Wilson and his wife to the Suttons'. Have begun Binet and Ferre's "Animal Magnetism." What strange, deep waters these are! Results, results, results—and the cause an absolute mystery. It is stimulating to the imagination, but I must be on my guard against that. Let us have no inferences nor deductions, and nothing but solid facts. I *know* that the mesmeric trance is true; I *know* that mesmeric suggestion is true; I *know* that I am myself sensitive to this force. That is my present position. I have a large new notebook which shall be devoted entirely to scientific detail.

Long talk with Agatha and Mrs. Marden in the evening about our marriage. We think that the summer vac. (the beginning of it) would be the best time for the wedding. Why should we delay? I grudge even those few months. Still, as Mrs. Marden says, there are a good many things to be arranged.

March 28. Mesmerized again by Miss Penelosa. Experience much the same as before, save that insensibility came on more quickly. See Notebook A for temperature of room, barometric pressure, pulse, and respiration as taken by Professor Wilson.

March 29. Mesmerized again. Details in Notebook A.

March 30. Sunday, and a blank day. I grudge any interruption of our experiments. At present they merely embrace the physical signs which go with slight, with complete, and with extreme insensibility. Afterwards we hope to pass on to the phenomena of suggestion and of lucidity. Professors have demonstrated these things upon women at Nancy and at the Salpêtrière. It will be more convincing when a woman demonstrates it upon a professor, with a second professor as a witness. And that I should be the subject—I, the sceptic, the materialist! At least, I have shown that my devotion to science is greater than to my own personal consistency. The eating of our own words is the greatest sacrifice which truth ever requires of us.

My neighbour, Charles Sadler, the handsome young demonstrator of anatomy, came in this evening to return a volume of Virchow's "Archives" which I had lent him. I call him young, but, as a matter of fact, he is a year older than I am.

"I understand, Gilroy," said he, "that you are being experimented upon by Miss Penelosa.

"Well," he went on, when I had acknowledged it, "if I were you, I should not let it go any further. You will think me very impertinent, no doubt, but, none the less, I feel it to be my duty to advise you to have no more to do with her."

Of course I asked him why.

"I am so placed that I cannot enter into particulars as freely as I could wish," said he. "Miss Penelosa is the friend of my friend, and my position is a delicate one. I can only say this: that I have myself been the subject of some of the woman's experiments, and that they have left a most unpleasant impression upon my mind."

He could hardly expect me to be satisfied with that, and I tried hard to get something more definite out of him, but without success. Is it conceivable that he could be jealous at my having superseded him? Or is he one of those men of science who feel personally injured when facts run counter to their preconceived opinions? He cannot seriously suppose that because he has some vague grievance I am, therefore, to abandon a series of experiments which promise to be so fruitful of results. He appeared to be annoyed at the light way in which I treated his shadowy warnings, and we parted with some little coldness on both sides.

March 31. Mesmerized by Miss P.

April 1. Mesmerized by Miss P. (Notebook A.)

April 2. Mesmerized by Miss P. (Sphygmographic chart taken by Professor Wilson.)

April 3. It is possible that this course of mesmerism may be a little trying to the general constitution. Agatha says that I am thinner and darker under the eyes. I am conscious of a nervous irritability, which I had not observed in myself before. The least noise, for example, makes me start, and the stupidity of a student causes me exasperation instead of amusement. Agatha wishes me to stop, but I tell her that every course of study is trying, and that one can never attain a result without paying some price for it. When she sees the sensation which my forthcoming paper on "The Relation between Mind and Matter" may make, she will understand that it is worth a little nervous wear and tear. I should not be surprised if I got my F.R.S. over it.

Mesmerized again in the evening. The effect is produced more rapidly now, and the subjective visions are less marked. I keep full notes of each sitting. Wilson is leaving for town for a week or ten days, but we shall not interrupt the experiments, which depend for their value as much upon my sensations as on his observations.

April 4. I must be carefully on my guard. A complication has crept into our experiments which I had not reckoned upon. In my eagerness for scientific facts I have been foolishly blind to the human relations between Miss Penelosa and myself. I can write here what I would not breathe to a living soul. The unhappy woman appears to have formed an attachment for me.

I should not say such a thing, even in the privacy of my own intimate journal, if it had not come to such a pass that it is impossible to ignore it. For some time—that is, for the last week—there have been signs which I have brushed aside and refused to think of. Her brightness when I come, her dejection when I go, her eagerness that I should come often, the expression of her eyes, the tone of her voice—I tried to think that they meant nothing, and were, perhaps, only her ardent West Indian manner. But last night, as I awoke from the mesmeric sleep, I put out my hand, unconsciously, involuntarily, and clasped hers. When I came fully to myself, we were sitting with them locked, she looking up at me with an expectant smile. And the horrible thing was that I felt impelled to say what she expected me to say. What a false wretch I should have been! How I should have loathed myself today had I yielded to the temptation of that moment! But, thank God, I was strong enough to spring up and hurry from the room. I was rude, I fear, but I could not, no, I *could* not, trust myself another moment. I, a gentleman, a man of honour, engaged to one of the sweetest girls in England—and yet in a moment of reasonless passion I nearly professed love for this woman whom I hardly know. She is far older than myself and a cripple. It is monstrous, odious; and yet the impulse was so strong that, had I stayed another minute in her presence, I should have committed myself. What was it? I have to teach others the workings of our organism, and what do I know of it myself? Was it the sudden upcropping of some lower stratum in my nature—a brutal primitive instinct suddenly asserting itself? I could almost believe the tales of obsession by evil spirits, so overmastering was the feeling.

Well, the incident places me in a most unfortunate position. On the one hand, I am very loath to abandon a series of experiments which have already gone so far, and which promise such brilliant results. On the other, if this unhappy woman has conceived a passion for me—but surely even now I must have made some hideous mistake. She, with her age and her deformity! It is impossible. And then she knew about Agatha. She understood how I was placed. She only smiled out of amusement, perhaps, when in my dazed state I seized her hand. It was my half-mesmerized brain which gave it a meaning, and sprang with such bestial swiftness to meet it. I wish I could persuade myself that it was indeed so. On the whole, perhaps, my wisest plan would be to postpone our other experiments until Wilson's return. I have written a note to Miss Penelosa, therefore, making no allusion to last night, but saying that a press of work would cause me to interrupt our sittings for a few days. She has answered, formally enough, to say that if I should change my mind I should find her at home at the usual hour.

10 p.m. Well, well, what a thing of straw I am! I am coming to know myself better of late, and the more I know the lower I fall in my own estimation. Surely I was not always so weak as this. At four o'clock I should have smiled had anyone told me that I should go to Miss Penelosa's tonight, and yet, at eight, I was at Wilson's door as usual. I don't know how it occurred. The influence of habit, I suppose. Perhaps there is a mesmeric craze as there is an opium craze, and I am a victim to it. I only know that as I worked in my study I became more and more uneasy. I fidgeted. I worried. I could not concentrate my mind upon the papers in front of me. And then, at last, almost before I knew what I was doing, I seized my hat and hurried round to keep my usual appointment.

We had an interesting evening. Mrs. Wilson was present during most of the time, which prevented the embarrassment which one at least of us must have felt. Miss Penelosa's manner was quite the same as usual, and she expressed no surprise at my having come in spite of my note. There was nothing in her bearing to show that yesterday's incident had made any impression upon her, and so I am inclined to hope that I overrated it.

April 6 (evening). No, no, no, I did not overrate it. I can no longer attempt to conceal from myself that this woman has conceived a passion for me. It is monstrous, but it is true. Again, tonight, I awoke from the mesmeric trance to find my hand in hers, and to suffer that odious feeling which urges me to throw away my honour, my career, everything, for the sake of this creature who, as I can plainly see when I am away from her influence, possesses no single charm upon earth. But when I am near her, I do not feel this. She rouses something in me, something evil, something I had rather not think of. She paralyzes my better nature, too, at the moment when she stimulates my worse. Decidedly it is not good for me to be near her.

Last night was worse than before. Instead of flying I actually sat for some time with my hand in hers talking over the most intimate subjects with her. We spoke of Agatha, among other things. What could I have been dreaming of? Miss Penelosa said that she was conventional, and I agreed with her. She spoke once or twice in a disparaging way of her, and I did not protest. What a creature I have been!

Weak as I have proved myself to be, I am still strong enough to bring this sort of thing to an end. It shall not happen again. I have sense enough to fly when I cannot fight. From this Sunday night onward I shall never sit with Miss Penelosa again. Never! Let the experiments go, let the research come to an end; anything is better than facing this monstrous temptation which drags me so low. I have said nothing to Miss Penelosa, but I shall simply stay away. She can tell the reason without any words of mine.

April 7. Have stayed away, as I said. It is a pity to ruin

such an interesting investigation, but it would be a greater pity still to ruin my life, and I *know* that I cannot trust myself with that woman.

11 p.m. God help me! What is the matter with me? Am I going mad? Let me try and be calm and reason with myself. First of all I shall set down exactly what occurred.

It was nearly eight when I wrote the lines with which this day begins. Feeling strangely restless and uneasy, I left my rooms and walked round to spend the evening with Agatha and her mother. They both remarked that I was pale and haggard. About nine Professor Pratt-Haldane came in, and we played a game of whist. I tried hard to concentrate my attention upon the cards, but the feeling of restlessness grew and grew until I found it impossible to struggle against it. I simply *could* not sit still at the table. At last, in the very middle of a hand, I threw my cards down and, with some sort of incoherent apology about having an appointment, I rushed from the room. As if in a dream I have a vague recollection of tearing through the hall, snatching my hat from the stand, and slamming the door behind me. As if in a dream, too, I have the impression of the double line of gas-lamps, and my bespattered boots tell me that I must have run down the middle of the road. It was all misty and strange and unnatural. I came to Wilson's house; I saw Mrs. Wilson and I saw Miss Penelosa. I hardly recall what we talked about, but I do remember that Miss P. shook the head of her crutch at me in a playful way, and accused me of being late and of losing interest in our experiments. There was no mesmerism, but I stayed some time and have only just returned.

My brain is quite clear again now, and I can think over what has occurred. It is absurd to suppose that it is merely weakness and force of habit. I tried to explain it in that way the other night, but it will no longer suffice. It is something much deeper and more terrible than that. Why, when I was at the Mardens' whist-table, I was dragged away as if the noose of a rope had been cast round me. I can no longer disguise it from myself. The woman has her grip upon me. I am in her clutch. But I must keep my head and reason it out and see what is best to be done.

But what a blind fool I have been! In my enthusiasm over my research I have walked straight into the pit, although it lay gaping before me. Did she not herself warn me? Did she not tell me, as I can read in my own journal, that when she has acquired power over a subject she can make him do her will? And she has acquired that power over me. I am for the moment at the beck and call of this creature with the crutch. I must come when she wills it. I must do as she wills. Worst of all, I must feel as she wills. I loathe her and fear her, yet, while I am under the spell, she can doubtless make me love her.

There is some consolation in the thought, then, that those odious impulses for which I have blamed myself do not really come from me at all. They are all transferred from her, little as I could have guessed it at the time. I feel cleaner and lighter for the thought.

April 8. Yes, now, in broad daylight, writing coolly and with time for reflection, I am compelled to confirm everything which I wrote in my journal last night. I am in a horrible position, but, above all, I must not lose my head. I must pit my intellect against her powers. After all, I am no silly puppet, to dance at the end of a string. I have energy, brains, courage. For all her devil's tricks I may beat her yet. May! I *must*, or what is to become of me?

Let me try to reason it out! This woman, by her own explanation, can dominate my nervous organism. She can project herself into my body and take command of it. She has a parasite soul; yes, she is a parasite, a monstrous parasite. She creeps into my frame as the hermit crab does into the whelk's shell. I am powerless. What can I do? I am dealing with forces of which I know nothing. And I can tell no one of my trouble. They would set me down as a madman. Certainly, if it got noised abroad, the university would say that they had no need of a devil-ridden professor. And Agatha! No, no, I must face it alone.

III

I read over my notes of what the woman said when she spoke about her powers. There is one point which fills me with dismay. She implies that when the influence is slight the subject knows what he is doing, but cannot control himself, whereas when it is strongly exerted he is absolutely unconscious. Now, I have always known what I did, though less so last night than on the previous occasions. That seems to mean that she has never yet exerted her full powers upon me. Was ever a man so placed before?

Yes, perhaps there was, and very near me, too. Charles Sadler must know something of this! His vague words of warning take a meaning now. Oh, if I had only listened to him then, before I helped by these repeated sittings to forge the links of the chain which binds me! But I will see him today. I will apologize to him for having treated his warning so lightly. I will see if he can advise me.

4 p.m. No, he cannot. I have talked with him, and he showed such surprise at the first words in which I tried to express my unspeakable secret that I went no further. As far as I can gather (by hints and inferences rather than by any statement), his own experience was limited to some words or looks such as I have myself endured. His abandonment of Miss Penelosa is in itself a sign that he was

never really in her toils. Oh, if he only knew his escape! He has to thank his phlegmatic Saxon temperament for it. I am dark and Celtic, and this hag's clutch is deep in my nerves. Shall I ever get it out? Shall I ever be the same man that I was just one short fortnight ago?

Let me consider what I had better do. I cannot leave the university in the middle of the term. If I were free, my course would be obvious. I should start at once and travel in Persia. But would she allow me to start? And could her influence not reach me in Persia, and bring me back to within touch of her crutch? I can only find out the limits of this hellish power by my own bitter experience. I will fight and fight and fight—and what can I do more?

I know very well that about eight o'clock tonight that craving for her society, that irresistible restlessness, will come upon me. How shall I overcome it? What shall I do? I must make it impossible for me to leave the room. I shall lock the door and throw the key out of the window. But, then, what am I to do in the morning? Never mind about the morning. I must at all costs break this chain which holds me.

April 9. Victory! I have done splendidly! At seven o'clock last night I took a hasty dinner, and then locked myself up in my bedroom and dropped the key into the garden. I chose a cheery novel, and lay in bed for three hours trying to read it, but really in a horrible state of trepidation, expecting every instant that I should become conscious of the impulse. Nothing of the sort occurred, however, and I awoke this morning with the feeling that a black nightmare had been lifted off me. Perhaps the creature realized what I had done, and understood that it was useless to try to influence me. At any rate, I have beaten her once, and if I can do it once, I can do it again.

It was most awkward about the key in the morning.

Luckily, there was an under-gardener below, and I asked him to throw it up. No doubt he thought I had just dropped it. I will have doors and windows screwed up and six stout men to hold me down in my bed before I will surrender myself to be hag-ridden in this way.

I had a note from Mrs. Marden this afternoon asking me to go round and see her. I intended to do so in any case, but had not expected to find bad news waiting for me. It seems that the Armstrongs, from whom Agatha has expectations, are due home from Adelaide in the *Aurora*, and that they have written to Mrs. Marden and her to meet them in town. They will probably be away for a month or six weeks, and, as the *Aurora* is due on Wednesday, they must go at once—tomorrow, if they are ready in time. My consolation is that when we meet again there will be no more parting between Agatha and me.

"I want you to do one thing, Agatha," said I, when we were alone together. "If you should happen to meet Miss Penelosa, either in town or here, you must promise me never again to allow her to mesmerize you."

Agatha opened her eyes.

"Why, it was only the other day that you were saying how interesting it all was, and how determined you were to finish your experiments."

"I know, but I have changed my mind since then."

"And you won't have it any more?"

"No."

"I am so glad, Austin. You can't think how pale and worn you have been lately. It was really our principal objection to going to London now that we did not wish to leave you when you were so pulled down. And your manner has been so strange occasionally—especially that night when you left poor Professor Pratt-Haldane to play dummy. I am convinced that these experiments are very bad for your nerves."

"I think so, too, dear."

"And for Miss Penelosa's nerves as well. You have heard that she is ill?"

"No."

"Mrs. Wilson told us so last night. She described it as a nervous fever. Professor Wilson is coming back this week, and of course Mrs. Wilson is very anxious that Miss Penelosa should be well again then, for he has quite a programme of experiments which he is anxious to carry out."

I was glad to have Agatha's promise, for it was enough that this woman should have one of us in her clutch. On the other hand, I was disturbed to hear about Miss Penelosa's illness. It rather discounts the victory which I appeared to win last night. I remember that she said that loss of health interfered with her power. That may be why I was able to hold my own so easily. Well, well, I must take the same precautions tonight and see what comes of it. I am childishly frightened when I think of her.

April 10. All went well last night. I was amused at the gardener's face when I had again to hail him this morning and to ask him to throw up my key. I shall get a name among the servants if this sort of thing goes on. But the great point is that I stayed in my room without the slightest inclination to leave it. I do believe that I am shaking myself clear of this incredible bond—or is it only that the woman's power is in abeyance until she recovers her strength? I can but pray for the best.

The Mardens left this morning, and the brightness seems to have gone out of the spring sunshine. And yet it is very beautiful also as it gleams on the green chestnuts opposite my windows, and gives a touch of gaiety to the heavy, lichen-mottled walls of the old colleges. How sweet and gentle and soothing is Nature! Who would think that lurked in her also such vile forces, such odious possibilities! For of course I understand that this dreadful thing which has sprung out at me is neither supernatural nor even preternatural. No, it is a natural force which this woman can use and society is ignorant of. The mere fact that it ebbs with her strength shows how entirely it is subject to physical laws. If I had time, I might probe it to the bottom and lay my hands upon its antidote. But you cannot tame the tiger when you are beneath his claws. You can but try to writhe away from him. Ah, when I look in the glass and see my own dark eyes and clear-cut Spanish face, I long for a vitriol splash or a bout of the smallpox. One or the other might have saved me from this calamity.

I am inclined to think that I may have trouble tonight. There are two things which make me fear so. One is that I met Mrs. Wilson in the street, and she tells me that Miss Penelosa is better, though still weak. I find myself wishing in my heart that the illness had been her last. The other is that Professor Wilson comes back in a day or two, and his presence would act as a constraint upon her. I should not fear our interviews if a third person were present. For both these reasons I have a presentiment of trouble tonight, and I shall take the same precautions as before.

April 10. No, thank God, all went well last night. I really could not face the gardener again. I locked my door and thrust the key underneath it, so that I had to ask the maid to let me out in the morning. But the precaution was really not needed, for I never had any inclination to go out at all. Three evenings in succession at home! I am surely near the end of my troubles, for Wilson will be home again either today or tomorrow. Shall I tell him of what I have gone through or not? I am convinced that I should not have the slightest sympathy from him. He would look upon me as an interesting case, and read a paper about me at the next meeting of the Psychical Society, in which he would gravely discuss the possibility of my being a deliberate liar, and weigh it against the chances of my being in an early stage of lunacy. No, I shall get no comfort out of Wilson.

I am feeling wonderfully fit and well. I don't think I ever lectured with greater spirit. Oh, if I could only get this shadow off my life, how happy I should be! Young, fairly wealthy, in the front rank of my profession, engaged to a beautiful and charming girl—have I not everything which a man could ask for? Only one thing to trouble me, but what a thing it is!

Midnight. I shall go mad. Yes, that will be the end of it. I shall go mad. I am not far from it now. My head throbs as I rest it on my hot hand. I am quivering all over like a scared horse. Oh, what a night I have had! And yet I have some cause to be satisfied also.

At the risk of becoming the laughing-stock of my own servant, I again slipped my key under the door, imprisoning myself for the night. Then, finding it too early to go to bed, I lay down with my clothes on and began to read one of Dumas's novels. Suddenly I was gripped—gripped and dragged from the couch. It is only thus that I can describe the overpowering nature of the force which pounced upon me. I clawed at the coverlet. I clung to the woodwork. I believe that I screamed out in my frenzy. It was all useless, hopeless, I must go. There is no way out of it. It was only at the outset that I resisted. The force soon became too overmastering for that. I thank goodness that there were no watchers there to interfere with me. I could not have answered for myself if there had been. And, besides the determination to get out, there came to me also, the keenest and coolest judgment in choosing means. I lit a candle and endeavoured, kneeling in front of the door, to pull the key through with the feather-end of a quill pen. It was just short and pushed it further away. Then with quiet persistence I got a paper-knife out of one of the drawers, and with that I managed to draw the key back. I opened the door, stepped into my study, took a photograph of myself from the bureau, wrote something across it, placed it in the inside pocket of my coat, and then started off for Wilson's.

It was all wonderfully clear, and yet disassociated from the rest of my life, as the incidents of even the most vivid dream might be. A peculiar double consciousness possessed me. There was the predominant alien will, which was bent upon drawing me to the side of its owner, and there was the feebler protesting personality, which I recognized as being myself, tugging feebly at the overmastering impulse as a led terrier might at its chain. I can remember recognizing these two conflicting forces, but I recall nothing of my walk, nor of how I was admitted to the house.

Very vivid, however, is my recollection of how I met Miss Penelosa. She was reclining on the sofa in the little boudoir in which our experiments had usually been carried out. Her head was rested on her hand, and a tiger-skin rug had been partly drawn over her. She looked up expectantly as I entered, and, as the lamp-light fell upon her face, I could see that she was very pale and thin, with dark hollows under her eyes. She smiled at me, and pointed to a stool beside her. It was with her left hand that she pointed, and I, running eagerly forward, seized it—I loathe myself as I think of it—and pressed it passionately to my lips. Then, seating myself upon the stool, and still retaining her hand, I gave her the photograph which I had brought with me, and talked and talked and talked—of my love for her, of my grief over her illness, of my joy at her recovery, of the misery it was to be absent a single evening from her side. She lay quietly looking down at me with imperious eyes and her provocative smile. Once I remember that she passed her hand over my hair as one caresses a dog; and it gave me pleasure—the caress. I thrilled under it. I was her slave, body and soul, and for the moment I rejoiced in my slavery.

And then came the blessed change. Never tell me that there is not a Providence! I was on the brink of perdition. My feet were on the edge. Was it a coincidence that at that very instant help should come? No, no, no; there is a Providence, and its hand has drawn me back. There is something in the universe stronger than this devil woman with her tricks. Ah, what a balm to my heart it is to think so!

As I looked up at her I was conscious of a change in her. Her face, which had been pale before, was now ghastly. Her eyes were dull, and the lids dropped heavily over them. Above all, the look of serene confidence had gone from her features. Her mouth had weakened. Her forehead had puckered. She was frightened and undecided. And as I watched the change my own spirit fluttered and struggled, trying hard to tear itself from the grip which held it—a grip which, from moment to moment, grew less secure.

"Austin," she whispered, "I have tried to do too much. I was not strong enough. I have not recovered yet from my illness. But I could not live longer without seeing you. You won't leave me, Austin? This is only a passing weakness. If you will only give me five minutes, I shall be myself again. Give me the small decanter from the table in the window."

But I had regained my soul. With her waning strength

the influence had cleared away from me and left me free. And I was aggressive—bitterly, fiercely aggressive. For once at least I could make this woman understand what my real feelings toward her were. My soul was filled with a hatred as bestial as the love against which it was a reaction. It was the savage, murderous passion of the revolted serf. I could have taken the crutch from her side and beaten her face in with it. She threw her hands up, as if to avoid a blow, and cowered away from me into the corner of the settee.

"The brandy!" she gasped. "The brandy!"

I took the decanter and poured it over the roots of a palm in the window. Then I snatched the photograph from her hand and tore it into a hundred pieces.

"You vile woman," I said, "if I did my duty to society, you would never leave this room alive!"

"I love you, Austin; I love you!" she wailed.

"Yes," I cried, "and Charles Sadler before. And how many others before that?"

"Charles Sadler!" she gasped. "He has spoken to you? So, Charles Sadler, Charles Sadler!" Her voice came through her white lips like a snake's hiss.

"Yes, I know you, and others shall know you, too. You shameless creature! You knew how I stood. And yet you used your vile power to bring me to your side. You may, perhaps, do so again, but at least you will remember that you have heard me say that I love Miss Marden from the bottom of my soul, and that I loathe you, abhor you! The very sight of you and the sound of your voice fill me with horror and disgust. The thought of you is repulsive. That is how I feel toward you, and if it pleases you by your tricks to draw me again to your side as you have done tonight, you will at least, I should think, have little satisfaction in trying to make a lover out of a man who has told you his real opinion of you. You may put what words you will into my mouth, but you cannot help remembering—"

I stopped, for the woman's head had fallen back, and she had fainted. She could not bear to hear what I had to say to her! What a glow of satisfaction it gives me to think that, come what may, in the future she can never misunderstand my true feelings toward her. But what will occur in the future? What will she do next? I dare not think of it. Oh, if only I could hope that she will leave me alone! But when I think of what I said to her—Never mind; I have been stronger than she for once.

April 11. I hardly slept last night, and found myself in the morning so unstrung and feverish that I was compelled to ask Pratt-Haldane to do my lecture for me. It is the first that I have ever missed. I rose at midday, but my head is aching, my hands quivering, and my nerves in a pitiable state.

Who should come round this evening but Wilson. He has just come back from London, where he has lectured, read papers, convened meetings, exposed a medium, conducted a series of experiments on thought transference, entertained Professor Richet of Paris, spent hours gazing into a crystal, and obtained some evidence as to the passage of matter through matter. All this he poured into my ears in a single gust.

"But you!" he cried at last. "You are not looking well. And Miss Penelosa is quite prostrated today. How about the experiments?"

"I have abandoned them."

"Tut, tut! Why?"

"The subject seems to me a dangerous one."

Out came his big brown notebook.

"This is of great interest," said he. "What are your grounds for saying that it is a dangerous one? Please give your facts in chronological order, with approximate dates and names of reliable witnesses with their permanent addresses."

"First of all," I asked, "would you tell me whether you have collected any cases where the mesmerist has gained a command over the subject and has used it for evil purposes?"

"Dozens!" he cried exultantly. "Crime by suggestion—"

"I don't mean suggestion. I mean where a sudden impulse comes from a person at a distance—an uncontrollable impulse."

"Obsession!" he shrieked, in an ecstasy of delight. "It is the rarest condition. We have eight cases, five well attested. You don't mean to say—" His exultation made him hardly articulate.

"No, I don't," I said. "Good evening! You will excuse me, but I am not very well tonight." And so at last I got rid of him, still brandishing his pencil and his notebook. My troubles may be bad to bear, but at least it is better to hug them to myself than to have myself exhibited by Wilson, like a freak at a fair. He has lost sight of human beings. Everything to him is a case and a phenomenon. I will die before I speak to him again upon the matter.

April 12. Yesterday was a blessed day of quiet, and I enjoyed an uneventful night. Wilson's presence is a great consolation. What can the woman do now? Surely, when she has heard me say what I have said, she will conceive the same disgust for me which I have for her. She could not, no, she *could* not, desire to have a lover who had insulted her so. No, I believe I am free from her love—but how about her hate? Might she not use these powers of hers for revenge? Tut! Why should I frighten myself over shadows? She will forget about me, and I shall forget about her, and all will be well.

April 13. My nerves have quite recovered their tone. I really believe that I have conquered the creature. But I must confess to living in some suspense. She is well again, for I hear that she was driving with Mrs. Wilson in the High Street in the afternoon.

April 14. I do wish I could get away from the place altogether. I shall fly to Agatha's side the very day that the term closes. I suppose it is pitiably weak of me, but this woman gets upon my nerves most terribly. I have seen her again, and I have spoken with her.

It was just after lunch, and I was smoking a cigarette in my study, when I heard the step of my servant Murray in the passage. I was languidly conscious that a second step was audible behind, and had hardly troubled myself to speculate who it might be, when suddenly a slight noise brought me out of my chair with my skin creeping with apprehension. I had never particularly observed before what sort of sound the tapping of a crutch was, but my quivering nerves told me that I heard it now in the sharp wooden clack which alternated with the muffled thud of the foot-fall. Another instant and my servant had shown her in.

I did not attempt the usual conventions of society, nor did she. I simply stood with the smouldering cigarette in my hand, and gazed at her. She in turn looked silently at me, and at her look I remembered how in these very pages I had tried to define the expression of her eyes, whether they were furtive or fierce. Today they were fierce—coldly and inexorably so.

"Well," she said, at last, "are you still of the same mind as when I saw you last?"

"I have always been of the same mind."

"Let us understand each other, Professor Gilroy," said she slowly. "I am not a very safe person to trifle with, as you should realize by now. It was you who asked me to enter into a series of experiments with you, it was you who won my affections, it was you who professed your love for me, it was you who brought me your own photograph with words of affection upon it, and, finally, it was you who on the very same evening thought it fit to insult me most outrageously, addressing me as no man has ever dared to speak to me yet. Tell me that those words came from you in a moment of passion and I am prepared to forget and forgive them. You did not mean what you said, Austin? You do not really hate me?"

I might have pitied this deformed woman—such a longing for love broke suddenly through the menace of her eyes. But then I thought of what I had gone through, and my heart set like flint.

"If ever you heard me speak of love," said I, "you know very well that it was your own voice which spoke, and not mine. The only words of truth which I have ever been able to say to you are those which you heard when last we met."

"I know. Someone has set you against me. It was he!" She tapped with her crutch upon the floor. "Well, you know very well that I could bring you this minute crouching like a spaniel to my feet. You will not find me again in my hour of weakness, when you can insult me with impunity. Have a care what you are doing, Professor Gilroy. You stand in a terrible position. You have not yet realized the hold which I have upon you."

I shrugged my shoulders and turned away.

"Well," said she, after a pause, "if you despise my love, I must see what can be done with fear. You smile, but the day will come when you will come screaming to me for pardon. Yes, you will grovel on the ground before me, proud as you are, and you will curse the day that ever you turned me from your best friend into your most bitter enemy. Have a care, Professor Gilroy!" I saw a white hand shaking in the air, and a face which was scarcely human, so convulsed was it with passion. An instant later she was gone, and I heard the quick hobble and tap receding down the passage.

But she has left a weight upon my heart. Vague presentiments of coming misfortune lie heavy upon me. I try in vain to persuade myself that these are only words of empty anger. I can remember those relentless eyes too clearly to think so. What shall I do—ah, what shall I do? I am no longer master of my own soul. At any moment this loathsome parasite may creep into me, and then—? I must tell someone my hideous secret—I must tell it or go mad. If I had someone to sympathize and advise! Wilson is out of the question. Charles Sadler would understand me only so far as his own experience carries him. Pratt-Haldane! He is a well-balanced man, a man of great common sense and resource. I will go to him. I will tell him everything. God grant that he may be able to advise me!

IV

6:45 p.m. No, it is useless. There is no human help for me; I must fight this out single-handed. Two courses lie before me. I might become this woman's lover. Or I must endure such persecutions as she can inflict upon me. Even if none come, I shall live in a well of apprehension. But she may torture me, she may drive me mad, she may kill me: I will never, never, never give in. What can she inflict which would be worse than the loss of Agatha, and the knowledge that I am a perjured liar, and have forfeited the name of gentleman?

Pratt-Haldane was most amiable, and listened with all politeness to my story. But when I looked at his heavy-set features, his slow eyes, and the ponderous study furniture which surrounded him, I could hardly tell him what I had come to say. It was all so substantial, so material. And, besides, what would I myself have said a short month ago if one of my colleagues had come to me with a story of demonic possession? Perhaps I should have been less patient than he was. As it was, he took notes of my statement, asked me how much tea I drank, how many hours I slept, whether I had been overworking much, had I had sudden pains in the head, evil dreams, singing in the ears, flashing before the eyes—all questions which pointed to his belief that brain congestion was at the bottom of my trouble. Finally he dismissed me with a great many platitudes about open-air exercise, and avoidance of nervous excitement. His prescription, which was for chloral and bromide, I rolled up and threw into the gutter.

No, I can look for no help from any human being. If I consult any more, they may put their heads together and I may find myself in an asylum. I can but grip my courage with both hands, and pray that an honest man may not be abandoned.

April 15. It is the sweetest spring within the memory of man. So green, so mild, so beautiful! Ah, what a contrast between nature without and my own soul so torn with doubt and terror! It has been an uneventful day, but I know that I am on the edge of an abyss. I know it, and yet I go on with the routine of my life. The one bright spot is that Agatha is happy and well and out of all danger. If this creature had a hand on each of us, what might she not do?

April 16. The woman is ingenious in her torments. She knows how fond I am of my work, and how highly my lectures are thought of. So it is from that point that she now attacks me. It will end, I can see, in my losing my professorship, but I will fight to the finish. She shall not drive me out of it without a struggle.

I was not conscious of any change during my lecture this morning save that for a minute or two I had a dizziness and swimminess which rapidly passed away. On the contrary, I congratulated myself upon having made my subject (the functions of the red corpuscles) both interesting and clear. I was surprised, therefore, when a student came into my laboratory immediately after the lecture, and complained of being puzzled by the discrepancy between my statements and those in the textbooks. He showed me his notebook, in which I was reported as having in one portion of the lecture championed the most outrageous and unscientific heresies. Of course I denied it, and declared that he had misunderstood me, but on comparing his notes with those of his companions, it became clear that he was right, and that I really had made some most preposterous statements. Of course I shall explain it away as being the result of a moment of aberration, but I feel only too sure that it will be the first of a series. It is but a month now to the end of the session, and I pray that I may be able to hold out until then.

April 26. Ten days have elapsed since I have had the heart to make any entry in my journal. Why should I record my own humiliation and degradation? I had vowed never to open it again. And yet the force of habit is strong, and here I find myself taking up once more the record of my own dreadful experiences—in much the same spirit in which a suicide has been known to take notes of the effects of the poison which killed him.

Well, the crash which I had foreseen has come—and that no further back than yesterday. The university authorities have taken my lectureship away from me. It has been done in the most delicate way, purporting to be a temporary measure to relieve me from the effects of overwork, and to give me the opportunity of recovering my health. None the less, it has been done, and I am no longer Professor Gilroy. The laboratory is still in my charge, but I have little doubt that that also will soon go.

The fact is that my lectures had become the laughing-stock of the university. My class was crowded with students who came to see and hear what the eccentric professor would do or say next. I cannot go into the detail of my humiliation. Oh, that devilish woman! There is no depth of buffoonery and imbecility to which she has not forced me. I would begin my lecture clearly and well, but always with the sense of a coming eclipse. Then as I felt the influence I would struggle against it, striving with clenched hands and beads of sweat upon my brow to get the better of it, while the students, hearing my incoherent words and watching my contortions, would roar with laughter at the antics of their professor. And then, when she had once fairly mastered me, out would come the most outrageous things—silly jokes, sentiments as though I were proposing a toast, snatches of ballads, personal abuse even against some member of my class. And then in a moment my brain would clear again, and my lecture would proceed decorously to the end. No wonder that my conduct has been the talk of the colleges. No wonder that the University Senate has been compelled to take official notice of such a scandal. Oh, that devilish woman!

And the most dreadful part of it all is my own loneliness. Here I sit in a commonplace English bow-window, looking out upon a commonplace English street with its garish buses and its lounging policeman, and behind me there hangs a shadow which is out of all keeping with the age and place. In the home of knowledge I am weighed down and tortured by a power of which science knows nothing. No magistrate would listen to me. No paper would discuss my case. No doctor would believe my symptoms. My own most intimate friends would only look upon it as a sign of brain derangement. I am out of all touch with my kind. Oh, that devilish woman! Let her have a care! She may push me too far. When the law cannot help a man, he may make a law for himself.

She met me in the High Street yesterday evening and spoke to me. It was as well for her, perhaps, that it was not between the hedges of a lonely country road. She asked me with her cold smile whether I had been chastened yet. I did not deign to answer her. "We must try another turn of the screw," said she. Have a care, my lady, have a care! I had her at my mercy once. Perhaps another chance may come.

April 28. The suspension of my lectureship has had the effect also of taking away her means of annoying me, and so I have enjoyed two blessed days of peace. After all, there is no reason to despair. Sympathy pours in to me from all sides, and everyone agrees that it is my devotion to science and the arduous nature of my researches which have shaken my nervous system. I have had the kindest message from the council advising me to travel abroad, and expressing the confident hope that I may be able to resume all my duties by the beginning of the summer term. Nothing could be more flattering than their allusions to my career and to my services to the university. It is only in misfortune that one can test one's own popularity. This creature may weary of tormenting me, and then all may yet be well. May God grant it!

April 29. Our sleepy little town has had a small sensation. The only knowledge of crime which we ever have is when a rowdy undergraduate breaks a few lamps or comes to blows with a policeman. Last night, however, there was an attempt made to break into the branch of the Bank of England, and we are all in a flutter in consequence.

Parkinson, the manager, is an intimate friend of mine, and I found him very much excited when I walked round there after breakfast. Had the thieves broken into the counting-house, they would still have had the safes to reckon with, so that the defence was considerably stronger than the attack. Indeed, the latter does not appear to have ever been very formidable. Two of the lower windows have marks as if a chisel or some such instrument had been pushed under them to force them open. The police should have a good clue, for the woodwork had been done with green paint only the day before, and from the smears it is evident that some of it has found its way on to the criminal's hands or clothes.

4:30 p.m. Ah, that accursed woman! That thrice accursed woman! Never mind! She shall not beat me! No, she shall not! But, oh, the she-devil! She has taken my professorship. Now she would take my honour. Is there nothing I can do against her, nothing save—Ah, but, hard pushed as I am, I cannot bring myself to think of that!

It was about an hour ago that I went into my bedroom, and was brushing my hair before the glass, when suddenly my eyes lit upon something which left me so sick and cold that I sat down upon the edge of the bed and began to cry. It is many a long year since I shed tears, but all my nerve was gone, and I could but sob and sob in impotent grief and anger. There was my house jacket, the coat I usually wear after dinner, hanging on its peg by the wardrobe, with the right sleeve thickly crusted from wrist to elbow with daubs of green paint.

So this was what she meant by another turn of the screw! She had made a public imbecile of me. Now she would brand me as a criminal. This time she has failed. But how about the next? I dare not think of it—and of Agatha and my poor old mother! I wish that I were dead!

Yes, this is the other turn of the screw. And this is also what she meant, no doubt, when she said that I had not realized yet the power she has over me. I look back at my account of my conversation with her, and I see how she declared that with a slight exertion of her will her subject would be conscious, and with a stronger one unconscious. Last night I was unconscious. I could have sworn that I slept soundly in my bed without so much as a dream. And yet those stains tell me that I dressed, made my way out, attempted to open the bank windows, and returned. Was I observed? Is it possible that someone saw me do it and followed me home? Ah, what a hell my life has become! I have no peace, no rest. But my patience is nearing its end.

10 p.m. I have cleaned my coat with turpentine. I do not think that anyone could have seen me. It was with my screwdriver that I made the marks. I found it all crusted with paint, and I have cleaned it. My head aches as if it would burst, and I have taken five grains of antipyrine. If it were not for Agatha, I should have taken fifty and had an end of it.

May 3. Three quiet days. This hell-fiend is like a cat with a mouse. She lets me loose only to pounce upon me again. I am never so frightened as when everything is still. My physical state is deplorable—perpetual hiccough and ptosis of the left eyelid.

I have heard from the Mardens that they will be back the day after tomorrow. I do not know whether I am glad or sorry. They were safe in London. Once here they may be drawn into the miserable network in which I am myself struggling. And I must tell them of it. I cannot marry Agatha so long as I know that I am not responsible for my own actions. Yes, I must tell them, even if it brings everything to an end between us.

Tonight is the university ball, and I must go. God knows I never felt less in the humour for festivity, but I must not have it said that I am unfit to appear in public. If I am seen there, and have speech with some of the elders of the university it will go a long way toward showing them that it would be unjust to take my chair away from me.

11:30 p.m. I have been to the ball. Charles Sadler and I went together, but I have come away before him. I shall wait up for him, however, for, indeed, I fear to go to sleep these nights. He is a cheery, practical fellow, and a chat with him will steady my nerves. On the whole, the evening was a great success. I talked to everyone who has influence, and I think that I made them realize that my chair is not vacant quite yet. The creature was at the ball—unable to dance, of course, but sitting with Mrs. Wilson. Again and again her eyes rested upon me. They were almost the last things I saw before I left the room. Once, as I sat sideways to her, I watched her, and saw that her gaze was following someone else. It was Sadler, who was dancing at the time with the second Miss Thurston. To judge by her expression, it is well for him that he is not in her grip as I am. He does not know the escape he has had. I think I hear his step in the street now, and I will go down and let him in. If he will—

May 4. Why did I break off in this way last night? I never went downstairs after all—at least, I have no recollection of doing so. But, on the other hand, I cannot remember going to bed. One of my hands is greatly swollen this morning, and yet I have no remembrance of injuring it yesterday. Otherwise, I am feeling all the better for last night's festivity. But I cannot understand how it is that I did not meet Charles Sadler when I so fully intended to do so. Is it possible—My God, it is only too probable! Has she been leading me in some devil's dance again? I will go down to Sadler and ask him.

Midday. The thing has come to a crisis. My life is not worth living. But, if I am to die, then she shall come also. I will not leave her behind, to drive some other man mad as she has me. No, I have come to the limit of my endurance. She has made me as desperate and dangerous a man as walks the earth. God knows I have never had the heart to hurt a fly, and yet, if I had my hands now upon that woman, she should never leave this room alive. I shall see her this very day, and she shall learn what she has to expect of me.

I went to Sadler and found him, to my surprise, in bed. As I entered he sat up and turned a face toward me which sickened me as I looked at it.

"Why, Sadler, what has happened?" I cried, but my heart turned cold as I said it.

"Gilroy," he answered, mumbling with his swollen lips, "I have for some weeks been under the impression that you are a madman. Now I know it, and that you are a dangerous one as well. If it were not that I am unwilling to make a scandal in the college, you would now be in the hands of the police."

"Do you mean—" I cried.

"I mean that as I opened the door last night you rushed out upon me, struck me with both your fists in the face, knocked me down, kicked me furiously in the side, and left me lying almost unconscious in the street. Look at your own hand bearing witness against you."

Yes, there it was, puffed up, with sponge-like knuckles, as after some terrific blow. What could I do? Though he put me down as a madman, I must tell him all. I sat by his bed and went over all my troubles from the beginning. I poured them out with quivering hands and burning words which might have carried conviction to the most sceptical. "She hates you and she hates me!" I cried. "She revenged herself last night on both of us at once. She saw me leave the ball, and she must have seen you also. She knew how long it would take you to reach home. Then she had but to use her wicked will. Ah, your bruised face is a small thing beside my bruised soul!"

He was struck by my story. That was evident. "Yes, yes, she watched me out of the room," he muttered. "She is capable of it. But is it possible that she has really reduced you to this? What do you intend to do?"

"To stop it!" I cried. "I am perfectly desperate; I shall give her fair warning today, and the next time will be the last."

"Do nothing rash," said he.

"Rash!" I cried. "The only rash thing is that I should postpone it another hour." With that I rushed to my room, and here I am on the eve of what may be the great crisis of my life. I shall start at once. I have gained one thing today, for I have made one man, at least, realize the truth of this monstrous experience of mine. And, if the worst should happen, this diary remains as a proof of the goad that has driven me.

Evening. When I came to Wilson's, I was shown up, and found that he was sitting with Miss Penelosa. For half an hour I had to endure his fussy talk about his recent research into the exact nature of the spiritualistic rap, while the creature and I sat in silence looking across the room at each other. I read a sinister amusement in her eyes, and she must have seen hatred and menace in mine. I had almost despaired of having speech with her when he was called from the room, and we were left for a few moments together.

"Well, Professor Gilroy—or is it Mr. Gilroy?" said she, with that bitter smile of hers. "How is your friend Mr. Charles Sadler after the ball?"

"You fiend!" I cried. "You have come to the end of your tricks now. I will have no more of them. Listen to what I say." I strode across and shook her roughly by the shoulder. "As sure as there is a God in heaven, I swear that if you try another of your devilries upon me, I will have your life for it. Come what may, I will have your life. I have come to the end of what a man can endure."

"Accounts are not quite settled between us," said she, with a passion that equalled my own. "I can love, and I can hate. You had your choice. You chose to spurn the first; now you must test the other. It will take a little more to break your spirit, I see, but broken it shall be. Miss Marden comes back tomorrow, as I understand."

"What has that to do with you?" I cried. "It is a pollution that you should dare even to think of her. If I thought that you would harm her—"

She was frightened, I could see, though she tried to brazen it out. She read the black thought in my mind, and cowered away from me.

"She is fortunate in having such a champion," said she. "He actually dares to threaten a lonely woman. I must really congratulate Miss Marden upon her protector."

The words were bitter, but the voice and manner were more acid still.

"There is no use talking," said I. "I only came here to tell you—and to tell you most solemnly—that your next outrage upon me will be your last." With that, as I heard Wilson's step upon the stair, I walked from the room. Ay, she may look venomous and deadly, but, for all that, she is beginning to see now that she has as much to fear from me as I can have from her. Murder! It has an ugly sound. But you don't talk of murdering a snake or of murdering a tiger. Let her have a care now.

May 5. I met Agatha and her mother at the station at eleven o'clock. She is looking so bright, so happy, so beautiful. And she was so overjoyed to see me. What have I done to deserve such love? I went back home with them, and we lunched together. All the troubles seem in a moment to have been shredded back from my life. She tells me that I am looking pale and worried and ill. The dear child puts it down to my loneliness and the perfunctory attention of a housekeeper. I pray that she may never know the truth! May the shadow, if shadow there must be, lie ever black across my life and leave hers in the sunshine. I have just come back from them, feeling a new man. With her by my side I think that I could show a bold face to anything which life might send.

5 p.m. Now, let me try to be accurate. Let me try to say exactly how it occurred. It is fresh in my mind, and I can set it down correctly, though it is not likely that the time will ever come when I shall forget the doings of today.

I had returned from the Mardens' after lunch, and was cutting some microscopic sections in my freezing microtome, when in an instant I lost consciousness in the sudden hateful fashion which has become only too familiar to me of late.

When my senses came back to me I was sitting in a small chamber, very different from the one in which I had been working. It was cosy and bright, with chintz-covered settees, coloured hangings, and a thousand pretty little trifles upon the wall. A small ornamental clock ticked in front of me, and the hands pointed to half-past three. It was all quite familiar to me, and yet I stared about for a moment in a half-dazed way until my eyes fell upon a cabinet photograph of myself upon the top of the piano. On the other side stood one of Mrs. Marden. Then, of course, I remembered where I was. It was Agatha's boudoir.

But how came I there, and what did I want? A horrible sinking came to my heart. Had I been sent there on some devilish errand? Had that errand already been done? Surely it must; otherwise, why should I be allowed to come back to consciousness? Oh, the agony of that moment! What had I done? I sprang to my feet in my despair, and as I did so a small glass bottle fell from my knees onto the carpet.

It was unbroken, and I picked it up. Outside was written "Sulphuric Acid. Fort." When I drew the round glass stopper, a thick fume rose slowly up, and a pungent, choking smell pervaded the room. I recognized it as one which I kept for chemical testing in my chambers. But why had I brought a bottle of vitriol into Agatha's chamber? Was it not this thick, reeking liquid with which jealous women had been known to mar the beauty of their rivals? My heart stood still as I held the bottle to the light. Thank God, it was full! No mischief had been done as yet. But had Agatha come in a minute sooner, was it not certain that the hellish parasite within me would have dashed the stuff into her—Ah, it will not bear to be thought of! But it must have been for that. Why else should I have brought it? At the thought of what I might have done my worn nerves broke down, and I sat shivering and twitching, the pitiable wreck of a man.

It was the sound of Agatha's voice and the rustle of her dress which restored me. I looked up, and saw her blue eyes, so full of tenderness and pity, gazing down at me.

"We must take you away to the country, Austin," she said. "You want rest and quiet. You look wretchedly ill."

"Oh, it is nothing!" said I, trying to smile. "It was only a momentary weakness. I am all right again now."

"I am so sorry to keep you waiting. Poor boy, you must have been here quite half an hour! The vicar was in the drawing-room, and, as I knew that you did not care for him, I thought it better that Jane should show you up here. I thought the man would never go!"

"Thank God he stayed! Thank God he stayed!" I cried hysterically.

"Why, what is the matter with you, Austin?" she asked, holding my arm as I staggered up from the chair. "Why are you glad that the vicar stayed? And what is this little bottle in your hand?"

"Nothing," I cried, thrusting it into my pocket. "But I must go. I have something important to do."

"How stern you look, Austin! I have never seen your face like that. You are angry?"

"Yes, I am angry."

"But not with me?"

"No, no, my darling! You would not understand."

"But you have not told me why you came."

"I came to ask you whether you would always love me—no matter what I did, or what shadow might fall on my name. Would you believe in me and trust me however black appearances might be against me?"

"You know that I would, Austin."

"Yes. I know that you would. What I do I shall do for you. I am driven to it. There is no other way out, my darling!" I kissed her and rushed from the room.

The time for indecision was at an end. As long as the creature threatened my own prospects and my honour there might be a question as to what I should do. But now, when Agatha—my innocent Agatha—was endangered, my duty lay before me like a turnpike road. I had no weapon, but I never paused for that. What weapon should I need, when I felt every muscle quivering with the strength of a frenzied man? I ran through the streets, so set upon what I had to do that I was only dimly conscious of the faces of friends whom I met—dimly conscious also that Professor Wilson met me, running with equal precipitance in the opposite direction. Breathless but resolute I reached the house and rang the bell. A white-cheeked maid opened the door, and turned whiter yet when she saw the face that looked in at her.

"Show me up at once to Miss Penelosa," I demanded.

"Sir," she gasped, "Miss Penelosa died this afternoon at half-past three!"

THE GIAOUR

✦✦✦

LORD BYRON

A FRAGMENT OF A TURKISH TALE

A turban carved in coarsest stone,
A pillar with rank weeds o'ergrown,
Whereon can now be scarcely read
The Koran verse that mourns the dead,
Point out the spot where Hassan fell
A victim in that lonely dell.
There sleeps as true an Osmanlie
As e'er at Mecca bent the knee;
As ever scorn'd forbidden wine,
Or pray'd with face towards the shrine,
In orisons resumed anew
At solemn sound of "Alla Hu!"
Yet died he by a stranger's hand,
And stranger in his native land;
Yet died he as in arms he stood,
And unavenged, at least in blood.
But him the maids of Paradise
Impatient to their halls invite,
And the dark Heaven of Houris' eyes
On him shall glance for ever bright;
They come—their kerchiefs green they wave,
And welcome with a kiss the brave!
Who falls in battle 'gainst a Giaour
Is worthiest an immortal bower.

But thou, false Infidel! shall writhe
Beneath avenging Monkir's scythe;
And from its torments 'scape alone
To wander round lost Eblis' throne;
And fire unquench'd, unquenchable,
Around, within, thy heart shall dwell;
Nor ear can hear nor tongue can tell
The tortures of that inward hell!
But first, on earth as Vampire sent,
Thy corse shall from its tomb be rent:
Then ghastly haunt thy native place,
And suck the blood of all thy race;
There from thy daughter, sister, wife,
At midnight drain the stream of life;
Yet loathe the banquet which perforce
Must feed thy livid living corse:
Thy victims ere they yet expire
Shall know the demon for their sire,
As cursing thee, thou cursing them,
Thy flowers are withered on the stem.
But one that for thy crime must fall,
The youngest, most beloved of all,
Shall bless thee with a father's name—
That word shall wrap thy heart in flame!
Yet must thou end thy task, and mark
Her cheek's last tinge, her eye's last spark,
And the last glassy glance must view
Which freezes o'er its lifeless blue;
Then with unhallow'd hand shalt tear
The tresses of her yellow hair,
Of which in life a lock when shorn
Affection's fondest pledge was worn,
But now is borne away by thee,
Memorial of thine agony!

Wet with thine own best blood shall drip
Thy gnashing tooth and haggard lip;
Then stalking to thy sullen grave,
Go—and with Gouls and Afrits rave;
Till these in horror shrink away
From Spectre more accursed than they!

THE MASTER OF RAMPLING GATE

♦♦♦

ANNE RICE

Rampling Gate: It was so real to us in those old pictures, rising like a fairy tale castle out of its own dark wood. A wilderness of gables and chimneys between those two immense towers, grey stone walls mantled in ivy, mullioned windows reflecting the drifting clouds.

But why had Father never gone there? Why had he never taken us? And why on his deathbed, in those grim months after Mother's passing, did he tell my brother, Richard, that Rampling Gate must be torn down stone by stone? Rampling Gate that had always belonged to Ramplings, Rampling Gate which had stood for over four hundred years.

We were in awe of the task that lay before us, and painfully confused. Richard had just finished four years at Oxford. Two whirlwind social seasons in London had proven me something of a shy success. I still preferred scribbling poems and stories in the quiet of my room to dancing the night away, but I'd kept that a good secret, and though we were not spoilt children, we had enjoyed the best of everything our parents could give. But now the carefree years were ended. We had to be careful and wise.

And our hearts ached as, sitting together in Father's book-lined study, we looked at the old pictures of Rampling Gate before the small coal fire. "Destroy it, Richard, as soon as I am gone," Father had said.

"I just don't understand it, Julie," Richard confessed, as he filled the little crystal glass in my hand with sherry. "It's the genuine article, that old place, a real fourteenth-century manor house in excellent repair. A Mrs. Blessington, born and reared in the village of Rampling, has apparently managed it all these years. She was there when Uncle Baxter died, and he was the last Rampling to live under that roof."

"Do you remember," I asked, "the year that Father took all these pictures down and put them away?"

"I shall never forget that," Richard said. "How could I? It was so peculiar, and so unlike Father, too." He sat back, drawing slowly on his pipe. "There had been that bizarre incident in Victoria Station, when he had seen that young man."

"Yes, exactly," I said, snuggling back into the velvet chair and looking into the tiny dancing flames in the grate. "You remember how upset Father was?"

Yet it was a simple incident. In fact nothing really happened at all. We couldn't have been more than six and eight at the time and we had gone to the station with Father to say farewell to friends. Through the window of a train Father saw a young man who startled and upset him. I could remember the face clearly to this day. Remarkably handsome, with a narrow nose and well-drawn eyebrows, and a mop of lustrous brown hair. The large black eyes had regarded Father with the saddest expression as Father had drawn us back and hurried us away.

"And the argument that night, between Father and Mother," Richard said thoughtfully. "I remember that we listened on the landing and we were so afraid."

"And Father said *he* wasn't content to be master of Rampling Gate anymore; *he* had come to London and revealed himself. An unspeakable horror, that is what he called it, that *he* should be so bold."

"Yes, exactly, and when Mother tried to quiet him, when she suggested that he was imagining things, he went into a perfect rage."

"But who could it have been, the master of Rampling Gate, if Father wasn't the master? Uncle Baxter was long dead by then."

"I just don't know what to make of it," Richard murmured. "And there's nothing in Father's papers to explain any of it at all." He examined the most recent of the pictures, a lovely tinted engraving that showed the house perfectly reflected in the azure water of its lake. "But I tell you, the worst part of it, Julie," he said shaking his head, "is that we've never even seen the house ourselves."

I glanced at him and our eyes met in a moment of confusion that quickly passed to something else. I leant forward:

"He did not say we couldn't go there, did he, Richard?" I demanded. "That we couldn't visit the house before it was destroyed."

"No, of course he didn't!" Richard said. The smile broke over his face easily. "After all, don't we owe it to the others, Julie? Uncle Baxter who spent the last of his fortune restoring the house, even this old Mrs. Blessington that has kept it all these years?"

"And what about the village itself?" I added quickly. "What will it mean to these people to see Rampling Gate destroyed? Of course we must go and see the place ourselves."

"Then it's settled. I'll write to Mrs. Blessington immediately. I'll tell her we're coming and that we can not say how long we will stay."

"Oh, Richard, that would be too marvelous!" I couldn't keep from hugging him, though it flustered him and he pulled on his pipe just exactly the way Father would have done. "Make it at least a fortnight," I said. "I want so to know the place, especially if . . ."

But it was too sad to think of Father's admonition. And much more fun to think of the journey itself. I'd pack my manuscripts, for who knew, maybe in that melancholy and exquisite setting I'd find exactly the inspiration I required. It was almost a wicked exhilaration I felt, breaking the gloom that had hung over us since the day that Father was laid to rest.

"It is the right thing to do, isn't it, Richard?" I asked uncertainly, a little disconcerted by how much I wanted to go. There was some illicit pleasure in it, going to Rampling Gate at last.

" 'Unspeakable horror,' " I repeated Father's words with a little grimace. What did it all mean? I thought again of the strange, almost exquisite young man I'd glimpsed in that railway carriage, gazing at us all with that wistful expression on his lean face. He had worn a black greatcoat with a red woollen cravat, and I could remember how pale he had been against that dash of red. Like bone china his complexion had been. Strange to remember it so vividly, even to the tilt of his head, and that long luxuriant brown hair. But he had been a blaze against that window. And I realized now that, in those few remarkable moments, he had created for me an ideal of masculine beauty which I had never questioned since. But Father had been so angry in those moments . . . I felt an unmistakable pang of guilt.

"Of course it's the right thing, Julie," Richard answered. He at the desk, already writing the letters, and I was at a loss to understand the full measure of my thoughts.

. . .

It was late afternoon when the wretched old trap carried us up the gentle slope from the little railway station, and we had at last our first real look at that magnificent house. I think I was holding my breath. The sky had paled to a deep rose hue beyond a bank of softly gilded clouds, and the last rays of the sun struck the uppermost panes of the leaded windows and filled them with solid gold.

"Oh, but it's too majestic," I whispered, "too like a great cathedral, and to think that it belongs to us." Richard gave me the smallest kiss on the cheek. I felt mad suddenly and eager somehow to be laid waste by it, through fear or enchantment I could not say, perhaps a sublime mingling of both.

I wanted with all my heart to jump down and draw near on foot, letting those towers grow larger and larger above me, but our old horse had picked up speed. And the little line of stiff starched servants had broken to come forward, the old withered housekeeper with her arms out, the men to take down the boxes and the trunks.

Richard and I were spirited into the great hall by the tiny, nimble figure of Mrs. Blessington, our footfalls echoing loudly on the marble tile, our eyes dazzled by the dusty shafts of light that fell on the long oak table and its heavily carved chairs, the sombre, heavy tapestries that stirred ever so slightly against the soaring walls.

"It is an enchanted place," I cried, unable to contain myself. "Oh, Richard, we are home!" Mrs. Blessington laughed gaily, her dry hand closing tightly on mine.

Her small blue eyes regarded me with the most curiously vacant expression despite her smile. "Ramplings at Rampling Gate again, I can not tell you what a joyful day this is for me. And yes, my dear," she said as if reading my mind that very second, "I am, and have been for many years, quite blind. But if you spy a thing out of place in this house, you're to tell me at once, for it would be the exception, I assure you, and not the rule." And such warmth emanated from her wrinkled little face that I adored her at once.

We found our bedchambers, the very finest in the house, well aired with snow white linen and fires blazing cozily to dry out the damp that never left the thick walls. The small diamond pane windows opened on a glorious view of the water and the oaks that enclosed it and the few scattered lights that marked the village beyond.

That night, we laughed like children as we supped at the great oak table, our candles giving only a feeble light. And afterwards, it was a fierce battle of pocket billiards in the game room which had been Uncle Baxter's last renovation, and a little too much brandy, I fear.

It was just before I went to bed that I asked Mrs. Blessington if there had been anyone in this house since Uncle Baxter died. That had been the year 1838, almost fifty years ago, and she was already housekeeper then.

"No, my dear," she said quickly, fluffing the feather pillows. "Your father came that year as you know, but he stayed for no more than a month or two and then went on home."

"There was never a young man after that . . ." I pushed, but in truth I had little appetite for anything to disturb the happiness I felt. How I loved the Spartan cleanliness of this bedchamber, the stone walls bare of paper or ornament, the high luster of the walnut-paneled bed.

"A young man?" She gave an easy, almost hearty laugh as with unerring certainty of her surroundings. She lifted the poker and stirred the fire. "What a strange thing for you to ask."

I sat silent for a moment looking in the mirror, as I took the last of the pins from my hair. It fell down heavy and warm around my shoulders. It felt good, like a cloak under which I could hide. But she turned as if sensing some uneasiness in me, and drew near.

"Why do you say a young man, Miss?" she asked. Slowly, tentatively, fingers examined the long tresses that lay over my shoulders. She took the brush from my hands.

I felt perfectly foolish telling her the story, but I managed a simplified version, somehow, our meeting unexpectedly a devilishly handsome young man whom my Father in anger had later called the master of Rampling Gate.

"Handsome, was he?" she asked as she brushed out the tangles in my hair gently. It seemed she hung upon every word as I described him again.

"There were no intruders in this house, then, Mrs. Blessington?" I asked. "No mysteries to be solved . . ."

She gave the sweetest laugh.

"Oh, no, darling, this house is the safest place in the world," she said quickly. "It is a happy house. No intruder would dare to trouble Rampling Gate!"

Nothing, in fact, troubled the serenity of the days that followed. The smoke and noise of London, and our Father's dying words, became a dream. What was real were our long walks together through the overgrown gardens, our trips in the little skiff to and fro across the lake. We had tea under the hot glass of the empty conservatory. And early evening found us on our way upstairs with the best of the books from Uncle Baxter's library to read by candlelight in the privacy of our rooms.

And all our discreet inquiries in the village met with

more or less the same reply: the villagers loved the house and carried no old or disquieting tales. Repeatedly, in fact, we were told that Rampling was the most contented hamlet in all England, that no one dared—Mrs. Blessington's very words—to make trouble here.

"It's our guardian angel, that old house," said the old woman at the bookshop where Richard stopped for the London papers. "Was there ever the town of Rampling without the house called Rampling Gate?"

How were we going to tell them of Father's edict? How were we going to remind ourselves? But we spoke not one word about the proposed disaster, and Richard wrote to his firm to say that we should not be back in London till fall.

He was finding a wealth of classical material in the old volumes that had belonged to Uncle Baxter, and I had set up my writing in the little study that opened off the library which I had all to myself.

Never had I known such peace and quiet. It seemed the atmosphere of Rampling Gate permeated my simplest written descriptions and wove its way richly into the plots and characters I created. The Monday after our arrival I had finished my first short story and went off to the village on foot to boldly post it to editors of *Blackwood's Magazine*.

It was a glorious morning, and I took my time as I came back on foot.

What had disturbed our father so about this lovely corner of England, I wondered? What had so darkened his last hours that he laid upon this spot his curse?

My heart opened to this unearthly stillness, to an undeniable grandeur that caused me utterly to forget myself. There were times here when I felt I was a disembodied intellect drifting through a fathomless silence, up and down garden paths and stone corridors that had witnessed too much to take cognizance of one small and fragile young woman who in random moments actually talked aloud to the suits of armour around her, to the broken statues in the garden, the fountain cherubs who had not had water to pour from their conches for years and years.

But was there in this loveliness some malignant force that was eluding us still, some untold story to explain all? Unspeakable horror . . . In my mind's eye I saw that young man, and the strangest sensation crept over me, that some enrichment of the picture had taken place in my memory or imagination in the recent past. Perhaps in dream I had reinvented him, given a ruddy glow to his lips and his cheeks. Perhaps in my re-creation for Mrs. Blessington, I had allowed him to raise his hand to that red cravat and had seen the fingers long and delicate and suggestive of a musician's hand.

It was all very much on my mind when I entered the house again, soundlessly, and saw Richard in his favorite leather wing chair by the fire.

The air was warm coming through the open garden doors, and yet the blaze was cheerful, making the vast room with its towering shelves of leatherbound volumes appear inviting and almost small.

"Sit down," Richard said gravely, scarcely giving me a glance. "I want to read you something right now." He held a long narrow ledger in his hands. "This was Uncle Baxter's," he said, "and at first I thought it was only an account book he kept during the renovations, but I've found some actual diary entries made in the last weeks of his life. They're hasty, almost indecipherable, but I've managed to make them out."

"Well, do read them to me," I said, but I felt a little tug

of fear. I didn't want to know anything terrible about this place. If we could have remained here forever . . . but that was out of the question, to be sure.

"Now listen to this," Richard said, turning the page carefully. " 'Fifth of May, 1838: He is here, I am sure of it. He is come back again.' And days later: 'He thinks this is his house, he does, and he would drink my wine and smoke my cigars if only he could. He reads my books and my papers and I will not stand for it. I have given orders that everything is to be locked.' And finally, the last entry written the morning before he died: 'Weary, weary, unto death and he is no small cause of my weariness. Last night I beheld him with my own eyes. He stood in this very room. He moves and speaks exactly as a mortal man, and dares tell me his secrets, and he a demon wretch with the face of a seraph and I a mere mortal, how am I to bear with him!' "

"Good Lord," I whispered slowly. I rose from the chair where I had settled, and standing behind him, read the page for myself. It was scrawl, the writing, the very last notation in the book. I knew that Uncle Baxter's heart had given out. He had not died by violence, but peacefully enough in this very room with his prayer book in his hand.

"Could it be the very same person Father spoke of that night?" Richard asked.

In spite of the sun pouring through the open doors, I experienced a violent chill. For the first time I felt wary of this house, wary of our boldness in coming here, heedful of our Father's words.

"But that was years before, Richard . . ." I said. "And what could this mean, this talk of a supernatural being! Surely the man was mad! It was no spirit I saw in that railway carriage!"

I sank down into the chair opposite and tried to quiet the beating of my heart.

"Julie," Richard said gently, shutting the ledger. "Mrs. Blessington has lived here contentedly for years. There are six servants asleep every night in the north wing. Surely there is nothing to all of this."

"It isn't very much fun, though, is it?" I said timidly. "Not at all like swapping ghost stories the way we used to do, and peopling the dark with imaginary beings, and laughing at friends at school who were afraid."

"All my life," he said, his eyes fixing me steadily, "I've heard tales of spooks and spirits, some imagined, some supposedly true, and almost invariably there is some mention of the house in question feeling haunted, of having an atmosphere to it that fills one with foreboding, some sense of menace or alarm . . ."

"Yes, I know, and there is no such poisonous atmosphere here at all."

"On the contrary, I've never been more at ease in my life." He shoved his hand into his pocket to extract the inevitable match to light his pipe which had gone out. "As a matter of fact, Julie, I don't know how in the world I'm going to comply with Father's last wish to tear down this place."

I nodded sympathetically. The very same thing had been on my mind since we'd arrived. Even now, I felt so comfortable, natural, quite safe.

I was wishing suddenly, irrationally, that he had not found the entries in Uncle Baxter's book.

"I should talk to Mrs. Blessington again!" I said almost crossly. "I mean quite seriously . . ."

"But I have, Julie," he said. "I asked her about it all this morning when I first made the discovery, and she only laughed. She swears she's never seen anything unusual here, and that there's no one left alive in the village who can tell tales of this place. She said again how glad she was that we'd come home to Rampling Gate. I don't think she has an inkling we mean to destroy the house. Oh, it would destroy her heart if she did."

"Never seen anything unusual?" I asked. "That is what she said? But what strange words for her to use, Richard, when she can not see at all."

But he had not heard me. He had laid the ledger aside and risen slowly, almost sluggishly, and he was wandering out of the double doors into the little garden and was looking over the high hedge at the oaks that bent their heavy elbowed limbs almost to the surface of the lake. There wasn't a sound at this early hour of the day, save the soft rustle of the leaves in the moving air, the cry now and then of a distant bird.

"Maybe it's gone, Julie," Richard said, over his shoulder, his voice carrying clearly in the quiet, "if it was ever here. Maybe there is nothing any longer to frighten anyone at all. You don't suppose you could endure the winter in this house, do you? I suppose you'd want to be in London again by then." He seemed quite small against the towering trees, the sky broken into small gleaming fragments by the canopy of foliage that gently filtered the light.

Rampling Gate had him. And I understood perfectly, because it also had me. I could very well endure the winter here, no matter how bleak or cold. I never wanted to go home.

And the immediacy of the mystery only dimmed my sense of everything and every place else.

After a long moment, I rose and went out into the garden, and placed my hand gently on Richard's arm.

"I know this much, Julie," he said just as if we had been talking to each other all the while. "I swore to Father that I would do as he asked, and it is tearing me apart. Either way, it will be on my conscience forever, obliterating this house or going against my own father and the charge he laid down to me with his dying breath."

"We must seek help, Richard. The advice of our lawyers, the advice of Father's clergymen. You must write to them and explain the whole thing. Father was feverish when he gave the order. If we could lay it out before them, they would help us decide."

It was three o'clock when I opened my eyes. But I had been awake for a long time. I had heard the dim chimes of the clock below hour by hour. And I felt not fear lying here alone in the dark but something else. Some vague and relentless agitation, some sense of emptiness and need that caused me finally to rise from my bed. What was required to dissolve this tension, I wondered. I stared at the simplest things in the shadows. The little arras that hung over the fireplace with it's slim princes and princesses lost in fading fiber and thread. The portrait of an Elizabethan ancestor gazing with one almond-shaped eye from his small frame.

What was this house, really? Merely a place or a state of mind? What was it doing to my soul? Why didn't the entries in Uncle Baxter's book send us flying back to London? Why had we stayed so late in the great hall together after supper, speaking not a single word?

I felt overwhelmed suddenly, and yet shut out of some great and dazzling secret, and wasn't that the very word that Uncle Baxter had used?

Conscious only of an unbearable restlessness, I pulled

on my woollen wrapper, buttoning the lace collar and tying the sash. And putting on my slippers, I went out into the hall.

The moon fell full on the oak stairway, and on the deeply recessed door to Richard's room. On tiptoe I approached and, peering in, saw the bed was empty, the covers completely undisturbed.

So he was off on his own tonight the same as I. Oh, if only he had come to me, asked me to go with him.

I turned and made my way soundlessly down the long stairs.

The great hall gaped like a cavern before me, the moonlight here and there touching upon a pair of crossed swords, or a mounted shield. But far beyond the great hall, in the alcove just outside the library, I saw unmistakably a flickering light. And a breeze moved briskly through the room, carrying with it the sound and the scent of a wood fire.

I shuddered with relief. Richard was there. We could talk. Or perhaps we could go exploring together, guarding our fragile candle flames behind cupped fingers as we went from room to room? A sense of well-being pervaded me and quieted me, and yet the dark distance between us seemed endless, and I was desperate to cross it, hurrying suddenly past the long supper table with its massive candlesticks, and finally into the alcove before the library doors.

Yes, Richard was there. He sat with his eyes closed, dozing against the inside of the leather wing chair, the breeze from the garden blowing the fragile flames of the candles on the stone mantel and on the table at his side.

I was about to go to him, about to shut the doors, and kiss him gently and ask did he not want to go up to bed, when quite abruptly I saw in the corner of my eye that there was someone else in the room.

In the far left corner at the desk stood another figure, looking down at the clutter of Richard's papers, his pale hands resting on the wood.

I knew that it could not be so. I knew that I must be dreaming, that nothing in this room, least of all this figure, could be real. For it was the same young man I had seen fifteen years ago in the railway carriage and not a single aspect of that taut young face had been changed. There was the very same hair, thick and lustrous and only carelessly combed as it hung to the thick collar of his black coat, and the skin so pale it was almost luminous in the shadows, and those dark eyes looking up suddenly and fixing me with the most curious expression as I almost screamed.

We stared at one another across the dark vista of that room, I stranded in the doorway, he visibly and undeniably shaken that I had caught him unawares. My heart stopped.

And in a split second he moved towards me, closed the gap between us, towering over me, those slender white fingers gently closing on my arms.

"Julie!" he whispered, in a voice so low it seemed my own thoughts speaking to me. But this was no dream. He was real. He was holding to me and the scream had broken loose from me, deafening, uncontrollable and echoing from the four walls.

I saw Richard rising from the chair. I was alone. Clutching to the door frame, I staggered forward, and then again in a moment of perfect clarity I saw the young intruder, saw him standing in the garden, looking back over his shoulder, and then he was gone.

I could not stop screaming. I could not stop even as Richard held me and pleaded with me, and sat me down in the chair.

And I was still crying when Mrs. Blessington finally came.

She got a glass of cordial for me at once, as Richard begged me once more to tell what I had seen.

"But you know who it was!" I said to Richard almost hysterically. "It was he, the young man from the train. Only he wore a frockcoat years out of fashion and his silk tie was open at his throat. Richard, he was reading your papers, turning them over, reading them in the pitch dark."

"All right," Richard said, gesturing with his hand up for calm. "He was standing at the desk. And there was no light there so you could not see him well."

"Richard, it was he! Don't you understand? He touched me, he held my arms." I looked imploringly to Mrs. Blessington, who was shaking her head, her little eyes like blue beads in the light. "He called me Julie," I whispered. "He knows my name!"

I rose, snatching up the candle, and all but pushing Richard out of the way went to the desk. "Oh, dear God," I said. "Don't you see what's happened? It's your letters to Dr. Partridge, and Mrs. Sellers, about tearing down the house!"

Mrs. Blessington gave a little cry and put her hand to her cheek. She looked like a withered child in her night-cap as she collapsed into the straight-backed chair by the door.

"Surely you don't believe it was the same man, Julie, after all these years . . ."

"But he had not changed, Richard, not in the smallest detail. There is no mistake, Richard, it was he, I tell you, the very same."

"Oh, dear, dear . . ." Mrs. Blessington whispered. "What will he do if you try to tear it down? What will he do now?"

"What will who do?" Richard asked carefully, narrowing his eyes. He took the candle from me and approached her. I was staring at her, only half realizing what I had heard.

"So you know who he is!" I whispered.

"Julie, stop it!" Richard said.

But her face had tightened, gone blank, and her eyes had become distant and small.

"You knew he was here!" I insisted. "You must tell us at once!"

With an effort she climbed to her feet. "There is nothing in this house to hurt *you*," she said, "nor any of us." She turned, spurning Richard as he tried to help her, and wandered into the dark hallway alone. "You've no need of me here any longer," she said softly, "and if you should tear down this house built by your forefathers, then you should do it without need of me."

"Oh, but we don't mean to do it, Mrs. Blessington!" I insisted. But she was making her way through the gallery back towards the north wing. "Go after her, Richard. You heard what she said. She knows who he is."

"I've had quite enough of this tonight," Richard said almost angrily. "Both of us should go up to bed. By the light of day we will dissect this entire matter and search this house. Now come."

"But he should be told, shouldn't he?" I demanded.

"Told what? Of whom do you speak!"

"Told that we will not tear down this house!" I said clearly, loudly, listening to the echo of my own voice.

. . .

The next day was indeed the most trying since we had come. It took the better part of the morning to convince Mrs. Blessington that we had no intention of tearing down Rampling Gate. Richard posted his letters and resolved that we should do nothing until help came.

And together we commenced a search of the house. But darkness found us only half finished, having covered the south tower and the south wing, and the main portion of house itself. There remained still the north tower, in a dreadful state of disrepair, and some rooms beneath the ground which in former times might have served as dungeons and were now sealed off. And there were closets and private stairways everywhere that we had scarce looked into, and at times we lost all track of where precisely we had been.

But it was also quite clear by supper time that Richard was in a state of strain and exasperation, and that he did not believe that I had seen anyone in the study at all.

He was further convinced that Uncle Baxter had been mad before he died, or else his ravings were a code for some mundane happening that had him extraordinarily overwrought.

But I knew what I had seen. And as the day progressed, I became ever more quiet and withdrawn. A silence had fallen between me and Mrs. Blessington. And I understood only too well the anger I'd heard in my father's voice on that long ago night when we had come home from Victoria Station and my mother had accused him of imagining things.

Yet what obsessed me more than anything else was the gentle countenance of the mysterious man I had glimpsed, the dark almost innocent eyes that had fixed on me for one moment before I had screamed.

"Strange that Mrs. Blessington is not afraid of him," I

said in a low distracted voice, no longer caring if Richard heard me. "And that no one here seems in fear of him at all . . ." The strangest fancies were coming to me. The careless words of the villagers were running through my head. "You would be wise to do one very important thing before you retire," I said. "Leave out in writing a note to the effect that you do not intend to tear down the house."

"Julie, you have created an impossible dilemma," Richard demanded. "You insist we reassure this apparition that the house will not be destroyed, when in fact you verify the existence of the very creature that drove our father to say what he did."

"Oh, I wish I had never come here!" I burst out suddenly.

"Then we should go, both of us, and decide this matter at home."

"No, that's just it. I could never go without knowing . . . 'his secrets' . . . 'the demon wretch.' I could never go on living without knowing now!"

Anger must be an excellent antidote to fear, for surely something worked to alleviate my natural alarm. I did not undress that night, nor even take off my shoes, but rather sat in that dark hollow bedroom gazing at the small square of diamond-paned window until I heard all of the house fall quiet. Richard's door at last closed. There came those distant echoing booms that meant other bolts had been put in place.

And when the grandfather clock in the great hall chimed the hour of eleven, Rampling Gate was as usual fast asleep.

I listened for my brother's step in the hall. And when I did not hear him stir from his room, I wondered at it, that curiosity would not impel him to come to me, to say that we must go together to discover the truth.

It was just as well. I did not want him to be with me. And I felt a dark exultation as I imagined myself going out of the room and down the stairs as I had the night before. I should wait one more hour, however, to be certain. I should let the night reach its pitch. Twelve, the witching hour. My heart was beating too fast at the thought of it, and dreamily I recollected the face I had seen, the voice that had said my name.

Ah, why did it seem in retrospect so intimate, that we had known each other, spoken together, that it was someone I recognized in the pit of my soul?

"What is your name?" I believe I whispered aloud. And then a spasm of fear startled me. Would I have the courage to go in search of him, to open the door to him? Was I losing my mind? Closing my eyes, I rested my head against the high back of the damask chair.

What was more empty than this rural night? What was more sweet?

I opened my eyes. I had been half dreaming or talking to myself, trying to explain to Father why it was necessary that we comprehend the reason ourselves. And I realized, quite fully realized—I think before I was even awake—that *he* was standing by the bed.

The door was open. And he was standing there, dressed exactly as he had been the night before, and his dark eyes were riveted on me with that same obvious curiosity, his mouth just a little slack like that of a schoolboy, and he was holding to the bedpost almost idly with his right hand. Why, he was lost in contemplating me. He did not seem to know that I was looking at him.

But when I sat forward, he raised his finger as if to quiet me, and gave a little nod of his head.

"Ah, it is you!" I whispered.

"Yes," he said in the softest, most unobtrusive voice.

But we had been talking to each other, hadn't we? I had been asking him questions, no, telling him things. And I felt suddenly I was losing my equilibrium or slipping back into a dream.

No. Rather I had all but caught the fragment of some dream from the past. That rush of atmosphere that can engulf one at any moment of the day following when something evokes the universe that absorbed one utterly in sleep. I mean I heard our voices for an instant, almost in argument, and I saw Father in his top hat and black overcoat rushing alone through the streets of the West End, peering into one door after another, and then, rising from the marble-top table in the dim smoky music hall you . . . your face.

"Yes . . ."

Go back, Julie! It was Father's voice.

". . . to penetrate the soul of it," I insisted, picking up the lost thread. But did my lips move? "To understand what it is that frightened him, enraged him. He said, 'Tear it down!' "

". . . you must never, never, can't do that." His face was stricken, like that of a schoolboy about to cry.

"No, absolutely, we don't want to, either of us, you know it . . . and you are not a spirit!" I looked at his mud-spattered boots, the faintest smear of dust on that perfect white cheek.

"A spirit?" he asked almost mournfully, almost bitterly. "Would that I were."

Mesmerized I watched him come towards me and the room darkened, and I felt his cool silken hands on my face. I had risen. I was standing before him, and I looked up into his eyes.

I heard my own heartbeat. I heard it as I had the night before, right at the moment I had screamed. Dear God, I was talking to him! He was in my room and I was talking to him! And I was in his arms.

"Real, absolutely real!" I whispered, and a low zinging sensation coursed through me so that I had to steady myself against the bed.

He was peering at me as if trying to comprehend something terribly important to him, and he didn't respond. His lips did have a ruddy look to them, a soft look for all his handsomeness, as if he had never been kissed. And a slight dizziness had come over me, a slight confusion in which I was not at all sure that he was even there.

"Oh, but I am," he said softly. I felt his breath against my cheek, and it was almost sweet. "I am here, and you are with me, Julie . . ."

"Yes . . ."

My eyes were closing. Uncle Baxter sat hunched over his desk and I could hear the furious scratch of his pen. "Demon wretch!" he said to the night air coming in the open doors.

"No!" I said. Father turned in the door of the music hall and cried my name.

"Love me, Julie," came that voice in my ear. I felt his lips against my neck. "Only a little kiss, Julie, no harm . . ." And the core of my being, that secret place where all desires and all commandments are nurtured, opened to him without a struggle or a sound. I would have fallen if he had not held me. My arms closed about him, my hands slipping into the soft silken mass of his hair.

I was floating, and there was as there had always been at Rampling Gate an endless peace. It was Rampling Gate I felt around me, it was that timeless and impenetrable soul that had opened itself at last . . . A power within me of enormous ken . . . To see as a god sees, and take the depth of things as nimbly as the outward eyes can size and shape pervade . . . Yes, I whispered aloud, those words from Keats, those words . . . To cease upon the midnight without pain . . .

No. In a violent instant we had parted, he drawing back as surely as I.

I went reeling across the bedroom floor and caught hold of the frame of the window, and rested my forehead against the stone wall.

For a long moment I stood with my eyes closed. There was a tingling pain in my throat that was almost pleasurable where his lips had touched me, a delicious throbbing that would not stop.

Then I turned, and I saw all the room clearly, the bed, the fireplace, the chair. And he stood still exactly as I'd left him and there was the most appalling distress in his face.

"What have they done to me?" he whispered. "Have they played the cruelest trick of all?"

"Something of menace, unspeakable menace," I whispered.

"Something ancient, Julie, something that defies understanding, something that can and will go on."

"But why, what are you?" I touched that pulsing pain with the tips of my fingers and, looking down at them, gasped. "And you suffer so, and you are so seemingly innocent, and it is as if you can love!"

His face was rent as if by a violent conflict within. And he turned to go. With my whole will, I stood fast not to follow him, not to beg him to turn back. But he did turn, bewildered, struggling and then bent upon his purpose as he reached for my hand. "Come with me," he said.

He drew me to him ever so gently, and slipping his arm around me guided me to the door.

Through the long upstairs corridor we passed hurriedly, and through a small wooden doorway to a screw stairs that I had never seen before.

I soon realized we were ascending the north tower of the house, the ruined portion of the structure that Richard and I had not investigated before.

Through one tiny window after another I saw the gently rolling landscape moving out from the forest that surrounded us, and the small cluster of dim lights that marked the village of Rampling and the pale streak of white that was the London road.

Up and up we climbed until we had reached the topmost chamber, and this he opened with an iron key. He held back the door for me to enter and I found myself in a spacious room whose high narrow windows contained no glass. A flood of moonlight revealed the most curious mixture of furnishings and objects, the clutter that suggests an attic and a sort of den. There was a writing table, a great shelf of books, soft leather chairs and scores of old yellowed and curling maps and framed pictures affixed to the walls. Candles were everywhere stuck in the bare stone niches or to the tables and the shelves. Here and there a barrel served as a table, right alongside the finest old Elizabethan chair. Wax had dripped over everything, it seemed, and in the very midst of the clutter lay rumpled copies of the most recent papers, the *Mercure de Paris*; the London *Times*.

There was no place for sleeping in this room.

And when I thought of that, where he must lie when he went to rest, a shudder passed over me and I felt, quite vividly, his lips touching my throat again, and I felt the sudden urge to cry.

But he was holding me in his arms, he was kissing my cheeks and my lips again ever so softly, and then he guided me to a chair. He lighted the candles about us one by one.

I shuddered, my eyes watering slightly in the light. I saw more unusual objects: telescopes and magnifying glasses and a violin in its open case, and a handful of gleaming and exquisitely shaped sea shells. There were jewels lying about, and a black silk top hat and a walking stick, and a bouquet of withered flowers, dry as straw, and daguerreotypes and tintypes in their little velvet cases, and opened books.

But I was too distracted now by the sight of him in the light, the gloss of his large black eyes, and the gleam of his hair. Not even in the railway station had I seen him so clearly as I did now amid the radiance of the candles. He broke my heart.

And yet he looked at me as though I were the feast for his eyes, and he said my name again and I felt the blood rush to my face. But there seemed a great break suddenly in the passage of time. I had been thinking, yes, what are you, how long have you existed . . . And I felt dizzy again.

I realized that I had risen and I was standing beside him at the window and he was turning me to look down and the countryside below had unaccountably changed. The lights of Rampling had been subtracted from the darkness that lay like a vapor over the land. A great wood, far older and denser than the forest of Rampling Gate, shrouded the hills, and I was afraid suddenly, as if I were slipping into a maelstrom from which I could never, of my own will, return.

There was that sense of us talking together, talking and talking in low agitated voices and I was saying that I should not give in.

"Bear witness, that is all I ask of you . . ."

And there was in me some dim certainty that by knowledge alone I should be fatally changed. It was the reading of a forbidden book, the chanting of a forbidden charm.

"No, only what was," he whispered.

And then even the shape of the land itself eluded me. And the very room had lost its substance, as if a soundless wind of terrific force had entered this place and was blowing it apart.

We were riding in a carriage through the night. We had long ago left the tower, and it was late afternoon and the sky was the color of blood. And we rode into a forest whose trees were so high and so thick that scarcely any sun at all broke to the soft leafstrewn ground.

We had no time to linger in this magical place. We had come to the open country, to the small patches of tilled earth that surrounded the ancient village of Knorwood with its gabled roofs and its tiny crooked streets. We saw the walls of the monastery of Knorwood and the little church with the bell chiming Vespers under the lowering sky. A great bustling life resided in Knorwood, a thousand hearts beat in Knorwood, a thousand voices gave forth their common prayer.

But far beyond the village on the rise above the forest stood the rounded tower of a truly ancient castle, and to that ruined castle, no more than a shell of itself anymore, as darkness fell in earnest, we rode. Through its empty chambers we roamed, impetuous children, the horse and the road quite forgotten, and to the Lord of the Castle, a gaunt and white-skinned creature standing before the roaring fire of the roofless hall, we came. He turned and fixed us with his narrow and glittering eyes. A dead thing he was, I understood, but he carried within himself a priceless magic. And my young companion, my innocent young man passed by me into the Lord's arms. I saw the kiss. I saw the young man grow pale and struggle to turn away. It was as I had done this very night, beyond this dream, in my own bedchamber; and from the Lord he retreated, clutching to the sharp pain in his throat.

I understood. I knew. But the castle was dissolving as surely as anything in this dream might dissolve, and we were in some damp and close place.

The stench was unbearable to me, it was that most terrible of all stenches, the stench of death. And I heard my steps on the cobblestones and I reached to steady myself against the wall. The tiny square was deserted; the doors and windows gaped open to the vagrant wind. Up one side and down the other of the crooked street I saw the marks on the houses. And I knew what the marks meant. The Black Death had come to the village of Knorwood. The Black Death had laid it waste. And in a moment of suffocating horror I realized that no one, not a single person, was left alive.

But this was not quite right. There was someone walking in fits and starts up the narrow alleyway. Staggering he was, almost falling, as he pushed in one door after another, and at last came to a hot, stinking place where a child screamed on the floor. Mother and Father lay dead in the bed. And the great fat cat of the household, unharmed, played with the screaming infant, whose eyes bulged from its tiny sunken face.

"Stop it," I heard myself gasp. I knew that I was holding my head with both hands. "Stop it, stop it please!" I was screaming and my screams would surely pierce the vision and this small crude little room should collapse around me, and I should rouse the household of Rampling Gate to me, but I did not. The young man turned and stared at me, and in the close stinking room, I could not see his face.

But I knew it was he, my companion, and I could smell his fever and his sickness and the stink of the dying infant, and see the sleek, gleaming body of the cat as it pawed at the child's outstretched hand.

"Stop it, you've lost control of it!" I screamed surely with all my strength, but the infant screamed louder. "Make it stop!"

"I can not . . ." he whispered. "It goes on forever! It will never stop!"

And with a great piercing shriek I kicked at the cat and sent it flying out of the filthy room, overturning the milk pail as it went, jetting like a witch's familiar over the stones.

Blanched and feverish, the sweat soaking his crude jerkin, my companion took me by the hand. He forced me back out of the house and away from the crying child and into the street.

Death in the parlour, death in the bedroom, death in the cloister, death before the high altar, death in the open fields. It seemed the Judgment of God that a thousand souls had died in the village of Knorwood—I was sobbing, begging to be released—it seemed the very end of Creation itself.

And at last night came down over the dead village and he was alive still, stumbling up the slopes, through the forest, towards that rounded tower where the Lord stood with his hand on the stone frame of the broken window waiting for him to come.

"Don't go!" I begged him. I ran alongside him crying, but he didn't hear. Try as I might, I could not affect these things.

The Lord stood over him smiling almost sadly as he watched him fall, watched the chest heave with its last breaths. Finally the lips moved, calling out for salvation when it was damnation the Lord offered, when it was damnation that the Lord would give.

"Yes, damned then, but living, breathing!" the young man cried, rising in a last spasmodic movement. And the Lord, who had remained still until that instant, bent to drink.

The kiss again, the lethal kiss, the blood drawn out of the dying body, and then the Lord lifting the heavy head of the young man to take the blood back again from the body of the Lord himself.

I was screaming again, *Do not, do not drink.* He turned and looked at me. His face was now so perfectly the visage of death that I couldn't believe there was animation left in him, yet he asked: What would you do? Would you go back to Knorwood, would you open those doors one after another, would you ring the bell in the empty church, and if you did would the dead rise?

He didn't wait for my answer. And I had none now to give. He had turned again to the Lord who waited for him, locked his innocent mouth to that vein that pulsed with every semblance of life beneath the Lord's cold and translucent flesh. And the blood jetted into the young body, vanquishing in one great burst the fever and the sickness that had wracked it, driving it out with the mortal life.

He stood now in the hall of the Lord alone. Immortality was his and the blood thirst he would need to sustain it, and that thirst I could feel with my whole soul. He stared at the broken walls around him, at the fire licking the blackened stones of the giant fireplace, at the night sky over the broken roof, throwing out its endless net of stars.

And each and every thing was transfigured in his vision, and in my vision—the vision he gave now to me—to the exquisite essence of itself. A wordless and eternal voice spoke from the starry veil of heaven; it sang in the wind that rushed through the broken timbers; it sighed in the flames that ate the sooted stones of the hearth.

It was the fathomless rhythm of the universe that played beneath every surface, as the last living creature—that tiny child—fell silent in the village below.

A soft wind sifted and scattered the soil from the new-turned furrows in the empty fields. The rain fell from the black and endless sky.

Years and years passed. And all that had been Knorwood melted into the very earth. The forest sent out its silent sentinels, and mighty trunks rose where there had been huts and houses, where there had been monastery walls.

Finally nothing of Knorwood remained: not the little cemetery, not the little church, not even the name of Knorwood lived still in the world. And it seemed the horror beyond all horrors that no one anymore should know of a thousand souls who had lived and died in that small and insignificant village, that not anywhere in the great archives in which all history is recorded should a mention of that town remain.

Yet one being remained who knew, one being who had witnessed, and stood now looking down upon the very spot where his mortal life had ended, he who had scrambled up on his hands and knees from the pit of Hell that had been that disaster; it was the young man who stood beside me, the master of Rampling Gate.

And all through the walls of his old house were the stones of the ruined castle, and all through the ceilings and floors the branches of those ancient trees.

What was solid and majestic here, and safe within the minds of those who slept tonight in the village of Rampling, was only the most fragile citadel against horror, the house to which he clung now.

A great sorrow swept over me. Somewhere in the drift of images I had relinquished myself, lost all sense of the point in space from which I saw. And in a great rush of lights and noise I was enlivened now and made whole as I had been when we rode together through the forest, only it was into the world of now, this hour, that we passed. We were flying it seemed through the rural darkness along the railway towards London, where the nighttime city burst like an enormous bubble in a shower of laughter, and motion, and glaring light. He was walking with me under the gas lamps, his face all but shimmering with that same dark innocence, that same irresistible warmth. And it seemed we were holding tight to one another in the very midst of a crowd. And the crowd was a living thing, a writhing thing, and everywhere there came a dark rich aroma from it, the aroma of fresh blood. Women in white fur and gentlemen in opera capes swept into the brightly lighted doors of the theatre; the blare of the music hall inundated us, then faded away. Only a thin soprano voice was left, singing a high, plaintive song. I was in his arms, and his lips were covering mine, and there came that dull zinging sensation again, that great uncontrollable opening within myself. Thirst, and the promise of satiation measured only by the intensity of that thirst. Up stairs we fled together, into high-ceilinged bedrooms papered in red damask where the loveliest women reclined on brass bedsteads, and the aroma was so strong now I could not bear it, and before me they offered themselves, they opened their arms. "Drink," he whispered, yes, drink. And I felt the warmth filling me, charging me, blurring my vision, until we broke again, free and light and invisible it seemed as we moved over the rooftops and down again through rain-drenched streets. But the rain did not touch us; the falling snow did not chill us; we had within ourselves a great and indissoluble heat. And together in the carriage, we talked to each other in low, exuberant rushes of language; we were lovers; we were constant; we were immortal. We were as enduring as Rampling Gate.

I tried to speak; I tried to end the spell. I felt his arms around me and I knew we were in the tower room together, and some terrible miscalculation had been made.

"Do not leave me," he whispered. "Don't you understand what I am offering you? I have told you everything; and all the rest is but the weariness, the fever and the fret, those old words from the poem. Kiss me, Julie, open to me. Against your will I will not take you . . ." Again I heard my own scream. My hands were on his cool white skin, his lips were gentle yet hungry, his eyes yielding and ever young. Father turned in the rain-drenched London street and cried out: "Julie!" I saw Richard lost in the crowd as if searching for someone, his hat shadowing his dark eyes, his face haggard, old. Old!

I moved away. I was free. And I was crying softly and we were in this strange and cluttered tower room. He stood against the backdrop of the window, against the distant drift of pale clouds. The candle-light glimmered in his eyes. Immense and sad and wise they seemed, and oh, yes, innocent as I have said again and again. "I revealed myself to them," he said. "Yes, I told my secret. In rage or bitterness, I know not which, I made them my dark co-conspirators and always I won. They could not move against me, and neither will you. But they would triumph still. For they torment me now with their fairest flower. Don't turn away from me, Julie. You are mine, Julie, as Rampling Gate is mine. Let me gather the flower to my heart."

. . .

Nights of argument. But finally Richard had come round. He would sign over to me his share of Rampling Gate, and I should absolutely refuse to allow the place torn down. There would be nothing he could do then to obey Father's command. I had given him the legal impediment he needed, and of course I should leave the house to him and his children. It should always be in Rampling hands.

A clever solution, it seemed to me, as Father had not told *me* to destroy the place, and I had no scruples in the matter now at all.

And what remained was for him to take me to the little train station and see me off for London, and not worry about me going home to Mayfair on my own.

"You stay here as long as you wish, and do not worry," I said. I felt more tenderly towards him than I could ever express. "You knew as soon as you set foot in the place that Father was all wrong. Uncle Baxter put it in his mind, undoubtedly, and Mrs. Blessington has always been right. There is nothing to harm there, Richard. Stay, and work or study as you please."

The great black engine was roaring past us, the carriages slowing to a stop. "Must go now, darling, kiss me," I said.

"But what came over you, Julie, what convinced you so quickly . . . ?"

"We've been through it all, Richard," I said. "What matters is that we are all happy, my dear." And we held each other close.

I waved until I couldn't see him anymore. The flickering lamps of the town were lost in the deep lavender light of the early evening, and the dark hulk of Rampling Gate appeared for one uncertain moment like the ghost of itself on the nearby rise.

I sat back and closed my eyes. Then I opened them

slowly, savouring this moment for which I had waited too long.

He was smiling, seated there as he had been all along, in the far corner of the leather seat opposite, and now he rose with a swift, almost delicate movement and sat beside me and enfolded me in his arms.

"It's five hours to London," he whispered in my ear.

"I can wait," I said, feeling the thirst like a fever as I held tight to him, feeling his lips against my eyelids and my hair. "I want to hunt the London streets tonight," I confessed, a little shyly, but I saw only approbation in his eyes.

"Beautiful Julie, my Julie . . ." he whispered.

"You'll love the house in Mayfair," I said.

"Yes . . ." he said.

"And when Richard finally tires of Rampling Gate, we shall go home."

THE VAMPIRE MAID

◆◆◆

HUME NISBET

It was the exact kind of abode that I had been looking after for weeks, for I was in that condition of mind when absolute renunciation of society was a necessity. I had become diffident of myself, and wearied of my kind. A strange unrest was in my blood; a barren dearth in my brains. Familiar objects and faces had grown distasteful to me. I wanted to be alone.

This is the mood which comes upon every sensitive and artistic mind when the possessor has been overworked or living too long in one groove. It is Nature's hint for him to seek pastures new; the sign that a retreat has become needful.

If he does not yield, he breaks down and becomes whimsical and hypochondriacal, as well as hypercritical. It is always a bad sign when a man becomes over-critical and censorious about his own or other people's work, for it means that he is losing the vital portions of work, freshness and enthusiasm.

Before I arrived at the dismal stage of criticism I hastily packed up my knapsack, and taking the train to Westmorland I began my tramp in search of solitude, bracing air, and romantic surroundings.

Many places I came upon during that early summer wandering that appeared to have almost the required conditions, yet some petty drawback prevented me from deciding. Sometimes it was the scenery that I did not take kindly to. At other places I took sudden antipathies to the landlady or landlord, and felt I would abhor them before a week was spent under their charge. Other places which might have suited me I could not have, as they did not want a lodger. Fate was driving me to this Cottage on the Moor, and no one can resist destiny.

One day I found myself on a wide and pathless moor near the sea. I had slept the night before at a small hamlet, but that was already eight miles in my rear, and since I had turned my back upon it I had not seen any signs of humanity; I was alone with a fair sky above me, a balmy ozone-filled wind blowing over the stony and heather-clad mounds, and nothing to disturb my meditations.

How far the moor stretched I had no knowledge; I only knew that by keeping in a straight line I would come to the ocean cliffs, then perhaps after a time arrive at some fishing village.

I had provisions in my knapsack, and being young did not fear a night under the stars. I was inhaling the delicious summer air and once more getting back the vigour and happiness I had lost; my city-dried brains were again becoming juicy.

Thus hour after hour slid past me, with the paces, until I had covered about fifteen miles since morning, when I saw before me in the distance a solitary stone-built cottage with roughly slated roof. "I'll camp there if possible," I said to myself as I quickened my steps towards it.

To one in search of a quiet, free life, nothing could have possibly been more suitable than this cottage. It stood on the edge of lofty cliffs, with its front door facing the moor and the back-yard wall overlooking the ocean. The sound of the dancing waves struck upon my ears like a lullaby as I drew near; how they would thunder when the autumn gales came on and the seabirds fled shrieking to the shelter of the sedges.

A small garden spread in front, surrounded by a dry-stone wall just high enough for one to lean lazily upon when inclined. This garden was a flame of colour, scarlet predominating, with those other soft shades that cultivated poppies take on in their blooming, for this was all that the garden grew.

As I approached, taking notice of this singular assortment of poppies, and the orderly cleanness of the windows, the front door opened and a woman appeared who impressed me at once favourably as she leisurely came along the pathway to the gate, and drew it back as if to welcome me.

She was of middle age, and when young must have been remarkably good-looking. She was tall and still shapely, with smooth clear skin, regular features and a calm expression that at once gave me a sensation of rest.

To my inquiries she said that she could give me both a sitting-room and bedroom, and invited me inside to see them. As I looked at her smooth black hair, and cool brown eyes, I felt that I would not be too particular about the accommodation. With such a landlady, I was sure to find what I was after here.

The rooms surpassed my expectation, dainty white curtains and bedding with the perfume of lavender about them, a sitting-room homely yet cosy without being crowded. With a sigh of infinite relief I flung down my knapsack and clinched the bargain.

She was a widow with one daughter, whom I did not see the first day, as she was unwell and confined to her own room, but on the next day she was somewhat better, and then we met.

The fare was simple, yet it suited me exactly for the

time, delicious milk and butter with home-made scones, fresh eggs and bacon; after a hearty tea I went early to bed in a condition of perfect content with my quarters.

Yet happy and tired out as I was I had by no means a comfortable night. This I put down to the strange bed. I slept certainly, but my sleep was filled with dreams so that I woke late and unrefreshed; a good walk on the moor, however, restored me, and I returned with a fine appetite for breakfast.

Certain conditions of mind, with aggravating circumstances, are required before even a young man can fall in love at first sight, as Shakespeare has shown in his Romeo and Juliet. In the city, where many fair faces passed me every hour, I had remained like a stoic, yet no sooner did I enter the cottage after that morning walk than I succumbed instantly before the weird charms of my landlady's daughter, Ariadne Brunnell.

She was somewhat better this morning and able to meet me at breakfast, for we had our meals together while I was their lodger. Ariadne was not beautiful in the strictly classical sense, her complexion being too lividly white and her expression too set to be quite pleasant at first sight; yet, as her mother had informed me, she had been ill for some time, which accounted for that defect. Her features were not regular, her hair and eyes seemed too black with that strangely white skin, and her lips too red for any except the decadent harmonies of an Aubrey Beardsley.

Yet my fantastic dreams of the preceding night, with my morning walk, had prepared me to be enthralled by this modern poster-like invalid.

The loneliness of the moor, with the singing of the ocean, had gripped my heart with a wistful longing. The incongruity of those flaunting and evanescent poppy flowers, dashing their giddy tints in the face of that sober heath, touched me with a shiver as I approached the cottage, and lastly that weird embodiment of startling contrasts completed my subjugation.

She rose from her chair as her mother introduced her, and smiled while she held out her hand. I clasped that soft snowflake, and as I did so a faint thrill tingled over me and rested on my heart, stopping for the moment its beating.

This contact seemed also to have affected her as it did me; a clear flush, like a white flame, lighted up her face, so that it glowed as if an alabaster lamp had been lit; her black eyes became softer and more humid as our glances crossed, and her scarlet lips grew moist. She was a living woman now, while before she had seemed half a corpse.

She permitted her white slender hand to remain in mine longer than most people do at an introduction, and then she slowly withdrew it, still regarding me with steadfast eyes for a second or two afterwards.

Fathomless velvety eyes these were, yet before they were shifted from mine they appeared to have absorbed all my willpower and made me her abject slave. They looked like deep dark pools of clear water, yet they filled me with fire and deprived me of strength. I sank into my chair almost as languidly as I had risen from my bed that morning.

Yet I made a good breakfast, and although she hardly tasted anything, this strange girl rose much refreshed and with a slight glow of colour on her cheeks, which improved her so greatly that she appeared younger and almost beautiful.

I had come here seeking solitude, but since I had seen Ariadne it seemed as if I had come for her only. She was not very lively; indeed, thinking back, I cannot recall any spontaneous remark of hers; she answered my questions by monosyllables and left me to lead in words; yet she was insinuating and appeared to lead my thoughts in her direction and speak to me with her eyes. I cannot describe her minutely, I only know that from the first glance and touch she gave me I was bewitched and could think of nothing else.

It was a rapid, distracting, and devouring infatuation that possessed me; all day long I followed her about like a dog, every night I dreamed of that white glowing face, those steadfast black eyes, those moist scarlet lips, and each morning I rose more languid than I had been the day before. Sometimes I dreamt that she was kissing me with those red lips, while I shivered at the contact of her silky black tresses as they covered my throat; sometimes that we were floating in the air, her arms about me and her long hair enveloping us both like an inky cloud, while I lay supine and helpless.

She went with me after breakfast on that first day to the moor, and before we came back I had spoken my love and received her assent. I held her in my arms and had taken her kisses in answer to mine, nor did I think it strange that all this had happened so quickly. She was mine, or rather I was hers, without a pause. I told her it was fate that had sent me to her, for I had no doubts about my love, and she replied that I had restored her to life.

Acting upon Ariadne's advice, and also from a natural shyness, I did not inform her mother how quickly matters had progressed between us, yet although we both acted as circumspectly as possible, I had no doubt Mrs. Brunnell could see how engrossed we were in each other. Lovers are not unlike ostriches in their modes of concealment. I was not afraid of asking Mrs. Brunnell for her daughter, for she already showed her partiality towards me, and had bestowed upon me some confidences regarding her own position in life, and I therefore knew that, so far as social position was concerned, there could be no real objection to our marriage. They lived in this lonely spot for the sake of their health, and kept no servant because they could not get any to take service so far away from other humanity. My coming had been opportune and welcome to both mother and daughter.

For the sake of decorum, however, I resolved to delay my confession for a week or two and trust to some favourable opportunity of doing it discreetly.

Meantime Ariadne and I passed our time in a thoroughly idle and lotus-eating style. Each night I retired to bed meditating starting work next day, each morning I rose languid from those disturbing dreams with no thought for anything outside my love. She grew stronger every day, while I appeared to be taking her place as the invalid, yet I was more frantically in love than ever, and only happy when with her. She was my lode-star, my only joy—my life.

We did not go great distances, for I liked best to lie on the dry heath and watch her glowing face and intense eyes while I listened to the surging of the distant waves. It was love made me lazy, I thought, for unless a man has all he longs for beside him, he is apt to copy the domestic cat and bask in the sunshine.

I had been enchanted quickly. My disenchantment came as rapidly, although it was long before the poison left my blood.

One night, about a couple of weeks after my coming to the cottage, I had returned after a delicious moonlight walk with Ariadne. The night was warm and the moon at the full, therefore I left my bedroom window open to let in what little air there was.

I was more than usually fagged out, so that I had only strength enough to remove my boots and coat before I flung myself wearily on the coverlet and fell almost instantly asleep without tasting the nightcap draught that was constantly placed on the table, and which I had always drained thirstily.

I had a ghastly dream this night. I thought I saw a monster bat, with the face and tresses of Ariadne, fly into the open window and fasten its white teeth and scarlet lips on my arm. I tried to beat the horror away, but could not, for I seemed chained down and thralled also with drowsy delight as the beast sucked my blood with a gruesome rapture.

I looked out dreamily and saw a line of dead bodies of young men lying on the floor, each with a red mark on their arms, on the same part where the vampire was then sucking me, and I remembered having seen and wondered at such a mark on my own arm for the past fortnight. In a flash I understood the reason for my strange weakness, and at the same moment a sudden prick of pain roused me from my dreamy pleasure.

The vampire in her eagerness had bitten a little too deeply that night, unaware that I had not tasted the drugged draught. As I woke I saw her fully revealed by the midnight moon, with her black tresses flowing loosely, and with her red lips glued to my arm. With a shriek of horror I dashed her backwards, getting one last glimpse of her savage eyes, glowing white face, and blood-stained red lips; then I rushed out to the night, moved on by my fear and hatred, nor did I pause in my mad flight until I had left miles between me and that accursed Cottage on the Moor.

SPECIAL

◆◆◆

RICHARD LAYMON

The outlaw women, wailing and shrieking, fled from the encampment. All but one, who stayed to fight.

She stood by the campfire, a sleek arm reaching up to pull an arrow from the quiver on her back. She stood alone as the men began to fall beneath the quick fangs of the dozen raiding vampires.

"She's mine!" Jim shouted.

None of his fellow Guardians gave him argument. Maybe they wanted no part of her. They raced into the darkness of the woods to chase down the others.

Jim rushed the woman.

You get her and you get her.

She looked innocent, fierce, glorious. Calmly nocking the arrow. Her thick hair was golden in the firelight. Her legs gleamed beneath the short leather skirt that hung low on her hips. Her vest spread open as she drew back her bowstring, sliding away from the tawny mound of her right breast.

Jim had never seen such a woman.

Get her!

She glanced at him. Without an instant of hesitation, she pivoted away and loosed her arrow.

Jim snapped his head sideways. The shaft flew at Strang's back. Hit him with a thunk. The vampire hurled the flapping body of an outlaw from his arms and whirled around, his black eyes fixing on the woman, blood spewing from his wide mouth as he bellowed, "Mine!"

Jim lurched to a halt.

Eyes narrowed, lips a tight line, the woman reached up for another arrow as Strang staggered toward her. Jim was near enough to hear breath hissing through her nostrils. He gazed at her, fascinated, as she fit the arrow onto the bowstring. Her eyes were on Strang. She pulled the string back to her jaw. Her naked breast rose and fell as she panted for air.

She didn't let the arrow fly.

Strang took one more stumbling stride, foamy blood gushing from his mouth, arms outstretched as if to reach beyond the campfire and grab her head. Then he pitched forward. His face crushed the flaming heap of wood, sending up a flurry of sparks. His hair began to blaze.

The woman met Jim's eyes.

Get her and you get her.

He'd never wanted any woman so much.

"Run!" he whispered. "Save yourself."

"Eat shit and die," she muttered, and released her arrow. It whizzed past his arm.

Going for her, Jim couldn't believe that she had missed. But he heard the arrow punch into someone, heard the roar of a wounded vampire, and knew that she'd found her target. For the second time, she had chosen to take down a vampire rather than protect herself from him. And she hadn't run when he'd given her the chance. What kind of woman *is* this?

With his left hand, he knocked the bow aside. With his right, he swung at her face. His fist clubbed her cheek. Her head snapped sideways, mouth dropping open, spit spraying out. The punch spun her. The bow flew from her hand. Her legs tangled and she went down. She pushed at the ground, got to her hands and knees, and scurried away from Jim.

Let her go?

He hurried after her, staring at her legs. Shadows and firelight fluttered on them. Sweat glistened. The skirt was so short it barely covered her rump and groin.

You get her and you get her.

She thrust herself up.

I'm gonna let her go, Jim thought. They'll kill me, and they'll probably get her anyway, but . . .

Instead of making a break for the woods, she whirled around, jerked a knife from the sheath at her hip, and threw herself at Jim. The blade ripped the front of his shirt. Before she could bring it back across, he caught her wrist. He yanked her arm up high and drove a fist into her belly. Her breath exploded out. The blow picked her up. The power of it would've hurled her backward and slammed her to the ground, but Jim kept his grip on her wrist. She dangled in front of him, writhing and wheezing. Her sweaty face was twisted with agony.

One side of her vest hung open.

She might've had a chance.

I got her, I get her.

Jim cupped her warm, moist breast, felt its nipple pushing against his palm.

Her fist crashed into his nose. He saw it coming, but had no time to block it. Pain exploded behind his eyes. But he kept his grip, stretched her high by the trapped arm, and punched her belly until he could no longer hold her up.

Blinking tears from his eyes, sniffing up blood, he let her go. She dropped to her knees in front of him and slumped forward, her face hitting the ground between his feet. Crouching, he pulled a pair of handcuffs from his belt. Blood splashed the back of her vest as he picked up her limp arms, pulled them behind her, and snapped the cuffs around her wrists.

"That one put up a hell of a scrap," Roger said.

Jim, sitting on the ground beside the crumpled body of the woman, looked up at the grinning vampire. "She was pretty tough," he said. He sniffed and swallowed some more blood. "Sorry I couldn't stop her quicker."

Roger patted him on the head. "Think nothing of it. Strang was always a pain in the ass, anyway, and Winthrop was such an atrocious brown-noser. I'm better off without them. I'd say, taken all 'round, that we've had a banner night."

Roger crouched in front of the woman, clutched the hair on top of her head, and lifted her to her knees. Her eyes were shut. By the limp way she hung there, Jim guessed she must still be unconscious.

"A looker," Roger said. "Well worth a broken nose, if you ask me." He chuckled. "Of course, it's not *my* nose. But if I were you, I'd be a pretty damn happy fellow about now." He eased her down gently and walked off to join the other vampires.

While they waited for all the Guardians to return with the female prisoners, they searched the bodies of the outlaws, took whatever possessions they found interesting, and stripped the corpses. They tossed the clothing into the campfire, not one of them bothering to remove Strang from the flames.

Joking and laughing quite a bit, they hacked the bodies to pieces. The banter died away as they began to suck the remaining blood from severed heads, stumps of necks and arms and legs, from various limbs and organs. Jim turned his eyes away. He looked at the woman. She was lucky to be out cold. She couldn't see the horrible carnage. She couldn't hear the grunts and sighs of pleasure, the sloppy wet sounds, the occasional belch from the vampires relishing their feast. Nor could she hear the women who'd been captured and brought in by the other Guardians. They were weeping, pleading, screaming, vomiting.

When he finally looked away from her, he saw that all the Guardians had returned. Each had a prisoner. Bart and Harry both had two. Most of the women looked as if they'd been beaten. Most had been stripped of their clothes.

They looked to Jim like a sorry bunch.

Not one stood proud and defiant.

I got the best of the lot, he thought.

Roger rose to his feet, tossed a head into the fire, and rubbed the back of his hand across his mouth. "Well, folks," he said, "how's about heading on back to the old homestead?"

Jim picked up the woman. Carrying her on his shoulder, he joined the procession through the woods. Other Guardians complimented him on his catch. Some made lewd suggestions about her. A few peeked under her skirt. Several offered to trade, and grumbled when Jim refused.

At last, they found their way to the road. They hiked up its moonlit center until they came to the bus. Biff and Steve, Guardians who'd stayed behind to protect it from outlaws and vampire gangs, waved greetings from its roof.

On the side of the black bus, in huge gold letters that glimmered with moonlight, was painted: ROGER'S ROWDY RAIDERS.

The vampires, Guardians, and prisoners climbed aboard.

Roger drove.

An hour later, they passed through the gates of his fortified estate.

The next day, Jim slept late. When he woke up, he lay in bed for a long time, thinking about the woman. Remembering her courage and beauty, the way her breast had felt in his hand, her weight and warmth and smoothness while she hung over his shoulder on the way to the bus.

He hoped she was all right. She'd seemed to be unconscious during the entire trip. Of course, she might've been pretending. Jim, sitting beside her, had savored the way she looked in the darkness and felt quick rushes of excitement each time a break in the trees permitted moonlight to wash across her.

The other Guardians were all busy ravishing their prisoners during the bus ride. Some had poked fun at him, asked if he'd gone queer like Biff and Steve, offered to pay him for a chance to screw Sleeping Beauty.

He wasn't sure why he had left her alone during the trip. In the past, he'd never hesitated to enjoy his prisoners.

But this woman was different. Special. Proud and strong. She deserved better than to be molested while out cold and in the presence of others.

Jim would have her soon. In privacy. She would be alert, brave, and fierce.

Soon.

But not today.

For today, the new arrivals would be in the care of Doc and his crew. They would be deloused and showered, then examined. Those judged incapable of bearing children would go to the Doner Ward. Each Doner had a twofold job: to give a pint of blood daily for the estate's stockroom, and to provide sexual services not only for the

Guardian who captured her but also for any others, so inclined, once he'd finished.

The other prisoners would find themselves in the Specialty Suite.

It wasn't a suite, just a barracklike room similar to the Doner Ward. But those assigned to it did receive special treatment. They weren't milked for blood. They were fed well.

And each Special could only be used by the Guardian who had captured her.

Mine will be a Special, Jim thought. She's gotta be. She *will* be. She's young and strong.

She'll be mine. All mine.

At least till Delivery Day.

He felt a cold, spreading heaviness.

That's a long time from now, he told himself. Don't think about it.

Moaning, he climbed out of bed.

He was standing guard in the north tower at ten the next morning when the two-way radio squawked and Doc's voice came through the speaker. "Harmon, you're up. Specialty Suite, Honors Room Three. Bennington's on his way to relieve you."

Jim thumbed the speak button on his mike. "Roger," he said.

Heart pounding, he waited for Bennington. He'd found out last night that his prisoner, named Diane, had been designated a Special. He'd hoped this would be the day, but he hadn't counted on it; Doc only gave the okay if the timing was right. In Doc's opinion, it was only right during about two weeks of each woman's monthly cycle.

Jim couldn't believe his luck.

Finally, Bennington arrived. Jim climbed down from the tower and made his way across the courtyard toward the Specialty Suite. He had a hard time breathing. His legs felt weak and shaky.

He'd been in Honors Rooms before. With many different outlaw women. But he'd never felt like this: excited, horribly excited, but also nervous. Petrified.

Honors Room Three had a single large bed with red satin sheets. The plush carpet was red. So were the curtains that draped the barred windows, and the shades of the twin lamps on either side of the bed.

Jim sat down on a soft, upholstered armchair. And waited. Trembling.

Calm down, he told himself. This is crazy. She's just a woman.

Yeah, sure.

Hearing footfalls from the corridor, he leapt to his feet. He turned to the door. Watched it open.

Diane stumbled in, shoved from behind by Morgan and Donner, Doc's burly assistants. She glared at Jim.

"Key," Jim said.

Morgan shook his head. "I wouldn't, if were you."

"I brought her in, didn't I?"

"She'll bust more than your nose, you give her half a chance."

Jim held out his hand. Morgan, shrugging, tossed him the key to the shackles. Then the two men left the room. The door bumped shut, locking automatically.

And he was alone with Diane.

From the looks of her, she'd struggled on the way to the Honors Room. Her thick hair was mussed, golden wisps hanging down her face. Her blue satin robe had fallen off one shoulder. Its cloth belt was loose, allowing a narrow gap from her waist to the hem at her knees. She was naked beneath the robe.

Jim slipped a finger under the belt. He pulled until its half-knot came apart. Then he spread the robe and slipped it down her arms until it was stopped by the wrist shackles.

Guilt subdued his excitement when he saw the livid smudges on her belly. "I'm sorry about that," he murmured.

"Do what you're going to do," she said. Though she was trying to sound tough, he heard a slight tremor in her voice.

"I'll take these shackles off," he said. "But if you fight me, I'll be forced to hurt you again. I don't want to do that."

"Then don't take them off."

"It'll be easier on you without them."

"Easier *for* you."

"Do you know why you're here?"

"It seems pretty obvious."

"It's not that obvious," Jim said, warning himself to speak with care. The room was bugged. A Guardian in the Security Center would be eavesdropping, and Roger himself was fond of listening to the Honors Room tapes. "This isn't . . . just so I can have fun and games with you. The thing is . . . I've got to make you pregnant."

Her eyes narrowed. She caught her lower lip between her teeth. She said nothing.

"What that means," Jim went on, "is that we'll be seeing each other every day. At least during your fertile times. Every day until you conceive. Do you understand?"

"Why do they want me pregnant?" she asked.

"They need more humans. For guards and staff and things. As it is, there aren't enough of us."

She gazed into his eyes. He couldn't tell whether or not she believed the lie.

"If you don't become pregnant, they'll put you in with the Doners. It's much better for you here. The Doners . . . all the Guardians can have them whenever they want."

"So, it's either you or the whole gang, huh?"

"That's right."

"Okay."

"Okay?"

She nodded.

Jim began taking off his clothes, excited but uncomfortably aware of the scorn in her eyes.

"You must be a terrible coward," she said.

He felt heat spread over his skin.

"You don't seem evil. So you must be a coward. To serve such beasts."

"Roger treats us very well," he said.

"If you were a man, you'd kill him and all his kind. Or die trying."

"I have a good life here."

"The life of a dog."

Naked, he crouched in front of Diane. His face was inches from her tuft of golden down. Aching with a hot confusion of lust and shame, he lowered his eyes to the short length of chain stretched taut between her feet. "I'm no coward," he said, and removed the steel cuffs.

As the shackles fell to the carpet, she pumped a knee into his forehead. Not a powerful blow, but enough to knock him off balance. His rump hit the floor. He caught himself with both hands while Diane dropped backward, curling, jamming her thighs tight against her chest. Before he could get up, she somehow slipped the hand shackles and trapped robe under her buttocks and up the backs of her legs. They cleared her feet. Her hands were suddenly in front of her, cuffs and chain hidden under the draping robe.

As her heels thudded the floor, Jim rushed her. She spread her legs wide, raised her knees, and stretched her arms out straight overhead. The robe was a glossy curtain molded to her face and breasts.

Jim dove, slamming down on her. She grunted. Clamped her legs around him. He reached for her arms. They were too quick for him. The covered chain swept past his eyes. Went tight around his throat. Squeezed.

Choking, he found her wrists. They were crossed behind his head. He tugged at them. Parted them. Felt the chain loosen. Forced them down until the chain pressed into Diane's throat.

Her face had come uncovered. Her eyes bulged. Her lips peeled back. She twisted and bucked and squirmed.

When he entered her, tears shimmered in her eyes.

The next day, Jim let Morgan and Donner chain her to the bed frame before leaving.

She didn't say a word. She didn't struggle. She lay motionless and glared at Jim as he took her.

When he was done but still buried in her tight heat, he whispered, "I'm sorry." He hoped the microphone didn't pick it up.,

For an instant, the look of hatred in her eyes changed to something else. Curiosity? Hope?

. . .

"What are you sorry about, Jim?"

"Sorry?"

"You apologized. What did you apologize for?"

"To who?"

"You've gone soft on her," Roger said. "Can't say I blame you. She's quite a looker. Feisty too. But she's obviously messing you up. I'm afraid someone else'll have to take over. We'll work a trade with Phil. You can do his gal, and he'll do yours. It'll be better for everyone."

"Yes, sir."

Phil's gal was named Betsy. She was a brunette. She was pretty. She was stacked. She was not just compliant, but enthusiastic. She said that she'd hated being an outlaw, living in the wilds, often hungry and always afraid. This, she said, was like paradise.

Jim had her once a day.

Each time, he closed his eyes and made believe she was Diane.

He longed for her. He dreamed about her. But she was confined to the Specialty Suite, available only to Phil, so he would probably never have a chance to see her again. It ate at him. He began to hope she would fail to conceive. In that case, she would eventually be sent to the Doner Ward.

A terrible fate for someone with her spirit. But at least Jim would be able to see her, go to her, touch her, have her. And she would be spared the final horror which awaited the Specials. Doc had judged her to be fertile, however, so Jim knew there was little chance of ever seeing her again.

Jim was in the Mess Hall a week after being reassigned to Betsy, trying to eat lunch though he had no appetite, when the alarm suddenly blared. The PA boomed, "Guardian down, Honors Room One! Make it snappy, men!"

Jim and six others ran from the Mess Hall. Sprinting across the courtyard, he took over the lead. He found Donner waiting in the corridor. The man, gray and shaky, pointed at the closed door of Honors Room One.

Jim threw the door open.

Instead of a bed, this room was equipped with a network of steel bars from which the Special could be suspended, stretched, and spread in a variety of positions.

Diane hung by her wrists from a high bar. There were no restraints on her feet. She was swinging and twisting at the ends of her chains as she kicked at Morgan. Her face wore a fierce grimace. Her hair clung to her face. Her skin, apparently oiled by Phil, gleamed and poured sweat. The shackles had cut into her wrists, and blood streamed down her arms and sides.

Phil lay motionless on the floor beneath her wild, kicking body. His head was turned. Too much.

She'd broken his neck?

How could she?

Even as Jim wondered, he saw Morgan lurch forward and grab one of her darting ankles. Diane shot her other leg high. With a cry of pain, she twisted her body and hooked her foot behind Morgan's head. The big man stumbled toward her, gasping with alarm. He lost his hold on her ankle. That leg flew up. In an instant, he was on his knees, his head trapped between her thighs.

Morgan's dilemma seemed to snap the audience of Guardians out of their stunned fascination.

Jim joined the others in their rush to the rescue.

He grabbed one leg. Bart grabbed the other. They forced her thighs apart, freeing Morgan. The man slumped on top of Phil's body, made a quick little whimpery sound, and scurried backward.

"Take Phil out of here," said Rooney, the head Guardian.

The body was dragged from under Diane and taken from the room.

"What'll we do with her?" Jim asked.

"Let her hang," Rooney said. "We'll wait for tonight and let Roger take care of her."

They released her legs and backed up quickly.

She dangled, swaying back and forth, her eyes fixed on Jim.

He paused in the doorway. He knew he would never see her again.

He was wrong.

He saw her a month later when he relieved Biff and began his new duty of monitoring video screens in the Security Center. Diane was on one of the dozen small screens. Alone. In the Punishment Room.

Jim couldn't believe his eyes. He'd been certain that Roger had killed her—probably torturing her, allowing the other vampires small samples of her blood before draining her himself. Jim had seen that done, once, to a Doner who tried to escape. Diane's crime had been much worse. She'd murdered a Guardian.

Instead of taking her life, however, Roger had merely sent her to the Punishment Room. Which amounted to little more than solitary confinement.

Incredible. Wonderful.

. . .

Night after night, alone in the Security Center, Jim watched her.

He watched her sleep on the concrete floor, a sheet wrapped around her naked body. He watched her sit motionless, cross-legged, gazing at the walls. He watched her squat on a metal bucket to relieve herself. Sometimes, she gave herself sponge baths.

Frequently, she exercised. For hours at a time, she would stretch, run in place, kick and leap, do sit-ups and push-ups and handstands. Jim loved to watch her quick, graceful motions, the flow of her sleek muscles, the way her hair danced and how her breasts jiggled and swayed. He loved the sheen of sweat that made her body glisten.

He could never see enough of her.

Every day, he waited eagerly for the hour when he could relieve Biff and be alone with Diane.

When he had to go on night raids, he was miserable. But he did his duty. He rounded up outlaw women. Some became Specials, and he visited them in Honors Rooms, but when he was with them he always tried to pretend they were Diane.

Then one night, watching her exercise, he noticed that her belly didn't look quite flat.

"No," he murmured.

Throughout the winter, he watched her grow. Every night, she seemed larger. Her breasts swelled and her belly became a bulging mound.

He often wondered whose child she was bearing. It might be his. It might be Phil's.

He worried, always, about Delivery Day.

. . .

During his free time, he began making solitary treks into the woods surrounding the estate.

He took his submachine gun and machete.

He often came back with game, which he delivered afterward to Jones in the kitchen. The grinning chef was always delighted to receive the fresh meat. He was glad to have Jim's company while he prepared it for the Guardians' evening meal.

Spring came. One morning at six, just as Bart entered the Security Center to relieve Jim of his watch, Diane flinched awake grimacing. She drew her knees up. She clutched her huge belly through the sheet.

"What gives?" Bart asked.

Jim shook his head.

Bart studied the monitor. "She's starting contractions. I'd better ring up Doc."

Bart made the call. Then he took over Jim's seat in front of the video screens.

"I think I'll stick around," Jim said.

Bart chuckled. "Help yourself."

He stayed. He watched the monitor. Soon, Doc and Morgan and Donner entered the cell. They flung the sheet aside. Morgan and Donner forced Diane's legs apart. Doc inspected her. Then they lifted her onto a gurney and strapped her down. They rolled the gurney out of the cell.

"I'll pick 'em up in the Prep Room," Bart muttered. "That's what you want to see, right?" He leered over his shoulder.

Jim forced a smile. "You got it."

Bart fingered some buttons. The deserted Punishment

Room vanished from the screen, and the Prep Room appeared.

Doc and his assistants rolled the gurney in.

He soaked a pad with chloroform and pressed it against Diane's nose and mouth until she passed out. Then the straps were unfastened. After being sprayed with water, she was rubbed with white foam. All three men went at her with razors.

"Wouldn't mind that job," Bart said.

Jim watched the razors sweep paths through the foam, cutting away not only Diane's thick golden hair, but also the fine down. The passage of the blades left her skin shiny and pink. After a while, she was turned over so the rest of her body could be lathered and shaved.

Then the men rinsed her and dried her with towels.

They carried her from the gurney to the wheeled, oak serving table. The table, a rectangle large enough to seat only six, was bordered by brass gutters for catching the runoff. At the corners of one end—Roger's end—were brass stirrups.

Feeling sick, Jim watched the men lift Diane's limp body onto the table. They bent her legs. They strapped her feet into the stirrups. They slid her forward to put her within easy reach of Roger. Then they cinched a belt across her chest, just beneath her breasts. They stretched her arms overhead and strapped her wrists to the table.

"That's about it for now," Bart said. "If you drop by around seven tonight, that's about when they'll be basting her. She'll be awake then too. That's about the time the panic really hits them. It's usually quite a sight to behold."

"I've seen," Jim muttered, and left the room.

. . .

He returned to the barracks and tried to sleep. It was no use. Finally, he got up and armed himself. Steve let him out the front gate. He wandered the woods for hours. With his submachine gun, he bagged three squirrels.

In the late afternoon, he ducked into the hiding place he'd found in a clump of bushes. He lashed together the twenty wooden spears which he'd fashioned during the past weeks. He pocketed the small pouch containing the nightcap mushrooms which he had gathered and ground to fine powder.

He carried the spears to the edge of the forest. Leaving them propped against a tree, he stepped into the open. He smiled and waved his squirrels at the north tower. The gate opened, and he entered the estate.

He took the squirrels to Jones in the kitchen. And helped the cheerful chef prepare stew for the Guardians' supper.

Just after sunset, Jim went to the Security Center and knocked.

"Yo." Biff's voice.

"It's Jim. I want to see the basting."

"You're a little early," Biff said. Moments later, he opened the door. He exhaled sharply and folded over as Jim rammed a knife into his stomach.

Diane was awake, sweaty and grunting, struggling against the restraints, gritting her teeth and flinching rigid each time a contraction hit her.

Jim stared at the screen. Without hair and eyebrows, she looked so *odd.* Freakish. Even her figure, misshapen by the distended belly and swollen breasts, seemed alien. But her eyes were pure Diane. In spite of her pain and terror, they were proud, unyielding.

Doc entered the Prep Room, examined her for a few moments, then went away.

Jim checked the other screens.

In the Doner Ward, the women had been locked down for the Guardians' evening mealtime. Some slept. Others chatted with friends in neighboring beds. Jim made a quick count.

In the Specialty Suite, Morgan and Donner were just returning a woman from an Honors Room. They led her to one of the ten empty beds, shoved her down on it, and shackled her feet to the metal frame. Jim counted heads.

Thirty-two Doners. Only sixteen Specials. Generally, however, the Doners were older women who'd been weakened by the daily loss of blood and by regular mistreatment at the hands of the Guardians. The Specials were fewer in number, but younger and stronger. Though some appeared to be in the late stages of their pregnancies, most were not very far along, and many of the newer ones had probably not even conceived yet.

It'll be the Specials, Jim decided.

He watched Morgan and Donner leave the suite.

In the mess hall, Guardians began to eat their stew.

In the floodlit courtyard, Steven and Bennington climbed stairs to the north and west towers, carrying pots of dinner to the men on watch duty. When they finished there, they should be heading for the other two towers.

Morgan and Donner entered the mess hall. They sat down, and Jones brought them pots of stew.

Doc entered the Prep Room. He set a bowl of shimmering red fluid onto the table beside Diane's hip. He dipped in a brush. He began to paint her body. The blood coated her like paint.

In the mess hall, Baxter groaned and staggered away from the table, clutching his belly.

In the Banquet Room, there was no camera. But Jim knew that Roger and his pals would be there, waiting and eager. The absence of the usual table would've already tipped them off that tonight would be special. Even now, Roger was probably picking five to sit with him at the serving table. The unfortunate four would only get to watch and dine on their usual fare of Doner blood.

In the mess hall, Guardians were stumbling about, falling down, rolling on the floor.

In the Prep Room, Doc set aside the brush and bowl. He rolled the serving table toward the door. Diane shook her crimson, hairless head from side to side and writhed against the restraints.

Jim rushed out of the Security Center.

"All hell's broken loose!" he shouted as he raced up the stairs to the north tower. "Don't touch your food! Jones poisoned it!"

"Oh shit!" Harris blurted, and spat out a mouthful.

"Did you swallow any?" Jim asked, rushing toward him.

"Not much, but . . ."

Jim jerked the knife from the back of his belt and slashed Harris's throat. He punched a button on the control panel.

By the time he reached the front gate, it was open. He ran out, dashed across the clear area beyond the wall, and grabbed the bundle of spears.

The gate remained open for him. Apparently, the poison had taken care of the Guardian on the west tower.

Rushing across the courtyard, he saw two Guardians squirming on the ground.

At the outer door of the Specialty Suite, Jim snatched the master key off its nail. He threw the door open and rushed in.

"All right, ladies! Listen up! We're gonna kill some vampires!"

Blasts pounding his ears, Jim blew apart the lock. He threw his gun aside, kicked the door, and charged into the Banquet Room.

Followed by sixteen naked Specials yelling and brandishing spears.

For just an instant, the vampires around the serving table continued to go about their business—greedily lapping the brown, dry blood from Diane's face and breasts and legs as Roger groped between her thighs. The four who watched, goblets in hand, were the first to respond.

Then, roaring, they all abandoned the table and attacked.

All except Roger.

Roger stood where he was. He met Jim's eyes. "*You dumb fuck!*" he shouted. "Take care of him, guys!"

The vampires tried. They all rushed Jim.

But were met, first, by Specials. Some went down with spears in their chests while others tossed the women away or slammed them to the floor or snapped their spines or ripped out their throats.

Jim rushed through the melee. He halted at the near end of the table as Roger cried out, "Is *this* why you're here?" His hands delved. Came up a moment later with a tiny, gleaming infant. "Not enough to share, I'm afraid." Grinning, he raised the child to his mouth. With a quick nip, he severed its umbilical cord.

One hand clutching the baby's feet, he raised it high and tilted back his head. His mouth opened wide. His other hand grasped the top of its head.

Ready to twist it off. Ready to enjoy his special, rare treat.

"No!" Diane shrieked.

Jim hurled his spear. Roger's hand darted down. He caught the shaft, stopping its flight even as the wooden point touched his chest. "Dickhead," he said. "You didn't really think . . ."

Jim launched himself at Diane. He flew over her body, smashed down on her, slid through the wide *v* of her spread legs and reached high and grabbed the spear and rammed it deep into Roger's chest.

The vampire bellowed. He staggered backward. Coughed. Blood exploded from his mouth, spraying Jim's face and arms. He dropped to his knees and looked up at the infant that he still held high. He lowered its head toward his wide, gushing mouth.

Jim flung himself off the end of the table and landed on the spear. As its shaft snapped under his weight, bloody vomit cascaded over his head. Pushing himself up, he saw the baby dangling over Roger's mouth. The vampire snapped futilely at its head. Jim scurried forward and grabbed the child as Roger let go and slumped against the floor.

Afterward, the Doners were released.

They helped with the burials.

Eleven dead Specials were buried in the courtyard, their graves marked by crosses fashioned of spears.

Morgan, Donner, and the Guardians, who'd all succumbed to the poison, were buried beyond the south wall of the estate.

The corpses of Roger and his fellow vampires were taken into the woods to a clearing where two trails crossed. The heads were severed. The torsos were buried with the spears still in place. The heads were carried a mile away to another crossing in the trail. There, they were burned. The charred skulls were crushed, then buried.

After a vote by the women, Doc and three Guardians who'd missed the poisoned squirrels were put to death. Jones had also missed the meal. But the women seemed to like him. He was appointed chef. Jim was appointed leader.

He chose Diane to be his assistant.

The child was a girl. They named her Glory. She had Diane's eyes, and ears that stuck out in very much the same way as Jim's.

The small army lived in Roger's estate, and seemed happy.

Frequently, when the weather was good, a squad of well-armed volunteers would board the bus. Jim driving, they would follow roads deep into the woods. They would park the bus and wander about, searching. Sometimes they found vampires and took them down with a shower of arrows. Sometimes they found bands of outlaws and welcomed these strangers into their ranks.

One morning, when a commotion in the courtyard drew Jim's attention, he looked down from the north tower and saw Diane gathered around the bus with half a dozen other women. Instead of their usual leather skirts and vests, they were dressed in rags.

Diane saw him watching, and waved. Her hair had grown, but it was still quite short. It shone like gold in the sunlight.

She looked innocent, glorious.

She and her friends were painting the bus pink.

A WEEK IN THE UNLIFE

♦♦♦

DAVID J. SCHOW

I

When you stake a bloodsucker, the heartblood pumps out thick and black, the consistency of honey. I saw it make bubbles as it glurped out. The creature thrashed and squirmed and tried to pull out the stake—they always do, if you leave on their arms for the kill—but by the third whack it was, as Stoker might say, dispatched well and duly.

I lost count a long time ago. Doesn't matter. I no longer think of them as being even *former* human beings, and feel no anthropomorphic sympathy. In their eyes I see no tragedy, no romance, no seductive pulp appeal. Merely lust, rage at being outfoxed, and debased appetite, focused and sanguine.

People usually commit journals as legacy. So be it. Call me sentry, vigilante if you like. When they sleep their comatose sleep, I stalk and terminate them. When they walk, I hide. Better than they do.

They're really not as smart as popular fiction and films would lead you to believe. They do have cunning, an animalistic savvy. But I'm an experienced tracker; I know their spoor, the traces they leave, the way their presence charges the air. Things invisible or ephemeral to ordinary citizens, blackly obvious to me.

The journal is so you'll know, just in case my luck runs out. Sundown. Nap time.

II

Naturally the police think of me as some sort of homicidal crackpot. That's a given; always has been for my predecessors. More watchers to evade. Caution comes reflexively to me these days. Police are slow and rational; they deal in the minutiae of a day-to-day world, deadly enough without the inclusion of bloodsuckers.

The police love to stop and search people. Fortunately for me, mallets and stakes and crosses and such are not yet illegal in this country. Lots of raised eyebrows and jokes and nudging but no actual arrests. When the time comes for them to recognize the plague that has descended upon their city, they will remember me, perhaps with grace.

My lot is friendless, solo. I know and expect such. It's okay.

City by city. I'm good at ferreting out the nests. To me, their kill-patterns are like a flashing red light. The police only see presumed loonies, draw no linkages; they bust and imprison mortals and never see the light.

I am not foolhardy enough to leave bloodsuckers lying. Even though the mean corpus usually dissolves, the stakes might be discovered. Sometimes there is other residue. City dumpsters and sewers provide adequate and fitting disposal for the leftovers of my mission.

The enemy casualties.

I wish I could advise the authorities, work hand-in-hand with them. Too complicated. Too many variables. Not a good control situation. Bloodsuckers have a maddening knack for vanishing into crevices, even hairline splits in logic.

Rule: Trust no one.

III

A female one, today. Funny. There aren't as many of them as you might suppose.

She had courted a human lover, so she claimed, like Romeo and Juliet—she could only visit him at night, and only after feeding, because bloodsuckers too can get carried away by passion.

I think she was intimating that she was a physical lover of otherworldly skill; I think she was fighting hard to tempt me not to eliminate her by saying so.

She did not use her mouth to seduce mortal men. I drove the stake into her brain, through the mouth. She was of recent vintage and did not melt or vaporize. When I fucked her remains, I was surprised to find her warm inside, not cold, like a cadaver. Warm.

With some of them, the human warmth is longer in leaving. But it always goes.

IV

I never met one before that gave up its existence without a struggle, but today I did, one that acted like he had been expecting me to wander along and relieve him of the burden of unlife. He did not deny what he was, nor attempt to trick me. He asked if he could talk a bit, before.

In a third-floor loft, the windows of which had been spray-painted flat black, he talked. Said he had always hated the taste of blood: said he preferred pineapple juice, or even coffee. He actually brewed a pot of coffee while we talked.

I allowed him to finish his cup before I put the ashwood length to his chest and drove deep and let his blackness gush. It dribbled, thinned by the coffee he had consumed.

V

Was thinking this afternoon perhaps I should start packing a Polaroid or somesuch, to keep a visual body count, just in case this journal becomes public record someday. It'd be good to have illustrations, proof. I was thinking of that line you hear overused in the movies. I'm sure you know it: "*But there's no such THING as a vampire!*" What a howler; ranks right up there alongside "*It's crazy—but it just might work!*" and "*We can't stop now for a lot of silly native superstitions!*"

Right; shoot cozy little memory snaps, in case they whizz to mist or drop apart to smoking goo. That bull about how you're not supposed to be able to record their images is from the movies, too. There's so much misleading information running loose that the bloodsuckers—the real ones—have no trouble at all moving through any urban center, *with impunity*, as they say on cop shows.

Maybe it would be a good idea to tape record the sounds they make when they die. Videotape them begging not to be exterminated. That would bug the eyes of all those monster movie fans, you bet.

VI

So many of them beleaguering this city, it's easy to feel outnumbered. Like I said, I've lost count.

Tonight might be a good window for moving on. Like them, I become vulnerable if I remain too long, and it's prudent operating procedure not to leave patterns or become predictable.

It's easy. I don't own much. Most of what I carry, I carry inside.

VII

They pulled me over on Highway Ten, outbound, for a broken left tail-light. A datafax photo of me was clipped to the visor in the Highway Patrol car. The journal book itself has been taken as evidence, so for now it's a felt-tip and high school notebook paper, which notes I hope to append to the journal proper later.

I have a cell with four bunks all to myself. The door is solid gray, with a food slot, unlike the barred cage of the bullpen. On the way back I noticed they had caught themselves a bloodsucker. Probably an accident; they probably don't even know what they have. There is no sunrise or sunset in the block, so if he gets out at night, they'll never know what happened. But I already know. Right now I will not say anything. I am exposed and at a disadvantage. The one I let slip today I can eliminate tenfold, next week.

VIII

New week. And I am vindicated at last.

I relaxed as soon as they showed me the photographs. How they managed documentation on the last few bloodsuckers I trapped, I have no idea. But I was relieved. Now I don't have to explain the journal—which, as you can see, they returned to me immediately. They had thousands of questions. They needed to know about the mallets, the stakes, the preferred method of killstrike. I cautioned them not to attempt a sweep and clear at night, when the enemy is stronger.

They paid serious attention this time, which made me feel much better. Now the fight can be mounted en masse.

They also let me know I wouldn't have to stay in the cell. Just some paperwork to clear, and I'm out among them again. One of the officials—not a cop, but a doctor—congratulated me on a stout job well done. He shook my hand, on behalf of all of them, he said, and mentioned writing a book on my work. This is exciting!

As per my request, the bloodsucker in the adjacent solitary cell was moved. I told them that to be really sure, they should use one of my stakes. It was simple vanity, really, on my part. I turn my stakes out of ashwood on a lathe. I made sure they knew I'd permit my stakes to be used as working models for the proper manufacture of all they would soon need.

When the guards come back I really must ask how they managed such crisp 8×10s of so many bloodsuckers. All those names and dates. First class documentation.

I'm afraid I may be a bit envious.

PRINCESS OF DARKNESS

♦♦♦

FREDERICK COWLES

I

In the spring of 1938 I was sent to Budapest on a rather delicate mission. For some years diplomatic circles, in at least five European countries, had been somewhat puzzled about a certain Princess Bessenyei who made sporadic appearances in the Hungarian capital, and was vaguely suspected of being involved in international espionage. The lady first attracted notice early in 1925 when she suddenly appeared in Budapest and just as suddenly departed after dazzling her admirers for little more than two months. Nearly a year passed before she was again seen in public and thereafter, at varying intervals, she was back in the capital for periods of from six weeks to three months at a time.

Lots of ugly rumours were whispered about the Princess. It was said that her departures from the city always coincided with the mysterious deaths of men who were reputed to have been her lovers. There were those who even asserted that a woman, strangely like the Princess, had been closely associated with Bela Kun, the notorious Communist leader, and had inspired many of the bloody orgies perpetrated by his regime. This suggestion was treated as idle gossip, for who could credit a story which linked such a proud aristocrat with the lowest of the vile criminals who, for a brief time, held in their incompetent hands the reins of government in Hungary?

No one could speak with any certainty of encountering the lady prior to 1925. The only facts one could accept with any degree of certainty were that the Princess was a member of a very ancient Hungarian family and that she appeared to have unlimited wealth at her disposal. Her claim to possess an estate on the borders of Transylvania was unquestioned as a place called Bessenyei appeared on the map. The story that she was a spy was difficult to believe as, so far as could be ascertained, Budapest was the only city she favoured with her presence. Yet the suggestion was taken seriously in certain quarters and my journey to Hungary must have been backed by some definite information. My task was simply to become acquainted with the Princess and to discover, if possible, something of her background.

Budapest, in the years between wars, was a favourite rendezvous for crooks of all types, as well as a very popular tourist resort. It was a lovable and romantic city and I remember, with nostalgic pleasure, the twinkling lights along the Danube, the great flood-lit statue of St. Gellert, and the eternal Gypsy music throbbing through the night.

Istvan Zichy was one of our agents in those days and we had become fairly close friends during my many visits to his country. He was an attractive young man and, being a Count, moved in the best society. His greeting was very warm when he met me at the *Nyugati Pályaudvar*, and he chattered of trifling things as we drove to the *Dunapalota* where accommodation had been reserved for me. He became more serious in the privacy of my suite and I was surprised to find that he regarded my mission with some uneasiness.

"I don't like it, my friend," he said. "There is something

uncanny about the woman, but it is all nonsense to suggest she is a spy. For myself I am of the opinion that she is thoroughly evil and a worshipper of the devil." He made a quick sign of the Cross and, catching an involuntary smile on my face, continued. "Ah! You laugh at me and think that Istvan grows superstitious. I am a Hungarian and I know that in this country the old beliefs die hard. What do we know of this Princess Bessenyei? For a few months she stays with us in Budapest and then back she goes to her castle near Arad—a castle which no one has ever visited and which, to my certain knowledge, is little more than a ruin. She leaves the city and immediately some young man who has enjoyed her favours dies in a strange fashion. Wait until you have seen the lady. I think you will find that cold shivers will go down your spine."

"But," I protested, "I have been led to believe that the Princess is very beautiful."

"Certainly she is lovely," he replied. "But I do not like her kind of beauty. A snake is a splendid thing—to those who like snakes. There is another queer point to which I must draw your attention. Why has this Princess no relatives to show? Often she speaks of her father but he never comes with her to Budapest, nor have I known of any person who has ever met him."

"Relations can be an awful nuisance at times," I laughed. "Perhaps the lady prefers to keep hers in the background."

"Possibly she prefers to keep a lot of other things in the background," he replied. "Well, my friend, I will help you all I can, but I do not envy you the job. Everything is arranged for you to meet the Princess tomorrow night and you can form your own conclusions. For myself I think that if she is a spy, the government for which she works is ruled over by a gentleman with horns on his head."

II

The following evening, at the *Astoria*, I was presented to the Princess. Istvan had carefully paved the way for the encounter and I had been spoken of as a wealthy English nobleman visiting Hungary on my way to Constantinople.

It is not easy to describe the Princess nor to set down my first impression of her. She was a slim woman of medium height, with auburn hair and piercing green eyes. She appeared to be about thirty years of age, and her face and hands were so pale that they seemed quite bloodless, although her lips were unnaturally red. I noticed that the hand she extended for me to kiss was intensely cold and, when she smiled, sharp fang-like teeth were revealed. As the night advanced and I was able to examine the woman more closely, I became more and more uncertain about her. Although, when animated, her face was that of a young woman, in repose there was an indefinable air of age about it. Not a single wrinkle marred its loveliness and yet, in those odd moments, it was old in the way that a flawless piece of ivory may have been carved centuries ago. Then, whilst her eyes were definitely green when the light reflected upon them, in the shadow they appeared almost black.

For most of the time she kept up a lively flow of conversation, discussing all manner of topics from the international situation to the play then running at the *Nemzeti Szinház.* She ate nothing but a couple of peaches and drank only aerated water. This, I afterwards discovered, was her invariable practice, and no one had ever seen her eat a more substantial meal. The leader of the Gypsy orchestra seemed to avoid her as much as possible and, in his perambulations of the tables, seldom paused by our party. When he did he was careful to stand behind the

Princess. Once she snapped a remark at him and I am sure I saw fear in the man's eyes.

During the next few days I encountered the Princess on several occasions and she always seemed pleased to see me. Within a week or so we were on fairly intimate terms and, to tell the truth, I found her very fascinating although, in some unaccountable way, I was afraid of her. One night we had been dancing at the *Hungaria* and I was taking her back to the flat she rented in one of the old palaces in Buda. We had just crossed the *Széchenyi Lánchid* when the taxi lurched and threw her against me. I put out my arm to steady her and she pressed herself against me, lifting her face with such obvious invitation in her eyes that I bent over and kissed her red lips. Her mouth opened and I felt her sharp teeth pierce my lower lip. It all happened in a moment and, just as quickly, she drew away from me with a long, satisfied sigh. Then she laughed softly. It was an unpleasant sound with no humour in it, and I felt that she was secretly gloating over gaining some purpose of her own. This impression was confirmed when we were parting and she said very quietly, "Now you are mine for ever. I think you will dream of me tonight."

I did dream about her and it was not a nice experience. As is my usual practice I read for about half an hour and then switched off the light and settled down to sleep. I suppose I must have dozed off for what followed could only have been a dream in spite of its seeming reality. I thought a ray of dull green light suddenly shone through the window and upon it, floating into the room, came the Princess Bessenyei. She was dressed in a long white robe, her teeth appeared abnormally long, and her eyes blazed like cold emeralds. I was powerless to stir or to utter one word, although I knew that those teeth would soon be fixed upon my throat. Closer she came, her mouth dripping with saliva in a most repulsive manner. She lifted the bed-clothes and then, like a snake darting upon its victim, she bent down to my neck. There was a sudden jar of metal upon bone, and I realized her teeth had struck the little silver crucifix which I always wear about my neck. With a bitter, frustrated cry she stood erect and I saw her pale face change in a most horrible manner. The cheeks sunk inwards, the eyes became hollow sockets, the mouth a gaping hole—I was gazing upon the ghastly head of a corpse. From this nightmare I awakened in a cold perspiration to find the window wide open and the curtains billowing in the breeze. I did not get to sleep again that night.

The following evening Istvan and I attended a gala performance at the Opera. The Princess was there with a party from the German Embassy. During the interval we went to the box to pay our respects and the first thing I noticed was that her mouth was disfigured by a thin white scar—a mark which might have been made by a thin piece of hot metal. She observed my glance and, with a forced laugh, said something about being careless with a cigarette.

Nearly a week passed before we met again and then it was an accidental encounter in the *Allatkert*—the Budapest Zoological Garden. The park was almost deserted, for it was a chilly day, and I came upon the Princess by the house in which the Siberian wolves are kept. She had climbed inside the barrier and was stroking the animals through the bars of the cage. I was amazed to see the ferocious beasts behaving like huge dogs—grovelling at her touch and licking her hands.

"Be careful," I exclaimed as I approached. "Surely it is hardly safe to tempt them with such dainty morsels."

"They will not hurt me," she replied. "I am used to wolves and know when they are dangerous."

She swung herself through the rail and came to my side. For a few moments we stood looking at the animals and then I invited her to take some refreshment with me in the restaurant. She excused herself, saying she never ate between meals, but suggested she should sit with me whilst I drank a coffee. We went into the almost empty café and, sitting at a table against the wall, talked trivialities for a time. Suddenly she said, "Tell me, are you a Catholic?" I admitted the fact and she went on, "Then perhaps you have such a thing as a small cross or holy medal you would give me for a keepsake. Tomorrow I must go away and we may never meet again."

"I have a little crucifix which I always wear," I replied. "But it has a sentimental value and I would not care to part with it. Let us go into the city and I will buy you a small souvenir of our friendship."

"No," she exclaimed rather pettishly. "I want something that has a real personal association—something you wear. You see I have a fondness for you and would wish to remember these happy days."

I surprised a hard gleam in those green eyes and knew that she was anxious to obtain possession of my cross and that nothing else would satisfy her. I also realized that the crucifix was my shield against some unknown danger and, without it, I should be at the mercy of a power I did not understand. As casually as possible I changed the subject and we chatted amiably for another ten or fifteen minutes. Then I escorted her to the gates where she called a taxi and held out her hand in farewell. As I kissed the cold fingers she whispered, "You have refused my request, but the cross will not save you. You are mine for ever and I can afford to wait." The red lips parted in a mirthless smile as she gave a sharp instruction to the driver and was borne away.

I was sufficiently disturbed by the events of the morning to seek out Istvan and recount them to him. He listened without comment as I told of the Princess's familiarity with the wolves and of her desire to possess my little crucifix. I also gave him a brief account of my unpleasant dream.

"It all confirms my suspicions," he said when I had finished. "This apparently attractive woman is not what she seems. If I were to tell you exactly what I believe her to be I am afraid it would tax your credulity. I am, however, convinced that, in your own interest, some immediate action must be taken to put a stop to something that is devilish. Will you do me the favour of telling your experiences to my friend Professor Otto Nemetz?"

"Do you mean the famous psychical investigator and the author of so many learned books and monographs on occult subjects?" I enquired.

"The very same. The Professor is very interested in our friend the Princess and may feel disposed to give you some surprising information regarding the lady."

"I shall be delighted to meet Nemetz," I replied. "I have read many of his works and, if the man is only half as interesting as his writings, he should be a remarkable individual."

"I promise that you will not be disappointed," said Istvan.

III

My friend took me along to Otto Nemetz's apartment and, having performed the necessary introductions, pleaded another engagement and left me alone with my host. The

Professor was utterly unlike what I had pictured him to be. Instead of the tall, scholarly man with a slightly sinister air which I had imagined, I found a small, rotund individual with merry twinkling eyes. When Istvan had departed, Nemetz drew me over to the wide window and enthused about the wonderful vista of the Danube. It was certainly a marvellous scene from that fourth floor balcony—the silver ribbon of the stream far below, the Royal Palace and the Coronation church beyond, and, to the north, the blue heights of the encircling mountains.

Suddenly the Professor pulled me back into the room, closed the window, and said, "Now let us get down to business." He piloted me to a chair and, taking a bunch of keys from his pocket, unlocked a drawer in his desk. Carefully withdrawing a parcel wrapped in green baize, he removed the covering and placed a small oil-painting in my hands. It was a portrait of the Princess Bessenyei and the artist had caught, with uncanny skill, the wicked gleam of the green eyes and the bitter curl of the red lips.

"It is a remarkable likeness," I exclaimed. "Who is the artist?"

"You mean who *was* the artist. It was painted by Nicholas Erdösi and he, it may surprise you to know, died in 1502."

"But that is impossible," I protested somewhat feebly. "It is certainly a portrait of the Princess Bessenyei but, according to your statement, it is over four hundred years old."

"Exactly," replied the Professor drawing his chair closer to mine and speaking in a low tone. "That, in my opinion, is the age of the Princess. I believe that this woman has troubled the world for over four hundred years. Don't think me mad. Listen to what I have to say before you decide to dismiss my theories as fantastic dreams."

He passed me the cigarettes and lit his own pipe before he continued.

"In parts of Hungary, more especially in the Transylvanian district, a belief in vampires still exists. Throughout the centuries it has been held that certain persons can, by evil arts, retain a semblance of life within the tomb. I need only refer you to Johann Christofer Herenberg's *Philosophicae et Christianae Cogitationes de Vampiris* as proof of the fact that this belief has been seriously studied by learned men. The unholy dead nourish their bodies upon the blood of living men and women and, when this sustenance is available, can walk the world and behave like normal people. Time and distance mean nothing to the vampire and, after a period of quiet rest in the grave, it is capable of living like a human being for as long as six months at a time. In its lust for living blood it is inspired by a passion which often resembles love, and its victims are frequently wooed by an artful courtship. Usually the vampire does not care to be away from its home for a long period and, in fact, it cannot manage this unless it obtains the nourishment it requires. Yet, in the grave, it can retain the appearance of healthy life for hundreds of years providing it rises, from time to time, to drink human blood.

"It is a recognized fact that certain families in this part of Europe were, in the Middle Ages, brought under the vampire curse through their own criminal activities. The Bessenyeis were one of these. In the fifteenth century certain members of this family dabbled in the black arts and Prince Lóránd was the worst of them all. He undoubtedly sold his soul to the Evil One and initiated his daughter, the Princess Gizella, in all the foul rites of Satanism. She became the terror of the countryside—an avowed murderess who was eventually executed for her misdeeds in 1506.

Unfortunately, having regard for her rank, her body was interred in the chapel of Bessenyei Castle. If it had been burned much trouble would have been saved, for I am convinced that she and her father have been as active from the tomb as they were in life. At different times throughout the centuries this woman has appeared in the world, and she is the person you know as the Princess Bessenyei."

"But surely such a tale is ridiculous," I interrupted. "I am prepared to swear that the Princess is a woman of flesh and blood, and I cannot believe that your theory will bear scientific investigation. After all this is the twentieth century."

"She is certainly a creature of flesh and blood," replied Nemetz. "But that flesh and blood is over four centuries old. I know it all sounds like a medieval fantasy and yet I believe it to be true. I am so convinced that I am determined to prove my contention and, in doing so, to rid the world of a devilish evil. Hungarians are naturally superstitious and I should find it difficult to persuade any person in this country to give me the assistance I require. You are an Englishman and can help me if you will."

"How is that possible?" I asked in some trepidation for, remembering the strange incidents connected with my short acquaintance with the Princess, I felt myself becoming convinced against my will.

"Come with me to the Castle of Bessenyei," suggested the little Professor. "I can guarantee you protection against the undead, but I do not promise that the sights I may reveal will be pleasant. You are, I take it, a man with good nerves and are not afraid of things which may live in your memory for ever."

"I am not afraid of anything I can understand, but this is quite beyond me," I replied. "I have to find out all I can about the woman and, for this reason if for no other, I am prepared to help you even to the extent of accompanying you to Bessenyei."

"Good," cried Nemetz. "No time must be wasted and we will start at nine o'clock in the morning. Meanwhile it may be as well for us to visit the *Országos Levéltár*—the department of State Archives—to see if we can obtain any information about the home of the Bessenyeis."

He seized his hat and stick and presently we were hurrying along the *Horthy Miklos Ut.* By the bridge the Professor signalled a taxi which carried us across the river to Buda, by the Coronation church, to the modern building in the *Bécsikapu Tér* where all documents of the Hungarian State are housed. Soon we were closeted with a courteous official who, in the pleasant fashion of the country, produced a bottle of wine before he dealt with our enquiry.

"Yes," he said. "I have heard of the castle but, so far as I can recollect, it is situated in disputed territory. I will, however, let you have all the information that is available." He rang a bell and instructed the subordinate, who answered the summons, to bring certain documents and maps. When these were before him he gave us the startling intelligence that the Bessenyei family, at least that branch of it which owned the castle, had become extinct in 1723.

"But," I said, "there is certainly a Princess Bessenyei who is well known in Budapest society."

"She probably comes from another branch of the family," he replied. "Bessenyei Castle, with its estates, seems to have become State property about the middle of the last century. The building can be little more than a picturesque ruin and I see from our records that a caretaker was maintained there until the outbreak of the last war. Since the Treaty of Trianon we have had no official connection with the estate which appears to be in territory still the subject of litigation. If you wish to visit the place you will encounter no difficulties, although I think it most unlikely that any custodian is on the premises. Certainly we have met no charges for maintenance during the past twenty or thirty years."

Thanking him for his assistance we parted with mutual expressions of goodwill, and Nemetz and I returned to Pest.

IV

Punctually at nine o'clock the following day the professor was at my hotel. He came up to my suite and, spreading a map on the table, pointed out the road we had to follow.

"The actual distance," he said, "is little more than a hundred English miles. But I am afraid the latter part of the journey will be by bad roads and we cannot expect to arrive at our destination before late evening. It may be helpful if we can spend the night in the castle. Do you think you can face such an ordeal?"

"Having undertaken this adventure," I replied, "I am in your hands. If you think we should spend the night in the building I am quite agreeable."

"Excellent! One more thing before we start. Are you wearing the crucifix about your neck?"

I showed him the cross on its thin silver chain and he gave a grunt of approval. He led me out to the waiting car which he was driving himself. I noticed two travelling cases in the back seat, also a small crowbar.

On the whole it was a pleasant drive with brief stops at Kecskemét and Szeged. At the latter place we had a meal and inspected the splendid votive church. From Makó the roads were little more than dusty tracks through cornfields and vineyards. At last we came to a gloomy forest and, upon the edge of it, was a Gypsy encampment. Nemetz pulled up and called out to one of the men, asking if he could direct us to the castle. The fellow came over to the car and appeared to be afraid to answer the question. On the Professor repeating his request the Gypsy burst into a torrent of words accompanied by urgent gestures. So far as I could make out the castle was in the forest, but it was only a deserted ruin. It was an evil place and we would be well advised to give it a wide berth. Nemetz laughed and said something about calling on the Princess. This remark served to increase the man's agitation and his incoherent warnings rang in our ears as we drove away.

"You see," said my companion, "even the Gypsies are afraid of the castle and know it to be the home of evil things."

It was so dark under the trees that we had to switch on the headlights to enable us to see the way. After about a couple of miles there was a break in the trees and a pair of ruined columns, one still surmounted by a heraldic device, indicated the approach to a large house. In the distance we could see the outline of a tower, but the drive was overgrown and hardly distinguishable from the surrounding fields. Dusk was falling as we turned into the entrance and suddenly there was a blood-curdling howl and a gaunt grey wolf leaped from the shadows and bounded along at the side of the car. Nemetz applied the brakes, pulled out a revolver, and fired three rounds at the animal. At such short range he could hardly have failed to hit it. But, with a howl of rage, it reared up on its hind legs and then ran off among the trees. Then, from all over the forest, came the answering cries of a pack of wolves howling in anger.

Beyond the shattered gates the track led through a wilderness which must have originally been parkland. A few stunted trees hung above a reedy lake into which flowed the waters of a dark moat, which we crossed by a crumbling bridge.

As we neared the castle I could see that it was little more than a shell, with a round tower on the western side and, beyond it, a detached building which looked like a chapel. Drawing up before the main doorway the Professor handed me a powerful electric torch and, carrying a bag each, we climbed the broken steps.

"There is just a chance that there may be a caretaker in the place," said Nemetz, "although I think it most unlikely." He pulled a chain which hung from a pillar and, far away inside the building, a bell tolled with a hollow sound. As its echoes died we heard the sound of shuffling footsteps and the heavy door swung open. On the threshold stood a tall man dressed in the dark costume of an old-fashioned retainer. He held a lighted candle in his hand and the light fell upon a bearded face in which the eyes glowed with a curious red glow. I confess that I was afraid and wished myself back in the pleasant comfort of the *Dunapalota*. But the Professor did not appear unduly alarmed.

"You are the custodian I presume?" he asked. The man gave a barely perceptible nod and Nemetz went on. "We are two travellers who desire shelter for the night. Can it be arranged?"

"The accommodation is poor," was the reply in a thin, fluting voice. "But you are welcome to such as it is. Enter, gentlemen. Enter of your own free will and become the guests of Castle Bessenyei."

He stood aside, holding the candle high, and we entered the building. The hall, which appeared to be in a tolerable state of repair, stank of damp and decay. A ragged tapestry fluttered on one wall, but the others were green with mildew. Our guide gave us little chance to examine our surroundings for, after slamming the door, he led the way up a wide staircase, along a narrow corridor on the first floor, and ushered us into a room at the end of it. It was apparently a large apartment and the feeble light of the candle revealed a bare floor, a heavy table, two chairs, and an oak settle.

"This is the best we can offer," said the strange custodian. "I trust you have food with you, for there is none in the castle. You will, I hope, find this better than a night spent in the forest." With a soft chuckle he added, "It is many years since last we entertained guests in Castle Bessenyei."

"Can you light a fire?" demanded the Professor. "The room is as cold as a tomb."

"I regret there is no fuel in the castle," was the reply. "This is all we can provide—a roof over your heads and chairs in which you can await the dawn. Even a tomb is not so cold as the living believe." As he spoke, the howl of a wolf sounded from under the windows. With a muttered word of apology he grabbed the candle and hurried from the room, leaving us in the semi-darkness.

The door had hardly closed when Nemetz quietly opened it again and, beckoning me to follow, led the way along the passage to the head of the stairs. The old man was descending and his candle cast queer shadows on the damp walls. Moving with a strange gliding motion he hurried over to the heavy door and flung it open. At once a long grey shape bounded over the threshold and I started back in fear. But immediately, before our eyes, the wolf changed into a woman. It was the Princess Bessenyei. We heard the muttering of low conversation and then the woman raised her eyes and looked to where we were standing. The Professor pulled me back into the deeper shadow and we watched as the two figures below moved towards a door near the foot of the stairs and vanished through it. We waited a few moments and then silently crept back to our room.

"Now we know exactly where we stand," said the Professor, driving home the rusty bolt on the door. "The Princess is here and it is obvious that the custodian is not what he pretends to be. We must prepare ourselves for the night."

From the first case he unpacked a portable electric lamp which was powerful enough to illuminate the sombre chamber. We saw that the dust of years covered the floor and the barred windows were festooned with cobwebs. A coat of arms was carved above the wide stone fireplace and this was repeated over each of the two windows. Nemetz then produced handfuls of garlic and spread the herb on the threshold of the rooms and on the windowsills. On the table he placed a pair of brass candle-sticks containing long yellow tapers which he lighted.

"We are now safe from direct attack," he explained. "For some reason the undead loathe the smell of garlic and it has always been considered a sure protection against their spells. The candles were blessed by the archbishop last Candlemas Day and, to make things doubly sure, I shall now sprinkle the room with holy water."

He took a flask from his pocket and, reciting the prayer of the *Asperges*, sprayed drops of the blessed water into every corner of the apartment. We then drew the chairs up to the table and ate a light meal of sandwiches washed down with a bottle of seltzer water.

"It will be safe enough to sleep," said the little man when we had finished our repast. "But on no account must you attempt to leave the room or to open the door or windows."

For a while we chatted of ordinary things which seemed ridiculously unreal in those sinister surroundings. But I was very tired and could feel my lids growing heavier. After a time I saw that my companion was finding it difficult to remain awake. Suddenly he slumped over the table and settled his head on his arm. I also must have fallen asleep and yet it seemed that I never closed my eyes. I became aware of a reddish glow which appeared to come from the fireplace and eventually resolved itself into minute particles of gleaming dust which danced in the light of the electric lamp. Gradually they took shape, misty at first and then more clearly defined until the Princess Bessenyei stood before me. Her green eyes were tender and inviting, and she beckoned me to follow her. I knew that I must remove the crucifix from my neck before I could rise from the chair. But I found it impossible to lift my hands—I was chained to the spot and could not move. The woman's face changed as she watched my fruitless efforts to obey her unspoken command. Angry frustration blazed from her eyes, her mouth twisted into a horrible dribbling leer, and she bared the white fangs of her teeth. Then the figure became blurred and a cloud of red dust hung in the light of the lamp before it faded away. The hungry cry of a wolf, echoing through the ruined castle, awakened me. Nemetz was already on his feet and he put his finger to his lips to enjoin silence. From beyond the door came the sibilant whisper of voices and then the wolf's howl rang out again.

"There is nothing to fear," the Professor assured me. He went on to explain that the vampire frequently assumes the shape of a wolf and, in this guise, is able to satisfy its lust for blood. I suppose the even murmur of his voice must have lulled me off to sleep again. When I awakened next time it was morning and the sun blazed through the dirty windows. The little man was bending over a primus stove and the warm, friendly aroma of coffee pervaded the apartment.

V

We made a good breakfast, for Nemetz had brought a liberal supply of food. I noticed, however, that no meat was provided and this was explained when the Professor remarked that, in dealing with the occult, it was best to avoid flesh-meat. After the meal we packed everything back into the cases in readiness to carry them out to the car.

"The real business of our visit remains to be performed," said my companion. "The task we have set ourselves is to rid the world of this evil creature and we shall require all our courage if we are to succeed. God grant we do not fail."

He opened the door and we were carrying our things into the passage when I stopped with a sudden exclamation. Just over the threshold, written in the dust on the floor, were the words, "You are mine for ever." Nothing I had experienced during my association with the Princess had affected me as did that strange message. I literally trembled with fear and it took all Nemetz's assurances to restore some of my self-control. Even then I would have backed out of the business if I could have done so honourably.

There was no sign of the old man we had seen on the previous evening and, in the cold light of day, the castle looked an utterly abandoned ruin. We peeped into some of the rooms on the ground floor and, apart from a few broken articles of antique furniture, they were quite empty. In what had evidently been the dining hall some of the carved panelling had been roughly ripped from the walls and birds were nesting in the crevices.

Before we packed the bags into the car Nemetz removed certain articles and placed them in his capacious pockets. These included a wooden crucifix, a wicked-looking dagger, a handful of garlic, and the bottle of holy water. Taking the crowbar in his hand he led the way towards the chapel.

The little building probably dated from the early fourteenth century and was graceful in design. The door opened to our touch and a wave of cold, dank air greeted us. The interior was filthy and littered with fallen masonry. A few fragments of coloured glass remained in the windows and there was a stone altar at the east end. The Professor mounted the steps and examined the slab. It was covered with the droppings of birds and, scraping some of the dirt away, he pointed to dark brown patches which stained the centre of the table. He also showed me that the five consecration crosses had been roughly obliterated and the receptacle for relics was empty.

"Here are the marks of unholy sacrifices," he said, "and proofs that this altar has been used for the wicked blasphemy of the Black Mass."

At the back of the altar we found a flight of narrow steps leading down into the depths of the earth. At the bottom was a small door marked with the same coat of arms we had seen in the castle.

"Now comes the real test," said Nemetz. "This is the burial vault of the Bessenyei family and here we shall find the evidence we seek. Let us pray for strength to enable us to finish this awful business."

Beside the desecrated altar we knelt and asked heaven

to bless our efforts and to shield us from evil. Then the Professor led the way down the steps and tried the door of the vault. It was apparently secured, but the rusty lock soon gave way before the crowbar and the door swung inwards. With a wild shriek which froze the blood in our veins, something flapped out of the darkness and soared towards the roof of the chapel. It was only a great white owl but our nerves, keyed almost to breaking point, were badly shaken. Speaking for myself I would, at that moment, gladly have abandoned the task we had set ourselves. But the Professor soon recovered himself and, with a self-conscious laugh, directed the beam of his torch into the vault. A ghastly sight met our eyes. Coffins of all shapes and sizes were ranged in niches around the walls and most of them had been broken open. Here and there bones protruded and the floor was covered with fragments of human bodies, some of them with dried scraps of flesh still adhering. In the centre of the place two great leaden coffins stood side by side.

"These are the ones we want," said the Professor advancing into the vault. "The others are of no importance for we can see that their inmates have suffered the normal course of corruption."

He placed the torch in my hands and motioned me to hold it so that the light fell upon the first of the two coffins. Then, with the crowbar, he prised the lid and found that it was not sealed in any way. He moved it a little so that he could get a grip on the edges. Evidently it was not so weighty as he had anticipated, for he lifted it off with comparative ease. There, before us in the leaden casket, was the body of the man we had taken to be the caretaker of the castle. He appeared to be sleeping and, in repose, the cruel lines of his mouth were set in an evil grin.

"Just as I suspected," muttered Nemetz. "This is Prince

Lóránd who is supposed to have died in the fifteenth century. You see for yourself how he lives in the grave and can arise when occasion demands. Now let us look at the other."

We turned to the second coffin and, without any difficulty, the two of us lifted the lid and placed it on the floor. I was more or less prepared for the sight that met our gaze but, even so, it gave me a nasty shock. The light of the torch showed us the Princess Bessenyei to all intents and purposes resting quietly in the tomb. She could hardly be described as sleeping, for her wicked eyes were wide open and gleamed with mocking scorn. Looking upon that beautiful face it was hard to believe that this woman had roamed the earth for over four centuries and that the source of her immunity from death was the blood of the innocent people who became her victims. Yet I was convinced at last.

We turned back to the first coffin and the Professor drew his dagger. Whispering to me to hold the torch steady he raised his arm and plunged the weapon deep into the heart of the thing in the casket. An unearthly scream of agony came from the twisted lips, the body writhed in grotesque fashion for a few moments and then, before our eyes, it turned to dust. Nemetz, who seemed quite unmoved, put a few bulbs of garlic into the coffin and sprinkled it with holy water. We were bending to lift the lid when I dropped the torch and plunged the vault into darkness. Before I could retrieve it a burst of harsh laughter rang out. We both sprang round and there, framed in the narrow doorway and wrapped in a pale, phosphorescent glow, was the Princess with her green eyes blazing with hellish anger. In a second the Professor had drawn his revolver and emptied it into the figure. He might have spared himself the trouble for the shots had no effect at all.

Lifting her hand in a commanding gesture which seemed to paralyse us into immobility, the Princess addressed us.

"You, Professor Nemetz," she said, "have taken my father from me and, for this, you shall pay the penalty. You have failed to destroy me and nothing can save you from my vengeance when the hour comes, for the undead do not forget." Then turning to me she smiled a slow mysterious smile. "There is no need for me to tell you again that you will be mine in the end. Your lips have touched mine and, although years may pass and seas may divide us, I shall come for you in my own good time."

With these words she vanished from our sight. Power was suddenly restored to our limbs and we rushed up the steps into the chapel. There was no sign of the Princess but, with a hoot of derision and a flapping of wings, the great white owl swooped down and flew back into the vault.

The Professor seemed very badly shaken. "Too late," he groaned. "Too late. I should have realized that she is too skilled in her evil arts to allow herself to be destroyed by the usual methods."

We made our way back to the car and were soon driving through the forest. Nemetz hardly spoke a word. He drove as if trying desperately to escape from a pursuing terror and we were back in Budapest by the late afternoon. I gave him a stiff brandy in my room, but all life seemed to have gone out of him.

"I must again seriously warn you of the danger in which you stand," he said before we parted. "This creature has a passion for you which resembles, to some degree, the passion of violent love. It will never be content until you have become its victim—even if it has to wait many years. I can only urge you to protect yourself by every means in your power. I fear for you and I also fear for myself. The Princess has promised to have her revenge and I am convinced it will not be long before the attack comes. God be with you, my friend. If all is well I will call upon you in the morning."

I never saw Professor Nemetz alive again. That same night he was killed in the most brutal fashion. The authorities decided that some wild animal had gained access to the poor man's apartment, though how it was impossible to determine, for he was literally savaged to death. But I know how and why he died. I saw the glazed terror in his dead eyes and remembered the gaunt grey wolf of Bessenyei.

My turn will come. I feel safe with the little cross around my neck, but she will find some way of overcoming its power. I write down this story so that the truth may be known and perhaps, in God's good time, someone will be brave enough to again attempt the destruction of the undead. I leave this city with fear in my heart, for I know she will follow me to the ends of the earth.

POSTSCRIPT BY DR. REGINALD STAINES,
MEDICAL OFFICER IN CHARGE OF
EASTDOWN MENTAL HOME, DEVON.

The foregoing manuscript was written by Harvey Gorton, a former member of the Diplomatic Service, who was admitted to this institution on 10th November 1939. His was a case of psychosis, the chief feature of which was a fixed delusion that he was being hunted by the woman he called the Princess Bessenyei. Apart from this he was apparently normal and never caused any trouble. I found him a most cultured man and we often chatted together about the international situation. He was very perturbed about the war and seemed particularly anxious that Hungary, for which country he had a great affection, should not be drawn into the conflict. In the ordinary course of events I think we should have effected a complete cure within a few months.

On 2nd December, after a light fall of snow, he was walking in the grounds when he stumbled over the root of a tree and fell some five or six feet down an embankment, injuring his left shoulder. He was evidently in great pain and an X-ray revealed a fracture in a bad position at the upper end of the humerus. It was decided to give an anaesthetic for reduction. Gorton always wore a little crucifix at his neck and I noticed that, when the surgeon lifted it aside to enable him to examine the shoulder more carefully, the man became unduly agitated and protested that the cross must on no account be removed. We injected Pentothal into a vein in the arm and, as Gorton was becoming unconscious, the nurse, by some clumsy movement, broke the chain on which the cross was suspended and it fell to the floor. The patient was only out for about forty seconds and, when he was taken back to his room, the crucifix was apparently forgotten. Later he became very anxious about the loss and worked himself up into such a state that I gave instructions for it to be restored to him. Unfortunately the operating theatre had been swept and, although the cross had been found, it had been locked up in the desk of the Matron. She had gone off duty and it was impossible for us to secure the thing until she returned.

I tried to soothe Gorton, but he made a terrible fuss about the business and demanded that the desk should be broken open. As he seemed likely to become violent I gave him a strong sleeping draught as the best way out of the difficulty.

Later in the evening, having ascertained that the patient was sleeping soundly, I went over to the vicarage for an hour to discuss with the vicar's wife the formation of some First Aid classes. I had hardly settled down when the telephone rang and I was recalled to the Home.

The whole place was in confusion. My deputy, Doctor Snell, reported that, about five minutes after I had left, a woman, speaking with a foreign accent, had called at the Home and asked to see Gorton. She was shown into a waiting room whilst the nurse went to inform Snell of the request. He naturally said it was quite impossible for Gorton to be seen and the nurse, returning to inform the visitor, found the waiting room empty. At that moment she heard a terrified scream and members of the staff, rushing upstairs, discovered the door of Gorton's room wide open. The poor wretch was lying half in and half out of bed and was already dead. When I came to examine the corpse I found that it was almost entirely drained of blood—a most difficult condition to describe or explain. The only wound on the body was a tiny double puncture in the throat.

THE GIRL WITH THE HUNGRY EYES

◆◆◆

FRITZ LEIBER

All right, I'll tell you why the Girl gives me the creeps. Why I can't stand to go downtown and see the mob slavering up at her on the tower, with that pop bottle or pack of cigarettes or whatever it is beside her. Why I hate to look at magazines any more because I know she'll turn up somewhere in a brassiere or a bubble bath. Why I don't like to think of millions of Americans drinking in that poisonous half-smile. It's quite a story—more story than you're expecting.

No, I haven't suddenly developed any long-haired indignation at the evils of advertising and the national glamour-girl complex. That'd be a laugh for a man in my racket, wouldn't it? Though I think you'll agree there's something a little perverted about trying to capitalize on sex that way. But it's okay with me. And I know we've had the Face and the Body and the Look and what not else, so why shouldn't someone come along who sums it all up so completely, that we have to call her the Girl and blazon her on all the billboards from Times Square to Telegraph Hill?

But the Girl isn't like any of the others. She's unnatural. She's morbid. She's unholy.

Oh it's 1948, is it, and the sort of thing I'm hinting at went out with witchcraft? But you see I'm not altogether sure myself what I'm hinting at, beyond a certain point.

There are vampires and vampires, and not all of them suck blood.

And there were the murders, if they were murders.

Besides, let me ask you this. Why, when America is obsessed with the Girl, don't we find out more about her? Why doesn't she rate a *Time* cover with a droll biography inside? Why hasn't there been a feature in *Life* or the *Post*? A profile in *The New Yorker*? Why hasn't *Charm* or *Mademoiselle* done her career saga? Not ready for it? Nuts!

Why haven't the movies snapped her up? Why hasn't she been on *Information, Please*? Why don't we see her kissing candidates at political rallies? Why isn't she chosen queen of some sort of junk or other at a convention?

Why don't we read about her tastes and hobbies, her views of the Russian situation? Why haven't the columnists interviewed her in a kimono on the top floor of the tallest hotel in Manhattan, and told us who her boyfriends are?

Finally—and this is the real killer—why hasn't she ever been drawn or painted?

Oh, no she hasn't. If you knew anything about commercial art you'd know that. Every blessed one of those pictures was worked up from a photograph. Expertly? Of course. They've got the top artists on it. But that's how it's done.

And now I'll tell you the *why* of all that. It's because from the top to the bottom of the whole world of advertising, news, and business, there isn't a solitary soul who knows where the Girl came from, where she lives, what she does, who she is, even what her name is.

You heard me. What's more, not a single solitary soul ever *sees* her—except one poor damned photographer, who's making more money off her than he ever hoped to in his life and who's scared and miserable as hell every minute of the day.

No, I haven't the faintest idea who he is or where he has his studio. But I know there has to be such a man and I'm morally certain he feels just like I *said*.

Yes, I might be able to find her, if I tried. I'm not sure though—by now she probably has other safeguards. Besides, I don't want to.

Oh, I'm off my rocker, am I? That sort of thing can't happen in this Year of our Atom 1948? People can't keep out of sight that way, not even Garbo?

Well I happen to know they can, because last year I was that poor damned photographer I was telling you about. Yes, last year, in 1947, when the Girl made her first poisonous splash right here in this big little city of ours.

Yes, I knew you weren't here last year and you don't know about it. Even the Girl had to start small. But if you hunted through the files of the local newspapers, you'd find some ads, and I might be able to locate you some of the old displays—I think Lovelybelt is still using one of them. I used to have a mountain of photos myself, until I burned them.

Yes, I made my cut off her. Nothing like what that other photographer must be making, but enough so it still bought this whiskey. She was funny about money. I'll tell you about that.

But first picture me in 1947. I had a fourth-floor studio in that rathole the Hauser Building, catty-corner from Ardleigh Park.

I'd been working at the Marsh-Mason studios until I'd got my bellyful of it and decided to start in for myself. The Hauser Building was crummy—I'll never forget how the stairs creaked—but it was cheap and there was a skylight.

Business was lousy. I kept making the rounds of all the advertisers and agencies, and some of them didn't object to me too much personally, but my stuff never clicked. I was pretty near broke. I was behind on my rent. Hell, I didn't even have enough money to have a girl.

It was one of those dark gray afternoons. The building was awfully quiet—even with the storage they can't half rent the Hauser. I'd just finished developing some pix I was doing on speculation for Lovelybelt Girdles and Buford's Pool and Playground—the last a faked-up beach scene. My model had left. A Miss Leon. She was a civics teacher at one of the high schools and modeled for me on the side, just lately on speculation too. After one look at the prints, I decided that Miss Leon probably wasn't just what Lovelybelt was looking for—or my photography either. I was about to call it a day.

And then the street door slammed four storeys down and there were steps on the stairs and she came in.

She was wearing a cheap, shiny black dress. Black pumps. No stockings. And except that she had a gray cloth coat over one of them, those skinny arms of hers were bare. Her arms are pretty skinny, you know, or can you see things like that any more?

And then the thin neck, the slightly gaunt, almost prim face, the tumbling mass of dark hair, and looking out from under it the hungriest eyes in the world.

That's the real reason she's plastered all over the country today, you know—those eyes. Nothing vulgar, but just the same they're looking at you with a hunger that's all sex and something more than sex. That's what everybody's been looking for since the Year One—something a little more than sex.

Well, boys, there I was, along with the Girl, in an office that was getting shadowy, in a nearly empty building. A situation that a million male Americans have undoubtedly pictured to themselves with various lush details. How was I feeling? Scared.

I know sex can be frightening. That cold, heart-thumping when you're alone with a girl and feel you're going to touch her. But if it was sex this time, it was overlaid with something else.

At least I wasn't thinking about sex.

I remember that I took a backward step and that my hand jerked so that the photos I was looking at sailed to the floor.

There was the faintest dizzy feeling like something was being drawn out of me. Just a little bit.

That was all. Then she opened her mouth and everything was back to normal for a while.

"I see you're a photographer, mister," she said. "Could you use a model?"

Her voice wasn't very cultivated.

"I doubt it," I told her, picking up the pix. You see, I wasn't impressed. The commercial possibilities of her eyes hadn't registered on me yet, by a long shot. "What have you done?"

Well, she gave me a vague sort of story and I began to check her knowledge of model agencies and studios and rates and what not and pretty soon I said to her, "Look here, you never modeled for a photographer in your life. You just walked in here cold."

Well, she admitted that was more or less so.

All along through our talk I got the idea she was feeling her way, like someone in a strange place. Not that she was uncertain of herself, or of me, but just of the general situation.

"And you think anyone can model?" I asked her pityingly.

"Sure," she said.

"Look," I said, "a photographer can waste a dozen negatives trying to get one halfway human photo of an average woman. How many do you think he'd have to waste before he got a real catchy, glamorous pix of her?"

"I think I could do it," she said.

Well, I should have kicked her out right then. Maybe I admired the cool way she stuck to her dumb little guns. Maybe I was touched by her underfed look. More likely I was feeling mean on account of the way my pix had been snubbed by everybody and I wanted to take it out on her by showing her up.

"Okay, I'm going to put you on the spot," I told her. "I'm going to try a couple of shots of you. Understand, it's strictly on spec. If somebody should ever want to use a photo of you, which is about one chance in two million, I'll pay you regular rates for your time. Not otherwise."

She gave me a smile. The first. "That's swell by me," she said.

Well, I took three or four shots, close-ups of her face since I didn't fancy her cheap dress, and at least she stood up to my sarcasm. Then I remembered I still had the Lovelybelt stuff and I guess the meanness was still working in me because I handed her a girdle and told her to go behind the screen and get into it and she did, without getting flustered as I'd expected, and since we'd gone that far I figured we might as well shoot the beach scene to round it out, and that was that.

All this time I wasn't feeling anything particular in one way or the other except every once in a while I'd get one of those faint dizzy flashes and wonder if there was something wrong with my stomach or if I could have been a bit careless with my chemicals.

Still, you know, I think the uneasiness was in me all the while.

I tossed her a card and pencil. "Write your name and address and phone," I told her and made for the darkroom.

A little later she walked out. I didn't call any good-byes. I was irked because she hadn't fussed around or seemed anxious about her poses, or even thanked me, except for that one smile.

I finished developing the negatives, made some prints, glanced at them, decided they weren't a great deal worse than Miss Leon. On an impulse I slipped them in with the pix I was going to take on the rounds next morning.

By now I'd worked long enough so I was a bit fagged and nervous, but I didn't dare waste enough money on liquor to help that. I wasn't very hungry. I think I went to a cheap movie.

I didn't think of the Girl at all, except maybe to wonder faintly why in my present womanless state I hadn't made a pass at her. She had seemed to belong to a, well, distinctly more approachable social stratum than Miss Leon. But then of course there were all sorts of arguable reasons for my not doing that.

Next morning I made the rounds. My first step was Munsch's Brewery. They were looking for a "Munsch Girl." Papa Munsch had a sort of affection for me, though he razzed my photography. He had a good natural judgment about that, too. Fifty years ago he might have been one of the shoestring boys who made Hollywood.

Right now he was out in the plant pursuing his favorite occupation. He put down the beaded can, smacked his lips, gabbled something technical to someone about hops, wiped his fat hands on the big apron he was wearing, and grabbed my thin stack of pix.

He was about halfway through, making noises with his tongue and teeth, when he came to her. I kicked myself for even having stuck her in.

"That's her," he said. "The photography's not so hot, but that's the girl."

It was all decided. I wondered now why Papa Munsch sensed what the girl had right away, while I didn't. I think it was because I saw her first in the flesh, if that's the right word.

At the time I just felt faint.

"Who is she?" he asked.

"One of my new models." I tried to make it casual.

"Bring her out tomorrow morning," he told me. "And your stuff. We'll photograph her here. I want to show you.

"Here, don't look so sick," he added. "Have some beer."

Well, I went away telling myself it was just a fluke, so that she'd probably blow it tomorrow with her inexperience, and so on.

Just the same, when I reverently laid my next stack of pix on Mr. Fitch, of Lovelybelt's rose-colored blotter, I had hers on top.

Mr. Fitch went through the motions of being an art critic. He leaned over backward, squinted his eyes, waved his long fingers, and said, "Hmmm. What do you think, Miss Willow? Here, in this light. Of course the photograph doesn't show the bias cut. And perhaps we should use the Lovelybelt Imp instead of the Angel. Still, the girl . . . Come over here, Binns." More finger-waving. "I want a married man's reaction."

He couldn't hide the fact that he was hooked.

Exactly the same thing happened at Buford's Pool and Playground, except that Da Costa didn't need a married man's say-so.

"Hot stuff," he said, sucking his lips. "Oh, boy, you photographers!"

I hot-footed it back to the office and grabbed up the card I'd given to her to put down her name and address.

It was blank.

I don't mind telling you that the next five minutes were about the worst I ever went through, in an ordinary way. When next morning rolled around and I still hadn't got hold of her, I had to start stalling.

"She's sick," I told Papa Munsch over the phone.

"She's at a hospital?" he asked me.

"Nothing that serious," I told him.

"Get her out here then. What's a little headache?"

"Sorry, I can't."

Papa Munsch got suspicious. "You really got this girl?"

"Of course I have."

"Well, I don't know. I'd think it was some New York model, except I recognized your lousy photography."

I laughed.

"Well, look, you get her here tomorrow morning, you hear?"

"I'll try."

"Try nothing. You get her out here."

He didn't know half of what I tried. I went around to all the model and employment agencies. I did some slick detective work at the photographic and art studios. I used up some of my last dimes putting advertisements in all three papers. I looked at high school yearbooks and at employee photos in local house organs. I went to restaurants and drugstores, looking for waitresses, and to dime stores and department stores, looking at clerks. I watched the crowds coming out of movie theaters. I roamed the streets.

Evenings I spent quite a bit of time along Pick-up Row. Somehow that seemed the right place.

The fifth afternoon I knew I was licked. Papa Munsch's deadline—he'd given me several, but this was it—was due to run out at six o'clock. Mr. Fitch had already canceled.

I was at the studio window, looking out at Ardleigh Park.

She walked in.

I'd gone over this moment so often in my mind that I had no trouble putting on my act. Even the faint dizzy feeling didn't throw me off.

"Hello," I said, hardly looking at her.

"Hello," she said.

"Not discouraged yet?"

"No." It didn't sound uneasy or defiant. It was just a statement.

I snapped a look at my watch, and got up and said curtly, "Look here, I'm going to give you a chance. There's a client of mine looking for a girl your general type. If you do a real good job you may break into the modeling business.

"We can see him this afternoon if we hurry," I said. I picked up my stuff. "Come on. And next time, if you expect favors, don't forget to leave your phone number."

"Uh uh," she said, not moving.

"What do you mean?" I said.

"I'm not going to see any client of yours."

"The hell you aren't," I said. "You little nut, I'm giving you a break."

She shook her head slowly. "You're not fooling me, baby, you're not fooling me at all. They *want* me." And she gave me the second smile.

At the time I thought she must have seen my newspaper ad. Now I'm not so sure.

"And now I'll tell you how we're going to work," she went on. "You aren't going to have my name or address or phone number. Nobody is. And we're going to do all the pictures right here. Just you and me."

You can imagine the roar I raised at that. I was everything—angry, sarcastic, patiently explanatory, off my nut, threatening, pleading.

I would have slapped her face off, except it was photographic capital.

In the end all I could do was phone Papa Munsch and tell him her conditions. I knew I didn't have a chance, but I had to take it.

He gave me a really angry bawling out, said "no" several times, and hung up.

It didn't faze her. "We'll start shooting at ten o'clock tomorrow," she said.

It was just like her, using that corny line from the movie magazines.

About midnight Papa Munsch called me up.

"I don't know what insane asylum you're renting this girl from," he said, "but I'll take her. Come around tomorrow morning and I'll try to get it through your head just how I want the pictures. And I'm glad I got you out of bed!"

After that it was a breeze. Even Mr. Fitch reconsidered and after taking two days to tell me it was quite impossible, he accepted the conditions too.

Of course you're all under the spell of the Girl, so you can't understand how much self-sacrifice it represented on Mr. Fitch's part when he agreed to forgo supervising the photography of my model in the Lovelybelt Imp or Vixen or whatever it was we finally used.

Next morning she turned up on time according to her schedule, and we went to work. I'll say one thing for her, she never got tired and she never kicked at the way I fussed over shots. I got along okay except I still had the feeling of something being shoved away gently. Maybe you've felt it just a little, looking at her picture.

When we finished I found out there were still more rules. It was about the middle of the afternoon. I started down with her to get a sandwich and coffee.

"Uh uh," she said, "I'm going down alone. And look, baby, if you ever try to follow me, if you ever so much as stick your head out that window when I go, you can hire yourself another model."

You can imagine how all this crazy stuff strained my temper—and my imagination. I remember opening the window after she was gone—I waited a few minutes first—and standing there getting some fresh air and trying to figure out what could be back of it, whether she was hiding from the police, or was somebody's ruined daughter, or maybe had got the idea it was smart to be temperamental, or more likely Papa Munsch was right and she was partly nuts.

But I had my pix to finish up.

Looking back it's amazing to think how fast her magic began to take hold of the city after that. Remembering what came after I'm frightened of what's happening to the whole country—and maybe the world. Yesterday I read something in *Time* about the Girl's picture turning up on billboards in Egypt.

The rest of my story will help show you why I'm frightened in that big general way. But I have a theory, too, that helps explain, though it's one of those things that's beyond that "certain point." It's about the Girl. I'll give it to you in a few words.

You know how modern advertising gets everybody's

mind set in the same direction, wanting the same things, imagining the same things. And you know the psychologists aren't so skeptical of telepathy as they used to be.

Add up the two ideas. Suppose the identical desires of millions of people focused on one telepathic person. Say a girl. Shaped her in their image.

Imagine her knowing the hiddenmost hungers of millions of men. Imagine her seeing deeper into those hungers than the people that had them, seeing the hatred and the wish for death behind the lust. Imagine her shaping herself in that complete image, keeping herself as aloof as marble. Yet imagine the hunger she might feel in answer to their hunger.

But that's getting a long way from the facts of my story. And some of those facts are darn solid. Like money. We made money.

That was the funny thing I was going to tell you. I was afraid the Girl was going to hold me up. Sh really had me over a barrel, you know.

But she didn't ask for anything but the regular rates. Later on I insisted on pushing more money at her, a whole lot. But she always took it with that same contemptuous look, as if she were going to toss it down the first drain when she got outside.

Maybe she did.

At any rate, I had money. For the first time in months I had money enough to get drunk, buy new clothes, take taxicabs. I could make a play for any girl I wanted to. I only had to pick.

And so of course I had to go and pick—

But first let me tell you about Papa Munsch.

Papa Munsch wasn't the first of the boys to try to meet my model but I think he was the first to really go soft on her. I could watch the change in his eyes as he looked at her pictures. They began to get sentimental, reverent. Mama Munsch had been dead for two years.

He was smart about the way he planned it. He got me to drop some information which told him when she came to work, and then one morning he came pounding up the stairs a few minutes before.

"I've got to see her, Dave," he told me.

I argued with him, I kidded him. I explained he didn't know just how serious she was about her crazy ideas. I pointed out he was cutting both our throats. I even amazed myself by bawling him out.

He didn't take any of it in his usual way. He just kept repeating, "But, Dave, I've got to see her."

The street door slammed.

"That's her," I said, lowering my voice. "You've got to get out."

He wouldn't, so I shoved him in the darkroom. "And keep quiet," I whispered. "I'll tell her I can't work today."

I knew he'd try to look at her and probably come busting in, but there wasn't anything else I could do.

The footsteps came to the fourth floor. But she never showed at the door. I got uneasy.

"Get that bum out of there!" she yelled suddenly from beyond the door. Not very loud, but in her commonest voice.

"I'm going up to the next landing," she said, "and if that fat-bellied bum doesn't march straight down to the street, he'll never get another pix of me except spitting in his lousy beer."

Papa Munsch came out of the darkroom. He was white. He didn't look at me as he went out. He never looked at her pictures in front of me again.

That was Papa Munsch. Now it's me I'm telling about.

I talked about the subject with her, I hinted, eventually I made my pass.

She lifted my hand off her as if it were a damp rag.

"Nix, baby," she said. "This is working time."

"But afterward . . ." I pressed.

"The rules still hold." And I got what I think was the fifth smile.

It's hard to believe, but she never budged an inch from that crazy line. I mustn't make a pass at her in the office, because our work was very important and she loved it and there mustn't be any distractions. And I couldn't see her anywhere else, because if I tried to, I'd never snap another picture of her—and all this with more money coming in all the time and me never so stupid as to think my photography had anything to do with it.

Of course I wouldn't have been human if I hadn't made more passes. But they always got the wet-rag treatment and there weren't any more smiles.

I changed. I went sort of crazy and light-headed—only sometimes I felt my head was going to burst. And I started to talk to her all the time. About myself.

It was like being in a constant delirium that never interfered with business. I didn't pay attention to the dizzy feeling. It seemed natural.

I'd walk around and for a moment the reflector would look like a sheet of white-hot steel, or the shadows would seem like armies of moths, or the camera would be a big black coal car. But the next instant they'd come all right again.

I think sometimes I was scared to death of her. She'd seem the strangest, horriblest person in the world. But other times . . .

And I talked. It didn't matter what I was doing—lighting her, posing her, fussing with props, snapping my pix—

or where she was—on the platform, behind the screen, relaxing with a magazine—I kept up a steady gab.

I told her everything I knew about myself. I told her about my first girl. I told her about my brother Bob's bicycle. I told her about running away on a freight and the licking Pa gave me when I came home. I told her about shipping to South America and the blue sky at night. I told her about Betty. I told her about my mother dying of cancer. I told her about being beaten up in a fight in an alley behind a bar. I told her about Mildred. I told her about the first picture I ever sold. I told her how Chicago looked from a sailboat. I told her about the longest drunk I was ever on. I told her about Marsh-Mason. I told her about Gwen. I told her about how I met Papa Munsch. I told her about hunting her. I told her about how I felt now.

She never paid the slightest attention to what I said. I couldn't even tell if she heard me.

It was when we were getting our first nibble from national advertisers that I decided to follow her when she went home.

Wait, I can place it better than that. Something you'll remember from the out-of-town papers—those maybe-murders I mentioned. I think there were six.

I say "maybe" because the police could never be sure they weren't heart attacks. But there's bound to be suspicion when heart attacks happen to people whose hearts have been okay, and always at night when they're alone and away from home and there's a question of what they were doing.

The six deaths created one of those "mystery poisoner" scares. And afterward there was a feeling that they hadn't really stopped, but were being continued in a less suspicious way.

That's one of the things that scares me now.

But at that time my only feeling was relief that I'd decided to follow her.

I made her work until dark one afternoon. I didn't need any excuses, we were snowed under with orders. I waited until the street door slammed, then I ran down. I was wearing rubber-soled shoes. I'd slipped on a dark coat she'd never seen me in, and a dark hat.

I stood in the doorway until I spotted her. She was walking by Ardleigh Park toward the heart of town. It was one of those warm fall nights. I followed her on the other side of the street. My idea for tonight was just to find out where she lived. That would give me a hold on her.

She stopped in front of a display window of Everly's department store, standing back from the glow. She stood there looking in.

I remembered we'd done a big photograph of her for Everly's, to make a flat model for a lingerie display. That was what she was looking at.

At that time it seemed all right to me that she should adore herself, if that was what she was doing.

When people passed she'd turn away a little or drift back farther into the shadows.

Then a man came by alone. I couldn't see his face very well, but he looked middle-aged. He stopped and stood looking in the window.

She came out of the shadows and stepped up beside him.

How would you boys feel if you were looking at a poster of the Girl and suddenly she was there beside you, her arm linked with yours?

This fellow's reaction showed plain as day. A crazy dream had come to life for him.

They talked for a moment. Then he waved a taxi to the curb. They got in and drove off.

I got drunk that night. It was almost as if she'd known I was following her and had picked that way to hurt me. Maybe she had. Maybe this was the finish.

But the next morning she turned up at the usual time and I was back in the delirium, only now with some new angles added.

That night when I followed her she picked a spot under a street lamp, opposite one of the Munsch Girl billboards.

Now it frightens me to think of her lurking that way.

After about twenty minutes a convertible slowed down going past her, backed up, swung in to the curb.

I was closer this time. I got a good look at the fellow's face. He was a little younger, about my age.

Next morning the same face looked up at me from the front page of the paper. The convertible had been found parked on a side street. He had been in it. As in the other maybe-murders, the cause of death was uncertain.

All kinds of thoughts were spinning in my head that day, but there were only two things I knew for sure. That I'd got the first real offer from a national advertiser, and that I was going to take the Girl's arm and walk down the stairs with her when we quit work.

She didn't seem surprised. "You know what you're doing?" she said.

"I know."

She smiled. "I was wondering when you'd get around to it."

I began to feel good. I was kissing everything good-bye, but I had my arm around hers.

It was another of those warm fall evenings. We cut across into Ardleigh Park. It was dark there, but all around the sky was a sallow pink from the advertising signs.

We walked for a long time in the park. She didn't say

anything and she didn't look at me, but I could see her lips twitching and after a while her hand tightened on my arm.

We stopped. We'd been walking across the grass. She dropped down and pulled me after her. She put her hands on my shoulders. I was looking down at her face. It was the faintest sallow pink from the glow in the sky. The hungry eyes were dark smudges.

I was fumbling with her blouse. She took my hand away, not like she had in the studio. "I don't want that," she said.

First I'll tell you what I did afterward. Then I'll tell you why I did it. Then I'll tell you what she said.

What I did was run away. I don't remember all of that because I was dizzy, and the pink sky was swinging against the dark trees. But after a while I staggered into the lights of the street. The next day I closed up the studio. The telephone was ringing when I locked the door and there were unopened letters on the floor. I never saw the Girl again in the flesh, if that's the right word.

I did it because I didn't want to die. I didn't want the life drawn out of me. There are vampires and vampires, and the ones that suck blood aren't the worst. If it hadn't been for the warning of those dizzy flashes, and Papa Munsch and the face in the morning paper, I'd have gone the way the others did. But I realized what I was up against while there was still time to tear myself away. I realized that wherever she came from, whatever shaped her, she's the quintessence of the horror behind the bright billboard. She's the smile that tricks you into throwing away your money and your life. She's the eyes that lead you on and on, and then show you death. She's the creature you give everything for and never really get. She's the being that takes everything you've got and gives nothing in return.

When you yearn toward her face on the billboards, remember that. She's the lure. She's the bait. She's the Girl.

And this is what she said: "I want you. I want your high spots. I want everything that's made you happy and everything that's hurt you bad. I want your first girl. I want that shiny bicycle. I want that licking. I want that pinhole camera. I want Betty's legs. I want the blue sky filled with stars. I want your mother's death. I want your blood on the cobblestones. I want Mildred's mouth. I want the first picture you sold. I want the lights of Chicago. I want the gin. I want Gwen's hands. I want your wanting me. I want your life. Feed me, baby, feed me."

THE ROOM IN THE TOWER

+++

E. F. BENSON

It is probable that everybody who is at all a constant dreamer has had at least one experience of an event or a sequence of circumstances which have come to his mind in sleep being subsequently realized in the material world. But, in my opinion, so far from this being a strange thing, it would be far odder if this fulfilment did not occasionally happen, since our dreams are, as a rule, concerned with people whom we know and places with which we are familiar, such as might very naturally occur in the awake and daylit world. True, these dreams are often broken into by some absurd and fantastic incident, which puts them out of court in regard to their subsequent fulfilment, but on the mere calculation of chances, it does not appear in the least unlikely that a dream imagined by anyone who dreams constantly should occasionally come true. Not long ago, for instance, I experienced such a fulfilment of a dream which seems to me in no way remarkable and to have no kind of psychical significance. The manner of it was as follows.

A certain friend of mine, living abroad, is amiable enough to write to me about once in a fortnight. Thus, when fourteen days or thereabouts have elapsed since I last heard from him, my mind, probably, either consciously or subconsciously, is expectant of a letter from him. One night last week I dreamed that as I was going upstairs to dress for dinner I heard, as I often heard, the sound of the postman's knock on my front door, and diverted my direction downstairs instead. There, among other correspondence, was a letter from him. Thereafter the fantastic entered, for on opening it I found inside the ace of diamonds, and scribbled across it in his well-known handwriting, "I am sending you this for safe custody, as you know it is running an unreasonable risk to keep aces in Italy." The next evening I was just preparing to go upstairs to dress when I heard the postman's knock, and did precisely as I had done in my dream. There, among other letters, was one from my friend. Only it did not contain the ace of diamonds. Had it done so, I should have attached more weight to the matter, which, as it stands, seems to me a perfectly ordinary coincidence. No doubt I consciously or subconsciously expected a letter from him, and this suggested to me my dream. Similarly, the fact that my friend had not written to me for a fortnight suggested to him that he should do so. But occasionally it is not so easy to find such an explanation, and for the following story I can find no explanation at all. It came out of the dark, and into the dark it has gone again.

All my life I have been a habitual dreamer: the nights are few, that is to say, when I do not find on awaking in the morning that some mental experience has been mine, and sometimes, all night long, apparently, a series of the most dazzling adventures befall me. Almost without exception these adventures are pleasant, though often merely trivial. It is of an exception that I am going to speak.

It was when I was about sixteen that a certain dream first came to me, and this is how it befell. It opened with my being set down at the door of a big red-brick house, where, I understood, I was going to stay. The servant who opened the door told me that tea was being served in the garden, and led me through a low dark-panelled hall, with a large open fireplace, on to a cheerful green lawn set round with flower beds. There were grouped about the tea-table a small party of people, but they were all strangers to me except one, who was a school-fellow called Jack Stone, clearly the son of the house, and he introduced me to his mother and father and a couple of sisters. I was, I remember, somewhat astonished to find myself here, for the boy in question was scarcely known to me, and I rather disliked what I knew of him; moreover, he had left school nearly a year before. The afternoon was very hot, and an intolerable oppression reigned. On the far side of the lawn ran a red-brick wall, with an iron gate in its center, outside which stood a walnut tree. We sat in the shadow of the house opposite a row of long windows, inside which I could see a table with cloth laid, glimmering with glass and silver. This garden front of the house was very long, and at one end of it stood a tower of three stories, which looked to me much older than the rest of the building.

Before long, Mrs. Stone, who, like the rest of the party, had sat in absolute silence, said to me, "Jack will show you your room: I have given you the room in the tower."

Quite inexplicably my heart sank at her words. I felt as if I had known that I should have the room in the tower, and that it contained something dreadful and significant. Jack instantly got up and I understood that I had to follow him. In silence we passed through the hall, and mounted a great oak staircase with many corners, and arrived at a small landing with two doors set in it. He pushed one of these open for me to enter, and without coming in himself, closed it after me. Then I knew that my conjecture had been right: there was something awful in the room, and with the terror of nightmare growing swiftly and enveloping me, I awoke in a spasm of terror.

Now that dream or variations on it occurred to me intermittently for fifteen years. Most often it came in exactly this form, the arrival, the tea laid out on the lawn, the deadly silence succeeded by that one deadly sentence, the mounting with Jack Stone up to the room in the tower where horror dwelt, and it always came to a close in the nightmare of terror at that which was in the room, though I never saw what it was. At other times I experienced variations on this same theme. Occasionally, for instance, we would be sitting at dinner in the dining-room, into the windows of which I had looked on the first night when the dream of this house visited me, but wherever we were, there was the same silence, the same sense of dreadful oppression and foreboding. And the silence I knew would always be broken by Mrs. Stone saying to me, "Jack will show you your room: I have given you the room in the tower." Upon which (this was invariable) I had to follow him up the oak staircase with many corners, and enter the place that I dreaded more and more each time that I visited it in sleep. Or, again, I would find myself playing cards still in silence in a drawing-room lit with immense chandeliers, that gave a blinding illumination. What the game was I have no idea; what I remember, with a sense of miserable anticipation, was that soon Mrs. Stone would get up and say to me, "Jack will show you your room: I have given you the room in the tower." This drawing-room where we played cards was next to the dining-room, and, as I have said, was always brilliantly illuminated, whereas the rest of the house was full of dusk and shadows. And yet, how often, in spite of those bouquets of lights, have I not pored over the cards that were dealt me, scarcely able for some reason to see them. Their designs, too, were strange: there were no red suits, but all were black, and among them there were certain cards which were black all over. I hated and dreaded those.

As this dream continued to recur, I got to know the greater part of the house. There was a smoking-room beyond the drawing-room, at the end of a passage with a green baize door. It was always very dark there, and as often as I went there I passed somebody whom I could not see in the doorway coming out. Curious developments, too, took place in the characters that peopled the dream as might happen to living persons. Mrs. Stone, for instance, who, when I first saw her, had been black-haired, became gray, and instead of rising briskly, as she had done at first when she said, "Jack will show you your room: I have given you the room in the tower," got up very feebly, as if the strength was leaving her limbs. Jack also grew up, and became a rather ill-looking young man, with a brown moustache, while one of the sisters ceased to appear, and I understood she was married.

Then it so happened that I was not visited by this dream for six months or more, and I began to hope, in such inexplicable dread did I hold it, that it had passed away for good. But one night after this interval I again found myself being shown out onto the lawn for tea, and Mrs. Stone was not there, while the others were all dressed in black. At once I guessed the reason, and my heart leaped at the thought that perhaps this time I should not have to sleep in the room in the tower, and though we usually all sat in silence, on this occasion the sense of relief made me talk and laugh as I had never yet done. But even then matters were not altogether comfortable, for no one else spoke, but they all looked secretly at each other.

And soon the foolish stream of my talk ran dry, and gradually an apprehension worse than anything I had previously known gained on me as the light slowly faded.

Suddenly a voice which I knew well broke the stillness, the voice of Mrs. Stone, saying, "Jack will show you your room: I have given you the room in the tower." It seemed to come from near the gate in the red-brick wall that bounded the lawn, and looking up, I saw that the grass outside was sown thick with gravestones. A curious greyish light shone from them, and I could read the lettering on the grave nearest me, and it was, "In evil memory of Julia Stone." And as usual Jack got up, and again I followed him through the hall and up the staircase with many corners. On this occasion it was darker than usual, and when I passed into the room in the tower I could only just see the furniture, the position of which was already familiar to me. Also there was a dreadful odor of decay in the room, and I woke screaming.

The dream, with such variations and developments as I have mentioned, went on at intervals for fifteen years. Sometimes I would dream it two or three nights in succession; once, as I have said, there was an intermission of six months, but taking a reasonable average, I should say that I dreamed it quite as often as once in a month. It had, as is plain, something of nightmare about it, since it always ended in the same appalling terror, which so far from getting less, seemed to me to gather fresh fear every time that I experienced it. There was, too, a strange and dreadful consistency about it. The characters in it, as I have mentioned, got regularly older, death and marriage visited this silent family, and I never in the dream, after Mrs. Stone had died, set eyes on her again. But it was always her voice that told me that the room in the tower was prepared for me, and whether we had tea out on the lawn, or the scene was laid in one of the rooms overlooking it, I could always see her gravestone standing just outside the iron gate. It was the same, too, with the married daughter; usually she was not present, but once or twice she returned again, in company with a man, whom I took to be her husband. He, too, like the rest of them, was always silent. But, owing to the constant repetition of the dream, I had ceased to attach, in my waking hours, any significance to it. I never met Jack Stone again during all those years, nor did I ever see a house that resembled this dark house of my dream. And then something happened.

I had been in London in this year, up till the end of July, and during the first week in August went down to stay with a friend in a house he had taken for the summer months, in the Ashdown Forest district of Sussex. I left London early, for John Clinton was to meet me at Forest Row Station, and we were going to spend the day golfing, and go to his house in the evening. He had his motor with him, and we set off, about five of the afternoon, after a thoroughly delightful day, for the drive, the distance being some ten miles. As it was still so early we did not have tea at the club house, but waited till we should get home. As we drove, the weather, which up till then had been, though hot, deliciously fresh, seemed to me to alter in quality, and become very stagnant and oppressive, and I felt that indefinable sense of ominous apprehension that I am accustomed to before thunder. John, however, did not share my views, attributing my loss of lightness to the fact that I had lost both my matches. Events proved, however, that I was right, though I do not think that the thunderstorm that broke that night was the sole cause of my depression.

Our way lay through deep high-banked lanes, and before we had gone very far I fell asleep, and was only awakened by the stopping of the motor. And with a sudden thrill, partly of fear but chiefly of curiosity, I found myself standing in the doorway of my house of dream. We went, I half wondering whether or not I was dreaming still, through a low oak-panelled hall, and out onto the lawn, where tea was laid in the shadow of the house. It was set in flower beds, a red-brick wall, with a gate in it, bounded one side, and out beyond that was a space of rough grass with a walnut tree. The façade of the house was very long, and at one end stood a three-storied tower, markedly older than the rest.

Here for the moment all resemblance to the repeated dream ceased. There was no silent and somehow terrible family, but a large assembly of exceedingly cheerful persons, all of whom were known to me. And in spite of the horror with which the dream itself had always filled me, I felt nothing of it now that the scene of it was thus reproduced before me. But I felt intensest curiosity as to what was going to happen.

Tea pursued its cheerful course, and before long Mrs. Clinton got up. And at that moment I think I knew what she was going to say. She spoke to me, and what she said was:

"Jack will show you your room: I have given you the room in the tower."

At that, for half a second, the horror of the dream took hold of me again. But it quickly passed, and again I felt nothing more than the most intense curiosity. It was not very long before it was amply satisfied.

John turned to me.

"Right up at the top of the house," he said, "but I think you'll be comfortable. We're absolutely full up. Would you like to go and see it now? By Jove, I believe that you are right, and that we are going to have a thunderstorm. How dark it has become."

I got up and followed him. We passed through the hall, and up the perfectly familiar staircase. Then he opened the door, and I went in. And at that moment sheer unreasoning terror again possessed me. I did not know for certain what I feared: I simply feared. Then like a sudden recollection, when one remembers a name which has long escaped the memory, I knew what I feared. I feared Mrs. Stone, whose grave with the sinister inscription, "In evil memory," I had so often seen in my dream, just beyond the lawn which lay below my window. And then once more the fear passed so completely that I wondered what there was to fear, and I found myself, sober and quiet and sane, in the room in the tower, the name of which I had so often heard in my dream, and the scene of which was so familiar.

I looked round it with a certain sense of proprietorship, and found that nothing had been changed from the dreaming nights in which I knew it so well. Just to the left of the door was the bed, lengthways along the wall, with the head of it in the angle. In a line with it was the fireplace and a small bookcase; opposite the door the outer wall was pierced by two lattice-paned windows, between which stood the dressing-table, while ranged along the fourth wall was the washing-stand and a big cupboard. My luggage had already been unpacked, for the furniture of dressing and undressing lay orderly on the wash-stand and toilet-table, while my dinner clothes were spread out on the coverlet of the bed. And then, with a sudden start of unexplained dismay, I saw that there were two rather conspicuous objects which I had not seen before in my dreams: one a life-sized oil painting of Mrs. Stone, the other a black-and-white sketch of Jack Stone, representing him as he had appeared to me only a week before in the last of the series of these repeated dreams, a rather secret and evil-looking man of about thirty. His picture hung between the windows, looking straight across the room to the other portrait, which hung at the side of the bed. At that I looked next, and as I looked I felt once more the horror of nightmare seize me.

It represented Mrs. Stone as I had seen her last in my dreams: old and withered and white-haired. But in spite of the evident feebleness of body, a dreadful exuberance and vitality shone through the envelope of flesh, an exuberance wholly malign, a vitality that foamed and frothed with unimaginable evil. Evil beamed from the narrow, leering eyes; it laughed in the demon-like mouth. The whole face was instinct with some secret and appalling mirth; the hands, clasped together on the knee, seemed shaking with suppressed and nameless glee. Then I saw also that it was signed in the left-hand bottom corner, and wondering who the artist could be, I looked more closely, and read the inscription, "Julia Stone by Julia Stone."

There came a tap at the door, and John Clinton entered. "Got everything you want?" he asked.

"Rather more than I want," said I, pointing to the picture.

He laughed.

"Hard-featured old lady," he said. "By herself, too, I remember. Anyhow she can't have flattered herself much."

"But don't you see?" said I. "It's scarcely a human face at all. It's the face of some witch, of some devil."

He looked at it more closely.

"Yes; it isn't very pleasant," he said. "Scarcely a bedside manner, eh? Yes; I can imagine getting the nightmare if I went to sleep with that close by my bed. I'll have it taken down if you like."

"I really wish you would," I said. He rang the bell, and with the help of a servant we detached the picture and carried it out onto the landing, and put it with its face to the wall.

"By Jove, the old lady is a weight," said John, mopping his forehead. "I wonder if she had something on her mind."

The extraordinary weight of the picture had struck me too. I was about to reply, when I caught sight of my own hand. There was blood on it, in considerable quantities, covering the whole palm.

"I've cut myself somehow," said I.

John gave a little startled exclamation.

"Why, I have too," he said.

Simultaneously the footman took out his handkerchief and wiped his hand with it. I saw that there was blood also on his handkerchief.

John and I went back into the tower room and washed the blood off; but neither on his hand nor on mine was there the slightest trace of a scratch or cut. It seemed to me that, having ascertained this, we both, by a sort of tacit consent, did not allude to it again. Something in my case had dimly occurred to me that I did not wish to think about. It was but a conjecture, but I fancied that I knew the same thing had occurred to him.

The heat and oppression of the air, for the storm we had expected was still undischarged, increased very much after dinner, and for some time most of the party, among whom were John Clinton and myself, sat outside on the path bounding the lawn, where we had had tea. The night was absolutely dark, and no twinkle of star or moon ray could penetrate the pall of cloud that overset the sky. By degrees our assembly thinned, the women went up to bed, men dispersed to the smoking or billiard room, and by eleven o'clock my host and I were the only two left. All the evening I thought that he had something on his mind, and as soon as we were alone he spoke.

"The man who helped us with the picture had blood on his hand, too, did you notice?" he said.

"I asked him just now if he had cut himself, and he said he supposed he had, but that he could find no mark of it. Now where did that blood come from?"

By dint of telling myself that I was not going to think about it, I had succeeded in not doing so, and I did not want, especially just at bedtime, to be reminded of it.

"I don't know," said I, "and I don't really care so long as the picture of Mrs. Stone is not by my bed."

He got up.

"But it's odd," he said. "Ha! Now you'll see another odd thing."

A dog of his, an Irish terrier by breed, had come out of the house as we talked. The door behind us into the hall was open, and a bright oblong of light shone across the lawn to the iron gate which led on to the rough grass outside, where the walnut tree stood. I saw that the dog had all his hackles up, bristling with rage and fright; his lips were curled back from his teeth, as if he was ready to spring at something, and he was growling to himself. He took not the slightest notice of his master or me, but stiffly and tensely walked across the grass to the iron gate. There he stood for a moment, looking through the bars and still growling. Then of a sudden his courage seemed to desert him: he gave one long howl, and scuttled back to the house with a curious crouching sort of movement.

"He does that half a dozen times a day," said John. "He sees something which he both hates and fears."

I walked to the gate and looked over it. Something was moving on the grass outside, and soon a sound which I could not instantly identify came to my ears. Then I remembered what it was: it was the purring of a cat. I lit a match, and saw the purrer, a big blue Persian, walking round and round in a little circle just outside the gate, stepping high and ecstatically, with tail carried aloft like a banner. Its eyes were bright and shining, and every now and then it put its head down and sniffed at the grass.

I laughed.

"The end of that mystery, I am afraid," I said. "Here's a large cat having Walpurgis night all alone."

"Yes, that's Darius," said John. "He spends half the day and all night there. But that's not the end of the dog mystery, for Toby and he are the best of friends, but the beginning of the cat mystery. What's the cat doing there? And why is Darius pleased, while Toby is terror-stricken?"

At that moment I remembered the rather horrible detail of my dreams when I saw through the gate, just where the cat was now, the white tombstone with the sinister inscription. But before I could answer the rain began, as suddenly and heavily as if a tap had been turned on, and simultaneously the big cat squeezed through the bars of the gate, and came leaping across the lawn to the house for shelter. Then it sat in the doorway, looking out eagerly into the dark. It spat and struck at John with its paw, as he pushed it in, in order to close the door.

Somehow, with the portrait of Julia Stone in the passage outside, the room in the tower had absolutely no alarm for me, and as I went to bed, feeling very sleepy and heavy, I had nothing more than interest for the curious incident about our bleeding hands, and the conduct of the cat and dog. The last thing I looked at before I put out my light was the square empty space by my bed where the portrait had been. Here the paper was of its original full tint of dark red: over the rest of the walls it had faded. Then I blew out my candle and instantly fell asleep.

My awaking was equally instantaneous, and I sat bolt upright in bed under the impression that some bright light had been flashed in my face, though it was now absolutely pitch dark. I knew exactly where I was, in the room which I had dreaded in dreams, but no horror that I ever felt when asleep approached the fear that now invaded and froze my brain. Immediately after a peal of thunder crackled just above the house, but the probability that it was only a flash of lightning which awoke me gave no reassurance to my galloping heart. Something I knew was in the room with me, and instinctively I put out my right hand, which was nearest the wall, to keep it away. And my hand touched the edge of a picture-frame hanging close to me.

I sprang out of bed, upsetting the small table that stood by it, and I heard my watch, candle, and matches clatter onto the floor. But for the moment there was no need of light, for a blinding flash leaped out of the clouds, and showed me that by my bed again hung the picture of Mrs. Stone. And instantly the room went into blackness again. But in that flash I saw another thing also, namely a figure that leaned over the end of my bed, watching me. It was dressed in some close-clinging white garment, spotted and stained with mold, and the face was that of the portrait.

Overhead the thunder cracked and roared, and when it ceased and the deathly stillness succeeded, I heard the rustle of movement coming nearer me, and, more horrible yet, perceived an odor of corruption and decay. And then a hand was laid on the side of my neck, and close beside my ear I heard quick-taken, eager breathing. Yet I knew that this thing, though it could be perceived by touch, by smell, by eye and by ear, was still not of this earth, but something that had passed out of the body and had power to make itself manifest. Then a voice, already familiar to me, spoke.

"I knew you would come to the room in the tower," it said. "I have been long waiting for you. At last you have come. Tonight I shall feast; before long we will feast together."

And the quick breathing came closer to me; I could feel it on my neck.

At that the terror, which I think had paralyzed me for the moment, gave way to the wild instinct of self-preservation. I hit wildly with both arms, kicking out at the same moment, and heard a little animal-squeal, and something soft dropped with a thud beside me. I took a couple of steps forward, nearly tripping up over whatever it was that lay there, and by the merest good-luck found the handle of the door. In another second I ran out on the landing, and had banged the door behind me. Almost at the same moment I heard a door open somewhere below, and John Clinton, candle in hand, came running upstairs.

"What is it?" he said. "I sleep just below you, and heard a noise as if—Good heavens, there's blood on your shoulder."

I stood there, so he told me afterwards, swaying from side to side, white as a sheet, with the mark on my shoulder as if a hand covered with blood had been laid there.

"It's in there," I said, pointing. "She, you know. The portrait is in there, too, hanging up on the place we took it from."

At that he laughed.

"My dear fellow, this is mere nightmare," he said.

He pushed by me, and opened the door, I standing there simply inert with terror, unable to stop him, unable to move.

"Phew! What an awful smell," he said.

Then there was silence; he had passed out of my sight behind the open door. Next moment he came out again, as white as myself, and instantly shut it.

"Yes, the portrait's there," he said, "and on the floor is a thing—a thing spotted with earth, like what they bury people in. Come away, quick, come away."

How I got downstairs I hardly know. An awful shuddering and nausea of the spirit rather than of the flesh had seized me, and more than once he had to place my feet upon the steps, while every now and then he cast glances of terror and apprehension up the stairs. But in time we came to his dressing-room on the floor below, and there I told him what I have here described.

The sequel can be made short; indeed, some of my readers have perhaps already guessed what it was, if they remember that inexplicable affair of the churchyard at West Fawley, some eight years ago, where an attempt was made three times to bury the body of a certain woman who had committed suicide. On each occasion the coffin was found in the course of a few days again protruding from the ground. After the third attempt, in order that the thing should not be talked about, the body was buried elsewhere in unconsecrated ground. Where it was buried was just outside the iron gate of the garden belonging to the house where this woman had lived. She had committed suicide in a room at the top of the tower in that house. Her name was Julia Stone.

Subsequently the body was again secretly dug up, and the coffin was found to be full of blood.

CARMILLA

✦✦✦

SHERIDAN LE FANU

Upon a paper attached to the narrative which follows, Doctor Hesselius has written a rather elaborate note, which he accompanies with a reference to his Essay on the strange subject which the Manuscript illuminates.

This mysterious subject he treats, in that Essay, with his usual learning and acumen, and with remarkable directness and condensation. It will form but one volume of the series of that extraordinary man's collected papers.

As I publish the case, in this volume, simply to interest the "laity," I shall in no way forestall the intelligent lady who relates it; and, after due consideration, I have determined, therefore, to abstain from presenting any *précis* of the learned Doctor's reasoning, or extract from his statement on a subject which he describes as "involving, not improbably, some of the profoundest arcana of our dual existence, and its intermediates."

I was anxious, on discovering this paper, to re-open the correspondence commenced by Doctor Hesselius, so many years before, with a person so clever and careful as his informant seems to have been. Much to my regret, however, I found that she had died in the interval.

She, probably, could have added little to the Narrative which she communicates in the following pages, with, so far as I can pronounce, such a conscientious particularity.

I. AN EARLY FRIGHT

Although we are by no means magnificent people, we inhabit a schloss, a castle in Styria. A small income, in that part of the world, goes a great way. Eight or nine hundred a year does wonders. Scantily enough ours would have answered among wealthy people at home. My father is English, and I bear an English name, although I never saw England. But here, in this lonely and primitive place, where everything is so marvelously cheap, I really don't see how ever so much more money would at all materially add to our comforts, or even luxuries.

My father was in the Austrian service, and retired upon a pension and his patrimony, and purchased this feudal residence, and the small estate on which it stands, a bargain.

Nothing can be more picturesque or solitary. It stands on a slight eminence in a forest. The road, very old and narrow, passes in front of its drawbridge, never raised in my time, and its moat, stocked with perch, and sailed over by many swans, and floating on its surface white fleets of water-lilies.

Over all this the schloss shows its many-windowed front, its towers, and its Gothic chapel.

The forest opens in an irregular and very picturesque glade before its gate, and at the right a steep Gothic bridge carries the road over a stream that winds in deep shadow through the wood.

I have said that this is a very lonely place. Judge whether I say truth. Looking from the hall door towards the road, the forest in which our castle stands extends fifteen miles to the right, and twelve to the left. The nearest inhabited village is about seven of your English miles to the left. The nearest inhabited schloss of any historic associations, is that of old General Spielsdorf, nearly twenty miles away to the right.

I have said "the nearest *inhabited* village," because there is, only three miles westward, that is to say in the direction of General Spielsdorf's schloss, a ruined village, with its quaint little church, now roofless, in the aisle of which are the moldering tombs of the proud family of Karnstein, now extinct, who once owned the equally-desolate château which, in the thick of the forest, overlooks the silent ruins of the town.

Respecting the cause of the desertion of this striking and melancholy spot, there is a legend which I shall relate to you another time.

I must tell you now, how very small is the party who constitute the inhabitants of our castle. I don't include servants or those dependents who occupy rooms in the buildings attached to the schloss. Listen, and wonder! My father, who is the kindest man on earth, but growing old; and I, at the date of my story, only nineteen. Eight years have passed since then. I and my father constituted the family at the schloss. My mother, a Styrian lady, died in my infancy, but I had a good-natured governess, who had been with me from, I might almost say, my infancy. I could not remember the time when her fat, benignant face was not a familiar picture in my memory. This was Madame Perrodon, a native of Berne, whose care and good nature in part supplied to me the loss of my mother, whom I do not even remember, so early did I lose her. She made a third at our little dinner party. There was a fourth, Mademoiselle De Lafontaine, a lady such as you term, I believe, a "finishing governess." She spoke French and German, Madame Perrodon French and broken English, to which my father and I added English, which, partly from patriotic motives, we spoke every day. The consequence was a Babel, at which strangers used to laugh, and which I shall make no attempt to reproduce in this narrative. And there were two or three young lady friends besides, pretty nearly of my own age, who were occasional visitors, for longer or shorter terms; and these visits I sometimes returned.

These were our regular social resources; but of course there were chance visits from "neighbors" of only five or six leagues' distance. My life was, notwithstanding, rather a solitary one, I can assure you.

My elders had just so much control over me as you might conjecture such sage persons would have in the case of a rather spoiled girl, whose only parent allowed her pretty nearly her own way in everything.

The first occurrence in my existence, which produced a terrible impression upon my mind, which, in fact, never has been effaced, was one of the very earliest incidents of my life which I can recollect. Some people will think it so trifling that it should not be recorded here. You will see, however, by-and-by, why I mention it. The nursery, as it was called, though I had it all to myself, was a large room in the upper story of the castle, with a steep oak roof. I can't have been more than six years old, when one night I awoke, and looking round the room from my bed, failed to see the nursery-maid. Neither was my nurse there; and I thought myself alone. I was not frightened, for I was one of those happy children who are studiously kept in ignorance of ghost stories, of fairy tales, and of all such lore as makes us cover up our heads when the door creaks suddenly, or the flicker of an expiring candle makes the shadow of a bed-post dance upon the wall, nearer to our faces. I was vexed and insulted at finding myself, as I conceived, neglected, and I began to whimper, preparatory to a hearty bout of roaring; when to my surprise, I saw a solemn, but very pretty face looking at me from the side of the bed. It was that of a young lady who was kneeling, with her hands under the coverlet. I looked at her with a kind of pleased wonder, and ceased whimpering. She caressed me with her hands, and lay down beside me on the bed, and drew me towards her, smiling; I felt immediately delightfully soothed, and fell asleep again. I was wakened by a sensation as if two needles ran into my breast very deep at the same moment, and I cried loudly. The lady started back, with her eyes fixed on me, and then slipped down upon the floor, and, as I thought, hid herself under the bed.

I was now for the first time frightened, and I yelled with all my might and main. Nurse, nursery-maid, housekeeper, all came running in, and hearing my story, they made light of it, soothing me all they could meanwhile. But, child as I was, I could perceive that their faces were pale with an unwonted look of anxiety, and I saw them look under the bed, and about the room, and peep under tables and pluck open cupboards; and the housekeeper whispered to the nurse: "Lay your hand along that hollow in the bed; some one *did* lie there, so sure as you did not; the place is still warm."

I remember the nursery-maid petting me, and all three examining my chest, where I told them I felt the puncture, and pronouncing that there was no sign visible that any such thing had happened to me.

The housekeeper and the two other servants who were in charge of the nursery, remained sitting up all night; and from that time a servant always sat up in the nursery until I was about fourteen.

I was very nervous for a long time after this. A doctor was called in, he was pallid and elderly. How well I remember his long saturnine face, slightly pitted with smallpox, and his chestnut wig. For a good while, every second day, he came and gave me medicine, which of course I hated.

The morning after I saw this apparition I was in a state of terror, and could not bear to be left alone, daylight though it was, for a moment.

I remember my father coming up and standing at the bedside, and talking cheerfully, and asking the nurse a number of questions, and laughing very heartily at one of the answers; and patting me on the shoulder, and kissing me, and telling me not to be frightened, that it was nothing but a dream and could not hurt me.

But I was not comforted, for I knew the visit of the strange woman was *not* a dream; and I was *awfully* frightened.

I was a little consoled by the nursery-maid's assuring me that it was she who had come and looked at me, and lain down beside me in the bed, and that I must have been half-dreaming not to have known her face. But this, though supported by the nurse, did not quite satisfy me.

I remember, in the course of that day, a venerable old man, in a black cassock, coming into the room with the nurse and housekeeper, and talking a little to them, and very kindly to me; his face was very sweet and gentle, and he told me they were going to pray, and joined my hands together, and desired me to say, softly, while they were praying, "Lord, hear all good prayers for us, for Jesus' sake." I think these were the very words, for I often repeated them to myself, and my nurse used for years to make me say them in my prayers.

I remember so well the thoughtful sweet face of that white-haired old man, in his black cassock, as he stood in that rude, lofty, brown room, with the clumsy furniture of a fashion three hundred years old, about him, and the scanty light entering its shadowy atmosphere through the small lattice. He kneeled, and the three women with him, and he prayed aloud with an earnest quavering voice for, what appeared to me, a long time. I forget all my life preceding that event, and for some time after it is all obscure also; but the scenes I have just described stand out vivid as the isolated pictures of the phantasmagoria surrounded by darkness.

II. A GUEST

I am now going to tell you something so strange that it will require all your faith in my veracity to believe my story. It is not only true, nevertheless, but truth of which I have been an eyewitness.

It was a sweet summer evening, and my father asked me, as he sometimes did, to take a little ramble with him along that beautiful forest vista which I have mentioned as lying in front of the schloss.

"General Spielsdorf cannot come to us so soon as I had hoped," said my father, as we pursued our walk.

He was to have paid us a visit of some weeks, and we had expected his arrival next day. He was to have brought with him a young lady, his niece and ward, Mademoiselle Rheinfeldt, whom I had never seen, but whom I had heard described as a very charming girl, and in whose society I had promised myself many happy days. I was more disappointed than a young lady living in a town, or a bustling neighborhood can possibly imagine. This visit, and the new acquaintance it promised, had furnished my day dream for many weeks.

"And how soon does he come?" I asked.

"Not till autumn. Not for two months, I dare say," he answered.

"And I am very glad now, dear, that you never knew Mademoiselle Rheinfeldt."

"And why?" I asked, both mortified and curious.

"Because the poor young lady is dead," he replied. "I quite forgot I had not told you, but you were not in the room when I received the General's letter this evening."

I was very much shocked. General Spielsdorf had mentioned in his first letter, six or seven weeks before, that she was not so well as he would wish her, but there was nothing to suggest the remotest suspicion of danger.

"Here is the General's letter," he said, handing it to me. "I am afraid he is in great affliction; the letter appears to me to have been written very nearly in distraction."

We sat down on a rude bench, under a group of magnificent lime trees. The sun was setting with all its melancholy splendor behind the sylvan horizon, and the stream that flows beside our home, and passes under the steep old bridge I have mentioned, wound through many a group of noble trees, almost at our feet, reflecting in its current the fading crimson of the sky. General Spielsdorf's letter was so extraordinary, so vehement, and in some places so self-contradictory, that I read it twice over—the second time aloud to my father—and was still unable to account for it, except by supposing that grief had unsettled his mind.

It said, "I have lost my darling daughter, for as such I loved her. During the last days of dear Bertha's illness I was not able to write to you. Before then I had no idea of her danger. I have lost her, and now learn *all*, too late. She died in the peace of innocence, and in the glorious hope of a blessed futurity. The fiend who betrayed our infatuated hospitality has done it all. I thought I was receiving into my house innocence, gaiety, a charming companion for my lost Bertha. Heavens! What a fool have I been! I thank God my child died without a suspicion of the cause of her sufferings. She is gone without so much as conjecturing the nature of her illness, and the accursed passion of the agent of all this misery. I devote my remaining days to tracking and extinguishing a monster. I am told I may hope to accomplish my righteous and merciful purpose. At present there is scarcely a gleam of light to guide me. I curse my conceited incredulity, my despicable affectation of superiority, my blindness, my obstinacy—all—too late. I cannot write or talk collectedly now. I am distracted. So soon as I shall have a little recovered, I mean to devote myself for a time to enquiry, which may possibly lead me as far as Vienna. Some time in the autumn, two months hence, or earlier if I live, I will see you—that is, if you permit me; I will then tell you all what I scarce dare put upon paper now. Farewell. Pray for me, dear friend."

In these terms ended this strange letter. Though I had never seen Bertha Rheinfeldt, my eyes filled with tears at the sudden intelligence; I was startled, as well as profoundly disappointed.

The sun had now set, and it was twilight by the time I had returned the General's letter to my father.

It was a soft clear evening, and we loitered, speculating upon the possible meanings of the violent and incoherent sentences which I had just been reading. We had nearly a mile to walk before reaching the road that passes the schloss in front, and by that time the moon was shining brilliantly. At the drawbridge we met Madame Perrodon and Mademoiselle De Lafontaine, who had come out, without their bonnets, to enjoy the exquisite moonlight.

We heard their voices gabbling in animated dialogue as we approached. We joined them at the drawbridge, and turned about to admire with them the beautiful scene.

The glade through which we had just walked lay before us. At our left the narrow road wound away under clumps of lordly trees, and was lost to sight amid the thickening forest. At the right the same road crosses the steep and picturesque bridge, near which stands a ruined tower, which once guarded that pass; and beyond the bridge an abrupt eminence rises, covered with trees, and showing in the shadow some grey ivy-clustered rocks.

Over the sward and low grounds, a thin film of mist was stealing like smoke, marking the distances with a transparent veil; and here and there we could see the river faintly flashing in the moonlight.

No softer, sweeter scene could be imagined. The news I had just heard made it melancholy; but nothing could disturb its character of profound serenity, and the enchanted glory and vagueness of the prospect.

My father, who enjoyed the picturesque, and I, stood looking in silence over the expanse beneath us. The two good governesses, standing a little way behind us, discoursed upon the scene, and were eloquent upon the moon.

Madame Perrodon was fat, middle-aged, and romantic, and talked and sighed poetically. Mademoiselle De Lafontaine—in right of her father, who was a German, assumed to be psychological, metaphysical, and something of a mystic—now declared that when the moon shone with a light so intense it was well known that it indicated a special spiritual activity. The effect of the full moon in such a state of brilliancy was manifold. It acted on dreams, it acted on lunacy, it acted on nervous people; it had marvelous physical influences connected with life.

Mademoiselle related that her cousin, who was mate of a merchant ship, having taken a nap on deck on such a night, lying on his back, with his face full in the light of the moon, had awakened, after a dream of an old woman clawing him by the cheek, with his features horribly drawn to one side; and his countenance had never quite recovered its equilibrium.

"The moon, this night," she said, "is full of odylic* and magnetic influence—and see, when you look behind you at the front of the schloss, how all its windows flash and twinkle with that silvery splendor, as if unseen hands had lighted up the rooms to receive fairy guests."

There are indolent states of the spirits in which, indisposed to talk ourselves, the talk of others is pleasant to our listless ears; and I gazed on, pleased with the tinkle of the ladies' conversation.

"I have got into one of my moping moods tonight," said my father, after a silence, and quoting Shakespeare, whom, by way of keeping up our English, he used to read aloud, he said:

> " '*In truth I know not why I am so sad;*
> *It wearies me; you say it wearies you;*
> *But how I got it—came by it.*'

"I forget the rest. But I feel as if some great misfortune were hanging over us. I suppose the poor General's afflicted letter has had something to do with it."

At this moment the unexpected sound of carriage wheels and many hoofs upon the road, arrested our attention.

*Od was a term given to a mysterious vital force in nature. See *The Odic Force* by Karl von Reichenbach, University Books Inc., 1968.

They seemed to be approaching from the high ground overlooking the bridge, and very soon the equipage emerged from that point. Two horsemen first crossed the bridge, then came a carriage drawn by four horses, and two men rode behind.

It seemed to be the travelling carriage of a person of rank; and we were all immediately absorbed in watching that very unusual spectacle. It became, in a few moments, greatly more interesting, for just as the carriage had passed the summit of the steep bridge, one of the leaders, taking fright, communicated his panic to the rest, and, after a plunge or two, the whole team broke into a wild gallop together, and dashing between the horsemen who rode in front, came thundering along the road towards us with the speed of a hurricane.

The excitement of the scene was made more painful by the clear, long-drawn screams of a female voice from the carriage window.

We all advanced in curiosity and horror; my father in silence, the rest with various ejaculations of terror.

Our suspense did not last long. Just before you reach the castle drawbridge, on the route they were coming, there stands by the roadside a magnificent lime tree, on the other stands an ancient stone cross, at the sight of which the horses, now going at a pace that was perfectly frightful, swerved so as to bring the wheel over the projecting roots of the tree.

I knew what was coming. I covered my eyes, unable to see it out, and turned my head away; at the same moment I heard a cry from my lady-friends, who had gone on a little.

Curiosity opened my eyes, and I saw a scene of utter confusion. Two of the horses were on the ground, the carriage lay upon its side, with two wheels in the air; the men were busy removing the traces, and a lady, with a commanding air and figure had got out, and stood with clasped hands, raising the handkerchief that was in them every now and then to her eyes. Through the carriage door was now lifted a young lady, who appeared to be lifeless. My dear old father was already beside the elder lady, with his hat in his hand, evidently tendering his aid and the resources of his schloss. The lady did not appear to hear him, or to have eyes for anything but the slender girl who was being placed against the slope of the bank.

I approached; the young lady was apparently stunned, but she was certainly not dead. My father, who prided himself on being something of a physician, had just had his fingers to her wrist and assured the lady, who declared herself her mother, that her pulse, though faint and irregular, was undoubtedly still distinguishable. The lady clasped her hands and looked upward, as if in a momentary transport of gratitude; but immediately she broke out again in that theatrical way which is, I believe, natural to some people.

She was what is called a fine-looking woman for her time of life, and must have been handsome; she was tall, but not thin, and dressed in black velvet, and looked rather pale, but with a proud and commanding countenance, though now agitated strangely.

"Was ever being so born to calamity?" I heard her say, with clasped hands, as I came up. "Here am I, on a journey of life and death, in prosecuting which to lose an hour is possibly to lose all. My child will not have recovered sufficiently to resume her route for who can say how long. I must leave her; I cannot, dare not, delay. How far on, sir, can you tell, is the nearest village? I must leave her there; and shall not see my darling, or even hear of her till my return, three months hence."

I plucked my father by the coat, and whispered earnestly in his ear, "Oh! Papa, pray ask her to let her stay with us—it would be so delightful. Do, pray."

"If Madame will entrust her child to the care of my daughter and of her good governess, Madame Perrodon, and permit her to remain as our guest, under my charge, until her return, it will confer a distinction and an obligation upon us, and we shall treat her with all the care and devotion which so sacred a trust deserves."

"I cannot do that, sir, it would be to task your kindness and chivalry too cruelly," said the lady, distractedly.

"It would, on the contrary, be to confer on us a very great kindness at the moment when we most need it. My daughter has just been disappointed by a cruel misfortune, in a visit from which she had long anticipated a great deal of happiness. If you confide this young lady to our care it will be her best consolation. The nearest village on your route is distant, and affords no such inn as you could think of placing your daughter at; you cannot allow her to continue her journey for any considerable distance without danger. If, as you say, you cannot suspend your journey, you must part with her tonight, and nowhere could you do so with more honest assurances of care and tenderness than here."

There was something in this lady's air and appearance so distinguished, and even imposing, and in her manner so engaging, as to impress one, quite apart from the dignity of her equipage, with a conviction that she was a person of consequence.

By this time the carriage was replaced in its upright position, and the horses, quite tractable, in the traces again.

The lady threw on her daughter a glance which I fancied was not quite so affectionate as one might have anticipated from the beginning of the scene; then she beckoned slightly to my father and withdrew two or three steps with him out of hearing; and talked to him with a fixed and stern countenance, not at all like that with which she had hitherto spoken.

I was filled with wonder that my father did not seem to perceive the change, and also unspeakably curious to learn what it could be that she was speaking, almost in his ear, with so much earnestness and rapidity.

Two or three minutes at most, I think, she remained thus employed, then she turned, and a few steps brought her to where her daughter lay, supported by Madame Perrodon. She kneeled beside her for a moment and whispered, as Madame supposed, a little benediction in her ear; then hastily kissing her, she stepped into her carriage, the door was closed, the footmen in stately liveries jumped up behind, the outriders spurred on, the postilions cracked their whips, the horses plunged and broke suddenly into a furious canter that threatened soon again to become a gallop, and the carriage whirled away, followed at the same rapid pace by the two horsemen in the rear.

III. WE COMPARE NOTES

We followed the *cortège* with our eyes until it was swiftly lost to sight in the misty wood; and the very sound of the hoofs and wheels died away in the silent night air.

Nothing remained to assure us that the adventure had not been an illusion for a moment but the young lady, who just at that moment opened her eyes. I could not see, for her face was turned from me, but she raised her head, evidently looking about her, and I heard a very sweet voice ask complainingly, "Where is mamma?"

Our good Madame Perrodon answered tenderly, and added some comfortable assurances.

I then heard her ask:

"Where am I? What is this place?" and after that she said, "I don't see the carriage; and Matska, where is she?"

Madame answered all her questions insofar as she understood them; and gradually the young lady remembered how the misadventure came about, and was glad to hear that no one in, or in attendance on, the carriage was hurt; and on learning that her mamma had left her here, till her return in about three months, she wept.

I was going to add my consolations to those of Madame Perrodon when Mademoiselle De Lafontaine placed her hand upon my arm, saying:

"Don't approach, one at a time is as much as she can at present converse with; a very little excitement would possibly overpower her now."

As soon as she is comfortably in bed, I thought, I will run up to her room and see her.

My father in the meantime had sent a servant on horseback for the physician, who lived about two leagues away; and a bedroom was being prepared for the young lady's reception.

The stranger now rose, and leaning on Madame's arm, walked slowly over the drawbridge and into the castle gate.

In the hall the servants waited to receive her, and she was conducted forthwith to her room.

The room we usually sat in as our drawing-room is long, having four windows, that looked over the moat and drawbridge, upon the forest scene I have just described.

It is furnished in old carved oak, with large carved cabinets, and the chairs are cushioned with crimson Utrecht velvet. The walls are covered with tapestry, and surrounded with great gold frames, the figures being as large as life, in ancient and very curious costume, and the subjects represented are hunting, hawking, and generally festive. It is not too stately to be extremely comfortable; and here we had our tea, for with his usual patriotic leanings he insisted that the national beverage should make its appearance regularly with our coffee and chocolate.

We sat here this night, and with candles lighted, were talking over the adventure of the evening.

Madame Perrodon and Mademoiselle De Lafontaine were both of our party. The younger stranger had hardly lain down in her bed when she sank into a deep sleep; and those ladies had left her in the care of a servant.

"How do you like our guest?" I asked, as soon as Madame entered. "Tell me all about her."

"I like her extremely," answered Madame, "she is, I almost think, the prettiest creature I ever saw; about your age, and so gentle and nice."

"She is absolutely beautiful," threw in Mademoiselle, who had peeped for a moment into the stranger's room.

"And such a sweet voice!" added Madame Perrodon.

"Did you remark a woman in the carriage, after it was set up again, who did not get out," inquired Mademoiselle, "but only looked from the window?"

No, we had not seen her.

Then she described a hideous black woman, with a sort of colored turban on her head, who was gazing all the time from the carriage window, nodding and grinning derisively towards the ladies, with gleaming eyes and large white eyeballs, and her teeth set as if in fury.

"Did you remark what an ill-looking pack of men the servants were?" asked Madame.

"Yes," said my father, who had just come in, "ugly, hangdog looking fellows, as ever I beheld in my life. I hope they mayn't rob the poor lady in the forest. They are clever rogues, however; they got everything to rights in a minute."

"I dare say they are worn out with too long travelling," said Madame. "Besides looking wicked, their faces were so strangely lean, and dark, and sullen. I am very curious, I own; but I dare say the young lady will tell us all about it tomorrow, if she is sufficiently recovered."

"I don't think she will," said my father, with a mysterious smile, and a little nod of his head, as if he knew more about it than he cared to tell us.

This made me all the more inquisitive as to what had passed between him and the lady in the black velvet, in the brief but earnest interview that had immediately preceded her departure.

We were scarcely alone, when I entreated him to tell me. He did not need much pressing.

"There is no particular reason why I should not tell you. She expressed a reluctance to trouble us with the care of her daughter, saying she was in delicate health, and nervous, but not subject to any kind of seizure—she volunteered that—nor to any illusion; being, in fact, perfectly sane."

"How very odd to say all that!" I interpolated. "It was so unnecessary."

"At all events it *was* said," he laughed, "and as you wish to know all that passed, which was indeed very little, I tell you. She then said, 'I am making a long journey of *vital* importance'—she emphasized the word—'rapid and secret; I shall return for my child in three months; in the meantime, she will be silent as to who we are, whence we come, and whither we are travelling.' That is all she said. She spoke very pure French. When she said the word 'secret,' she paused for a few seconds, looking sternly, her eyes fixed on mine. I fancy she makes a great point of that.

You saw how quickly she was gone. I hope I have not done a very foolish thing in taking charge of the young lady."

For my part, I was delighted. I was longing to see and talk to her; and only waiting till the doctor should give me leave. You who live in towns can have no idea how great an event the introduction of a new friend is, in such a solitude as surrounded us.

The doctor did not arrive till nearly one o'clock; but I could no more have gone to my bed and slept, than I could have overtaken, on foot, the carriage in which the princess in black velvet had driven away.

When the physician came down to the drawing-room, it was to report very favorably upon his patient. She was now sitting up, her pulse quite regular, apparently perfectly well. She had sustained no injury, and the little shock to her nerves had passed away quite harmlessly. There could be no harm certainly in my seeing her, if we both wished it; and, with this permission, I sent forthwith, to know whether she would allow me to visit her for a few minutes in her room.

The servant returned immediately to say that she desired nothing more.

You may be sure I was not long in availing myself of this permission.

Our visitor lay in one of the handsomest rooms in the schloss. It was, perhaps, a little stately. There was a somber piece of tapestry opposite the foot of the bed, representing Cleopatra with the asp to her bosom; and other solemn classic scenes were displayed, a little faded, upon the other walls. But there was gold carving, and rich and varied color enough in the other decorations of the room, to more than redeem the gloom of the old tapestry.

There were candles at the bedside. She was sitting up; her slender pretty figure enveloped in the soft silk dressing-gown, embroidered with flowers, and lined with thick quilted silk, which her mother had thrown over her feet as she lay upon the ground.

What was it that, as I reached the bedside and had just begun my little greeting, struck me dumb in a moment, and made me recoil a step or two from before her? I will tell you.

I saw the very face which had visited me in my childhood at night, which remained so fixed in my memory, and on which I had for so many years so often ruminated with horror, when no one suspected of what I was thinking.

It was pretty, even beautiful; and when I first beheld it, wore the same melancholy expression.

But this almost instantly lighted into a strange fixed smile of recognition.

There was a silence of fully a minute, and then at length *she* spoke; *I* could not.

"How wonderful!" she exclaimed. "Twelve years ago, I saw your face in a dream, and it has haunted me ever since."

"Wonderful indeed!" I repeated, overcoming with an effort the horror that had for a time suspended my utterances. "Twelve years ago, in vision or reality, *I* certainly saw you. I could not forget your face. It has remained before my eyes ever since."

Her smile had softened. Whatever I had fancied strange in it, was gone, and it and her dimpling cheeks were now delightfully pretty and intelligent.

I felt reassured, and continued more in the vein which hospitality indicated, to bid her welcome, and to tell her how much pleasure her accidental arrival had given us all, and especially what a happiness it was to me.

I took her hand as I spoke. I was a little shy, as lonely

people are, but the situation made me eloquent, and even bold. She pressed my hand, she laid hers upon it, and her eyes glowed, as, looking hastily into mine, she smiled again, and blushed.

She answered my welcome very prettily. I sat down beside her, still wondering; and she said:

"I must tell you my vision about you; it is so very strange that you and I should have had, each of the other so vivid a dream, that each should have seen, I you and you me, looking as we do now, when of course we both were mere children. I was a child about six years old, and I awoke from a confused and troubled dream, and found myself in a room, unlike my nursery, wainscoted clumsily in some dark wood, and with cupboards and bedsteads, and chairs, and benches placed about it. The beds were, I thought, all empty, and the room itself without any one but myself in it; and I, after looking about me for some time, and admiring especially an iron candlestick, with two branches, which I should certainly know again, crept under one of the beds to reach the window; but as I got from under the bed, I heard someone crying; and looking up, while I was still upon my knees, I saw *you*—most assuredly you—as I see you now; a beautiful young lady, with golden hair and large blue eyes, and lips—your lips—you, as you are here. Your looks won me; I climbed on the bed and put my arms about you, and I think we both fell asleep. I was aroused by a scream; you were sitting up screaming. I was frightened, and slipped down upon the ground, and, it seemed to me, lost consciousness for a moment; and when I came to myself, I was again in my nursery at home. Your face I have never forgotten since. I could not be misled by mere resemblance. You *are* the lady whom I then saw."

It was now my turn to relate my corresponding vision,

which I did, to the undisguised wonder of my new acquaintance.

"I don't know which should be most afraid of the other," she said, again smiling. "If you were less pretty I think I should be very much afraid of you, but being as you are, and you and I both so young, I feel only that I have made your acquaintance twelve years ago, and have already a right to your intimacy; at all events, it does seem as if we were destined, from our earliest childhood, to be friends. I wonder whether you feel as strangely drawn towards me as I do to you; I have never had a friend—shall I find one now?" She sighed, and her fine dark eyes gazed passionately on me.

Now the truth is, I felt rather unaccountably towards the beautiful stranger. I did feel, as she said, "drawn towards her," but there was also something of repulsion. In this ambiguous feeling, however, the sense of attraction immensely prevailed. She interested and won me; she was so beautiful and so indescribably engaging.

I perceived now something of languor and exhaustion stealing over her, and hastened to bid her goodnight.

"The doctor thinks," I added, "that you ought to have a maid to sit up with you tonight; one of ours is waiting, and you will find her a very useful and quiet creature."

"How kind of you, but I could not sleep, I never could with an attendant in the room. I shan't require any assistance—and, shall I confess my weakness, I am haunted with a terror of robbers. Our house was robbed once, and two servants murdered, so I always lock my door. It has become a habit—and you look so kind I know you will forgive me. I see there is a key in the lock."

She held me close in her pretty arms for a moment and whispered in my ear, "Goodnight, darling, it is very hard to part with you, but goodnight; tomorrow, but not early, I shall see you again."

She sank back on the pillow with a sigh, and her fine eyes followed me with a fond and melancholy gaze, and she murmured again, "Goodnight, dear friend."

Young people like, and even love, on impulse. I was flattered by the evident, though as yet undeserved, fondness she showed me. I liked the confidence with which she at once received me. She was determined that we should be very dear friends.

Next day came and we met again. I was delighted with my companion; that is to say, in many respects.

Her looks lost nothing in daylight—she was certainly the most beautiful creature I had ever seen, and the unpleasant remembrance of the face presented in my early dream, had lost the effect of the first unexpected recognition.

She confessed that she had experienced a similar shock on seeing me, and precisely the same faint antipathy that had mingled with my admiration of her. We now laughed together over our momentary horrors.

IV. HER HABITS—A SAUNTER

I told you that I was charmed with her in most particulars.

There were some that did not please me so well.

She was above the middle height of women. I shall begin by describing her. She was slender, and wonderfully graceful. Except that her movements were languid—*very* languid—indeed, there was nothing in her appearance to indicate an invalid. Her complexion was rich and brilliant; her features were small and beautifully formed; her eyes large, dark, and lustrous; her hair was quite wonderful, I never saw hair so magnificently thick and long when it was down about her shoulders; I have often placed my hands under it, and laughed with wonder at its weight. It was exquisitely fine and soft, and in color a rich very dark brown, with something of gold. I loved to let it down, tumbling with its own weight, as, in her room, she lay back in her chair talking in her sweet low voice, I used to fold and braid it, and spread it out and play with it. Heavens! If I had but known all!

I said there were particulars which did not please me. I have told you that her confidence won me the first night I saw her; but I found that she exercised with respect to herself, her mother, her history, everything in fact connected with her life, plans, and people an ever-wakeful reserve. I dare say I was unreasonable, perhaps I was wrong; I dare say I ought to have respected the solemn injunction laid upon my father by the stately lady in black velvet. But curiosity is a restless and unscrupulous passion, and no one girl can endure, with patience, that hers should be baffled by another. What harm could it do anyone to tell me what I so ardently desired to know? Had she no trust in my good sense or honor? Why would she not believe me when I assured her, so solemnly, that I would not divulge one syllable of what she told me to any mortal breathing?

There was a coldness, it seemed to me, beyond her years, in her smiling melancholy persistent refusal to afford me the least ray of light.

I cannot say we quarreled upon this point, for she would not quarrel upon any. It was, of course, very unfair of me to press her, very ill-bred, but I really could not help it; and I might just as well have let it alone.

What she did tell me amounted, in my unconscionable estimation—to nothing.

It was all summed up in three very vague disclosures.

First.—Her name was Carmilla.

Second.—Her family was very ancient and noble.

Third.—Her home lay in the direction of the west.

She would not tell me the name of her family, nor their armorial bearings, nor the name of the estate, nor even that of the country they lived in.

You are not to suppose that I worried her incessantly on these subjects. I watched opportunity, and rather insinuated than urged my inquiries. Once or twice, indeed, I did attack more directly. But no matter what my tactics, utter failure was invariably the result. Reproaches and caresses were all lost upon her. But I must add this, that her evasion was conducted with so pretty a melancholy and deprecation, and so many, and even passionate declarations of her liking for me, and trust in my honor, and with so many promises, that I should at last know all, that I could not find it in my heart long to be offended with her.

She used to place her pretty arms about my neck, draw me to her, and laying her cheek to mine, murmur with her lips near my ear, "Dearest, your little heart is wounded; think me not cruel because I obey the irresistible law of my strength and weakness; if your dear heart is wounded, my wild heart bleeds with yours. In the rapture of my enormous humiliation I live in your warm life, and you shall die—die, sweetly die—into mine. I cannot help it; as I draw near to you, you, in your turn, will draw near to others, and learn the rapture of that cruelty, which yet is love; so, for a while, seek to know no more of me and mine, but trust me with all your loving spirit."

And when she had spoken such a rhapsody, she would press me more closely in her trembling embrace, and her lips in soft kisses gently glow upon my cheek.

Her agitations and her language were unintelligible to me.

From these foolish embraces, which were not of very frequent occurrence, I must allow, I used to wish to extricate myself; but my energies seemed to fail me. Her murmured words sounded like a lullaby in my ear, and soothed my resistance into a trance, from which I only seemed to recover myself when she withdrew her arms.

In these mysterious moods I did not like her. I experienced a strange tumultuous excitement that was pleasurable, ever and anon, mingled with a vague sense of fear and disgust. I had no distinct thoughts about her while such scenes lasted, but I was conscious of a love growing into adoration, and also of abhorrence. This I know is paradox, but I can make no other attempt to explain the feeling.

I now write, after an interval of more than ten years, with a trembling hand, with a confused and horrible recollection of certain occurrences and situations, in the ordeal through which I was unconsciously passing; though with a vivid and very sharp remembrance of the main current of my story. But, I suspect, in all lives there are certain emotional scenes, those in which our passions have been most wildly and terribly roused, that are of all others the most vaguely and dimly remembered.

Sometimes after an hour of apathy, my strange and beautiful companion would take my hand and hold it with a fond pressure, renewed again and again; blushing softly, gazing in my face with languid and burning eyes, and breathing so fast that her dress rose and fell with the tumultuous respiration. It was like the ardor of a lover; it embarrassed me; it was hateful and yet overpowering; and with gloating eyes she drew me to her, and her hot lips travelled along my cheek in kisses; and she would whisper, almost in sobs, "You are mine, you *shall* be mine, and you and I are one for ever." Then she has thrown herself back in her chair, with her small hands over her eyes, leaving me trembling.

"Are we related?" I used to ask. "What can you mean by all this? I remind you perhaps of some one whom you love; but you must not, I hate it; I don't know you—I don't know myself when you look so and talk so."

She used to sigh at my vehemence, then turn away and drop my hand.

Respecting these very extraordinary manifestations I strove in vain to form any satisfactory theory—could not refer them to affectation or trick. It was unmistakably the momentary breaking out of suppressed instinct and emotion. Was she, notwithstanding her mother's volunteered denial, subject to brief visitations of insanity, or was there here a disguise and a romance? I had read in old story books of such things. What if a boyish lover had found his way into the house, and sought to make advances in masquerade, with the assistance of a clever old adventuress. But there were many things against this hypothesis, highly interesting as it was to my vanity.

I could boast of no little attentions such as masculine gallantry delights to offer. Between these passionate moments there were long intervals of commonplace, of gaiety, of brooding melancholy, during which, except that I detected her eyes so full of melancholy fire, following me, at times I might have been as nothing to her. Except in these brief periods of mysterious excitement her ways were girlish; and there was always a languor about her, quite incompatible with a masculine system in a state of health.

In some respects her habits were odd. Perhaps not so singular in the opinion of a town lady like you, as they appeared to us rustic people. She used to come down very late, generally not till one o'clock, she would then take a cup of chocolate, but eat nothing; we then went out for a walk, which was a mere saunter, and she seemed, almost immediately, exhausted, and either returned to the schloss or sat on one of the benches that were placed, here and there, among the trees. This was a bodily languor in which her mind did not sympathize. She was always an animated talker, and very intelligent.

She sometimes alluded for a moment to her own home, or mentioned an adventure or situation, or an early recollection, which indicated a people of strange manners, and described customs of which we knew nothing. I gathered from these chance hints that her native country was much more remote than I had at first fancied.

As we sat thus one afternoon under the trees, a funeral passed us by. It was that of a pretty young girl, whom I had often seen, the daughter of one of the rangers of the forest. The poor man was walking behind the coffin of his darling; she was his only child, and he looked quite heartbroken. Peasants walking two-and-two came behind, they were singing a funeral hymn.

I rose to mark my respect as they passed, and joined in the hymn they were very sweetly singing.

My companion shook me a little roughly, and I turned surprised.

She said brusquely, "Don't you perceive how discordant that is?"

"I think it is very sweet, on the contrary," I answered, vexed at the interruption, and very uncomfortable, lest the people who composed the little procession should observe and resent what was passing.

I resumed, therefore, instantly, and was again interrupted. "You pierce my ears," said Carmilla, almost angrily, and stopping her ears with her tiny fingers. "Besides, how can you tell that your religion and mine are the same; your forms wound me, and I hate funerals. What a fuss! Why, *you* must die—*everyone* must die; and all are happier when they do. Come home."

"My father has gone on with the clergyman to the churchyard. I thought you knew she was to be buried today."

"*She?* I don't trouble my head about peasants. I don't know who she is," answered Carmilla, with a flash from her fine eyes.

"She is the poor girl who fancied she saw a ghost a fortnight ago, and has been dying ever since, till yesterday, when she expired."

"Tell me nothing about ghosts. I shan't sleep tonight if you do."

"I hope there is no plague or fever coming; all this looks very like it," I continued. "The swineherd's young wife died only a week ago, and she thought something seized her by the throat as she lay in her bed, and nearly strangled her. Papa says such horrible fancies do accompany some forms of fever. She was quite well the day before. She sank afterwards, and died before a week."

"Well, *her* funeral is over, I hope, and *her* hymn sung; and our ears shan't be tortured with that discord and jargon. It has made me nervous. Sit down here, beside me; sit close; hold my hand; press it hard—hard—harder."

We had moved a little back, and had come to another seat.

She sat down. Her face underwent a change that alarmed and even terrified me for a moment. It darkened, and became horribly livid; her teeth and hands were clenched, and she frowned and compressed her lips, while she stared down upon the ground at her feet, and trembled all over with a continued shudder as irrepressible as ague. All her energies seemed strained to suppress a fit, with which she was then breathlessly tugging; and at length a low convulsive cry of suffering broke from her, and gradually the hysteria subsided. "There! That comes of strangling people with hymns!" she said at last. "Hold me, hold me still. It is passing away."

And so gradually it did; and perhaps to dissipate the somber impression which the spectacle had left upon me, she became unusually animated and talkative; and so we got home.

This was the first time I had seen her exhibit any definable symptoms of that delicacy of health which her mother had spoken of. It was the first time, also, I had seen her exhibit anything like temper.

Both passed away like a summer cloud; and never but once afterwards did I witness on her part a momentary sign of anger. I will tell you how it happened.

She and I were looking out of one of the long drawing-room windows, when there entered the courtyard, over the drawbridge, a figure of a wanderer whom I knew very well. He used to visit the schloss generally twice a year.

It was the figure of a hunchback, with the sharp lean features that generally accompany deformity. He wore a pointed black beard, and he was smiling from ear to ear, showing his white fangs. He was dressed in buff, black, and scarlet, and crossed with more straps and belts than I could count, from which hung all manner of things. Behind, he carried a magic-lantern, and two boxes, which I well knew, in one of which was a salamander, and in the other a mandrake. These monsters used to make my father laugh. They were compounded of parts of monkeys, parrots, squirrels, fish, and hedgehogs, dried and stitched together with great neatness and startling effect. He had a fiddle, a box of conjuring apparatus, a pair of foils and masks attached to his belt, several other mysterious cases dangling about him, and a black staff with copper ferrules in his hand. His companion was a rough spare dog, that followed at his heels, but stopped short, suspiciously, at the drawbridge, and in a little while began to howl dismally.

In the meantime, the mountebank, standing in the midst of the courtyard, raised his grotesque hat, and made us a very ceremonious bow, paying his compliments very volubly in execrable French, and German not much better. Then, disengaging his fiddle, he began to scrape a lively air, to which he sang with a merry discord, dancing with ludicrous airs and activity, that made me laugh, in spite of the dog's howling.

Then he advanced to the window with many smiles and salutations, and his hat in his left hand, his fiddle under his arm, and with a fluency that never took breath, he gabbled a long advertisement of all his accomplishments, and the resources of the various arts which he placed at our service, and the curiosities and entertainments which it was in his power, at our bidding, to display.

"Will your ladyships be pleased to buy an amulet against the vampire, which is going like the wolf, I hear, through these woods," he said, dropping his hat on the pavement. "They are dying of it right and left, and here is a charm that never fails; only pinned to the pillow, and you may laugh in his face."

These charms consisted of oblong slips of vellum, with cabalistic ciphers and diagrams upon them.

Carmilla instantly purchased one, and so did I.

He was looking up, and we were smiling down upon him, amused; at least, I can answer for myself. His piercing black eye, as he looked up in our faces, seemed to detect something that fixed for a moment his curiosity.

In an instant he unrolled a leather case, full of all manner of odd little steel instruments.

"See here, my lady," he said, displaying it, and addressing me, "I profess, among other things less useful, the art of dentistry. Plague take the dog!" he interpolated. "Silence, beast! He howls so that your ladyships can scarcely hear a word. Your noble friend, the young lady at your right, has the sharpest tooth—long, thin, pointed, like an awl, like a needle; ha, ha! With my sharp and long sight, as I look up, I have seen it distinctly; now if it happens to hurt the young lady, and I think it must, here am I, here are my file, my punch, my nippers; I will make it round and blunt, if her ladyship pleases; no longer the tooth of a fish, but of a beautiful young lady as she is. Hey? Is the young lady displeased? Have I been too bold? Have I offended her?"

The young lady, indeed, looked very angry as she drew back from the window.

"How dares that mountebank insult us so? Where is your father? I shall demand redress from him. My father would have had the wretch tied up to the pump, and flogged with a cartwhip, and burnt to the bones with the castle brand!"

She retired from the window a step or two, and sat down, and hardly lost sight of the offender, when her wrath subsided as suddenly as it had risen, and she gradually recovered her usual tone, and seemed to forget the little hunchback and his follies.

My father was out of spirits that evening. On coming in he told us that there had been another case similar to the two fatal ones which had lately occurred. The sister of a young peasant on his estate, only a mile away, was very ill, had been, as she described it, attacked very nearly in the same way, and was now slowly but steadily sinking.

"All this," said my father, "is strictly referable to natural causes. These poor people infect one another with their superstitions, and so repeat in imagination the images of terror that have infested their neighbors."

"But that very circumstance frightens one horribly," said Carmilla.

"How so?" inquired my father.

"I am so afraid of fancying I see such things; I think it would be as bad as reality."

"We are in God's hands; nothing can happen without His permission, and all will end well for those who love Him. He is our faithful creator; He has made us all, and will take care of us."

"Creator! *Nature!*" said the young lady in answer to my gentle father. "And this disease that invades the country is natural. Nature. All things proceed from Nature—don't they? All things in the heaven, in the earth, and under the earth, act and live as Nature ordains? I think so."

"The doctor said he would come here today," said my father, after a silence. "I want to know what he thinks about it, and what he thinks we had better do."

"Doctors never did me any good," said Carmilla.

"Then you have been ill?" I asked.

"More ill than ever you were," she answered.

"Long ago?"

"Yes, a long time. I suffered from this very illness; but I forget all but my pain and weakness, and they were not so bad as are suffered in other diseases."

"You were very young then?"

"I dare say; let us talk no more of it. You would not wound a friend?" She looked languidly in my eyes, and passed her arm round my waist lovingly, and led me out of the room. My father was busy over some papers near the window.

"Why does your papa like to frighten us?" said the pretty girl, with a sigh and a little shudder.

"He doesn't, dear Carmilla, it is the very furthest thing from his mind."

"Are you afraid, dearest?"

"I should be very much if I fancied there was any real danger of my being attacked as those poor people were."

"You are afraid to die?"

"Yes, every one is."

"But to die as lovers may—to die together, so that they may live together. Girls are caterpillars while they live in the world, to be finally butterflies when the summer comes; but in the meantime there are grubs and larvae, don't you see—each with their peculiar propensities, necessities and structure. So says Monsieur Buffon, in his big book, in the next room."

Later in the day the doctor came, and was closeted with papa for some time. He was a skilful man, of sixty and upwards, he wore powder, and shaved his pale face as smooth as a pumpkin. He and papa emerged from the room together, and I heard papa laugh, and say as they came out:

"Well, I do wonder at a wise man like you. What do you say to hippogriffs and dragons?"

The doctor was smiling, and made answer, shaking his head—

"Nevertheless, life and death are mysterious states, and we know little of the resources of either."

And so they walked on, and I heard no more. I did not then know what the doctor had been suggesting, but I think I guess it now.

V. A WONDERFUL LIKENESS

This evening there arrived from Gratz the grave, dark-faced son of the picture-cleaner, with a horse and cart laden with two large packing-cases, having many pictures in each. It was a journey of ten leagues, and whenever a messenger arrived at the schloss from our little capital of Gratz, we used to crowd about him in the hall, to hear the news.

This arrival created in our secluded quarters quite a sensation. The cases remained in the hall, and the messenger was taken charge of by the servants till he had eaten his supper. Then with assistants, and armed with hammer, ripping chisel, and turnscrew, he met us in the hall, where we had assembled to witness the unpacking of the cases.

Carmilla sat looking listlessly on, while one after the other the old pictures, nearly all portraits, which had undergone the process of renovation, were brought to light. My mother was of an old Hungarian family, and most of these pictures, which were about to be restored to their places, had come to us through her.

My father had a list in his hand, from which he read, as the artist rummaged out the corresponding numbers. I don't know that the pictures were very good, but they were, undoubtedly, very old, and some of them very curious also. They had, for the most part, the merit of being now seen by me, I may say, for the first time; for the smoke and dust of time had all but obliterated them.

"There is a picture that I have not seen yet," said my father. "In one corner, at the top of it, is the name, as well as I could read, 'Marcia Karnstein,' and the date '1698'; and I am curious to see how it has turned out."

I remembered it; it was a small picture, about a foot and a half high, and nearly square, without a frame; but it was so blackened by age that I could not make it out.

The artist now produced it, with evident pride. It was quite beautiful; it was startling; it seemed to live. It was the likeness of Carmilla!

"Carmilla, dear, here is an absolute miracle. Here you are, living, smiling, ready to speak, in this picture. Isn't it beautiful, papa? And see, even the little mole on her throat."

My father laughed, and said, "Certainly it is a wonderful likeness," but he looked away, and to my surprise seemed but little struck by it, and went on talking to the picture-cleaner, who was also something of an artist, and discoursed with intelligence about the portraits of other works, which his art had just brought into light and color, while *I* was more and more lost in wonder the more I looked at the picture.

"Will you let me hang this picture in my room, papa?" I asked.

"Certainly dear," said he, smiling, "I'm very glad you think it so like. It must be prettier even than I thought it, if it is."

The young lady did not acknowledge this pretty speech, did not seem to hear it. She was leaning back in her seat, her fine eyes under their long lashes gazing on me in contemplation, and she smiled in a kind of rapture.

"And now you can read quite plainly the name that is written in the corner. It is not Marcia; it looks as if it was done in gold. The name is Mircalla, Countess Karnstein, and this is a little coronet over it, and underneath A.D. 1698. I am descended from the Karnsteins; that is, mamma was."

"Ah!" said the lady, languidly, "so am I, I think, a very long descent, very ancient. Are there any Karnsteins living now?"

"None who bear the name, I believe. The family were ruined, I believe, in some civil wars, long ago, but the ruins of the castle are only about three miles away."

"How interesting!" she said, languidly. "But see what beautiful moonlight!" She glanced through the hall door, which stood a little open. "Suppose you take a little ramble round the court and look down at the road and river."

"It is so like the night you came to us," I said.

She sighed, smiling.

She rose, and each with her arm about the other's waist, we walked out upon the pavement.

In silence, slowly we walked down to the drawbridge, where the beautiful landscape opened before us.

"And so you were thinking of the night I came here?" she almost whispered. "Are you glad I came?"

"Delighted, dear Carmilla," I answered.

"And you asked for the picture you think like me, to hang in your room," she murmured with a sigh, as she drew her arm closer about my waist, and let her pretty head sink upon my shoulder.

"How romantic you are, Carmilla," I said. "Whenever you tell me your story, it will be made up chiefly of some one great romance."

She kissed me silently.

"I am sure, Carmilla, you have been in love; that there is, at this moment, an affair of the heart going on."

"I have been in love with no one, and never shall," she whispered, "unless it should be with you."

How beautiful she looked in the moonlight!

Shy and strange was the look with which she quickly hid her face in my neck and hair, with tumultuous sighs, that seemed to sob, and pressed in mine a hand that trembled.

Her soft cheek was glowing against mine. "Darling, darling," she murmured. "I live in you; and you would die for me, I love you so."

I started from her.

She was gazing on me with eyes from which all fire, all meaning had flown, and a face colorless and apathetic.

"Is there a chill in the air, dear?" she said drowsily. "I almost shiver; have I been dreaming? Let us come in. Come, come; come in."

"You look ill, Carmilla; a little faint. You certainly must take some wine," I said.

"Yes, I will. I'm better now. I shall be quite well in a few minutes. Yes, do give me a little wine," answered Carmilla, as we approached the door. "Let us look again for a moment; it is the last time, perhaps, I shall see the moonlight with you."

"How do you feel now, dear Carmilla? Are you really better?" I asked.

I was beginning to take alarm lest she should have been stricken with the strange epidemic that they said had invaded the country about us.

"Papa would be grieved beyond measure," I added, "if he thought you were ever so little ill, without immediately letting us know. We have a very skilful doctor near this, the physician who was with papa today."

"I'm sure he is. I know how kind you all are; but, dear child, I am quite well again. There is nothing ever wrong with me but a little weakness. People say I am languid; I am incapable of exertion; I can scarcely walk as far as a child of three years old; and every now and then the little strength I have falters, and I become as you have just seen me. But after all I am very easily set up again; in a moment I am perfectly myself. See how I have recovered."

So, indeed, she had; and she and I talked a great deal, and very animated she was; and the remainder of that evening passed without any recurrence of what I called her infatuations. I mean her crazy talk and looks, which embarrassed, and even frightened me.

But there occurred that night an event which gave my thoughts quite a new turn, and seemed to startle even Carmilla's languid nature into momentary energy.

VI. A VERY STRANGE AGONY

When we got into the drawing-room, and had sat down to our coffee and chocolate, although Carmilla did not take any, she seemed quite herself again, and Madame, and Mademoiselle De Lafontaine, joined us, and made a little card party, in the course of which papa came in for what he called his "dish of tea."

When the game was over he sat down beside Carmilla on the sofa, and asked her, a little anxiously, whether she had heard from her mother since her arrival.

She answered "No."

He then asked her whether she knew where a letter would reach her at present.

"I cannot tell," she answered, ambiguously, "but I have been thinking of leaving you; you have been already too hospitable and too kind to me. I have given you an infinity of trouble, and I should wish to take a carriage tomorrow and post in pursuit of her; I know where I shall ultimately find her, although I dare not yet tell you."

"But you must not dream of any such thing," exclaimed my father, to my great relief. "We can't afford to lose you so, and I won't consent to your leaving us, except under the care of your mother, who was so good as to consent to your remaining with us till she should herself return. I should be quite happy if I knew that you heard from her; but this evening the accounts of the progress of the mysterious disease that has invaded our neighborhood grow even more alarming; and my beautiful guest, I do feel the responsibility, unaided by advice from your mother, very much. But I shall do my best; and one thing is certain, that you must not think of leaving us without her distinct direction to that effect. We should suffer too much in parting from you to consent to it easily."

"Thank you, sir, a thousand times for your hospitality," she answered, smiling bashfully. "You have all been too kind to me; I have seldom been so happy in all my life before, as in your beautiful château, under your care, and in the society of your dear daughter."

So he gallantly, in his old-fashioned way, kissed her hand, smiling, and pleased at her little speech.

I accompanied Carmilla as usual to her room, and sat and chatted with her while she was preparing for bed.

"Do you think," I said, at length, "that you will ever confide fully in me?"

She turned round smiling, but made no answer, only continued to smile on me.

"You won't answer that?" I said. "You can't answer pleasantly; I ought not to have asked you."

"You were quite right to ask me that, or anything. You do not know how dear you are to me, or you could not think any confidence too great to look for. But I am under vows, no nun half so awfully, and I dare not tell my story yet, even to you. The time is very near when you shall know everything. You will think me cruel, very selfish, but love is always selfish; the more ardent the more selfish. How jealous I am you cannot know. You must come with me, loving me, to death; or else hate me, and still come with me, and *hating* me through death and after. There is no such word as indifference in my apathetic nature."

"Now, Carmilla, you are going to talk your wild nonsense again," I said hastily.

"Not I, silly little fool as I am, and full of whims and fancies; for your sake I'll talk like a sage. Were you ever at a ball?"

"No; how you do run on. What is it like? How charming it must be."

"I almost forget, it is years ago."

I laughed.

"You are not so old. Your first ball can hardly be forgotten yet."

"I remember everything about it—with an effort. I see it all, as divers see what is going on above them, through a medium, dense, rippling, but transparent. There occurred that night what has confused the picture, and made its colors faint. I was all but assassinated in my bed, wounded *here*," she touched her breast, "and never was the same since."

"Were you near dying?"

"Yes, very—a cruel love—strange love, that would have taken my life. Love will have its sacrifices. No sacrifice without blood. Let us go to sleep now, I feel so lazy. How can I get up just now and lock my door?"

She was lying with her tiny hands buried in her rich wavy hair, under her cheek, her little head upon the pillow, and her glittering eyes followed me wherever I moved, with a kind of shy smile that I could not decipher.

I bid her goodnight, and crept from the room with an uncomfortable sensation.

I often wondered whether our pretty guest ever said her prayers. *I* certainly had never seen her upon her knees. In the morning she never came down until long after our family prayers were over, and at night she never left the drawing-room to attend our brief evening prayers in the hall.

If it had not been that it had casually come out in one of our careless talks that she had been baptized, I should have doubted her being a Christian. Religion was a subject on which I had never heard her speak a word. If I had known the world better, this particular neglect or antipathy would not have so much surprised me.

The precautions of nervous people are infectious, and persons of a like temperament are pretty sure, after a time, to imitate them. I had adopted Carmilla's habit of locking her bedroom door, having taken into my head all her whimsical alarms about midnight invaders, and prowling assassins. I had also adopted her precaution of making a brief search through her room, to satisfy herself that no lurking assassin or robber was "ensconced."

These wise measures taken, I got into my bed and fell asleep. A light was burning in my room. This was an old habit, of very early date, and which nothing could have tempted me to dispense with.

Thus fortified I might take my rest in peace. But dreams come through stone walls, light up dark rooms, or darken light ones, and their persons make their exits and their entrances as they please, and laugh at locksmiths.

I had a dream that night that was the beginning of a very strange agony.

I cannot call it a nightmare, for I was quite conscious of being asleep. But I was equally conscious of being in my room, and lying in bed, precisely as I actually was. I saw, or fancied I saw, the room and its furniture just as I had seen it last, except that it was very dark, and I saw something moving round the foot of the bed, which at first I could not accurately distinguish. But I soon saw that it was a sooty-black animal that resembled a monstrous cat. It appeared to me about four or five feet long, for it measured fully the length of the hearth-rug as it passed over it; and it continued to-ing and fro-ing with the lithe sinister restlessness of a beast in a cage. I could not cry out, although as you may suppose, I was terrified. Its pace was growing faster, and the room rapidly darker and darker, and at length so dark that I could no longer see anything of it but its eyes. I felt it spring lightly on the bed. The two broad eyes approached my face, and suddenly I felt a stinging pain as if two large needles darted, an inch or two apart, deep into my breast. I awoke with a scream. The room was lighted by the candle that burnt there all through the night, and I saw a female figure standing at the foot of the bed, a little at the right side. It was in a dark loose dress, and its hair was down and covered its shoulders. A block of stone could not have been more still. There was not the slightest stir of respiration. As I stared at it, the figure appeared to have changed its place, and was now nearer the door; then, close to it, the door opened, and it passed out.

I was now relieved, and able to breathe and move. My first thought was that Carmilla had been playing me a trick, and that I had forgotten to secure my door. I hastened to it, and found it locked as usual on the inside. I was afraid to open it—I was horrified. I sprang into my bed and covered my head up in the bed-clothes, and lay there more dead than alive till morning.

VII. DESCENDING

It would be vain my attempting to tell you the horror with which, even now, I recall the occurrence of that night. It was no such transitory terror as a dream leaves behind it.

It seemed to deepen by time, and communicated itself to the room and the very furniture that had encompassed the apparition.

I could not bear next day to be alone for a moment. I should have told papa, but for two opposite reasons. At one time I thought he would laugh at my story, and I could not bear its being treated as a jest; and at another, I thought he might fancy that I had been attacked by the mysterious complaint which had invaded our neighborhood. I had myself no misgivings of the kind, and as he had been rather an invalid for some time, I was afraid of alarming him.

I was comfortable enough with my good-natured companions, Madame Perrodon, and the vivacious Mademoiselle Lafontaine. They both perceived that I was out of spirits and nervous and at length I told them what lay so heavy at my heart. Mademoiselle laughed, but I fancied that Madame Perrodon looked anxious.

"By-the-by," said Mademoiselle, laughing, "the long lime tree walk, behind Carmilla's bedroom window, is haunted!"

"Nonsense!" exclaimed Madame, who probably thought the theme rather inopportune, "and who tells that story, my dear?"

"Martin says that he came up twice, when the old yard-gate was being repaired before sunrise, and twice saw the same female figure walking down the lime tree avenue."

"So he well might, as long as there are cows to milk in the river fields," said Madame.

"I dare say; but Martin chooses to be frightened, and never did I see a fool *more* frightened."

"You must not say a word about it to Carmilla, because she can see down that walk from her room window," I interposed, "and she is, if possible, a greater coward than I."

Carmilla came down rather later than usual that day.

"I was so frightened last night," she said so soon as we were together, "and I am sure I should have seen something dreadful if it had not been for that charm I bought from the poor little hunchback whom I called such hard names. I had a dream of something black coming round my bed, and I awoke in a perfect horror, and I really thought, for some seconds, I saw a dark figure near the chimney piece, but I felt under my pillow for my charm, and the moment my fingers touched it, the figure disappeared, and I felt quite certain, only that I had it by me, that something frightful would have made its appearance, and perhaps, throttled me, as it did those poor people we heard of."

"Well, listen to me," I began, and recounted my adventure, at the recital of which she appeared horrified.

"And had you the charm near you?" she asked, earnestly.

"No, I had dropped it into a china vase in the drawing-room, but I shall certainly take it with me tonight, as you have so much faith in it."

At this distance of time I cannot tell you, or even understand, how I overcame my horror so effectually as to lie alone in my room that night. I remember distinctly that I pinned the charm to my pillow. I fell asleep almost immediately, and slept even more soundly than usual all night.

Next night I passed as well. My sleep was delightfully deep and dreamless. But I wakened with a sense of lassitude and melancholy which, however, did not exceed a degree that was almost luxurious.

"Well, I told you so," said Carmilla, when I described my quiet sleep, "I had such delightful sleep myself last night; I pinned the charm to the breast of my nightdress.

It was too far away the night before. I am quite sure it was all fancy, except the dreams. I used to think that evil spirits made dreams, but our doctor told me it is no such thing. Only a fever passing by, or some other malady, as they often do, he said, knocks at the door, and not being able to get in, passes on, with that alarm."

"And what do you think the charm is?" said I.

"It has been fumigated or immersed in some drug, and is an antidote against the malaria," she answered.

"Then it acts only on the body?"

"Certainly; you don't suppose that evil spirits are frightened by bits of ribbon, or the perfumes of a druggist's shop? No, these complaints, wandering in the air, begin by trying the nerves, and so infect the brain; but before they can seize upon you, the antidote repels them. That I am sure is what the charm has done for us. It is nothing magical, it is simply natural."

I should have been happier if I could quite have agreed with Carmilla, but I did my best, and the impression was a little losing its force.

For some nights I slept profoundly; but still every morning I felt the same lassitude, and a languor weighed upon me all day. I felt myself a changed girl. A strange melancholy was stealing over me, a melancholy that I would not have interrupted. Dim thoughts of death began to open, and an idea that I was slowly sinking took gentle, and, somehow, not unwelcome possession of me. If it was sad, the tone of mind which this induced was also sweet. Whatever it might be, my soul acquiesced in it.

I would not admit that I was ill, I would not consent to tell my papa, or to have the doctor sent for.

Carmilla became more devoted to me than ever, and her strange paroxysms of languid adoration more frequent. She used to dote on me with increasing ardor the more my strength and spirits waned. This always shocked me like a momentary glare of insanity.

Without knowing it, I was now in a pretty advanced stage of the strangest illness under which mortal ever suffered. There was an unaccountable fascination in its earlier symptoms that more than reconciled me to the incapacitating effect of that stage of the malady. This fascination increased for a time, until it reached a certain point, when gradually a sense of the horrible mingled itself with it, deepening, as you shall hear, until it discolored and perverted the whole state of my life.

The first change I experienced was rather agreeable. It was very near the turning point from which began the descent of Avernus.

Certain vague and strange sensations visited me in my sleep. The prevailing one was of that pleasant, peculiar cold thrill which we feel in bathing, when we move against the current of a river. This was soon accompanied by dreams that seemed interminable, and were so vague that I could never recollect their scenery and persons, or any one connected portion of their action. But they left an awful impression, and a sense of exhaustion, as if I had passed through a long period of great mental exertion and danger. After all these dreams there remained on waking a remembrance of having been in a place very nearly dark, and of having spoken to people whom I could not see; and especially of one clear voice, of a female's, very deep, that spoke as if at a distance, slowly, and producing always the same sensation of indescribable solemnity and fear. Sometimes there came a sensation as if a hand was drawn softly along my cheek and neck. Sometimes it was as if warm lips kissed me, and longer and more lovingly as they reached my throat, but there the caress fixed itself. My heart beat faster, my breathing rose and fell rapidly and full drawn; a sobbing, that rose into a sense of strangulation, supervened, and turned into a dreadful convulsion, in which my senses left me, and I became unconscious.

It was now three weeks since the commencement of this unaccountable state. My sufferings had, during the last week, told upon my appearance. I had grown pale, my eyes were dilated and darkened underneath, and the languor which I had long felt began to display itself in my countenance.

My father asked me often whether I was ill; but, with an obstinacy which now seems to me unaccountable, I persisted in assuring him that I was quite well.

In a sense this was true. I had no pain, I could complain of no bodily derangement. My complaint seemed to be one of the imagination, or the nerves, and, horrible as my sufferings were, I kept them, with a morbid reserve, very nearly to myself.

It could not be that terrible complaint which the peasants call the vampire, for I had now been suffering for three weeks, and they were seldom ill for much more than three days, when death put an end to their miseries.

Carmilla complained of dreams and feverish sensations, but by no means of so alarming a kind as mine. I say that mine were extremely alarming. Had I been capable of comprehending my condition, I would have invoked aid and advice on my knees. The narcotic of an unsuspected influence was acting upon me, and my perceptions were benumbed.

I am going to tell you now of a dream that led immediately to an odd discovery.

One night, instead of the voice I was accustomed to hear in the dark, I heard one, sweet and tender, and at the same time terrible, which said, "Your mother warns you to beware of the assassin." At the same time a light unexpectedly sprang up, and I saw Carmilla, standing, near the foot of my bed, in her white nightdress, bathed, from her chin to her feet, in one great stain of blood.

I wakened with a shriek, possessed with the one idea that Carmilla was being murdered. I remember springing from my bed, and my next recollection is that of standing on the lobby, crying for help.

Madame and Mademoiselle came scurrying out of their rooms in alarm; a lamp burned always on the lobby, and seeing me, they soon learned the cause of my terror.

I insisted on our knocking at Carmilla's door. Our knocking was unanswered. It soon became a pounding and an uproar. We shrieked her name but all was vain.

We all grew frightened, for the door was locked. We hurried back, in panic, to my room. There we rang the bell long and furiously. If my father's room had been at that side of the house, we would have called him up at once to our aid. But, alas! he was quite out of hearing, and to reach him involved an excursion for which we none of us had courage.

Servants, however, soon came running up the stairs; I had got on my dressing-gown and slippers meanwhile, and my companions were already similarly furnished. Recognizing the voices of the servants on the lobby, we sallied out together; and having renewed, as fruitlessly, our summons at Carmilla's door, I ordered the men to force the lock. They did so, and we stood, holding our lights aloft, in the doorway, and so stared into the room.

We called her by name; but there was still no reply. We looked round the room. Everything was undisturbed. It was exactly in the state in which I left it on bidding her goodnight. But Carmilla was gone.

VIII. SEARCH

At the sight of the room, perfectly undisturbed except for our violent entrance, we began to cool a little, and soon recovered our senses sufficiently to dismiss the men. It had struck Mademoiselle that possibly Carmilla had been wakened by the uproar at her door, and in her first panic had jumped from her bed, and hid herself in a press, or behind a curtain, from which she could not, of course, emerge until the majordomo and his men had withdrawn. We now recommenced our search, and began to call her by name again.

It was all to no purpose. Our perplexity and agitation increased. We examined the windows, but they were secured. I implored of Carmilla, if she had concealed herself, to play this cruel trick no longer—to come out, and to end our anxieties. It was all useless. I was by this time convinced that she was not in the room, nor in the dressing-room, the door of which was still locked on this side. She could not have passed it. I was utterly puzzled. Had Carmilla discovered one of those secret passages which the old housekeeper said were known to exist in the schloss, although the tradition of their exact situation had been lost? A little time would, no doubt, explain all—utterly perplexed as, for the present, we were.

It was past four o'clock, and I preferred passing the remaining hours of darkness in Madame's room. Daylight brought no solution of the difficulty.

The whole household, with my father at its head, was in a state of agitation next morning. Every part of the château was searched. The grounds were explored. Not a trace of the missing lady could be discovered. The stream was about to be dragged; my father was in distraction; what a tale to have to tell the poor girl's mother on her return.

I, too, was almost beside myself, though my grief was quite of a different kind.

The morning was passed in alarm and excitement. It was now one o'clock, and still no tidings. I ran up to Carmilla's room, and found her standing at her dressing-table! I was astounded. I could not believe my eyes. She beckoned me to her with her pretty finger, in silence. Her face expressed extreme fear.

I ran to her in an ecstasy of joy; I kissed and embraced her again and again. I ran to the bell and rang it vehemently, to bring others to the spot, who might at once relieve my father's anxiety.

"Dear Carmilla, what has become of you all this time? We have been in agonies of anxiety about you," I exclaimed. "Where have you been? How did you come back?"

"Last night has been a night of wonders," she said.

"For mercy's sake, explain all you can."

"It was past two last night," she said, "when I went to sleep as usual in my bed, with my doors locked, that of the dressing-room and that opening upon the gallery. My sleep was uninterrupted, and, so far as I know, dreamless; but I awoke just now on the sofa in the dressing-room there, and I found the door between the rooms open, and the other door forced. How could all this have happened without my being awakened? It must have been accompanied with a great deal of noise, and I am particularly easily wakened; and how could I have been carried out of my bed without my sleep having been interrupted, I whom the slightest stir startles?"

By this time, Madame, Mademoiselle, my father, and a number of the servants were in the room. Carmilla was, of course, overwhelmed with inquiries, congratulations, and welcomes. She had but one story to tell, and seemed the least able of all the party to suggest any way of accounting for what had happened.

My father took a turn up and down the room, thinking. I saw Carmilla's eye follow him for a moment with a sly, dark glance.

When my father had sent the servants away, Mademoiselle having gone in search of a little bottle of valerian and sal-volatile, and there being no one now in the room with Carmilla except my father, Madame, and myself, he came to her thoughtfully, took her hand very kindly, led her to the sofa, and sat down beside her.

"Will you forgive me, my dear, if I risk a conjecture, and ask a question?"

"Who can have a better right?" she said. "Ask what you please, and I will tell you everything. But my story is simply one of bewilderment and darkness. I know absolutely nothing. Put any question you please. But you know, of course, the limitations mamma has placed me under."

"Perfectly, my dear child. I need not approach the topics on which she desires our silence. Now, the marvel of last night consists in your having been removed from your bed and your room without being wakened, and this removal having occurred apparently while the windows were still secured, and the two doors locked upon the inside. I will tell you my theory, and first ask you a question."

Carmilla was leaning on her hand dejectedly; Madame and I were listening breathlessly.

"Now, my question is this. Have you ever been suspected of walking in your sleep?"

"Never since I was very young indeed."

"But you did walk in your sleep when you were young?"

"Yes; I know I did. I have been told so often by my old nurse."

My father smiled and nodded.

"Well, what has happened is this. You got up in your sleep, unlocked the door, not leaving the key, as usual, in the lock, but taking it out and locking it on the outside; you again took the key out, and carried it away with you to some one of the five-and-twenty rooms on this floor, or perhaps upstairs or downstairs. There are so many rooms and closets, so much heavy furniture, and such accumulations of lumber, that it would require a week to search this old house thoroughly. Do you see, now, what I mean?"

"I do, but not all," she answered.

"And how, papa, do you account for her finding herself on the sofa in the dressing-room, which we had searched so carefully?"

"She came there after you had searched it, still in her sleep, and at last awoke spontaneously, and was as much surprised to find herself where she was as anyone else. I wish all mysteries were as easily and innocently explained as yours, Carmilla," he said, laughing. "And so we may congratulate ourselves on the certainty that the most natural explanation of the occurrence is one that involves no drugging, no tampering with locks, no burglars, or poisoners, or witches—nothing that need alarm Carmilla, or any one else, for our safety."

Carmilla was looking charmingly. Nothing could be more beautiful than her tints. Her beauty was, I think, enhanced by that graceful languor that was peculiar to her. I think my father was silently contrasting her looks with mine, for he said:

"I wish my poor Laura was looking more like herself"; and he sighed.

So our alarms were happily ended, and Carmilla restored to her friends.

IX. THE DOCTOR

As Carmilla would not hear of an attendant sleeping in her room, my father arranged that a servant should sleep outside her door so that she could not attempt to make another such excursion without being arrested at her own door.

That night passed quietly; and next morning early, the doctor, whom my father had sent for without telling me a word about it, arrived to see me.

Madame accompanied me to the library; and there the grave little doctor, with white hair and spectacles, whom I mentioned before, was waiting to receive me.

I told him my story, and as I proceeded he grew graver and graver.

We were standing, he and I, in the recess of one of the windows, facing one another. When my statement was over, he leaned with his shoulders against the wall, and with his eyes fixed on me earnestly with an interest in which was a dash of horror.

After a minute's reflection, he asked Madame if he could see my father.

He was sent for accordingly, and as he entered, smiling, he said:

"I dare say, doctor, you are going to tell me that I am an old fool for having brought you here; I hope I am."

But his smile faded into shadow as the doctor, with a very grave face, beckoned him to him.

He and the doctor talked for some time in the same recess where I had just conferred with the physician. It seemed an earnest and argumentative conversation. The room is very large, and I and Madame stood together, burning with curiosity, at the further end. Not a word could we hear, however, for they spoke in a very low tone, and the deep recess of the window quite concealed the doctor from view, and very nearly my father, whose foot, arm, and shoulder only could we see; and the voices were, I suppose, all the less audible for the sort of closet which the thick wall and window formed.

After a time my father's face looked into the room; it was pale, thoughtful, and, I fancied, agitated.

"Laura, dear, come here for a moment. Madame, we shan't trouble you, the doctor says, at present."

Accordingly I approached, for the first time a little alarmed; for, although I felt very weak, I did not feel ill; and strength, one always fancies, is a thing that may be picked up when we please.

My father held out his hand to me as I drew near, but he was looking at the doctor, and he said:

"It certainly *is* very odd; I don't understand it quite. Laura, come here, dear; now attend to Doctor Spielsberg, and recollect yourself."

"You mentioned a sensation like that of two needles piercing the skin, somewhere about your neck, on the night when you experienced your first horrible dream. Is there still any soreness?"

"None at all," I answered.

"Can you indicate with your finger about the point at which you think this occurred?"

"Very little below my throat—*here*," I answered.

I wore a morning dress, which covered the place I pointed to.

"Now you can satisfy yourself," said the doctor. "You

won't mind your papa's lowering your dress a very little. It is necessary, to detect a symptom of the complaint under which you have been suffering."

I acquiesced. It was only an inch or two below the edge of my collar.

"God bless me!—so it is," exclaimed my father, growing pale.

"You see it now with your own eyes," said the doctor, with a gloomy triumph.

"What is it?" I exclaimed, beginning to be frightened.

"Nothing, my dear young lady, but a small blue spot, about the size of the tip of your little finger, and now," he continued, turning to papa, "the question is what is best to be done?"

"Is there any danger?" I urged, in great trepidation.

"I trust not, my dear," answered the doctor. "I don't see why you should not recover. I don't see why you should not begin *immediately* to get better. That is the point at which the sense of strangulation begins?"

"Yes," I answered.

"And—recollect as well as you can—the same point was a kind of center of that thrill which you described just now, like the current of a cold stream running against you?"

"It may have been; I think it was."

"Ay, you see?" he added, turning to my father. "Shall I say a word to Madame?"

"Certainly," said my father.

He called Madame to him, and said:

"I find my young friend here far from well. It won't be of any great consequence, I hope; but it will be necessary that some steps be taken, which I will explain by-and-by; but in the meantime, Madame, you will be so good as not to let Miss Laura be alone for one moment. That is the only direction I need give for the present. It is indispensable."

"We may rely upon your kindness, Madame, I know," added my father.

Madame satisfied him eagerly.

"And you, dear Laura, I know you will observe the doctor's direction."

"I shall have to ask your opinion upon another patient, whose symptoms slightly resemble those of my daughter, that have just been detailed to you—very much milder in degree, but I believe quite of the same sort. She is a young lady—our guest; but as you say you will be passing this way again this evening, you can't do better than take your supper here, and you can then see her. She does not come down till the afternoon."

"I thank you," said the doctor. "I shall be with you, then, at about seven this evening."

And then they repeated their directions to me and to Madame, and with this parting charge my father left us, and walked out with the doctor; and I saw them pacing together up and down between the road and the moat, on the grassy platform in front of the castle, evidently absorbed in earnest conversation.

The doctor did not return. I saw him mount his horse there, take his leave, and ride away eastward through the forest. Nearly at the same time I saw the man arrive from Dranfeld with the letters, and dismount and hand the bag to my father.

In the meantime, Madame and I were both busy, lost in conjecture as to the reasons of the singular and earnest direction which the doctor and my father concurred in imposing. Madame, as she afterwards told me, was afraid the doctor apprehended a sudden seizure, and that, without prompt assistance, I might either lose my life in a fit, or at least be seriously hurt.

This interpretation did not strike me; and I fancied, perhaps luckily for my nerves, that the arrangement was prescribed simply to secure a companion, who would prevent my taking too much exercise, or eating unripe fruit, or doing any of the fifty foolish things to which young people are supposed to be prone.

About half-an-hour after, my father came in—he had a letter in his hand—and said:

"This letter had been delayed; it is from General Spielsdorf. He might have been here yesterday, he may not come till tomorrow, or he may be here today."

He put the open letter into my hand; but he did not look pleased, as he used to when a guest, especially one so much loved as the General, was coming. On the contrary, he looked as if he wished him at the bottom of the Red Sea. There was plainly something on his mind which he did not choose to divulge.

"Papa, darling, will you tell me this?" said I, suddenly laying my hand on his arm, and looking, I am sure, imploringly in his face.

"Perhaps," he answered, smoothing my hair caressingly over my eyes.

"Does the doctor think me very ill?"

"No, dear; he thinks, if right steps are taken, you will be quite well again, at least on the high road to a complete recovery, in a day or two," he answered, a little drily. "I wish our good friend, the General, had chosen any other time; that, is, I wish you had been perfectly well to receive him."

"But do tell me, papa," I insisted, "*what* does he think is the matter with me?"

"Nothing; you must not plague me with questions," he answered, with more irritation than I ever remember him to have displayed before; and seeing that I looked wounded, I suppose, he kissed me, and added, "You shall know all about it in a day or two; that is, all that *I* know. In the meantime, you are not to trouble your head about it."

He turned and left the room, but came back before I had done wondering and puzzling over the oddity of all this; it was merely to say that he was going to Karnstein and had ordered the carriage to be ready at twelve, and that I and Madame should accompany him; he was going to see the priest who lived near those picturesque grounds, upon business, and as Carmilla had never seen them, she could follow, when she came down, with Mademoiselle, who would bring materials for what you call a picnic, which might be laid for us in the ruined castle.

At twelve o'clock, accordingly, I was ready, and not long after, my father, Madame and I set out upon our projected drive. Passing the drawbridge we turn to the right, and follow the road over the steep Gothic bridge westward, to reach the deserted village and ruined castle of Karnstein.

No sylvan drive can be fancied prettier. The ground breaks into gentle hills and hollows, all clothed with beautiful wood, totally destitute of the comparative formality which artificial planting and early culture and pruning impart.

The irregularities of the ground often lead the road out of its course, and cause it to wind beautifully round the sides of broken hollows and the steeper sides of the hills, among varieties of ground almost inexhaustible.

Turning one of these points, we suddenly encountered our old friend, the General, riding towards us, attended by a mounted servant. His portmanteaus were following in a hired wagon, such as we term a cart.

The General dismounted as we pulled up, and, after the usual greetings, was easily persuaded to accept the vacant seat in the carriage, and send his horse on with his servant to the schloss.

X. BEREAVED

It was about ten months since we had last seen him; but that time had sufficed to make an alteration of years in his appearance. He had grown thinner; something of gloom and anxiety had taken the place of that cordial serenity which used to characterize his features. His dark eyes, always penetrating, now gleamed with a sterner light from under his shaggy grey eyebrows. It was not such a change as grief alone usually induces, and angrier passions seemed to have had their share in bringing it about.

We had not long resumed our drive, when the General began to talk, with his usual soldierly directness, of the bereavement, as he termed it, which he had sustained in the death of his beloved niece and ward; and he then broke out in a tone of intense bitterness and fury, inveighing against the "hellish arts" to which she had fallen a victim, and expressing, with more exasperation than piety, his wonder that Heaven should tolerate so monstrous an indulgence of the lusts and malignity of hell.

My father, who saw at once that something very extraordinary had befallen, asked him, if not too painful to him, to detail the circumstances which he thought justified the strong terms in which he expressed himself.

"I should tell you all with pleasure," said the General, "but you would not believe me."

"Why should I not?" he asked.

"Because," he answered testily, "you believe in nothing but what consists with your own prejudices and illusions. I remember when I was like you, but I have learned better."

"Try me," said my father; "I am not such a dogmatist as you suppose. Besides which, I very well know that you generally require proof for what you believe, and am, therefore, very strongly predisposed to respect your conclusions."

"You are right in supposing that I have not been led lightly into a belief in the marvelous—for what I have experienced is marvelous—and I have been forced by extraordinary evidence to credit that which ran counter, diametrically, to all my theories. I have been made the dupe of a preternatural conspiracy."

Notwithstanding his professions of confidence in the General's penetration, I saw my father, at this point, glance at the General, with, as I thought, a marked suspicion of his sanity.

The General did not see it, luckily. He was looking gloomily and curiously into the glades and vistas of the woods that were opening before us.

"You are going to the Ruins of Karnstein?" he said. "Yes, it is a lucky coincidence; do you know I was going to ask you to bring me there to inspect them. I have a special object in exploring. There is a ruined chapel, isn't there, with a great many tombs of that extinct family?"

"So there are—highly interesting," said my father. "I hope you are thinking of claiming the title and estates?"

My father said this gaily, but the General did not recollect the laugh, or even the smile, which courtesy exacts for a friend's joke; on the contrary, he looked grave and even fierce, ruminating on a matter that stirred his anger and horror.

"Something very different," he said, gruffly. "I mean to unearth some of those fine people. I hope, by God's blessing, to accomplish a pious sacrilege here, which will relieve our earth of certain monsters, and enable honest people to sleep in their beds without being assailed by murderers. I have strange things to tell you, my dear friend, such as I myself would have scouted as incredible a few months since."

My father looked at him again, but this time not with a glance of suspicion—with an eye, rather, of keen intelligence and alarm.

"The house of Karnstein," he said, "has been long extinct: a hundred years at least. My dear wife was maternally descended from the Karnsteins. But name and title have long ceased to exist. The castle is a ruin; the very village is deserted; it is fifty years since the smoke of a chimney was seen there; not a roof left."

"Quite true. I have heard a great deal about that since I last saw you; a great deal that will astonish you. But I had better relate everything in the order in which it occurred," said the General. "You saw my dear ward—my child, I may call her. No creature could have been more beautiful and only three months ago none more blooming."

"Yes, poor thing! When I saw her last she certainly was quite lovely," said my father. "I was grieved and shocked more than I can tell you, my dear friend; I knew what a blow it was to you."

He took the General's hand, and they exchanged a kind pressure. Tears gathered in the old soldier's eyes. He did not seek to conceal them. He said:

"We have been very old friends; I knew you would feel for me, childless as I am. She had become an object of very dear interest to me, and repaid my care by affection that cheered my home and made my life happy. That is all gone. The years that remain to me on earth may not be very long; but by God's mercy I hope to accomplish a service to mankind before I die, and to subserve the vengeance of Heaven upon the fiends who have murdered my poor child in the spring of her hopes and beauty!"

"You said, just now, that you intended relating everything as it occurred," said my father. "Pray do; I assure you that it is not mere curiosity that prompts me."

By this time we had reached the point at which the Drunstall road, by which the General had come, diverges from the road which we were travelling to Karnstein.

"How far is it to the ruins?" inquired the General, looking anxiously forward.

"About half a league," answered my father. "Pray let us hear the story you were so good as to promise."

XI. THE STORY

"With all my heart," said the General, with an effort; and after a short pause in which to arrange his subject, he commenced one of the strangest narratives I ever heard.

"My dear child was looking forward with great pleasure to the visit you had been so good as to arrange for her to your charming daughter." Here he made me a gallant but melancholy bow.

"In the meantime we had an invitation to my old friend the Count Carlsfeld, whose schloss is about six leagues to the other side of Karnstein. It was to attend the series of fêtes which, you remember, were given by him in honor of his illustrious visitor, the Grand Duke Charles."

"Yes; and very splendid, I believe, they were," said my father.

"Princely! But then his hospitalities are quite regal. He has Aladdin's lamp. The night from which my sorrow dates was devoted to a magnificent masquerade. The grounds were thrown open, the trees hung with colored lamps. There was such a display of fireworks as Paris itself had never witnessed. And such music—music, you know, is my weakness—such ravishing music! The finest instrumental band, perhaps, in the world, and the finest singers who could be collected from all the great operas in Europe. As you wandered through these fantastically illuminated grounds, the moonlighted château throwing a rosy light from its long rows of windows, you would suddenly hear these ravishing voices stealing from the silence of some grove, or rising from boats upon the lake. I felt myself, as I looked and listened, carried back into the romance and poetry of my early youth.

"When the fireworks were ended, and the ball beginning, we returned to the noble suite of rooms that was thrown open to the dancers. A masked ball, you know, is a beautiful sight; but so brilliant a spectacle of the kind I never saw before.

"It was a very aristocratic assembly. I was myself almost the only 'nobody' present.

"My dear child was looking quite beautiful. She wore no mask. Her excitement and delight added an unspeakable charm to her features, always lovely. I remarked a young lady, dressed magnificently, but wearing a mask, who appeared to me to be observing my ward with extraordinary interest. I had seen her, earlier in the evening, in the great hall, and again, for a few minutes, walking near us, on the terrace under the castle windows, similarly employed. A lady, also masked, richly and gravely dressed, and with a stately air, like a person of rank, accompanied her as a chaperon. Had the young lady not worn a mask, I could, of course, have been much more certain upon the question whether she was really watching my poor darling. I am now well assured that she was.

"We were now in one of the *salons.* My poor dear child had been dancing, and was resting a little on one of the chairs near the door; I was standing near. The two ladies I have mentioned had approached, and the younger took the chair next to my ward; while her companion stood beside me, and for a little time addressed herself, in a low tone, to her charge.

"Availing herself of the privilege of her mask she turned to me, and in the tone of an old friend, and calling me by my name, opened a conversation with me, which piqued my curiosity a good deal. She referred to many scenes where she had met me—at Court, and at distinguished houses. She alluded to little incidents which I had long ceased to think of, but which, I found, had only lain in abeyance in my memory, for they instantly started into life at her touch.

"I became more and more curious to ascertain who she was, every moment. She parried my attempts to discover very adroitly and pleasantly. The knowledge she showed of many passages in my life seemed to me all but unaccountable; and she appeared to take a not unnatural pleasure in foiling my curiosity, and in seeing me flounder, in my eager perplexity, from one conjecture to another.

"In the meantime the young lady, whom her mother called by the odd name of Millarca, when she once or twice addressed her, had, with the same ease and grace, got into conversation with my ward.

"She introduced herself by saying that her mother was a very old acquaintance of mine. She spoke of the agreeable audacity which a mask rendered practicable; she talked like a friend; she admired her dress, and insinuated very prettily her admiration of her beauty. She amused her with laughing criticisms upon the people who crowded the ballroom, and laughed at my poor child's fun. She was very witty and lively when she pleased, and after a time they had grown very good friends, and the young stranger lowered her mask, displaying a remarkably beautiful face. I had never seen it before, neither had my dear child. But though it was new to us, the features were so engaging, as well as lovely, that it was impossible not to feel the attraction powerfully. My poor girl did so. I never saw anyone more taken with another at first sight, unless indeed, it was the stranger herself, who seemed quite to have lost her heart to her.

"In the meantime, availing myself of the license of a masquerade, I put not a few questions to the elder lady.

" 'You have puzzled me utterly,' I said, laughing. 'Is that not enough? Won't you, now consent to stand on equal terms, and do me the kindness to remove your mask?'

" 'Can any request be more unreasonable?' she replied. 'Ask a lady to yield an advantage! Besides, how do you know you should recognize me? Years make changes.'

" 'As you see,' I said, with a bow, and, I suppose, a rather melancholy little laugh.

" 'As philosophers tell us,' she said; 'and how do you know that a sight of my face would help you?'

" 'I should take chance for that,' I answered. 'It is vain trying to make yourself out an old woman; your figure betrays you.'

" 'Years, nevertheless, have passed since I saw you, rather since you saw me, for that is what I am considering. Millarca, there, is my daughter; I cannot then be young, even in the opinion of people whom time has taught to be indulgent, and I may not like to be compared with what you remember me. You have no mask to remove. You can offer me nothing in exchange.'

" 'My petition is to your pity, to remove it.'

" 'And mine to yours, to let it stay where it is,' she replied.

" 'Well, then, at least you will tell me whether you are French or German; you speak both languages so perfectly.'

" 'I don't think I shall tell you that, General; you intend a surprise, and are meditating the particular point of attack.'

" 'At all events, you won't deny this,' I said, 'that being honored by your permission to converse, I ought to know how to address you. Shall I say Madame la Comtesse!'

"She laughed, and she would, no doubt, have met me with another evasion—if, indeed, I can treat any occurrence in an interview every circumstance of which was prearranged, as I now believe, with the profoundest cunning, as liable to be modified by accident.

" 'As to that,' she began; but she was interrupted, almost as she opened her lips, by a gentleman, dressed in black, who looked particularly elegant and distinguished, with this drawback, that his face was the most deadly pale I ever saw, except in death. He was in no masquerade—in the plain evening dress of a gentleman; and he said, without a smile, but with a courtly and unusually low bow:

" 'Will Madame la Comtesse permit me to say a very few words which may interest her?'

"The lady turned quickly to him, and touched her lip in token of silence; she then said to me, 'Keep my place for me, General; I shall return when I have said a few words.'

"And with this injunction, playfully given, she walked

a little aside with the gentleman in black, and talked for some minutes, apparently very earnestly. They then walked away slowly together in the crowd, and I lost them for some minutes.

"I spent the interval in cudgelling my brains for conjecture as to the identity of the lady who seemed to remember me so kindly, and I was thinking of turning about and joining in the conversation between my pretty ward and the Countess's daughter, and trying whether, by the time she returned, I might not have a surprise in store for her, by having her name, title, château, and estates at my fingers' ends. But at this moment she returned, accompanied by the pale man in black, who said:

" 'I shall return and inform Madame la Comtesse when her carriage is at the door.'

"He withdrew with a bow."

XII. A PETITION

" 'Then we are to lose Madame la Comtesse, but I hope only for a few hours,' I said, with a low bow.

" 'It may be that only, or it may be a few weeks. It was very unlucky his speaking to me just now as he did. Do you now know me?'

"I assured her I did not.

" 'You shall know me,' she said, 'but not at present. We are older and better friends than, perhaps, you suspect. I cannot yet declare myself. I shall in three weeks pass your beautiful schloss about which I have been making inquiries. I shall then look in upon you for an hour or two, and renew a friendship which I never think of without a thousand pleasant recollections. This moment a piece of news has reached me like a thunderbolt. I must set out now, and travel by a devious route, nearly a hundred miles, with all the dispatch I can possibly make. My perplexities multiply. I am only deterred by the compulsory reserve I practice as to my name from making a very singular request of you. My poor child has not quite recovered her strength. Her horse fell with her, at a hunt which she had ridden out to witness, her nerves have not yet recovered the shock, and our physician says that she must on no account exert herself for some time to come. We came here, in consequence, by very easy stages—hardly six leagues a day. I must now travel day and night on a mission of life and death—a mission the critical and momentous nature of which I shall be able to explain to you when we meet, as I hope we shall, in a few weeks, without the necessity of any concealment.'

"She went on to make her petition, and it was in the tone of a person from whom such a request amounted to conferring, rather than seeking a favor. This only in manner, and, as it seemed, quite unconsciously. Than the terms in which it was expressed, nothing could be more deprecatory. It was simply that I would consent to take charge of her daughter during her absence.

"This was, all things considered, a strange, not to say, an audacious request. She in some sort disarmed me, by stating and admitting everything that could be urged against it, and throwing herself entirely upon my chivalry. At the same moment, by a fatality that seems to have predetermined all that happened, my poor child came to my side, and, in an undertone, besought me to invite her new friend, Millarca, to pay us a visit. She had just been sounding her, and thought, if her mamma would allow her, she would like it extremely.

"At another time I should have told her to wait a little, until, at least, we knew who they were. But I had not a moment to think in. The two ladies assailed me together, and I must confess the refined and beautiful face of the young lady, about which there was something extremely engaging, as well as the elegance and fire of high birth, determined me; and quite overpowered, I submitted, and undertook, too easily, the care of the young lady, whom her mother called Millarca.

"The Countess beckoned to her daughter, who listened with grave attention while she told her, in general terms, how suddenly and peremptorily she had been summoned, and also of the arrangement she had made for her under my care, adding that I was one of her earliest and most valued friends.

"I made, of course, such speeches as the case seemed to call for, and found myself, on reflection, in a position which I did not half like.

"The gentleman in black returned, and very ceremoniously conducted the lady from the room.

"The demeanor of this gentleman was such as to impress me with the conviction that the Countess was a lady of very much more importance than her modest title alone might have led me to assume.

"Her last charge to me was that no attempt was to be made to learn more about her than I might have already guessed, until her return. Our distinguished host, whose guest she was, knew her reasons.

" 'But here,' she said, 'neither I nor my daughter could safely remain for more than a day. I removed my mask imprudently for a moment, about an hour ago, and, too late, I fancied you saw me. So I resolved to seek an opportunity of talking a little to you. Had I found that you *had* seen me, I should have thrown myself on your high sense of honor to keep my secret for some weeks. As it is, I am satisfied that you did not see me; but if you now *suspect*, or, on reflection, *should* suspect, who I am, I commit myself, in like manner, entirely to your honor. My daughter will observe the same secrecy, and I well know that you will, from time to time, remind her, lest she should thoughtlessly disclose it.'

"She whispered a few words to her daughter, kissed her hurriedly twice, and went away, accompanied by the pale gentleman in black, and disappeared in the crowd.

" 'In the next room,' said Millarca, 'there is a window that looks upon the hall door. I should like to see the last of mamma, and to kiss my hand to her.'

"We assented, of course, and accompanied her to the window. We looked out, and saw a handsome old-fashioned carriage, with a troop of couriers and footmen. We saw the slim figure of the pale gentleman in black, as he held a thick velvet cloak, and placed it about her shoulders and threw the hood over her head. She nodded to him, and just touched his hand with hers. He bowed low repeatedly as the door closed, and the carriage began to move.

" 'She is gone,' said Millarca, with a sigh.

" 'She is gone,' I repeated to myself, for the first time—in the hurried moments that had elapsed since my consent—reflecting upon the folly of my act.

" 'She did not look up,' said the young lady, plaintively.

" 'The Countess had taken off her mask, perhaps, and did not care to show her face,' I said; 'and she could not know that you were in the window.'

"She sighed and looked in my face. She was so beautiful that I relented. I was sorry I had for a moment repented of my hospitality, and I determined to make her amends for the unavowed churlishness of my reception.

"The young lady, replacing her mask, joined my ward in persuading me to return to the grounds, where the concert was soon to be renewed. We did so, and walked up and down the terrace that lies under the castle windows. Millarca became very intimate with us, and amused us with lively descriptions and stories of most of the great people whom we saw upon the terrace. I liked her more and more every minute. Her gossip, without being ill-natured, was extremely diverting to me, who had been so long out of the great world. I thought what life she would give to our sometimes lonely evenings at home.

"This ball was not over until the morning sun had almost reached the horizon. It pleased the Grand Duke to dance till then, so loyal people could not go away, or think of bed.

"We had just got through a crowded saloon, when my ward asked me what had become of Millarca. I thought she had been by her side, and she fancied she was by mine. The fact was, we had lost her.

"All my efforts to find her were vain. I feared that she had mistaken, in the confusion of momentary separation from us, other people for her new friends, and had, possibly, pursued and lost them in the extensive grounds which were thrown open to us.

"Now, in its full force, I recognized a new folly in my having undertaken the charge of a young lady without so much as knowing her full name; and fettered as I was by promises, of the reasons for imposing which I knew nothing, I could not even point my inquiries by saying that the missing young lady was the daughter of the Countess who had taken her departure a few hours before.

"Morning broke. It was clear daylight before I gave up my search. It was not till near two o'clock next day that we heard anything of my missing charge.

"At about that time a servant knocked at my niece's door, to say that he had been earnestly requested by a young lady, who appeared to be in great distress, to make out where she could find the General Baron Spielsdorf and the young lady his daughter, in whose charge she had been left by her mother.

"There could be no doubt, notwithstanding the slight inaccuracy, that our young friend had turned up; and so she had. Would to Heaven we had lost her!

"She told my poor child a story to account for her having failed to recover us for so long. Very late, she said, she had got into the housekeeper's bedroom in despair of finding us, and had then fallen into a deep sleep which, long as it was, hardly sufficed to recruit her strength after the fatigues of the ball.

"That day Millarca came home with us. I was only too happy, after all, to have secured so charming a companion for my dear girl."

XIII. THE WOODSMAN

"There soon, however, appeared some drawbacks. In the first place, Millarca complained of extreme languor—the weakness that remained after her late illness—and she never emerged from her room till the afternoon was pretty far advanced. In the next place, it was accidentally discovered, although she always locked her door on the inside, and never disturbed the key from its place, till she admitted the maid to assist at her toilet, that she was undoubtedly sometimes absent from her room in the very early morning, and at various times later in the day, before she wished it to be understood that she was stirring. She was repeatedly seen from the windows of the schloss, in the first faint grey of the morning, walking through the trees, in an easterly direction, and looking like a person in a trance. This convinced me that she walked in her sleep. But this hypothesis did not solve the puzzle. How did she pass out from her room, leaving the door locked on the inside? How did she escape from the house without unbarring door or window?

"In the midst of my perplexities, an anxiety of a far more urgent kind presented itself.

"My dear child began to lose her looks and health, and that in a manner so mysterious, and even horrible, that I became thoroughly frightened.

"She was at first visited by appalling dreams; then, as she fancied, by a specter, something resembling Millarca, sometimes in the shape of a beast, indistinctly seen, walking round the foot of the bed, from side to side. Lastly came sensations. One not unpleasant, but very peculiar, she said, resembled the flow of an icy stream against her breast. At a later time, she felt something like a pair of large needles pierce her, a little below the throat with a very sharp pain. A few nights after, followed a gradual and convulsive sense of strangulation; then came unconsciousness."

I could hear distinctly every word the kind old General was saying, because by this time we were driving upon the short grass that spreads on either side of the road as you approach the roofless village which had not shown the smoke of a chimney for more than half a century.

You may guess how strangely I felt as I heard my own symptoms so exactly described in those which had been experienced by the poor girl who, but for the catastrophe which followed, would have been at that moment a visitor at my father's château. You may suppose, also, how I felt as I heard him detail habits and mysterious peculiarities which were, in fact, those of our beautiful guest, Carmilla!

A vista opened in the forest; we were on a sudden under the chimneys and gables of the ruined village, and the towers and battlements of the dismantled castle, round which gigantic trees are grouped, overhung us from a slight eminence.

In a frightened dream I got down from the carriage, and in silence, for we had each abundant matters for thinking; we soon mounted the ascent, and were among the spacious chambers, winding stairs, and dark corridors of the castle.

"And this was once the palatial residence of the Karnsteins!" said the old General at length, as from a great window he looked out across the village, and saw the wide, undulating expanse of forest. "It was a bad family, and here its bloodstained annals were written," he continued. "It is hard that they should, after death, continue to plague the human race with their atrocious lusts. That is the chapel of the Karnsteins, down there."

He pointed down to the grey walls of the Gothic building, partly visible through the foliage, a little way down the steep. "And I hear the axe of a woodsman," he added, "busy among the trees that surround it; he possibly may give us the information of which I am in search, and point out the grave of Mircalla, Countess of Karnstein. These rustics preserve the local traditions of great families, whose stories die out among the rich and titled so soon as the families themselves become extinct."

"We have a portrait, at home, of Mircalla, the Countess Karnstein; should you like to see it?" asked my father.

"Time enough, dear friend," replied the General. "I believe that I have seen the original; and one motive which has led me to you earlier than I at first intended, was to explore the chapel which we are now approaching."

"What! See the Countess Mircalla," exclaimed my father. "Why, she has been dead more than a century!"

"Not so dead as you fancy, I am told," answered the General.

"I confess, General, you puzzle me utterly," replied my father, looking at him, I fancied, for a moment with a return of the suspicion I detected before. But although there was anger and detestation, at times, in the old General's manner, there was nothing flighty.

"There remains to me," he said, as we passed under the heavy arch of the Gothic church—for its dimensions would have justified its being so styled—"but one object which can interest me during the few years that remain to me on earth, and that is to wreak on her the vengeance which, I thank God, may still be accomplished by a mortal arm."

"What vengeance can you mean?" asked my father, in increasing amazement.

"I mean, to decapitate the monster," he answered, with a fierce flush, and a stamp that echoed mournfully through the hollow ruin, and his clenched hand was at the same moment raised, as if it grasped the handle of an axe, while he shook it ferociously in the air.

"What!" exclaimed my father, more than ever bewildered.

"To strike her head off."

"Cut her head off!"

"Aye, with a hatchet, with a spade, or with anything that can cleave through her murderous throat. You shall hear," he answered, trembling with rage. And hurrying forward he said: "That beam will answer for a seat; your dead child is fatigued; let her be seated, and I will, in a few sentences, close my dreadful story."

The squared block of wood, which lay on the grass-grown pavement of the chapel, formed a bench on which I was very glad to seat myself, and in the meantime the

General called to the woodsman, who had been removing some boughs which leaned upon the old walls; and, axe in hand, the hardy old fellow stood before us.

He could not tell us anything of these monuments; but there was an old man, he said, a ranger of this forest, at present sojourning in the house of the priest, about two miles away, who could point out every monument of the old Karnstein family and, for a trifle, he undertook to bring him back with him, if we would lend him one of our horses, in little more than half-an-hour.

"Have you been long employed about this forest?" asked my father of the old man.

"I have been a woodsman here," he answered in his dialect, "under the forester, all my days; so has my father before me, and so on, as many generations as I can count up. I could show you the very house in the village here, in which my ancestors lived."

"How came the village to be deserted?" asked the General.

"It was troubled by ghosts, sir; several were tracked to their graves, there detected by the usual tests, and extinguished in the usual way, by decapitation, by the stake, and by burning; but not until many of the villagers were killed.

"But after all these proceedings according to law," he continued—"so many graves opened, and so many vampires deprived of their horrible animation—the village was not relieved. But a Moravian nobleman, who happened to be travelling this way, heard how matters were, and being skilled—as many people are in his country—in such affairs, he offered to deliver the village from its tormentor. He did so thus: There being a bright moon that night, he ascended, shortly after sunset, the tower of the chapel here, from whence he could distinctly see the churchyard beneath him; you can see it from that window. From this point he watched until he saw the vampire come out of his grave, and place near it the linen clothes in which he had been folded, and glide away towards the village to plague its inhabitants.

"The stranger, having seen all this, came down from the steeple, took the linen wrappings of the vampire, and carried them up to the top of the tower, which he again mounted. When the vampire returned from his prowlings and missed his clothes, he cried furiously to the Moravian, whom he saw at the summit of the tower, and who, in reply, beckoned him to ascend and take them. Whereupon the vampire, accepting his invitation, began to climb the steeple, and so soon as he had reached the battlements, the Moravian, with a stroke of his sword, split his skull in two, hurling him down to the churchyard, whither, descending by the winding stairs, the stranger followed and cut his head off, and next day delivered it and the body to the villagers, who duly impaled and burnt them.

"This Moravian nobleman had authority from the then head of the family to remove the tomb of Mircalla, Countess Karnstein, which he did effectually, so that in a little while its site was quite forgotten."

"Can you point out where it stood?" asked the General, eagerly.

The forester shook his head and smiled.

"Not a soul living could tell you that now," he said. "Besides they say her body was removed; but no one is sure of that either."

Having thus spoken, as time pressed, he dropped his axe and departed, leaving us to hear the remainder of the General's strange story.

XIV. THE MEETING

"My beloved child," he resumed, "was now growing rapidly worse. The physician who attended her had failed to produce the slightest impression upon her disease, for such I then supposed it to be. He saw my alarm, and suggested a consultation. I called in an abler physician, from Gratz. Several days elapsed before he arrived. He was a good and pious, as well as a learned man. Having seen my poor ward together, they withdrew to my library to confer and discuss. I, from the adjoining room, where I awaited their summons, heard these two gentlemen's voices raised in something sharper than a strictly philosophical discussion. I knocked at the door and entered. I found the old physician from Gratz maintaining his theory. His rival was combating it with undisguised ridicule, accompanied with bursts of laughter. This unseemly manifestation subsided and the altercation ended on my entrance.

" 'Sir,' said my first physician, 'my learned brother seems to think that you want a conjuror, and not a doctor.'

" 'Pardon me,' said the old physician from Gratz, looking displeased. 'I shall state my own view of the case in my own way another time. I grieve, Monsieur le Général, that by my skill and science I can be of no use. Before I go I shall do myself the honor to suggest something to you.'

"He seemed thoughtful, and sat down at a table, and began to write. Profoundly disappointed, I made my bow, and as I turned to go, the other doctor pointed over his shoulder to his companion who was writing, and then, with a shrug, significantly touched his forehead.

"This consultation, then, left me precisely where I was. I walked out into the grounds, all but distracted. The doctor from Gratz, in ten or fifteen minutes, overtook me. He apologized for having followed me, but said that he could not conscientiously take his leave without a few words more. He told me that he could not be mistaken; no natural disease exhibited the same symptoms; and that death was already very near. There remained, however, a day, or possibly two, of life. If the fatal seizure were at once arrested, with great care and skill her strength might possibly return. But all hung now upon the confines of the irrevocable. One more assault might extinguish the last spark of vitality which is, every moment, ready to die.

" 'And what is the nature of the seizure you speak of?' I entreated.

" 'I have stated all fully in this note, which I place in your hands, upon the distinct condition that you send for the nearest clergyman, and open my letter in his presence, and on no account read it till he is with you; you would despise it else, and it is a matter of life and death. Should the priest fail you, then, indeed, you may read it.'

"He asked me, before taking his leave finally, whether I would wish to see a man curiously learned upon the very subject, which, after I had read his letter, would probably interest me above all others, and he urged me earnestly to invite him to visit him there; and so took his leave.

"The ecclesiastic was absent, and I read the letter by myself. At another time, or in another case, it might have excited my ridicule. But into what quackeries will not people rush for a last chance, where all accustomed means have failed, and the life of a beloved object is at stake?

"Nothing, you will say, could be more absurd than the learned man's letter. It was monstrous enough to have consigned him to a madhouse. He said that the patient was suffering from the visits of a vampire! The punctures which she described as having occurred near the throat, were, he insisted, the insertion of those two long, thin, and sharp teeth which, it is well known, are peculiar to vampires; and there could be no doubt, he added, as to the well-defined presence of the small livid mark which all concurred in describing as that induced by the demon's lips, and every symptom described by the sufferer was in exact conformity with those recorded in every case of a similar visitation.

"Being myself wholly skeptical as to the existence of any such portent as the vampire, the supernatural theory of the good doctor furnished, in my opinion, but another instance of learning and intelligence oddly associated with some hallucination. I was so miserable, however, that, rather than try nothing, I acted upon the instructions of the letter.

"I concealed myself in the dark dressing-room, that opened upon the poor patient's room, in which a candle was burning, and watched there till she was fast asleep. I stood at the door, peeping through the small crevice, my sword laid on the table beside me, as my directions prescribed, until, a little after one, I saw a large black object, very ill-defined, crawl, as it seemed to me, over the foot of the bed, and swiftly spread itself up to the poor girl's throat, where it swelled, in a moment, into a great, palpitating mass.

"For a few moments I had stood petrified. I now sprang forward, with my sword in my hand. The black creature suddenly contracted toward the foot of the bed, glided over it, and, standing on the floor about a yard below the foot of the bed, with a glare of skulking ferocity and horror fixed on me, I saw Millarca. Speculating I know not what, I struck at her instantly with my sword; but I saw her standing near the door, unscathed. Horrified, I pursued, and struck again. She was gone! And my sword flew to splinters against the door.

"I can't describe to you all that passed on that horrible night. The whole house was up and stirring. The specter

Millarca was gone. But her victim was sinking fast, and before the morning dawned, she died."

The old General was agitated. We did not speak to him. My father walked to some little distance, and began reading the inscriptions on the tombstones; and thus occupied, he strolled into the door of a side chapel to pursue his researches. The General leaned against the wall, dried his eyes, and sighed heavily. I was relieved on hearing the voices of Carmilla and Madame, who were at that moment approaching. The voices died away.

In this solitude, having just listened to so strange a story, connected, as it was, with the great and titled dead, whose monuments were moldering amongst the dust and ivy round us, and every incident of which bore so awfully upon my own mysterious case—in this haunted spot, darkened by the towering foliage that rose on every side, dense and high above its noiseless walls—a horror began to steal over me, and my heart sank as I thought that my friends were, after all, now about to enter and disturb this sad and ominous scene.

The old General's eyes were fixed on the ground, as he leaned with his hand upon the basement of a shattered monument.

Under a narrow, arched doorway, surmounted by one of those demoniacal grotesques in which the cynical and ghastly fancy of old Gothic carving delights, I saw very gladly the beautiful face and figure of Carmilla enter the shadowy chapel.

I was just about to rise and speak, and nodded smiling, in answer to her peculiarly engaging smile; when, with a cry, the old man by my side caught up the woodsman's hatchet, and started forward. On seeing him a brutalized change came over her features. It was an instantaneous and horrible transformation, as she made a crouching step backwards. Before I could utter a scream, he struck at her with all his force, but she dived under his blow, and unscathed, caught him in her tiny grasp by the wrist. He struggled for a moment to release his arm, but his hand opened, the axe fell to the ground, and the girl was gone.

He staggered against the wall. His grey hair stood upon his head, and a moisture shone over his face, as if he were at the point of death.

The frightful scene had passed in a moment. The first thing I recollect after, is Madame standing before me, and impatiently repeating again and again, the question, "Where is Mademoiselle Carmilla?"

I answered at length, "I don't know—I can't tell—she went there," and I pointed to the door through which Madame had just entered, "only a minute or two since."

"But I have been standing there, in the passage, ever since Mademoiselle Carmilla entered; and she did not return."

She then began to call "Carmilla" through every door and passage and from the windows, but no answer came.

"She called herself Carmilla?" asked the General, still agitated.

"Carmilla, yes," I answered.

"Aye," he said, "that is Millarca. That is the same person who long ago was called Mircalla, Countess Karnstein. Depart from this accursed ground, my poor child, as quickly as you can. Drive to the clergyman's house, and stay there till we come. Begone! May you never behold Carmilla more; you will not find her here."

XV. ORDEAL AND EXECUTION

As he spoke, one of the strangest-looking men I ever beheld entered the chapel at the door through which

Carmilla had made her entrance and her exit. He was tall, narrow-chested, stooping, with high shoulders, and dressed in black. His face was brown and dried in with deep furrows; he wore an oddly-shaped hat with a broad leaf. His hair, long and grizzled, hung on his shoulders. He wore a pair of gold spectacles, and walked slowly, with an odd shambling gait, and his face sometimes turned up to the sky, and sometimes bowed down toward the ground, seemed to wear a perpetual smile; his long thin arms were swinging, and his lank hands, in old black gloves ever so much too wide for them, waving and gesticulating in utter abstraction.

"The very man!" exclaimed the General, advancing with manifest delight. "My dear Baron, how happy I am to see you, I had no hope of meeting you so soon." He signed to my father, who had by this time returned, and leading the fantastic old gentleman, whom he called the Baron, to meet him. He introduced him formally, and they at once entered into earnest conversation. The stranger took a roll of paper from his pocket, and spread it on the worn surface of a tomb that stood by. He had a pencil case in his fingers, with which he traced imaginary lines from point to point on the paper, which from their often glancing from it, together, at certain points of the building, I concluded to be a plan of the chapel. He accompanied, what I may term his lecture, with occasional readings from a dirty little book, whose yellow leaves were closely written over.

They sauntered together down the side aisle, opposite to the spot where I was standing, conversing as they went; then they began measuring distances by paces, and finally they all stood together, facing a piece of the side-wall, which they began to examine with great minuteness; pulling off the ivy that clung over it, and rapping the plaster with the ends of their sticks, scraping here, and knocking there. At length they ascertained the existence of a broad marble tablet, with letters carved in relief upon it.

With the assistance of the woodsman, who soon returned, a monument inscription, and carved escutcheon, were disclosed. They proved to be those of the long lost monument of Mircalla, Countess Karnstein.

The old General, though not I fear given to the praying mood, raised his hand and eyes to heaven, in mute thanksgiving for some moments.

"Tomorrow," I heard him say; "the commissioner will be here, and the Inquisition will be held according to law."

Then turning to the old man with the gold spectacles, whom I have described, he shook him warmly by both hands and said:

"Baron, how can I thank you? How can we all thank you? You will have delivered this region from a plague that has scourged its inhabitants for more than a century. The horrible enemy, thank God, is at last tracked."

My father led the stranger aside, and the General followed. I knew that he had led them out of hearing, that he might relate my case, and I saw them glance often quickly at me, as the discussion proceeded.

My father came to me, kissed me again and again, and leading me from the chapel, said:

"It is time to return, but before we go home, we must add to our party the good priest, who lives but a little way from this; and persuade him to accompany us to the schloss."

In this quest we were successful: and I was glad, being unspeakably fatigued when we reached home. But my satisfaction was changed to dismay, on discovering that there were no tidings of Carmilla. Of the scene that had occurred in the ruined chapel, no explanation was offered to me, and it was clear that it was a secret which my father for the present determined to keep from me.

The sinister absence of Carmilla made the remembrance of the scene more horrible to me. The arrangements for that night were singular. Two servants and Madame were to sit up in my room that night; and the ecclesiastic with my father kept watch in the adjoining dressing-room.

The priest had performed certain solemn rites that night, the purport of which I did not understand any more than I comprehended the reason of this extraordinary precaution taken for my safety during sleep.

I saw all clearly a few days later.

The disappearance of Carmilla was followed by the discontinuance of my nightly sufferings.

You have heard, no doubt, of the appalling superstition that prevails in Upper and Lower Styria, in Moravia, Silesia, in Turkish Serbia, in Poland, even in Russia; the superstition, so we must call it, of the vampire.

If human testimony, taken with every care and solemnity, judicially, before commissions innumerable, each consisting of many members, all chosen for integrity and intelligence, and constituting reports more voluminous perhaps than exist upon any one other class of cases, is worth anything, it is difficult to deny, or even to doubt the existence of such a phenomenon as the vampire.

For my part I have heard no theory by which to explain what I myself have witnessed and experienced other than that supplied by the ancient and well-attested belief of the country.

The next day the formal proceedings took place in the Chapel of Karnstein. The grave of the Countess Mircalla was opened; and the General and my father recognized each his perfidious and beautiful guest, in the face now disclosed to view. The features, though a hundred and fifty years had passed since her funeral, were tinted with the warmth of life. Her eyes were open; no cadaverous smell exhaled from the coffin. The two medical men, one officially present, the other on the part of the promoter of the inquiry, attested the marvelous fact, that there was a faint but appreciable respiration, and a corresponding action of the heart. The limbs were perfectly flexible, the flesh elastic; and the leaden coffin floated with blood, in which to a depth of seven inches, the body lay immersed. Here then, were all the admitted signs and proofs of vampirism. The body, therefore, in accordance with the ancient practice, was raised, and a sharp stake driven through the heart of the vampire, who uttered a piercing shriek at the moment, in all respects such as might escape from a living person in the last agony. Then the head was struck off, and a torrent of blood flowed from the severed neck. The body and head were next placed on a pile of wood, and reduced to ashes, which were thrown upon the river and borne away, and that territory has never since been plagued by the visits of a vampire.

My father has a copy of the report of the Imperial Commission with the signatures of all who were present at these proceedings attached in verification of the statement. It is from this official paper that I have summarized my account of this last shocking scene.

XVI. CONCLUSION

I write all this you suppose with composure. But far from it; I cannot think of it without agitation. Nothing but your earnest desire so repeatedly expressed, could have induced me to sit down to a task that has unstrung my nerves for months to come, and reinduced a shadow of the unspeakable horror which years after my deliverance continued to make my days and nights dreadful, and solitude insupportably terrific.

Let me add a word or two about that quaint Baron Vordenburg, to whose curious lore we were indebted for the discovery of the Countess Mircalla's grave.

He had taken up his abode in Gratz, where, living upon a mere pittance, which was all that remained to him of the once princely estates of his family, in Upper Styria, he devoted himself to the minute and laborious investigation of the marvelously authenticated tradition of vampirism. He had at his fingers' ends all the great and little works upon the subject. *Magia Posthuma, Phlegon de Mirabilibus, Augustinus de curâ pro Mortuis, Philosophicae et Christianae Cogitationes de Vampiris*, by John Christofer Herenberg; and a thousand others, among which I remember only a few of those which he lent to my father. He had a voluminous digest of all the judicial cases, from which he had extracted a system of principles that appear to govern—some always, and others occasionally only—the condition of the vampire. I may mention, in passing, that the deadly pallor attributed to that sort of *revenants*, is a mere melodramatic fiction. They present, in the grave, and when they show themselves in human society, the appearance of healthy life. When disclosed to light in their coffins, they exhibit all the symptoms that are enumerated as those which proved the vampire-life of the long-dead Countess Karnstein.

How they escape from their graves and return to them for certain hours every day, without displacing the clay or leaving any trace of disturbance in the state of the coffin or the cerements, has always been admitted to be utterly inexplicable. The amphibious existence of the vampire is sustained by daily renewed slumber in the grave. Its horrible lust for living blood supplies the vigor of its waking existence. The vampire is prone to be fascinated with an engrossing vehemence, resembling the passion of love, by particular persons. In pursuit of these it will exercise inexhaustible patience and stratagem, for access to a particular object may be obstructed in a hundred ways. It will never desist until it has satiated its passion, and drained the very life of its coveted victim. But it will, in these cases, husband and protract its murderous enjoyment with the refinement of an epicure, and heighten it by the gradual approaches of an artful courtship. In these cases it seems to yearn for something like sympathy and consent. In ordinary ones it goes direct to its object, overpowers with violence, and strangles and exhausts often at a single feast.

The vampire is, apparently, subject, in certain situations, to special conditions. In the particular instance of which I have given you a relation, Mircalla seemed to be limited to a name which, if not her real one, should at least reproduce, without the omission or addition of a single letter, those, as we say, anagrammatically, which compose it. *Carmilla* did this; so did *Millarca.*

My father related to the Baron Vordenburg, who remained with us for two or three weeks after the expulsion of Carmilla, the story about the Moravian nobleman and the vampire at Karnstein churchyard, and then he asked the Baron how he had discovered the exact position of the long-concealed tomb of the Countess Millarca. The Baron's grotesque features puckered up into a mysterious smile; he looked down, still smiling, on his worn spectacle-case and fumbled with it. Then looking up, he said:

"I have many journals, and other papers, written by that remarkable man; the most curious among them is one treating of the visit of which you speak, to Karnstein. The tradition, of course, discolors and distorts a little. He might have been termed a Moravian nobleman, for he had changed his bode to that territory, and was, beside, a noble. But he was, in truth, a native of Upper Styria. It is enough to say that in very early youth he had been a passionate and favored lover of the beautiful Mircalla, Countess Karnstein. Her early death plunged him into inconsolable grief. It is the nature of vampires to increase and multiply, but according to an ascertained and ghostly law.

"Assume, at starting, a territory perfectly free from that pest. How does it begin, and how does it multiply itself? I will tell you. A person, more or less wicked, puts an end to himself. A suicide, under certain circumstances, becomes a vampire. That specter visits living people in their slumbers; *they* die, and almost invariably, in the grave develop into vampires. This happened in the case of the beautiful Mircalla, who was haunted by one of those demons. My ancestor, Vordenburg, whose title I still bear, soon discovered this, and in the course of the studies to which he devoted himself, learned a great deal more.

"Among other things, he concluded that suspicion of vampirism would probably fall, sooner or later, upon the dead Countess, who in life had been his idol. He conceived a horror, be she what she might, of her remains being profaned by the outrage of a posthumous execution. He has left a curious paper to prove that the vampire, on its expulsion from its amphibious existence, is projected into a far more horrible life; and he resolved to save his once beloved Mircalla from this.

"He adopted the stratagem of a journey here, a pretended removal of her remains, and a real obliteration of her monument. When age had stolen upon him, and from the vale of years he looked back on the scenes he was leaving, he considered, in a different spirit, what he had done, and a horror took possession of him. He made the tracings and notes which have guided me to the very spot, and drew up a confession of the deception that he had practiced. If he had intended any further action in this matter, death prevented him; and the hand of a remote descendant has, too late for many, directed the pursuit to the lair of the beast."

We talked a little more, and among other things he said was this:

"One sign of the vampire is the power of the hand. The slender hand of Mircalla closed like a vise of steel on the General's wrist when he raised the hatchet to strike. But its power is not confined to its grasp; it leaves a numbness in the limb it seizes, which is slowly, if ever, recovered from."

The following Spring my father took me on a tour through Italy. We remained away for more than a year. It was long before the terror of recent events subsided; and to this hour the image of Carmilla returns to memory with ambiguous alternations—sometimes the playful, languid, beautiful girl; sometimes the writhing fiend I saw in the ruined church; and often from a reverie I have started, fancying I heard the light step of Carmilla at the drawing-room door.

THE SAD STORY OF A VAMPIRE

◆◆◆

ERIC (COUNT) STENBOCK

Vampire stories are generally located in Styria; mine is also. Styria is by no means the romantic kind of place described by those who have certainly never been there. It is a flat, uninteresting country, only celebrated by its turkeys, its capons, and the stupidity of its inhabitants. Vampires generally arrive at night, in carriages drawn by two black horses.

Our Vampire arrived by the commonplace means of the railway train, and in the afternoon. You must think I am joking, or perhaps that by the word "Vampire" I mean a financial vampire. No, I am quite serious. The Vampire of whom I am speaking, who laid waste our hearth and home, was a *real* vampire.

Vampires are generally described as dark, sinister-looking, and singularly handsome. Our Vampire was, on the contrary, rather fair, and certainly was not at first sight sinister-looking, and though decidedly attractive in appearance, not what one would call singularly handsome.

Yes, he desolated our home, killed my brother—the one object of my adoration—also my dear father. Yet, at the same time, I must say that I myself came under the spell of his fascination, and, in spite of all, have no ill-will towards him now.

Doubtless you have read in the papers *passim* of "the

Baroness and her beasts." It is to tell how I came to spend most of my useless wealth on an asylum for stray animals that I am writing this.

I am old now; what happened then was when I was a little girl of about thirteen. I will begin by describing our household. We were Poles; our name was Wronski: we lived in Styria, where we had a castle. Our household was very limited. It consisted, with the exclusion of domestics, of only my father, our governess—a worthy Belgian named Mademoiselle Vonnaert—my brother, and myself. Let me begin with my father: he was old, and both my brother and I were children of his old age. Of my mother I remember nothing: she died in giving birth to my brother, who is only one year, or not as much, younger than myself. Our father was studious, continually occupied in reading books, chiefly on recondite subjects and in all kinds of unknown languages. He had a long white beard, and wore habitually a black velvet skull-cap.

How kind he was to us! It was more than I could tell. Still it was not I who was the favorite. His whole heart went out to Gabriel—"Gabryel" as we spelled it in Polish. He was always called by the Russian abbreviation Gavril—I mean, of course, my brother, who had a resemblance to the only portrait of my mother, a slight chalk sketch which hung in my father's study. But I was by no means jealous: my brother was and has been the only love of my life. It is for his sake that I am now keeping in Westbourne Park a home for stray cats and dogs.

I was at that time, as I said before, a little girl; my name was Carmela. My long tangled hair was always all over the place, and never would be combed straight. I was not pretty—at least, looking at a photograph of me at that time, I do not think I could describe myself as such. Yet at the same time, when I look at the photograph, I think my expression may have been pleasing to some people: irregular features, large mouth, and large wild eyes.

I was by way of being naughty—not so naughty as Gabriel in the opinion of Mlle. Vonnaert. Mlle. Vonnaert, I may interpose, was a wholly excellent person, middle-aged, who really *did* speak good French, although she was a Belgian, and could also make herself understood in German, which, as you may or may not know, is the current language of Styria.

I find it difficult to describe my brother Gabriel; there was something about him strange and superhuman, or perhaps I should rather say praeter-human, something between the animal and the divine. Perhaps the Greek idea of the Faun might illustrate what I mean; but that will not do either. He had large, wild, gazelle-like eyes: his hair, like mine, was in a perpetual tangle—that point he had in common with me, and indeed, as I afterwards heard, our mother having been of gypsy race, it will account for much of the innate wildness there was in our natures. I was wild enough, but Gabriel was much wilder. Nothing would induce him to put on shoes and socks, except on Sundays—when he also allowed his hair to be combed, but only by me. How shall I describe the grace of that lovely mouth, shaped verily "en arc d'amour." I always think of the text in the Psalm, "Grace is shed forth on thy lips, therefore has God blessed thee eternally"—lips that seemed to exhale the very breath of life. Then that beautiful, lithe, living, elastic form!

He could run faster than any deer: spring like a squirrel to the topmost branch of a tree: he might have stood for the sign and symbol of vitality itself. But seldom could he be induced by Mlle. Vonnaert to learn lessons; but when he did so, he learned with extraordinary quickness. He would play upon every conceivable instrument, holding a violin here, there, and everywhere except the right place: manufacturing instruments for himself out of reeds—even sticks. Mlle. Vonnaert made futile efforts to induce him to learn to play the piano. I suppose he was what was called spoiled, though merely in the superficial sense of the word. Our father allowed him to indulge in every caprice.

One of his peculiarities, when quite a little child, was horror at the sight of meat. Nothing on earth would induce him to taste it. Another thing which was particularly remarkable about him was his extraordinary power over animals. Everything seemed to come tame to his hand. Birds would sit on his shoulder. Then sometimes Mlle. Vonnaert and I would lose him in the woods—he would suddenly dart away. Then we would find him singing softly or whistling to himself, with all manner of woodland creatures around him—hedgehogs, little foxes, wild rabbits, marmots, squirrels, and such like. He would frequently bring these things home with him and insist on keeping them. This strange menagerie was the terror of poor Mlle. Vonnaert's heart. He chose to live in a little room at the top of a turret; but which, instead of going upstairs, he chose to reach by means of a very tall chestnut tree, through the window. But in contradiction to all this, it was his custom to serve every Sunday Mass in the parish church, with hair nicely combed and with white surplice and red cassock. He looked as demure and tamed as possible. Then came the element of the divine. What an expression of ecstasy there was in those glorious eyes!

Thus far I have not been speaking about the Vampire. However, let me begin with my narrative at last. One day my father had to go to the neighboring town—as he frequently had. This time he returned accompanied by a guest. The gentleman, he said, had missed his train, through the late arrival of another at our station, which was a junction, and he would therefore, as trains were not frequent in our parts, have had to wait there all night. He had joined in conversation with my father in the too-late-arriving train from the town: and had consequently accepted my father's invitation to stay the night at our house. But of course, you know, in those out-of-the-way parts we are almost patriarchal in our hospitality.

He was announced under the name of Count Vardalek—the name being Hungarian. But he spoke German well enough: not with the monotonous accentuation of Hungarians, but rather, if anything, with a slight Slavonic intonation. His voice was peculiarly soft and insinuating. We soon afterwards found out he could talk Polish, and Mlle. Vonnaert vouched for his good French. Indeed he seemed to know all languages. But let me give my first impressions. He was rather tall, with fair wavy hair, rather long, which accentuated a certain effeminacy about his smooth face. His figure had something—I cannot say what—serpentine about it. The features were refined; and he had long, slender, subtle, magnetic-looking hands, a somewhat long sinuous nose, a graceful mouth, and an attractive smile, which belied the intense sadness of the expression of the eyes. When he arrived his eyes were half closed—indeed they were habitually so—so that I could not decide their color. He looked worn and wearied. I could not possibly guess his age.

Suddenly Gabriel burst into the room: a yellow butterfly was clinging to his hair. He was carrying in his arms a little squirrel. Of course he was bare-legged as usual. The stranger looked up at his approach; then I noticed his eyes. They were green: they seemed to dilate and grow larger. Gabriel stood stock-still, with a startled look, like that of a bird fascinated by a serpent. But nevertheless he held out his hand to the newcomer. Vardalek, taking his hand—I don't know why I noticed this trivial thing—pressed the pulse with his forefinger. Suddenly Gabriel darted from the room and rushed upstairs, going to his turret-room this time by the staircase instead of the tree. I was in terror what the Count might think of him. Great was my relief when he came down in his velvet Sunday suit, and shoes and stockings. I combed his hair, and set him generally right.

When the stranger came down to dinner his appearance had somewhat altered; he looked much younger. There was an elasticity of the skin, combined with a delicate complexion, rarely to be found in a man. Before, he had struck me as being very pale.

Well, at dinner we were all charmed with him, especially my father. He seemed to be thoroughly acquainted with all my father's particular hobbies. Once, when my father was relating some of his military experiences, he said something about a drummer-boy who was wounded in battle. His eyes opened completely again and dilated: this time with a particularly disagreeable expression, dull and dead, yet at the same time animated by some horrible excitement. But this was only momentary.

The chief subject of his conversation with my father was about certain curious mystical books which my father had just lately picked up, and which he could not make out, but Vardalek seemed completely to understand. At dessert-time my father asked him if he were in a great hurry to reach his destination: if not, would he not stay with us a little while: though our place was out of the way, he would find much that would interest him in his library.

He answered, "I am in no hurry. I have no particular reason for going to that place at all, and if I can be of service to you in deciphering these books, I shall be only too glad." He added with a smile which was bitter, very very bitter:

"You see I am a cosmopolitan, a wanderer on the face of the earth."

After dinner my father asked him if he played the piano. He said, "Yes, I can a little," and he sat down at the piano. Then he played a Hungarian csardas—wild, rhapsodic, wonderful.

That is the music which makes men mad. He went on in the same strain.

Gabriel stood stock-still by the piano, his eyes dilated and fixed, his form quivering. At last he said very slowly, at one particular motive—for want of a better word you may call it the *relâche* of a csardas, by which I mean that point where the original quasi-slow movement begins again—"Yes, I think I could play that."

Then he quickly fetched his fiddle and self-made xylophone, and did actually, alternating the instruments, render the same very well indeed.

Vardalek looked at him, and said in a very sad voice, "Poor child! You have the soul of music within you."

I could not understand why he should seem to commiserate instead of congratulate Gabriel on what certainly showed an extraordinary talent.

Gabriel was shy even as the wild animals who were tame to him. Never before had he taken to a stranger. Indeed, as a rule, if any stranger came to the house by any chance, he would hide himself, and I had to bring him up his food to the turret chamber. You may imagine what was my surprise when I saw him walking about hand in hand with Vardalek the next morning, in the garden, talking livelily with him, and showing his collection of pet animals, which he had gathered from the woods, and for which we had had to fit up a regular zoological gardens. He seemed utterly under the domination of Vardalek. What surprised us was (for otherwise we liked the stranger, especially for being kind to him) that he seemed, though not noticeably at first—except perhaps to me, who noticed everything with regard to him—to be gradually losing his general health and vitality. He did not become pale as yet; but there was a certain languor about his movements which certainly there was by no means before.

My father got more and more devoted to Count Vardalek. He helped him in his studies: and my father would hardly allow him to go away, which he did sometimes—to Trieste, he said: he always came back, bringing us presents of strange Oriental jewelry or textures.

I knew all kinds of people came to Trieste, Orientals included. Still, there was a strangeness and magnificence about these things which I was sure even then could not possibly have come from such a place as Trieste, memorable to me chiefly for its necktie shops.

When Vardalek was away, Gabriel was continually asking for him and talking about him. Then at the same time he seemed to regain his old vitality and spirits. Vardalek always returned looking much older, wan, and weary. Gabriel would rush to meet him, and kiss him on the mouth. Then he gave a slight shiver: and after a little while began to look quite young again.

Things continued like this for some time. My father would not hear of Vardalek's going away permanently. He came to be an inmate of our house. I indeed, and Mlle. Vonnaert also, could not help noticing what a difference there was altogether about Gabriel. But my father seemed totally blind to it.

One night I had gone downstairs to fetch something

which I had left in the drawing-room. As I was going up again I passed Vardalek's room. He was playing on a piano, which had been specially put there for him, one of Chopin's nocturnes, very beautifully: I stopped, leaning on the banisters to listen.

Something white appeared on the dark staircase. We believed in ghosts in our part. I was transfixed with terror, and clung to the banisters. What was my astonishment to see Gabriel walking slowly down the staircase, his eyes fixed as though in a trance! This terrified me even more than a ghost would. Could I believe my senses? Could that be Gabriel?

I simply could not move. Gabriel, clad in his long white nightshirt, came downstairs and opened the door. He left it open. Vardalek still continued playing, but talked as he played.

He said—this time speaking in Polish—*Nie umiem wyrazic jak ceihie kocham*—"My darling, I fain would spare thee; but thy life is my life, and I must live, I who would rather die. Will God not have *any* mercy on me? Oh! oh! life; oh the torture of life!" Here he struck one agonized and strange chord, then continued playing softly, "O Gabriel, my beloved! My life, yes *life*—oh, why life? I am sure this is but a little that I demand of thee. Surely thy superabundance of life can spare a little to one who is already dead. No, stay," he said now almost harshly, "what must be, must be!"

Gabriel stood there quite still, with the same fixed vacant expression, in the room. He was evidently walking in his sleep. Vardalek played on: then said, "Ah!" with a sigh of terrible agony. Then very gently, "Go now, Gabriel; it is enough." And Gabriel went out of the room and ascended the staircase at the same slow pace, with the same unconscious stare. Vardalek struck the piano, and although he did not play loudly, it seemed as though the strings would break. You never heard music so strange and so heart-rending!

I only know I was found by Mlle. Vonnaert in the morning, in an unconscious state, at the foot of the stairs. Was it a dream after all? I am sure now that it was not. I thought then it might be, and said nothing to any one about it. Indeed, what could I say?

Well, to let me cut a long story short, Gabriel, who had never known a moment's sickness in his life, grew ill: and we had to send to Gratz for a doctor, who could give no explanation of Gabriel's strange illness. Gradual wasting away, he said: absolutely no organic complaint. What could this mean?

My father at last became conscious of the fact that Gabriel was ill. His anxiety was fearful. The last trace of grey faded from his hair, and it became quite white. We sent to Vienna for doctors. But all with the same result.

Gabriel was generally unconscious, and when conscious, only seemed to recognize Vardalek, who sat continually by his bedside, nursing him with the utmost tenderness.

One day I was alone in the room: and Vardalek cried suddenly, almost fiercely, "Send for a priest at once, at once," he repeated. "It is now almost too late!"

Gabriel stretched out his arms spasmodically, and put them round Vardalek's neck. This was the only movement he had made for some time. Vardalek bent down and kissed him on the lips. I rushed downstairs: and the priest was sent for. When I came back Vardalek was not there. The priest administered extreme unction. I think Gabriel was already dead, although we did not think so at the time.

Vardalek had utterly disappeared; and when we looked for him he was nowhere to be found; nor have I seen or heard of him since.

My father died very soon afterwards: suddenly aged, and bent down with grief. And so the whole of the Wronski property came into my sole possession. And here I am, an old woman, generally laughed at for keeping, in memory of Gabriel, an asylum for stray animals—and—people do not, as a rule, believe in Vampires!

NECROS

✦✦✦

BRIAN LUMLEY

I

An old woman in a faded blue frock and black head-square paused in the shade of Mario's awning and nodded good-day. She smiled a gap-toothed smile. A bulky, slouch-shouldered youth in jeans and a stained yellow T-shirt—a slope-headed idiot, probably her grandson—held her hand, drooling vacantly and fidgeting beside her.

Mario nodded good-naturedly, smiled, wrapped a piece of stale *fucaccia* in greaseproof paper and came from behind the bar to give it to her. She clasped his hand, thanked him, turned to go.

Her attention was suddenly arrested by something she saw across the road. She started, cursed vividly, harshly, and despite my meager knowledge of Italian I picked up something of the hatred in her tone. "Devil's spawn!" She said it again. "Dog! Swine!" She pointed a shaking hand and finger, said yet again: "Devil's spawn!" before making the two-fingered, double-handed stabbing sign with which the Italians ward off evil. To do this it was first necessary that she drop her salted bread, which the idiot youth at once snatched up.

Then, still mouthing low, guttural imprecations, dragging the shuffling, *fucaccia*-munching cretin behind her, she hurried off along the street and disappeared into an alley. One word that she had repeated over and over again stayed in my mind: *"Necros! Necros!"* Though the word was new to me, I took it for a curse-word. The accent she put on it had been poisonous.

I sipped at my Negroni, remained seated at the small circular table beneath Mario's awning and stared at the object of the crone's distaste. It was a motorcar, a white convertible Rover and this year's model, inching slowly forward in a stream of holiday traffic. And it was worth looking at it only for the girl behind the wheel. The little man in the floppy white hat beside her—well, he was something else, too. But *she* was—just something else.

I caught just a glimpse, sufficient to feel stunned. That was good. I had thought it was something I could never know again: that feeling a man gets looking at a beautiful girl. Not after Linda. And yet—

She was young, say twenty-four or -five, some three or four years my junior. She sat tall at the wheel, slim, raven-haired under a white, wide-brimmed summer hat which just missed matching that of her companion, with a complexion cool and creamy enough to pour over peaches. I stood up—yes, to get a better look—and right then the traffic came to a momentary standstill. At that moment, too, she turned her head and looked at me. And if the profile had stunned me . . . well, the full frontal knocked me dead. The girl was simply, classically, beautiful.

Her eyes were of a dark green but very bright, slightly tilted and perfectly oval under straight, thin brows. Her cheeks were high, her lips a red Cupid's bow, her neck long and white against the glowing yellow of her blouse. And her smile—

—Oh, yes, she smiled.

Her glance, at first cool, became curious in a moment,

then a little angry, until finally, seeing my confusion—that smile. And as she turned her attention back to the road and followed the stream of traffic out of sight, I saw a blush of color spreading on the creamy surface of her cheek. Then she was gone.

Then, too, I remembered the little man who sat beside her. Actually, I hadn't seen a great deal of him, but what I had seen had given me the creeps. He too had turned his head to stare at me, leaving in my mind's eye an impression of beady bird eyes, sharp and intelligent in the shade of his hat. He had stared at me for only a moment, and then his head had slowly turned away; but even when he no longer looked at me, when he stared straight ahead, it seemed to me I could feel those raven's eyes upon me, and that a query had been written in them.

I believed I could understand it, that look. He must have seen a good many young men staring at him like that—or rather, at the girl. His look had been a threat in answer to my threat—and because he was practiced in it I had certainly felt the more threatened!

I turned to Mario, whose English was excellent. "She has something against expensive cars and rich people?"

"Who?" he busied himself behind his bar.

"The old lady, the woman with the idiot boy."

"Ah!" he nodded. "Mainly against the little man, I suspect."

"Oh?"

"You want another Negroni?"

"Okay—and one for yourself—but tell me about this other thing, won't you?"

"If you like—but you're only interested in the girl, yes?" He grinned.

I shrugged. "She's a good-looker . . ."

"Yes, I saw her." Now he shrugged. "That other thing—just old myths and legends, that's all. Like your English Dracula, eh?"

"Transylvanian Dracula," I corrected him.

"Whatever you like. And Necros: that's the name of the spook, see?"

"Necros is the name of a vampire?"

"A spook, yes."

"And this is a real legend? I mean, historical?"

He made a fifty-fifty face, his hands palms-up. "Local, I guess. Ligurian. I remember it from when I was a kid. If I was bad, old Necros sure to come and get me. Today," again the shrug, "it's forgotten."

"Like the bogeyman," I nodded.

"Eh?"

"Nothing. But why did the old girl go on like that?"

Again he shrugged. "Maybe she think that old man Necros, eh? She crazy, you know? Very backward. The whole family."

I was still interested. "How does the legend go?"

"The spook takes the life out of you. You grow old, spook grows young. It's a bargain you make: he gives you something you want, gets what he wants. What he wants is your youth. Except he uses it up quick and needs more. All the time, more youth."

"What kind of bargain is that?" I asked. "What does the victim get out of it?"

"Gets what he wants," said Mario, his brown face cracking into another grin. "In your case the girl, eh? *If* the little man was Necros . . ."

He got on with his work and I sat there sipping my Negroni. End of conversation. I thought no more about it—until later.

II

Of course, I should have been in Italy with Linda, but . . . I had kept her "Dear John" for a fortnight before shredding it, getting mindlessly drunk and starting in on the process of forgetting. That had been a month ago. The holiday had already been booked and I wasn't about to miss out on my trip to the sun. And so I had come out on my own. It was hot, the swimming was good, life was easy and the food superb. With just two days left to enjoy it, I told myself it hadn't been bad. But it would have been better with Linda.

Linda . . . She was still on my mind—at the back of it, anyway—later that night as I sat in the bar of my hotel beside an open bougainvillaea-decked balcony that looked down on the bay and the seafront lights of the town. And maybe she wasn't all that far back in my mind—maybe she was right there in front—or else I was just plain daydreaming. Whichever, I missed the entry of the lovely lady and her shriveled companion, failing to spot and recognize them until they were taking their seats at a little table just the other side of the balcony's sweep.

This was the closest I'd been to her, and—

Well, first impressions hadn't lied. This girl *was* beautiful. She didn't look quite as young as she'd first seemed—my own age, maybe—but beautiful she certainly was. And the old boy? He must be, could only be, her father. Maybe it sounds like I was a little naive, but with her looks this lady really didn't need an old man. And if she did need one it didn't have to be *this* one.

By now she'd seen me and my fascination with her must have been obvious. Seeing it she smiled and blushed at one and the same time, and for a moment turned her eyes away—but only for a moment. Fortunately her companion had his back to me or he must have known my feelings at once; for as she looked at me again—fully upon me this time—I could have sworn I read an invitation in her eyes, and in that same moment any bitter vows I may have made melted away completely and were forgotten. God, *please* let him be her father!

For an hour I sat there, drinking a few too many cocktails, eating olives and potato crisps from little bowls on the bar, keeping my eyes off the girl as best I could, if only for common decency's sake. But . . . all the time I worried frantically at the problem of how to introduce myself, and as the minutes ticked by it seemed to me that the most obvious way must also be the best.

But how obvious would it be to the old boy?

And the damnable thing was that the girl hadn't given me another glance since her original—invitation? Had I mistaken that look of hers?—or was she simply waiting for me to make the first move? *God, let him be her father!*

She was sipping Martinis, slowly; he drank a rich red wine, in some quantity. I asked a waiter to replenish their glasses and charge it to me. I had already spoken to the bar steward, a swarthy, friendly little chap from the South called Francesco, but he hadn't been able to enlighten me. The pair were not resident, he assured me; but being resident myself I was already pretty sure of that.

Anyway, my drinks were delivered to their table; they looked surprised; the girl put on a perfectly innocent expression, questioned the waiter, nodded in my direction and gave me a cautious smile, and the old boy turned his head to stare at me. I found myself smiling in return but avoiding his eyes, which were like coals now, sunken deep in his brown-wrinkled face. Time seemed suspended—if only for a second—then the girl spoke again to the waiter and he came across to me.

"Mr. Collins, sir, the gentleman and the young lady thank you and request that you join them." Which was everything I had dared hope for—for the moment.

Standing up I suddenly realized how much I'd had to drink. I willed sobriety on myself and walked across to their table. They didn't stand up but the little chap said, "Please sit." His voice was a rustle of dried grass. The waiter was behind me with a chair. I sat.

"Peter Collins," I said. "How do you do, Mr.—er?—"

"Karpethes," he answered. "Nichos Karpethes. And this is my wife, Adrienne." Neither one of them had made the effort to extend their hands, but that didn't dismay me. Only the fact that they were married dismayed me. He must be very, very rich, this Nichos Karpethes.

"I'm delighted you invited me over," I said, forcing a smile, "but I see that I was mistaken. You see, I thought I heard you speaking English, and I—"

"Thought we were English?" she finished it for me. "A natural error. Originally I am Armenian, Nichos is Greek, of course. We do not speak each other's tongue, but we do both speak English. Are you staying here, Mr. Collins?"

"Er, yes—for one more day and night. Then"—I shrugged and put on a sad look—"back to England, I'm afraid."

"Afraid?" the old boy whispered. "There is something to fear in a return to your homeland?"

"Just an expression," I answered. "I meant I'm afraid that my holiday is coming to an end."

He smiled. It was a strange, wistful sort of smile, wrinkling his face up like a little walnut. "But your friends will be glad to see you again. Your loved ones—?"

I shook my head. "Only a handful of friends—none of them really close—and no loved ones. I'm a loner, Mr. Karpethes."

"A loner?" His eyes glowed deep in their sockets and his hands began to tremble where they gripped the table's rim. "Mr. Collins, you don't—"

"We understand," she cut him off. "For although we are together, we too, in our way, are loners. Money has made Nichos lonely, you see? Also, he is not a well man and time is short. He will not waste what time he has on frivolous friendships. As for myself—people do not understand our being together, Nichos and I. They pry, and I withdraw. And so I too am a loner."

There was no accusation in her voice, but still I felt obliged to say: "I certainly didn't intend to pry, Mrs.—"

"Adrienne," she smiled. "Please. No, of course you didn't. I would not want you to think we thought that of you. Anyway I will *tell* you why we are together, and then it will be put aside."

Her husband coughed, seemed to choke, struggled to his feet. I stood up and took his arm. He at once shook me off—with some distaste, I thought—but Adrienne had already signaled to a waiter. "Assist Mr. Karpethes to the gentleman's room," she quickly instructed in very good Italian. "And please help him back to the table when he has recovered."

As he went Karpethes gesticulated, probably tried to say something to me by way of an apology, choked again, and reeled as he allowed the waiter to help him from the room.

"I'm . . . sorry," I said, not knowing what else to say.

"He has attacks." She was cool. "Do not concern yourself. I am used to it."

We sat in silence for a moment. Finally I began. "You were going to tell me—"

"Ah, yes! I had forgotten. It is a symbiosis."

"Oh?"

"Yes. I need the good life he can give me, and he needs . . . my youth? We supply each other's needs." And so, in a way, the old woman with the idiot boy hadn't been wrong after all. A sort of bargain had indeed been struck. Between Karpethes and his wife. As that thought crossed my mind I felt the short hairs at the back of my neck stiffen for a moment. Gooseflesh crawled on my arms. After all, "Nichos" was pretty close to "Necros," and now this youth thing again. Coincidence, of course. And after all, aren't all relationships bargains of sorts? Bargains struck for better or for worse.

"But for how long?" I asked. "I mean, how long will it work for you?"

She shrugged. "I have been provided for. And he will have me all the days of his life."

I coughed, cleared my throat, gave a strained, self-conscious laugh. "And here's me, the non-pryer!"

"No, not at all, I wanted you to know."

"Well," I shrugged, "—but it's been a pretty deep first conversation."

"First? Did you believe that buying me a drink would entitle you to more than one conversation?"

I almost winced. "Actually, I—"

But then she smiled and my world lit up. "You did not need to buy the drinks," she said. "There would have been some other way."

I looked at her inquiringly. "Some other way to—?"

"To find out if we were English or not."

"Oh!"

"Here comes Nichos now," she smiled across the room. "And we must be leaving. He's not well. Tell me, will you be on the beach tomorrow?"

"Oh—yes!" I answered after a moment's hesitation. "I like to swim."

"So do I. Perhaps we can swim out to the raft . . . ?"

"I'd like that very much."

Her husband arrived back at the table under his own steam. He looked a little stronger now, not quite so shriveled somehow. He did not sit but gripped the back of his chair with parchment fingers, knuckles white where the skin stretched over old bones. "Mr. Collins," he rustled, "—Adrienne, I'm sorry. . . ."

"There's really no need," I said, rising.

"We really must be going." She also stood. "No, you stay here, er, Peter? It's kind of you, but we can manage. Perhaps we'll see you on the beach." And she helped him to the door of the bar and through it without once looking back.

III

They weren't staying at my hotel, had simply dropped in for a drink. That was understandable (though I would have preferred to think that she had been looking for me) for *my* hotel was middling tourist-class while theirs was something else. They were up on the hill, high on the crest of a Ligurian spur where a smaller, much more exclusive place nested in Mediterranean pines. A place whose lights spelled money when they shone up there at night, whose music came floating down from a tiny open-air disco like the laughter of high-living elementals of the air. If I was poetic it was because of her. I mean, that beautiful girl and that weary, wrinkled, dried-up walnut of an old man. If anything I was sorry for him. And yet in another way I wasn't.

And let's make no pretense about it—if I haven't said it already, let me say it right now—I wanted her. Moreover, there had been that about our conversation, her beach invitation, which told me that she was available.

The thought of it kept me awake half the night. . . .

I was on the beach at 9:00 a.m.—they didn't show until 11:00. When they did, and when she came out of her tiny changing cubicle—

There wasn't a male head on the beach that didn't turn at least twice. Who could blame them? That girl, in *that* costume, would have turned the head of a sphynx. But—there was something, some little nagging thing different about her. A maturity beyond her years? She held herself like a model, a princess. But who was it for? Karpethes or me?

As for the old man: he was in a crumpled lightweight summer suit and sunshade hat as usual, but he seemed a bit more perky this morning. Unlike myself he'd doubtless had a good night's sleep. While his wife had been changing he had made his way unsteadily across the pebbly beach to my table and sun umbrella, taking the seat directly opposite me; and before his wife could appear he had opened with:

"Good morning, Mr. Collins."

"Good morning," I answered. "Please call me Peter."

"Peter, then," he nodded. He seemed out of breath, either from his stumbling walk over the beach or a certain urgency which I could detect in his movements, his hurried, almost rude "let's get down to it" manner.

"Peter, you said you would be here for one more day?"

"That's right," I answered, for the first time studying him closely where he sat like some strange garden gnome half in the shade of the beach umbrella. "This is my last day."

He was a bundle of dry wood, a pallid prune, a small, umber scarecrow. And his voice, too, was of straw, or autumn leaves blown across a shady path. Only his eyes were alive. "And you said you have no family, few friends, no one to miss you back in England?"

Warning bells rang in my head. Maybe it wasn't so much urgency in him—which usually implies a goal or ambition still to be realized—but eagerness in that the goal was in sight. "That's correct. I am, was, a student doctor. When I get home I shall seek a position. Other than that there's nothing, no one, no ties."

He leaned forward, bird eyes very bright, claw hand reaching across the table, trembling, and—

Her shadow suddenly fell across us as she stood there in that costume. Karpethes jerked back in his chair. His face was working, strange emotions twisting the folds and wrinkles of his flesh into stranger contours. I could feel my heart thumping against my ribs . . . why I couldn't say. I calmed myself, looked up at her, and smiled.

She stood with her back to the sun, which made a dark silhouette of her head and face. But in that blot of darkness her oval eyes were green jewels. "Shall we swim, Peter?"

She turned and ran down the beach, and of course I ran after her. She had a head start and beat me to the water, beat me to the raft, too. It wasn't until I hauled myself up beside her that I thought of Karpethes: how I hadn't even excused myself before plunging after her. But at least the water had cleared my head, bringing me completely awake and aware.

Aware of her incredible body where it stretched almost

touching mine, on the fiber deck of the gently bobbing raft.

I mentioned her husband's line of inquiry, gasping a little for breath as I recovered from the frantic exercise of our race. She, on the other hand, already seemed completely recovered. She carefully arranged her hair about her shoulders like a fan, to dry in the sunlight, before answering.

"Nichos is not really my husband," she finally said, not looking at me. "I am his companion, that's all. I could have told you last night, but . . . there was the chance that you really were curious only about our nationality. As for any veiled threats he might have issued: that is not unusual. He might not have the vitality of younger men, but jealousy is ageless."

"No," I answered, "he didn't threaten—not that I noticed. But jealousy? Knowing I have only one more day to spend here, what has he to fear from me?"

Her shoulders twitched a little, a shrug. She turned her face to me, her lips inches away. Her eyelashes were like silken shutters over green pools, hiding whatever swam in the deeps. "I am young, Peter, and so are you. And you are very attractive, very . . . eager? Holiday romances are not uncommon."

My blood was on fire. "I have very little money," I said. "We are staying at different hotels. He already suspects me. It is impossible."

"What is?" she innocently asked, leaving me at a complete loss.

But then she laughed, tossed back her hair, already dry, dangled her hands and arms in the water. "Where there's a will . . ." she said.

"You know that I want you—" The words spilled out before I could control or change them.

"Oh, yes. And I want you." She said it so simply, and yet suddenly I felt seared. A moth brushing the magnet candle's flame.

I lifted my head, looked toward the beach. Across seventy-five yards of sparkling water the beach umbrellas looked very large and close. Karpethes sat in the shade just as I had last seen him, his face hidden in shadow. But I knew that he watched.

"You can do nothing here," she said, her voice languid—but I noticed now that she, too, seemed short of breath.

"This," I told her with a groan, "is going to kill me!"

She laughed, laughter that sparkled more than the sun on the sea. "I'm sorry," she sobered. "It's unfair of me to laugh. But—your case is not hopeless."

"Oh?"

"Tomorrow morning, early, Nichos has an appointment with a specialist in Genova. I am to drive him into the city tonight. We'll stay at a hotel overnight."

I groaned my misery. "Then my case *is* quite hopeless. I fly tomorrow."

"But if I sprained my wrist," she said, "and so could not drive . . . and if he went into Genova by taxi while I stayed behind with a headache—because of the pain from my wrist—" Like a flash she was on her feet, the raft tilting, her body diving, striking the water into a spray of diamonds.

Seconds for it all to sink in—and then I was following her, laboring through the water in her churning wake. And as she splashed from the sea, seeing her stumble, go to her hands and knees in Ligurian shingle—and the pained look on her face, the way she held her wrist as she came to her feet. As easy as that!

Karpethes, struggling to rise from his seat, stared at

her with his mouth agape. Her face screwed up now as I followed her up the beach. And Adrienne holding her "sprained" wrist and shaking it, her mouth forming an elongated "O." The sinuous motion of her body and limbs, mobile marble with dew of ocean clinging saltily. . . .

If the tiny man had said to me: "I am Necros. I want ten years of your life for one night with her," at that moment I might have sealed the bargain. Gladly. But legends are legends and he wasn't Necros, and he didn't, and I didn't. After all, there was no need. . . .

IV

I suppose my greatest fear was that she might be "having me on," amusing herself at my expense. She was, of course, "safe" with me—insofar as I would be gone tomorrow and the "romance" forgotten, for her, anyway—and I could also see how she was starved for young companionship, a fact she had brought right out in the open from the word go.

But why me? Why should I be so lucky?

Attractive? Was I? I had never thought so. Perhaps it was because I *was* so safe: here today and gone tomorrow, with little or no chance of complications. Yes, that must be it. *If* she wasn't simply making a fool of me. She might be just a tease—

—But she wasn't.

At 8:30 that evening I was in the bar of my hotel—had been there for an hour, careful not to drink too much, unable to eat—when the waiter came to me and said there was a call for me on the reception telephone. I hurried out to reception where the clerk discreetly excused himself and left me alone.

"Peter?" Her voice was a deep well of promise. "He's gone. I've booked us a table, to dine at 9:00. Is that all right for you?"

"A table? Where?" my own voice breathless.

"Why, up here, of course! Oh, don't worry, it's perfectly safe. And anyway, Nichos knows."

"Knows?" I was taken aback, a little panicked. "What does he know?"

"That we're dining together. In fact he suggested it. He didn't want me to eat alone—and since this is your last night . . ."

"I'll get a taxi right away," I told her.

"Good. I look forward to . . . seeing you. I shall be in the bar."

I replaced the telephone in its cradle, wondering if she always took an *apéritif* before the main course. . . .

I had smartened myself up. That is to say, I was immaculate. Black bow tie, white evening jacket (courtesy of C & A), black trousers, and a lightly-frilled white shirt, the only one I had ever owned. But I might have known that my appearance would never match up to hers. It seemed that everything she did was just perfectly right. I could only hope that that meant literally everything.

But in her black lace evening gown with its plunging neckline, short wide sleeves, and delicate silver embroidery, she was stunning. Sitting with her in the bar, sipping our drinks—for me a large whiskey and for her a tall Cinzano—I couldn't take my eyes off her. Twice I reached out for her hand and twice she drew back from me.

"Discreet they may well be," she said, letting her oval green eyes flicker toward the bar, where guests stood and chatted, and back to me, "but there's really no need to give them occasion to gossip."

"I'm sorry, Adrienne," I told her, my voice husky and close to trembling, "but— "

"How is it," she demurely cut me off, "that a good-looking man like you is—how do you say it?—going short?"

I sat back, chuckled. "That's a rather unladylike expression," I told her.

"Oh? And what I've planned for tonight is ladylike?"

My voice went huskier still. "Just what is your plan?"

"While we eat," she answered, her voice low, "I shall tell you." At which point a waiter loomed, towel over his arm, inviting us to accompany him to the dining room.

Adrienne's portions were tiny, mine huge. She sipped a slender, light white wine, I gulped blocky rich red from a glass the waiter couldn't seem to leave alone. Mercifully I was hungry—I hadn't eaten all day—else that meal must surely have bloated me out. And all of it ordered in advance, the very best in quality cuisine.

"This," she eventually said, handing me her key, "fits the door of our suite." We were sitting back, enjoying liqueurs and cigarettes. "The rooms are on the ground floor. Tonight you enter through the door, tomorrow morning you leave via the window. A slow walk down to the seafront will refresh you. How is that for a plan?"

"Unbelievable!"

"You don't believe it?"

"Not my good fortune, no."

"Shall we say that we both have our needs?"

"I think," I said, "that I may be falling in love with you. What if I don't wish to leave in the morning?"

She shrugged, smiled, said: "Who knows what tomorrow may bring?"

How could I ever have thought of her simply as another girl? Or even an ordinary young woman? Girl she certainly was, woman, too, but so . . . *knowing*! Beautiful as a princess and knowing as a whore.

If Mario's old myths and legends were reality, and if Nichos Karpethes were really Necros, then he'd surely picked the right companion. No man born could ever have resisted Adrienne, of that I was quite certain. These thoughts were in my mind—but dimly, at the back of my mind—as I left her smoking in the dining room and followed her directions to the suite of rooms at the rear of the hotel. In the front of my mind were other thoughts, much more vivid and completely erotic.

I found the suite, entered, left the door slightly ajar behind me.

The thing about an Italian room is its size. An entire suite of rooms is vast. As it happened I was only interested in one room, and Adrienne had obligingly left the door to that one open.

I was sweating. And yet . . . I shivered.

Adrienne had said fifteen minutes, time enough for her to smoke another cigarette and finish her drink. Then she would come to me. By now the entire staff of the hotel probably knew I was in here, but this was Italy.

V

I shivered again. Excitement? Probably.

I threw off my clothes, found my way to the bathroom,

took the quickest shower of my life. Drying myself off, I padded back to the bedroom.

Between the main bedroom and the bathroom a smaller door stood ajar. I froze as I reached it, my senses suddenly alert, my ears seeming to stretch themselves into vast receivers to pick up any slightest sound. For there had been a sound, I was sure of it, from that room. . . .

A scratching? A rustle? A whisper? I couldn't say. But a sound, anyway.

Adrienne would be coming soon. Standing outside that door I slowly recommenced toweling myself dry. My naked feet were still firmly rooted, but my hands automatically worked with the towel. It was nerves, only nerves. There had been no sound, or at worst only the night breeze off the sea, whispering in through an open window.

I stopped toweling, took another step toward the main bedroom, heard the sound again. A small, choking rasp. A tiny gasping for air.

Karpethes? What the hell was going on?

I shivered violently, my suddenly chill flesh shuddering in an uncontrollable spasm. But . . . I forced myself to action, returned to the main bedroom, quickly dressed (with the exceptions of my tie and jacket), and crept back to the small room.

Adrienne must be on her way to me even now. She mustn't find me poking my nose into things, like a suspicious kid. I must kill off this silly feeling that had my skin crawling. Not that an attack of nerves was unnatural in the circumstances, on the contrary, but I wasn't about to let it spoil the night. I pushed open the door of the room, entered into darkness, found the lightswitch. Then—

—I held my breath, flipped the switch.

The room was only half as big as the others. It contained a small single bed, a bedside table, a wardrobe. Nothing more, or at least nothing immediately apparent to my wildly darting eyes. My heart, which was racing, slowed and began to settle toward a steadier beat. The window was open, external shutters closed—but small night sounds were finding their way in through the louvers. The distant sounds of traffic, the toot of horns—holiday sounds from below.

I breathed deeply and gratefully, and saw something projecting from beneath the pillow on the bed. A corner of card or of dark leather, like a wallet or—

—Or a passport!

A Greek passport, Karpethes', when I opened it. But how could it be? The man in the photograph was young, no older than me. His birthdate proved it. And there was his name: Nichos Karpethes. Printed in Greek, of course, but still plain enough. His son?

Puzzling over the passport had served to distract me. My nerves had steadied up. I tossed the passport down, frowned at it where it lay upon the bed, breathed deeply once more . . . and froze solid!

A scratching, a hissing, a dry grunting—from the wardrobe.

Mice? Or did I in fact smell a rat?

Even as the short hairs bristled on the back of my neck I knew anger. There were too many unexplained things here. Too much I didn't understand. And what was it I feared? Old Mario's myths and legends? No, for in my experience the Italians are notorious for getting things wrong. Oh, yes, notorious . . .

I reached out, turned the wardrobe's doorknob, yanked the doors open.

At first I saw nothing of any importance or significance. My eyes didn't know what they sought. Shoes, patent leather, two pairs, stood side by side below. Tiny suits, no bigger than boys' sizes, hung above on steel hangers. And—my God, my God—a waistcoat!

I backed out of that little room on rubber legs, with the silence of the suite shrieking all about me, my eyes bugging, my jaw hanging slack—

"Peter?"

She came in through the suite's main door, came floating toward me, eager, smiling, her green eyes blazing. Then blazing their suspicion, their anger as they saw my condition. "Peter!"

I lurched away as her hands reached for me, those hands I had never yet touched, which had never touched me. Then I was into the main bedroom, snatching my tie and jacket from the bed, (don't ask me why!) and out of the window, yelling some inarticulate, choking thing at her and lashing out frenziedly with my foot as she reached after me. Her eyes were bubbling green hells. *"Peter!"*

Her fingers closed on my forearm, bands of steel containing a fierce, hungry heat. And strong as two men she began to lift me back into her lair!

I put my feet against the wall, kicked, came free, and crashed backward into shrubbery. Then up on my feet, gasping for air, running, tumbling, crashing into the night, down madly tilting slopes, through black chasms of mountain pine with the Mediterranean stars winking overhead, and the beckoning, friendly lights of the village seen occasionally below . . .

In the morning, looking up at the way I had descended and remembering the nightmare of my panic-flight, I counted myself lucky to have survived it. The place was precipitous. In the end I *had* fallen, but only for a short distance. All in utter darkness, and my head striking something hard. But . . .

I did survive. Survived both Adrienne and my flight from her.

And waking with the dawn, and gently fingering my bruises and the massive bump on my forehead, I made my staggering way back to my still slumbering hotel, let myself in, and *locked* myself in my room—then sat there trembling and moaning until it was time for the coach.

Weak? Maybe I was, maybe I am.

But on my way into Genova, with people round me and the sun hot through the coach's windows, I could think again. I could roll up my sleeve and examine that claw mark of four slim fingers and a thumb, branded white into my suntanned flesh, where hair would never more grow on skin sere and wrinkled.

And seeing those marks I could also remember the wardrobe and the waistcoat—and what the waistcoat contained.

That tiny puppet of a man, alive still but barely, his stick-arms dangling through the waistcoat's armholes, his baby's head projecting, its chin supported by the tightly buttoned waistcoat's breast. And the large bull-dog clip over the hanger's bar, its teeth fastened in the loose, wrinkled skin of his walnut head, holding it up. And his skinny little legs dangling, twig-things twitching there; and his pleading, pleading eyes!

But eyes are something I mustn't dwell upon.

And green is a color I can no longer bear. . . .

HUMAN REMAINS

◆◆◆

CLIVE BARKER

Some trades are best practised by daylight, some by night. Gavin was a professional in the latter category. In midwinter, in midsummer, leaning against a wall, or poised in a doorway, a fire-fly cigarette hovering at his lips, he sold what sweated in his jeans to all comers.

Sometimes to visiting widows with more money than love, who'd hire him for a weekend of illicit meetings, sour, insistent kisses, and perhaps, if they could forget their dead partners, a dry hump on a lavender-scented bed. Sometimes to lost husbands, hungry for their own sex and desperate for an hour of coupling with a boy who wouldn't ask their name.

Gavin didn't much care which it was. Indifference was a trademark of his, even a part of his attraction. And it made leaving him, when the deed was done and the money exchanged, so much simpler. To say, "Ciao," or "Be seeing you," or nothing at all to a face that scarcely cared if you lived or died: that was an easy thing.

And for Gavin, the profession was not unpalatable, as professions went. One night out of four it even offered him a grain of physical pleasure. At worst it was a sexual abattoir, all steaming skins and lifeless eyes. But he'd got used to that over the years.

It was all profit. It kept him in good shoes.

By day he slept mostly, hollowing out a warm furrow in

the bed, and mummifying himself in his sheets, head wrapped up in a tangle of arms to keep out the light. About three or so, he'd get up, shave, and shower, then spend half an hour in front of the mirror, inspecting himself. He was meticulously self-critical, never allowing his weight to fluctuate more than a pound or two to either side of his self-elected ideal, careful to feed his skin if it was dry, or swab it if it was oily, hunting for any pimple that might flaw his cheek. Strict watch was kept for the smallest sign of venereal disease—the only type of lovesickness he ever suffered. The occasional dose of crabs was easily dispatched, but gonorrhoea, which he'd caught twice, would keep him out of service for three weeks, and that was bad for business; so he policed his body obsessively, hurrying to the clinic at the merest sign of a rash.

It seldom happened. Uninvited crabs aside there was little to do in that half-hour of self-appraisal but admire the collision of genes that had made him. He was wonderful. People told him that all the time. Wonderful. The face, oh the face, they would say, holding him tight as if they could steal a piece of his glamour.

Of course there were other beauties available, through the agencies, even on the streets if you knew where to search. But most of the hustlers Gavin knew had faces that seemed, beside his, unmade. Faces that looked like the first workings of a sculptor rather than the finished article: unrefined, experimental. Whereas he was made, entire. All that could be done had been; it was just a question of preserving the perfection.

Inspection over, Gavin would dress, maybe regard himself for another five minutes, then take the packaged wares out to sell.

He worked the street less and less these days. It was chancey; there was always the law to avoid, and the occasional psycho with an urge to clean up Sodom. If he was feeling really lazy he could pick up a client through the Escort Agency, but they always creamed off a fat portion of the fee.

He had regulars of course, clients who booked his favours month after month. A widow from Fort Lauderdale always hired him for a few days on her annual trip to Europe; another woman whose face he'd seen once in a glossy magazine called him now and then, wanting only to dine with him and confide her marital problems. There was a man Gavin called Rover, after his car, who would buy him once every few weeks for a night of kisses and confessions.

But on nights without a booked client he was out on his own finding a spec and hustling. It was a craft he had pulled off perfectly. Nobody else working the street had caught the vocabulary of invitation better; the subtle blend of encouragement and detachment, of putto and wanton. The particular shift of weight from left foot to right that presented the groin at the best angle: so. Never too blatant: never whorish. Just casually promising.

He prided himself that there was seldom more than a few minutes between tricks, and never as much as an hour. If he made his play with his usual accuracy, eyeing the right disgruntled wife, the right regretful husband, he'd have them feed him (clothe him sometimes), bed him, and bid him a satisfied goodnight all before the last tube had run on the Metropolitan Line to Hammersmith. The years of half-hour assignations, three blow-jobs and a fuck in one evening, were over. For one thing he simply didn't have the hunger for it any longer, for another he was preparing for his career to change course in the coming years: from street hustler to gigolo, from gigolo to kept boy, from kept boy to husband. One of these days, he knew it, he'd marry one of the widows; maybe the matron from Florida. She'd told him how she could picture him spread out beside her pool in Fort Lauderdale, and it was a fantasy he kept warm for her. Perhaps he hadn't got there yet, but he'd turn the trick of it sooner or later. The problem was that these rich blooms needed a lot of tending, and the pity of it was that so many of them perished before they came to fruit.

Still, this year. Oh yes, this year for certain, it had to be this year. Something good was coming with the autumn, he knew it for sure.

Meanwhile he watched the lines deepen around his wonderful mouth (it was, without doubt, wonderful) and calculated the odds against him in the race between time and opportunity.

It was nine-fifteen at night. September 29th, and it was chilly, even in the foyer of the Imperial Hotel. No Indian summer to bless the streets this year: autumn had London in its jaws and was shaking the city bare.

The chill had got to his tooth, his wretched, crumbling tooth. If he'd gone to the dentist's, instead of turning over in his bed and sleeping another hour, he wouldn't be feeling this discomfort. Well, too late now, he'd go tomorrow. Plenty of time tomorrow. No need for an appointment. He'd just smile at the receptionist, she'd melt and tell him she could find a slot for him somewhere, he'd smile again, she'd blush, and he'd see the dentist then and there instead of waiting two weeks like the poor nerds who didn't have wonderful faces.

For tonight he'd just have to put up with it. All he needed was one lousy punter—a husband who'd pay through the nose for taking it in the mouth—then he could retire to an all-night club in Soho and content himself with reflections. As long as he didn't find himself with a confession-freak on his hands, he could spit his stuff and be done by half ten.

But tonight wasn't his night. There was a new face on the reception desk of the Imperial, a thin, shot-at face with a mismatched rug perched (glued) on his pate, and he'd been squinting at Gavin for almost half an hour.

The usual receptionist, Madox, was a closet-case Gavin had seen prowling the bars once or twice, an easy touch if you could handle that kind. Madox was putty in Gavin's hand; he'd even bought his company for an hour a couple of months back. He'd got a cheap rate too—that was good politics. But this new man was straight, and vicious, and he was on to Gavin's game.

Idly, Gavin sauntered across to the cigarette machine, his walk catching the beat of the Muzak as he trod the maroon carpet. Lousy fucking night.

The receptionist was waiting for him as he turned from the machine, packet of Winston in hand.

"Excuse me . . . Sir." It was a practised pronounciation that was clearly not natural. Gavin looked sweetly back at him.

"Yes?"

"Are you actually a resident at this hotel . . . Sir?"

"Actually—"

"If not, the management would be obliged if you'd vacate the premises immediately."

"I'm waiting for somebody."

"Oh?"

The receptionist didn't believe a word of it.

"Well just give me the name—"

"No need."

"Give me the name," the man insisted, "and I'll gladly check to see if your . . . contact . . . is in the hotel."

The bastard was going to try and push it, which narrowed the options. Either Gavin could choose to play it cool, and leave the foyer, or play the outraged customer and stare the other man down. He chose, more to be bloodyminded than because it was good tactics, to do the latter.

"You don't have any right—" he began to bluster, but the receptionist wasn't moved.

"Look, sonny," he said, "I know what you're up to, so don't try and get snotty with me or I'll fetch the police." He'd lost control of his elocution: it was getting further south of the river with every syllable. "We've got a nice clientele here, and they don't want no truck with the likes of you, see?"

"Fucker," said Gavin very quietly.

"Well that's one up from a cocksucker, isn't it?"

Touché.

"Now, sonny—you want to mince out of here under your own steam or be carried out in cuffs by the boys in blue?"

Gavin played his last card.

"Where's Mr. Madox? I want to see Mr. Madox: he knows me."

"I'm sure he does," the receptionist snorted, "I'm bloody sure he does. He was dismissed for improper conduct—" the artificial accent was re-establishing itself "—so I wouldn't try dropping his name here if I were you. Okay? On your way."

Upper hand well and truly secured, the receptionist stood back like a matador and gestured for the bull to go by.

"The management thanks you for your patronage. Please don't call again."

Game, set, and match to the man with the rug. What the hell; there were other hotels, other foyers, other receptionists. He didn't have to take all this shit.

As Gavin pushed the door open he threw a smiling "Be seeing you" over his shoulder. Perhaps that would make the tick sweat a little one of these nights when he was walking home and he heard a young man's step on the street behind him. It was a petty satisfaction, but it was something.

The door swung closed, sealing the warmth in and Gavin out. It was colder, substantially colder, than it had been when he'd stepped into the foyer. A thin drizzle had begun, which threatened to worsen as he hurried down Park Lane towards South Kensington. There were a couple of hotels on the High Street he could hole up in for a while; if nothing came of that he'd admit defeat.

The traffic surged around Hyde Park Corner, speeding to Knightsbridge or Victoria, purposeful, shining. He pictured himself standing on the concrete island between the two contrary streams of cars, his fingertips thrust into his jeans (they were too tight for him to get more than the first joint into the pockets), solitary, forlorn.

A wave of unhappiness came up from some buried place in him. He was twenty-four and five months. He had hustled, on and off and on again, since he was seventeen, promising himself that he'd find a marriageable widow (the gigolo's pension) or a legitimate occupation before he was twenty-five.

But time passed and nothing came of his ambitions. He just lost momentum and gained another line beneath the eye.

And the traffic still came in shining streams, lights signalling this imperative or that, cars full of people with ladders to climb and snakes to wrestle, their passage isolating him from the bank, from safety, with its hunger for destination.

He was not what he'd dreamed he'd be, or promised his secret self.

And youth was yesterday.

Where was he to go now? The flat would feel like a prison tonight, even if he smoked a little dope to take the edge off the room. He wanted, no, he *needed* to be with somebody tonight. Just to see his beauty through somebody else's eyes. Be told how perfect his proportions were, be wined and dined and flattered stupid, even if it was by Quasimodo's richer, uglier brother. Tonight he needed a fix of affection.

The pick-up was so damned easy it almost made him forget the episode in the foyer of the Imperial. A guy of fifty-five or so, well-heeled: Gucci shoes, a very classy overcoat. In a word: quality.

Gavin was standing in the doorway of a tiny art-house cinema, looking over the times of the Truffaut movie they were showing, when he became aware of the punter staring at him. He glanced at the guy to be certain there was a pick-up in the offing. The direct look seemed to unnerve the punter; he moved on; then he seemed to change his mind, muttered something to himself, and retraced his steps, showing patently false interest in the movie schedule. Obviously not too familiar with this game, Gavin thought; a novice.

Casually Gavin took out a Winston and lit it, the flare of the match in his cupped hands glossing his cheekbones golden. He'd done it a thousand times, as often as not in the mirror for his own pleasure. He had the glance up from the tiny fire off pat: it always did the trick. This time when he met the nervous eyes of the punter, the other didn't back away.

He drew on the cigarette, flicking out the match and letting it drop. He hadn't made a pick-up like this in several months, but he was well satisfied that he still had the knack. The faultless recognition of a potential client, the implicit offer in eyes and lips, that could be construed as innocent friendliness if he'd made an error.

This was no error, however, this was the genuine article. The man's eyes were glued to Gavin, so enamoured of him he seemed to be hurting with it. His mouth was open, as though the words of introduction had failed him. Not much of a face, but far from ugly. Tanned too often, and too quickly: maybe he'd lived abroad. He was assuming the man was English: his prevarication suggested it.

Against habit, Gavin made the opening move.

"You like French movies?"

The punter seemed to deflate with relief that the silence between them had been broken.

"Yes," he said.

"You going in?"

The man pulled a face.

"I . . . I . . . don't think I will."

"Bit cold . . ."

"Yes. It is."

"Bit cold for standing around, I mean."

"Oh—yes."

The punter took the bait.

"Maybe . . . you'd like a drink?"

Gavin smiled.

"Sure, why not?"

"My flat's not far."

"Sure."

"I was getting a bit cheesed off, you know, at home."

"I know the feeling."

Now the other man smiled. "You are . . . ?"

"Gavin."

The man offered his leather-gloved hand. Very formal, businesslike. The grip as they shook was strong, no trace of his earlier hesitation remaining.

"I'm Kenneth," he said, "Ken Reynolds."

"Ken."

"Shall we get out of the cold?"

"Suits me."

"I'm only a short walk from here."

A wave of musty, centrally-heated air hit them as Reynolds opened the door of his apartment. Climbing the three flights of stairs had snatched Gavin's breath, but Reynolds wasn't slowed at all. Health freak maybe. Occupation? Something in the city. The handshake, the leather gloves. Maybe Civil Service.

"Come in, come in."

There was money here. Underfoot the pile of the carpet was lush, hushing their steps as they entered. The hallway was almost bare: a calendar hung on the wall, a small table with telephone, a heap of directories, a coat-stand.

"It's warmer in here."

Reynolds was shrugging off his coat and hanging it up. His gloves remained on as he led Gavin a few yards down the hallway and into a large room.

"Let's have your jacket," he said.

"Oh . . . sure."

Gavin took off his jacket, and Reynolds slipped out into the hall with it. When he came in again he was working off his gloves; a slick of sweat made it a difficult job. The guy was still nervous: even on his home ground. Usually they started to calm down once they were safe behind locked doors. Not this one: he was a catalogue of fidgets.

"Can I get you a drink?"

"Yeah; that would be good."

"What's your poison?"

"Vodka."

"Surely. Anything with it?"

"Just a drop of water."

"Purist, eh?"

Gavin didn't quite understand the remark.

"Yeah," he said.

"Man after my own heart. Will you give me a moment—I'll just fetch some ice."

"No problem."

Reynolds dropped the gloves on a chair by the door, and left Gavin to the room. It, like the hallway, was almost stiflingly warm, but there was nothing homely or welcoming about it. Whatever his profession, Reynolds was a collector. The room was dominated by displays of antiquities, mounted on the walls, and lined up on shelves. There was very little furniture, and what there was seemed odd: battered tubular frame chairs had no place in an apartment this expensive. Maybe the man was a university don, or a museum governor, something academic. This was no stockbroker's living room.

Gavin knew nothing about art, and even less about history, so the displays meant very little to him, but he went to have a closer look, just to show he was willing. The guy was bound to ask him what he thought of the stuff. The shelves were deadly dull. Bits and pieces of pottery and sculpture: nothing in its entirety, just fragments. On some of the shards there remained a glimpse of design, though age had almost washed the colours out. Some of the sculpture was recognisably human: part of a torso, or foot (all five toes in place), a face that was all but eaten away, no longer male or female. Gavin stifled a yawn. The heat, the exhibits, and the thought of sex made him lethargic.

He turned his dulled attention to the wall-hung pieces. They were more impressive than the stuff on the shelves but they were still far from complete. He couldn't see why anyone would want to look at such broken things; what was the fascination? The stone reliefs mounted on the wall were pitted and eroded, so that the skins of the figures looked leprous, and the Latin inscriptions were almost wiped out. There was nothing beautiful about them: too spoiled for beauty. They made him feel dirty somehow, as though their condition was contagious.

Only one of the exhibits struck him as interesting: a tombstone, or what looked to him to be a tombstone, which was larger than the other reliefs and in slightly better condition. A man on a horse, carrying a sword, loomed over his headless enemy. Under the picture, a few words in Latin. The front legs of the horse had been broken off, and the pillars that bounded the design were badly defaced by age, otherwise the image made sense. There was even a trace of personality in the crudely made face: a long nose, a wide mouth; an individual.

Gavin reached to touch the inscription, but withdrew his fingers as he heard Reynolds enter.

"No, please touch it," said his host. "It's there to take pleasure in. Touch away."

Now that he'd been invited to touch the thing, the desire had melted away. He felt embarrassed; caught in the act.

"Go on," Reynolds insisted.

Gavin touched the carving. Cold stone, gritty under his fingertips.

"It's Roman," said Reynolds.

"Tombstone?"

"Yes. Found near Newcastle."

"Who was he?"

"His name was Flavinus. He was a regimental standard-bearer."

What Gavin had assumed to be a sword was, on closer inspection, a standard. It ended in an almost erased motif: maybe a bee, a flower, a wheel.

"You an archaeologist, then?"

"That's part of my business. I research sites, occasionally oversee digs; but most of the time I restore artifacts."

"Like these?"

"Roman Britain's my personal obsession."

He put down the glasses he was carrying and crossed to the pottery-laden shelves.

"This is stuff I've collected over the years. I've never quite got over the thrill of handling objects that haven't seen the light of day for centuries. It's like plugging into history. You know what I mean?"

"Yeah."

Reynolds picked a fragment of pottery off the shelf.

"Of course all the best finds are claimed by the major collections. But if one's canny, one manages to keep a few pieces back. They were an incredible influence, the Romans. Civil engineers, road-layers, bridge builders."

Reynolds gave a sudden laugh at his burst of enthusiasm.

"Oh hell," he said, "Reynolds is lecturing again. Sorry. I get carried away."

Replacing the pottery-shard in its niche on the shelf,

he returned to the glasses, and started pouring drinks. With his back to Gavin, he managed to say: "Are you expensive?"

Gavin hesitated. The man's nervousness was catching and the sudden tilt of the conversation from the Romans to the price of a blow-job took some adjustment.

"It depends," he flannelled.

"Ah . . ." said the other, still busying himself with the glasses, "you mean what is the precise nature of my—er—requirement?"

"Yeah."

"Of course."

He turned and handed Gavin a healthy-sized glass of vodka. No ice.

"I won't be demanding of you," he said.

"I don't come cheap."

"I'm sure you don't," Reynolds tried a smile, but it wouldn't stick to his face, "and I'm prepared to pay you well. Will you be able to stay the night?"

"Do you want me to?"

Reynolds frowned into his glass.

"I suppose I do."

"Then yes."

The host's mood seemed to change, suddenly: indecision was replaced by a spurt of conviction.

"Cheers," he said, clinking his whisky-filled glass against Gavin's. "To love and life and anything else that's worth paying for."

The double-edged remark didn't escape Gavin: the guy was obviously tied up in knots about what he was doing.

"I'll drink to that," said Gavin and took a gulp of the vodka.

The drinks came fast after that, and just about his third vodka Gavin began to feel mellower than he'd felt in a hell of a long time, content to listen to Reynolds' talk of excavations and the glories of Rome with only one ear. His mind was drifting, an easy feeling. Obviously he was going to be here for the night, or at least until the early hours of the morning, so why not drink the punter's vodka and enjoy the experience for what it offered? Later, probably much later to judge by the way the guy was rambling, there'd be some drink-slurred sex in a darkened room, and that would be that. He'd had customers like this before. They were lonely, perhaps between lovers, and usually simple to please. It wasn't sex this guy was buying, it was company, another body to share his space awhile; easy money.

And then, the noise.

At first Gavin thought the beating sound was in his head, until Reynolds stood up, a twitch at his mouth. The air of well-being had disappeared.

"What's that?" asked Gavin, also getting up, dizzy with drink.

"It's all right—" Reynolds, palms were pressing him down into his chair. "Stay here—"

The sound intensified. A drummer in an oven, beating as he burned.

"Please, please stay here a moment. It's just somebody upstairs."

Reynolds was lying, the racket wasn't coming from upstairs. It was from somewhere else in the flat, a rhythmical thumping, that speeded up and slowed and speeded again.

"Help yourself to a drink," said Reynolds at the door, face flushed. "Damn neighbours . . ."

The summons, for that was surely what it was, was already subsiding.

"A moment only," Reynolds promised, and closed the door behind him.

Gavin had experienced bad scenes before: tricks whose lovers appeared at inappropriate moments; guys who wanted to beat him up for a price—one who got bitten by guilt in a hotel room and smashed the place to smithereens. These things happened. But Reynolds was different: nothing about him said weird. At the back of his mind, at the very back, Gavin was quietly reminding himself that the other guys hadn't seemed bad at the beginning. Ah hell; he put the doubts away. If he started to get the jitters every time he went with a new face he'd soon stop working altogether. Somewhere along the line he had to trust to luck and his instinct, and his instinct told him that this punter was not given to throwing fits.

Taking a quick swipe from his glass, he refilled it, and waited.

The noise had stopped altogether, and it became increasingly easier to rearrange the facts: maybe it had been an upstairs neighbour after all. Certainly there was no sound of Reynolds moving around in the flat.

His attention wandered around the room looking for something to occupy it awhile, and came back to the tombstone on the wall.

Flavinus the Standard-Bearer.

There was something satisfying about the idea of having your likeness, however crude, carved in stone and put up on the spot where your bones lay, even if some historian was going to separate bones and stone in the fullness of time. Gavin's father had insisted on burial rather than cremation: How else, he'd always said, was he going to be remembered? Who'd ever go to an urn, in a wall, and cry? The irony was that nobody ever went to his grave either: Gavin had been perhaps twice in the years since his father's death. A plain stone bearing a name, a date, and a platitude. He couldn't even remember the year his father died.

People remembered Flavinus though; people who'd never known him, or a life like his, knew him now. Gavin stood up and touched the standard-bearer's name, the crudely chased "FLAVINVS" that was the second word of the inscription.

Suddenly, the noise again, more frenzied than ever. Gavin turned away from the tombstone and looked at the door, half-expecting Reynolds to be standing there with a word of explanation. Nobody appeared.

"Damn it."

The noise continued, a tattoo. Somebody, somewhere, was very angry. And this time there could be no self-deception: the drummer was here, on this floor, a few yards away. Curiosity nibbled Gavin, a coaxing lover. He drained his glass and went out into the hall. The noise stopped as he closed the door behind him.

"Ken?" he ventured. The word seemed to die at his lips.

The hallway was in darkness, except for a wash of light from the far end. Perhaps an open door. Gavin found a switch to his right, but it didn't work.

"Ken?" he said again.

This time the enquiry met with a response. A moan, and the sound of a body rolling, or being rolled, over. Had Reynolds had an accident? Jesus, he could be lying incapacitated within spitting distance from where Gavin stood: he must help. Why were his feet so reluctant to move? He had the tingling in his balls that always came with nervous anticipation; it reminded him of childhood hide-and-seek: the thrill of the chase. It was almost pleasurable.

And pleasure apart, could he really leave now, without knowing what had become of the punter? He had to go down the corridor.

The first door was ajar; he pushed it open and the room beyond was a book-lined bedroom/study. Street lights through the curtainless window fell on a jumbled desk. No Reynolds, no thrasher. More confident now he'd made the first move Gavin explored further down the hallway. The next door—the kitchen—was also open. There was no light from inside. Gavin's hands had begun to sweat: he thought of Reynolds trying to pull his gloves off, though they stuck to his palm. What had he been afraid of? It was more than the pick-up: there was somebody else in the apartment: somebody with a violent temper.

Gavin's stomach turned as his eyes found the smeared hand-print on the door; it was blood.

He pushed the door, but it wouldn't open any further. There was something behind it. He slid through the available space, and into the kitchen. An unemptied waste bin, or a neglected vegetable rack, fouled the air. Gavin smoothed the wall with his palm to find the light switch, and the fluorescent tube spasmed into life.

Reynolds' Gucci shoes poked out from behind the door. Gavin pushed it to, and Reynolds rolled out of his hiding place. He'd obviously crawled behind the door to take refuge; there was something of the beaten animal in his tucked up body. When Gavin touched him he shuddered.

"It's all right . . . it's me." Gavin prised a bloody hand from Reynolds' face. There was a deep gouge running from his temple to his chin, and another, parallel with it but not as deep, across the middle of his forehead and his nose, as though he'd been raked by a two-pronged fork.

Reynolds opened his eyes. It took him a second only to focus on Gavin, before he said:

"Go away."

"You're hurt."

"Jesus' sake, go away. Quickly. I've changed my mind . . . You understand?"

"I'll fetch the police."

The man practically spat: "Get the fucking hell out of here, will you? Fucking bum-boy!"

Gavin stood up, trying to make sense out of all this. The guy was in pain, it made him aggressive. Ignore the insults and fetch something to cover the wound. That was it. Cover the wound, and then leave him to his own devices. If he didn't want the police that was his business. Probably he didn't want to explain the presence of a pretty-boy in his hot-house.

"Just let me get you a bandage—"

Gavin went back into the hallway.

Behind the kitchen door Reynolds said: "Don't," but the bum-boy didn't hear him. It wouldn't have made much difference if he had. Gavin liked disobedience. Don't was an invitation.

Reynolds put his back to the kitchen door, and tried to edge his way upright, using the door handle as purchase. But his head was spinning: a carousel of horrors, round and round, each horse uglier than the last. His legs doubled up under him, and he fell down like the senile fool he was. Damn. Damn. Damn.

Gavin heard Reynolds fall, but he was too busy arming himself to hurry back into the kitchen. If the intruder who'd attacked Reynolds was still in the flat, he wanted to be ready to defend himself. He rummaged through the reports on the desk in the study and alighted on a paper knife which was lying beside a pile of unopened correspondence. Thanking God for it, he snatched it up. It was light, and the blade was thin and brittle, but properly placed it could surely kill.

Happier now, he went back into the hall and took a moment to work out his tactics. The first thing was to locate the bathroom, hopefully there he'd find a bandage for Reynolds. Even a clean towel would help. Maybe then he could get some sense out of the guy, even coax him into an explanation.

Beyond the kitchen the hallway made a sharp left. Gavin turned the corner, and dead ahead the door was ajar. A light burned inside: water shone on tiles. The bathroom.

Clamping his left hand over the right hand that held the knife, Gavin approached the door. The muscles of his arms had become rigid with fear: would that improve his strike if it was required? he wondered. He felt inept, graceless, slightly stupid.

There was blood on the door-jamb, a palm-print that was clearly Reynolds'. This was where it had happened—Reynolds had thrown out a hand to support himself as he reeled back from his assailant. If the attacker was still in the flat, he must be here. There was nowhere else for him to hide.

Later, if there was a later, he'd probably analyse this situation and call himself a fool for kicking the door open, for encouraging this confrontation. But even as he contemplated the idiocy of the action he was performing it, and the door was swinging open across tiles strewn with water-blood puddles, and any moment there'd be a figure there, hook-handed, screaming defiance.

No. Not at all. The assailant wasn't here; and if he wasn't here, he wasn't in the flat.

Gavin exhaled, long and slow. The knife sagged in his hand, denied its pricking. Now, despite the sweat, the terror, he was disappointed. Life had let him down, again—snuck his destiny out of the back door and left him with a mop in his hand not a medal. All he could do was play nurse to the old man and go on his way.

The bathroom was decorated in shades of lime; the blood and tiles clashed. The translucent shower curtain, sporting stylised fish and seaweed, was partially drawn. It looked like the scene of a movie murder: not quite real. Blood too bright: light too flat.

Gavin dropped the knife in the sink, and opened the mirrored cabinet. It was well-stocked with mouth-washes, vitamin supplements, and abandoned toothpaste tubes, but the only medication was a tin of Elastoplast. As he closed the cabinet door he met his own features in the mirror, a drained face. He turned on the cold tap full, and lowered his head to the sink; a splash of water would clear away the vodka and put some colour in his cheeks.

As he cupped the water to his face, something made a noise behind him. He stood up, his heart knocking against his ribs, and turned off the tap. Water dripped off his chin and his eyelashes, and gurgled down the waste pipe.

The knife was still in the sink, a hand's-length away. The sound was coming from the bath, from *in* the bath, the inoffensive slosh of water.

Alarm had triggered flows of adrenalin, and his senses distilled the air with new precision. The sharp scent of lemon soap, the brilliance of the turquoise angel-fish flitting through lavender kelp on the shower curtain, the cold droplets on his face, the warmth behind his eyes: all sudden experiences, details his mind had passed over 'til now, too lazy to see and smell and feel to the limits of its reach.

You're living in the real world, his head said (it was a revelation), and if you're not very careful you're going to die there.

Why hadn't he looked in the bath? Asshole. Why not the bath?

"Who's there?" he asked, hoping against hope that Reynolds had an otter that was taking a quiet swim. Ridiculous hope. There was blood here, for Christ's sake.

He turned from the mirror as the lapping subsided—do it! do it!—and slid back the shower curtain on its plastic hooks. In his haste to unveil the mystery he'd left the knife in the sink. Too late now: the turquoise angels concertinaed, and he was looking down into the water.

It was deep, coming up to within an inch or two of the top of the bath, and murky. A brown scum spiralled on the surface, and the smell off it was faintly animal, like the wet fur of a dog. Nothing broke the surface of the water.

Gavin peered in, trying to work out the form at the bottom, his reflection floating amid the scum. He bent closer, unable to puzzle out the relation of shapes in the silt, until he recognised the crudely-formed fingers of a hand and he realised he was looking at a human form curled up into itself like a foetus, lying absolutely still in the filthy water.

He passed his hand over the surface to clear away the muck, his reflection shattered, and the occupant of the bath came clear. It was a statue, carved in the shape of a sleeping figure, only its head, instead of being tucked up tight, was cranked round to stare up out of the blur of sediment towards the surface. Its eyes were painted open, two crude blobs on a roughly carved face; its mouth was a slash, its ears ridiculous handles on its bald head. It was naked: its anatomy no better realised than its features: the work of an apprentice sculptor. In places the paint had been corrupted, perhaps by the soaking, and was lifting off the torso in grey, globular strands. Underneath, a core of dark wood was uncovered.

There was nothing to be frightened of here. An *objet d'art* in a bath, immersed in water to remove a crass paint-job. The lapping he'd heard behind him had been some bubbles rising from the thing, caused by a chemical reaction. There: the fright was explained. Nothing to panic over. Keep beating my heart, as the barman at the Ambassador used to say when a new beauty appeared on the scene.

Gavin smiled at the irony; this was no Adonis.

"Forget you ever saw it."

Reynolds was at the door. The bleeding had stopped, staunched by an unsavoury rag of a handkerchief pressed to the side of his face. The light of the tiles made his skin bilious: his pallor would have shamed a corpse.

"Are you all right? You don't look it."

"I'll be fine . . . just go, please."

"What happened?"

"I slipped. Water on the floor. I slipped, that's all."

"But the noise . . ."

Gavin was looking back into the bath. Something about the statue fascinated him. Maybe its nakedness, and that second strip it was slowly performing underwater: the ultimate strip: off with the skin.

"Neighbours, that's all."

"What is this?" Gavin asked, still looking at the unfetching doll-face in the water.

"It's nothing to do with you."

"Why's it all curled up like that? Is he dying?"

Gavin looked back to Reynolds to see the response to that question, the sourest of smiles, fading.

"You'll want money."

"No."

"Damn you! You're in business aren't you? There's notes beside the bed; take whatever you feel you deserve for your wasted time"—he was appraising Gavin—"and your silence."

Again the statue: Gavin couldn't keep his eyes off it, in all its crudity. His own face, puzzled, floated on the skin of the water, shaming the hand of the artist with its proportions.

"Don't wonder," said Reynolds.

"Can't help it."

"This is nothing to do with you."

"You stole it . . . is that right? This is worth a mint and you stole it."

Reynolds pondered the question and seemed, at last, too tired to start lying.

"Yes. I stole it."

"And tonight somebody came back for it—"

Reynolds shrugged.

"Is that it? Somebody came back for it?"

"That's right. I stole it . . ." Reynolds was saying the lines by rote, ". . . and somebody came back for it."

"That's all I wanted to know."

"Don't come back here, Gavin whoever-you-are. And don't try anything clever, because I won't be here."

"You mean extortion?" said Gavin, "I'm no thief."

Reynolds' look of appraisal rotted into contempt.

"Thief or not, be thankful. If it's in you." Reynolds stepped away from the door to let Gavin pass. Gavin didn't move.

"Thankful for what?" he demanded. There was an itch of anger in him; he felt, absurdly, rejected, as though he was being foisted off with a half-truth because he wasn't worthy enough to share this secret.

Reynolds had no more strength left for explanation. He was slumped against the door-frame, exhausted.

"Go," he said.

Gavin nodded and left the guy at the door. As he passed from bathroom into hallway a glob of paint must have been loosened from the statue. He heard it break surface, heard the lapping at the edge of the bath, could see, in his head, the way the ripples made the body shimmer.

"Goodnight," said Reynolds, calling after him.

Gavin didn't reply, nor did he pick up any money on his way out. Let him have his tombstones and his secrets.

On his way to the front door he stepped into the main room to pick up his jacket. The face of Flavinus the Standard-Bearer looked down at him from the wall. The man must have been a hero, Gavin thought. Only a hero would have been commemorated in such a fashion. He'd get no remembrance like that; no stone face to mark his passage.

He closed the front door behind him, aware once more that his tooth was aching, and as he did so the noise began again, the beating of a fist against a wall.

Or worse, the sudden fury of a woken heart.

The toothache was really biting the following day, and he went to the dentist mid-morning, expecting to coax the girl on the desk into giving him an instant appointment. But his charm was at a low ebb, his eyes weren't sparkling quite as luxuriantly as usual. She told him he'd have to wait until the following Friday, unless it was an emergency. He told her it was: she told him it wasn't. It was going to be a bad day: an aching tooth, a lesbian dentist receptionist, ice on the puddles, nattering women on every street corner, ugly children, ugly sky.

That was the day the pursuit began.

Gavin had been chased by admirers before, but never quite like this. Never so subtle, so surreptitious. He'd had people follow him round for days, from bar to bar, from street to street, so dog-like it almost drove him mad. Seeing the same longing face night after night, screwing up the courage to buy him a drink, perhaps offering him a watch, cocaine, a week in Tunisia, whatever. He'd rapidly come to loathe that sticky adoration that went bad as quickly as milk, and stank to high Heaven once it had. One of his most ardent admirers, a knighted actor he'd been told, never actually came near him, just followed him around, looking and looking. At first the attention had been flattering, but the pleasure soon became irritation, and eventually he'd cornered the guy in a bar and threatened him with a broken head. He'd been so wound up that night, so sick of being devoured by looks, he'd have done some serious harm if the pitiful bastard hadn't taken the hint. He never saw the guy again; half thought he'd probably gone home and hanged himself.

But this pursuit was nowhere near as obvious, it was scarcely more than a feeling. There was no hard evidence that he had somebody on his tail. Just a prickly sense, every time he glanced round, that someone was slotting themselves into the shadows, or that on a night street a walker was keeping pace with him, matching every click of his heel, every hesitation in his step. It was like paranoia, except that he wasn't paranoid. If he was paranoid, he reasoned, somebody would tell him.

Besides, there were incidents. One morning the cat woman who lived on the landing below him idly enquired who his visitor was: the funny one who came in late at night and waited on the stairs hour after hour, watching his room. He'd had no such visitor: and knew no-one who fitted the description.

Another day, on a busy street, he'd ducked out of the throng into the doorway of an empty shop and was in the act of lighting a cigarette when somebody's reflection, distorted through the grime on the window, caught his eye. The match burned his finger, he looked down as he dropped it, and when he looked up again the crowd had closed round the watcher like an eager sea.

It was a bad, bad feeling: and there was more where that came from.

Gavin had never spoken with Preetorius, though they'd exchanged an occasional nod on the street, and each asked after the other in the company of mutual acquaintances as though they were dear friends. Preetorius was a black, somewhere between forty-five and assassination, a glorified pimp who claimed to be descended from Napoleon. He'd been running a circle of women, and three or four boys, for the best part of a decade, and doing well from the business. When he first began work, Gavin had been strongly advised to ask for Preetorius' patronage, but he'd always been too much of a maverick to want that kind of help. As a result he'd never been looked upon kindly by Preetorius or his clan. Nevertheless, once he became a fixture on the scene, no-one challenged his right to be his own man. The word was that Preetorius even admitted a grudging admiration for Gavin's greed.

Admiration or no, it was a chilly day in Hell when Preetorius actually broke the silence and spoke to him.

"White boy."

It was towards eleven, and Gavin was on his way from a bar off St. Martin's Lane to a club in Covent Garden. The street still buzzed: there were potential punters amongst the theatre- and movie-goers, but he hadn't got the appetite for it tonight. He had a hundred in his pocket, which he'd made the day before and hadn't bothered to bank. Plenty to keep him going.

His first thought when he saw Preetorius and his piebald goons blocking his path was: they want my money.

"White boy."

Then he recognised the flat, shining face. Preetorius was no street thief; never had been, never would be.

"White boy, I'd like a word with you."

Preetorius took a nut from his pocket, shelled it in his palm, and popped the kernel into his ample mouth.

"You don't mind do you?"

"What do you want?"

"Like I said, just a word. Not too much to ask, is it?"

"Okay. What?"

"Not here."

Gavin looked at Preetorius' cohorts. They weren't gorillas, that wasn't the black's style at all, but nor were they ninety-eight-pound weaklings. This scene didn't look, on the whole, too healthy.

"Thanks, but no thanks." Gavin said, and began to walk, with as even a pace as he could muster, away from the trio. They followed. He prayed they wouldn't, but they followed. Preetorius talked at his back.

"Listen. I hear bad things about you," he said.

"Oh yes?"

"I'm afraid so. I'm told you attacked one of my boys."

Gavin took six paces before he answered. "Not me. You've got the wrong man."

"He recognised you, trash. You did him some serious mischief."

"I told you: not me."

"You're a lunatic, you know that? You should be put behind fucking bars."

Preetorius was raising his voice. People were crossing the street to avoid the escalating argument.

Without thinking, Gavin turned off St. Martin's Lane into Long Acre, and rapidly realised he'd made a tactical error. The crowds thinned substantially here, and it was a long trek through the streets of Covent Garden before he reached another centre of activity. He should have turned right instead of left, and he'd have stepped onto Charing Cross Road. There would have been some safety there. Damn it, he couldn't turn round, not and walk straight into them. All he could do was walk (not run; never run with a mad dog on your heels) and hope he could keep the conversation on an even keel.

Preetorius: "You've cost me a lot of money."

"I don't see—"

"You put some of my prime boy-meat out of commission. It's going to be a long time 'til I get that kid back on the market. He's shit scared, see?"

"Look . . . I didn't do anything to anybody."

"Why do you fucking lie to me, trash? What have I ever done to you, you treat me like this?"

Preetorius picked up his pace a little and came up level with Gavin, leaving his associates a few steps behind.

"Look . . ." he whispered to Gavin, "kids like that can be tempting, right? That's cool. I can get into that. You put a little boy-pussy on my plate I'm not going to turn my nose up at it. But you hurt him: and when you hurt one of my kids, I bleed too."

"If I'd done this like you say, you think I'd be walking the street?"

"Maybe you're not a well man, you know? We're not talking about a couple of bruises here, man. I'm talking about you taking a shower in a kid's blood, that's what I'm saying. Hanging him up and cutting him everywhere, then leaving him on my fuckin' stairs wearing a pair of fuckin' socks. You getting my message now, white boy? You read my message?"

Genuine rage had flared as Preetorius described the alleged crimes, and Gavin wasn't sure how to handle it. He kept his silence, and walked on.

"That kid idolised you, you know? Thought you were essential reading for an aspirant bum-boy. How'd you like that?"

"Not much."

"You should be fuckin' flattered, man, 'cause that's about as much as you'll ever amount to."

"Thanks."

"You've had a good career. Pity it's over."

Gavin felt iced lead in his belly: he'd hoped Preetorius was going to be content with a warning. Apparently not. They were here to damage him: Jesus, they were going to hurt him, and for something he hadn't done, didn't even know anything about.

"We're going to take you off the street, white boy. Permanently."

"I did nothing."

"The kid knew you, even with a stocking over your head he knew you. The voice was the same, the clothes were the same. Face it, you were recognised. Now take the consequences."

"Fuck you."

Gavin broke into a run. As an eighteen-year-old he'd

sprinted for his county: he needed that speed again now. Behind him Preetorius laughed (such sport!) and two sets of feet pounded the pavement in pursuit. They were close, closer—and Gavin was badly out of condition. His thighs were aching after a few dozen yards, and his jeans were too tight to run in easily. The chase was lost before it began.

"The man didn't tell you to leave," the white goon scolded, his bitten fingers digging into Gavin's biceps.

"Nice try." Preetorius smiled, sauntering towards the dogs and the panting hare. He nodded, almost imperceptibly, to the other goon.

"Christian?" he asked.

At the invitation Christian delivered a fist to Gavin's kidneys. The blow doubled him up, spitting curses.

Christian said: "Over there." Preetorius said: "Make it snappy," and suddenly they were dragging him out of the light into an alley. His shirt and his jacket tore, his expensive shoes were dragged through dirt, before he was pulled upright, groaning. The alley was dark and Preetorius' eyes hung in the air in front of him, dislocated.

"Here we are again," he said. "Happy as can be."

"I . . . didn't touch him," Gavin gasped.

The unnamed cohort, Not-Christian, put a ham hand in the middle of Gavin's chest, and pushed him back against the end wall of the alley. His heel slid in muck, and though he tried to stay upright his legs had turned to water. His ego too: this was no time to be courageous. He'd beg, he'd fall down on his knees and lick their soles if need be, anything to stop them doing a job on him. Anything to stop them spoiling his face.

That was Preetorius' favourite pastime, or so the street talk went: the spoiling of beauty. He had a rare way with him, could maim beyond hope of redemption in three strokes of his razor, and have the victim pocket his lips as a keepsake.

Gavin stumbled forward, palms slapping the wet ground. Something rotten-soft slid out of its skin beneath his hand.

Not-Christian exchanged a grin with Preetorius.

"Doesn't he look delightful?" he said.

Preetorius was crunching a nut. "Seems to me," he said, "the man's finally found his place in life."

"I didn't touch him," Gavin begged. There was nothing to do but deny and deny: and even then it was a lost cause.

"You're guilty as hell," said Not-Christian.

"Please."

"I'd really like to get this over with as soon as possible," said Preetorius, glancing at his watch. "I've got appointments to keep, people to pleasure."

Gavin looked up at his tormentors. The sodium-lit street was a twenty-five-yard dash away, if he could break through the cordon of their bodies.

"Allow me to rearrange your face for you. A little crime of fashion."

Preetorius had a knife in his hand. Not-Christian had taken a rope from his pocket, with a ball on it. The ball goes in the mouth, the rope goes round the head—you couldn't scream if your life depended on it. This was it.

Go!

Gavin broke from his grovelling position like a sprinter from his block, but the slops greased his heels, and threw him off balance. Instead of making a clean dash for safety he stumbled sideways and fell against Christian, who in turn fell back.

There was a breathless scrambling before Preetorius stepped in, dirtying his hands on the white trash, and hauling him to his feet.

"No way out, fucker," he said, pressing the point of the blade against Gavin's chin. The jut of the bone was clearest there, and he began the cut without further debate—tracing the jawline, too hot for the act to care if the trash was gagged or not. Gavin howled as blood washed down his neck, but his cries were cut short as somebody's fat fingers grappled with his tongue, and held it fast.

His pulse began to thud in his temples, and windows, one behind the other, opened and opened in front of him, and he was falling through them into unconsciousness.

Better to die. Better to die. They'd destroy his face: better to die.

Then he was screaming again, except that he wasn't aware of making the sound in his throat. Through the slush in his ears he tried to focus on the voice, and realised it was Preetorius' scream he was hearing, not his own.

His tongue was released; and he was spontaneously sick. He staggered back, puking, from a mess of struggling figures in front of him. A person, or persons, unknown had stepped in, and prevented the completion of his spoiling. There was a body sprawled on the floor, face up. Not-Christian, eyes open, life shut. God: someone had killed for him. *For him.*

Gingerly, he put his hand up to his face to feel the damage. The flesh was deeply lacerated along his jawbone, from the middle of his chin to within an inch of his ear. It was bad, but Preetorius, ever organised, had left the best delights to the last, and had been interrupted before he'd slit Gavin's nostrils or taken off his lips. A scar along his jawbone wouldn't be pretty, but it wasn't disastrous.

Somebody was staggering out of the mêlée towards him—Preetorius, tears on his face, eyes like golf-balls.

Beyond him Christian, his arms useless, was staggering towards the street.

Preetorius wasn't following: why?

His mouth opened; an elastic filament of saliva, strung with pearls, depended from his lower lip.

"Help me," he appealed, as though his life was in Gavin's power. One large hand was raised to squeeze a drop of mercy out of the air, but instead came the swoop of another arm, reaching over his shoulder and thrusting a weapon, a crude blade, into the black's mouth. He gargled it a moment, his throat trying to accommodate its edge, its width, before his attacker dragged the blade up and back, holding Preetorius' neck to steady him against the force of the stroke. The startled face divided, and heat bloomed from Preetorius' interior, warming Gavin in a cloud.

The weapon hit the alley floor, a dull clank. Gavin glanced at it. A short, wide-bladed sword. He looked back at the dead man.

Preetorius stood upright in front of him, supported now only by his executioner's arm. His gushing head fell forward, and the executioner took the bow as a sign, neatly dropping Preetorius' body at Gavin's feet. No longer eclipsed by the corpse, Gavin met his saviour face to face.

It took him only a moment to place those crude features: the startled, lifeless eyes, the gash of a mouth, the jug-handle ears. It was Reynolds' statue. It grinned, its teeth too small for its head. Milk-teeth, still to be shed before the adult form. There was, however, some improvement in its appearance, he could see that even in the gloom. The brow seemed to have swelled; the face was altogether better proportioned. It remained a painted doll, but it was a doll with aspirations.

The statue gave a stiff bow, its joints unmistakably creaking, and the absurdity, the sheer absurdity of this situation welled up in Gavin. It bowed, damn it, it smiled, it murdered: and yet it couldn't possibly be alive, could it? Later, he would disbelieve, he promised himself. Later he'd find a thousand reasons not to accept the reality in front of him: blame his blood-starved brain, his confusion, his panic. One way or another he'd argue himself out of this fantastic vision, and it would be as though it had never happened.

If he could just live with it a few minutes longer.

The vision reached across and touched Gavin's jaw, lightly, running its crudely carved fingers along the lips of the wound Preetorius had made. A ring on its smallest finger caught the light: a ring identical to his own.

"We're going to have a scar," it said.

Gavin knew its voice.

"Dear me: pity," it said. It was speaking with *his* voice. "Still, it could be worse."

His voice. God, his, his, his.

Gavin shook his head.

"Yes," it said, understanding that he'd understood.

"Not me."

"Yes."

"Why?"

It transferred its touch from Gavin's jawbone to its own, marking out the place where the wound should be, and even as it made the gesture its surface opened, and it grew a scar on the spot. No blood welled up: it had no blood.

Yet wasn't that his own, even brow it was emulating, and the piercing eyes, weren't they becoming his, and the wonderful mouth?

"The boy?" said Gavin, fitting the pieces together.

"Oh the boy . . ." It threw its unfinished glance to Heaven. "What a treasure he was. And how he snarled."

"You washed in his blood?"

"I need it." It knelt to the body of Preetorius and put its

fingers in the split head. "This blood's old, but it'll do. The boy was better."

It daubed Preetorius' blood on its cheek, like war-paint. Gavin couldn't hide his disgust.

"Is he such a loss?" the effigy demanded.

The answer was no, of course. It was no loss at all that Preetorius was dead, no loss that some drugged, cocksucking kid had given up some blood and sleep because this painted miracle needed to feed its growth. There were worse things than this every day, somewhere; huge horrors. And yet—

"You can't condone me," it prompted, "it's not in your nature is it? Soon it won't be in mine either. I'll reject my life as a tormentor of children, because I'll see through *your* eyes, share *your* humanity . . ."

It stood up, its movements still lacking flexibility.

"Meanwhile, I must behave as I think fit."

On its cheek, where Preetorius' blood had been smeared, the skin was already waxier, less like painted wood.

"I am a thing without a proper name," it pronounced. "I am a wound in the flank of the world. But I am also that perfect stranger you always prayed for as a child, to come and take you, call you beauty, lift you naked out of the street and through Heaven's window. Aren't I? Aren't I?"

How did it know the dreams of his childhood? How could it have guessed that particular emblem, of being hoisted out of a street full of plague into a house that was Heaven?

"Because I am yourself," it said, in reply to the unspoken question, "made perfectable."

Gavin gestured towards the corpses.

"You can't be me. I'd never have done this."

It seemed ungracious to condemn it for its intervention, but the point stood.

"Wouldn't you?" said the other. "I think you would."

Gavin heard Preetorius' voice in his ear. "A crime of fashion." Felt again the knife at his chin, the nausea, the helplessness. Of course he'd have done it, a dozen times over he'd have done it, and called it justice.

It didn't need to hear his accession, it was plain.

"I'll come and see you again," said the painted face. "Meanwhile—if I were you"—it laughed—"I'd be going."

Gavin locked eyes with it a beat, probing it for doubt, then started towards the road.

"Not that way. This!"

It was pointing towards a door in the wall, almost hidden behind festering bags of refuse. That was how it had come so quickly, so quietly.

"Avoid the main streets, and keep yourself out of sight. I'll find you again, when I'm ready."

Gavin needed no further encouragement to leave. Whatever the explanations of the night's events, the deeds were done. Now wasn't the time for questions.

He slipped through the doorway without looking behind him: but he could hear enough to turn his stomach. The thud of fluid on the ground, the pleasurable moan of the miscreant: the sounds were enough for him to be able to picture its toilet.

Nothing of the night before made any more sense the morning after. There was no sudden insight into the nature of the waking dream he'd dreamt. There was just a series of stark facts.

In the mirror, the fact of the cut on his jaw, gummed up and aching more badly than his rotted tooth.

In the newspapers, the reports of two bodies found in the Covent Garden area, known criminals viciously murdered in what the police described as a "gangland slaughter."

In his head, the inescapable knowledge that he would be found out sooner or later. Somebody would surely have seen him with Preetorius, and spill the beans to the police. Maybe even Christian, if he was so inclined, and they'd be there, on his step, with cuffs and warrants. Then what could he tell them, in reply to their accusations? That the man who did it was not a man at all, but an effigy of some kind, that was by degrees becoming a replica of himself? The question was not whether he'd be incarcerated, but which hole they'd lock him in, prison or asylum?

Juggling despair with disbelief, he went to the casualty department to have his face seen to, where he waited patiently for three and a half hours with dozens of similar walking wounded.

The doctor was unsympathetic. There was no use in stitches now, he said, the damage was done: the wound could and would be cleaned and covered, but a bad scar was now unavoidable. Why didn't you come last night, when it happened? the nurse asked. He shrugged: what the hell did they care? Artificial compassion didn't help him an iota.

As he turned the corner with his street, he saw the cars outside the house, the blue light, the cluster of neighbours grinning their gossip. Too late to claim anything of his previous life. By now they had possession of his clothes, his combs, his perfumes, his letters—and they'd be searching through them like apes after lice. He'd seen how thorough-going these bastards could be when it suited them, how completely they could seize and parcel up a man's identity. Eat it up, suck it up: they could erase you as surely as a shot, but leave you a living blank.

There was nothing to be done. His life was theirs now to sneer at and salivate over: even have a nervous moment, one or two of them, when they saw his photographs and wondered if perhaps they'd paid for this boy themselves, some horny night.

Let them have it all. They were welcome. From now on he would be lawless, because laws protect possessions and he had none. They'd wiped him clean, or as good as: he had no place to live, nor anything to call his own. He didn't even have fear: that was the strangest thing.

He turned his back on the street and the house he'd lived in for four years, and he felt something akin to relief, happy that his life had been stolen from him in its squalid entirety. He was the lighter for it.

Two hours later, and miles away, he took time to check his pockets. He was carrying a banker's card, almost a hundred pounds in cash, a small collection of photographs, some of his parents and sister, mostly of himself; a watch, a ring, and a gold chain round his neck. Using the card might be dangerous—they'd surely have warned his bank by now. The best thing might be to pawn the ring and the chain, then hitch North. He had friends in Aberdeen who'd hide him awhile.

But first—Reynolds.

It took Gavin an hour to find the house where Ken Reynolds lived. It was the best part of twenty-four hours since he'd eaten and his belly complained as he stood outside Livingstone Mansions. He told it to keep its peace, and slipped into the building. The interior looked less impressive by daylight. The tread of the stair carpet was worn, and the paint on the balustrade filthied with use.

Taking his time he climbed the three flights to Reynolds' apartment, and knocked.

Nobody answered, nor was there any sound of movement from inside. Reynolds had told him of course: don't come back—I won't be here. Had he somehow guessed the consequences of sicking that thing into the world?

Gavin rapped on the door again, and this time he was certain he heard somebody breathing on the other side of the door.

"Reynolds . . ." he said, pressing to the door, "I can hear you."

Nobody replied, but there was somebody in there, he was sure of it. Gavin slapped his palm on the door.

"Come on, open up. Open up, you bastard."

A short silence, then a muffled voice. "Go away."

"I want to speak to you."

"Go away, I told you, go away. I've nothing to say to you."

"You owe me an explanation, for God's sake. If you don't open this fucking door I'll fetch someone who will."

An empty threat, but Reynolds responded: "No! Wait. Wait."

There was the sound of a key in the lock, and the door was opened a few paltry inches. The flat was in darkness beyond the scabby face that peered out at Gavin. It was Reynolds sure enough, but unshaven and wretched. He smelt unwashed, even through the crack in the door, and he was wearing only a stained shirt and a pair of pants, hitched up with a knotted belt.

"I can't help you. Go away."

"If you'll let me explain—" Gavin pressed the door, and Reynolds was either too weak or too befuddled to stop him opening it. He stumbled back into the darkened hallway.

"What the fuck's going on in here?"

The place stank of rotten food. The air was evil with it. Reynolds let Gavin slam the door behind him before producing a knife from the pocket of his stained trousers.

"You don't fool me," Reynolds gleamed, "I know what you've done. Very fine. Very clever."

"You mean the murders? It wasn't me."

Reynolds poked the knife towards Gavin.

"How many blood-baths did it take?" he asked, tears in his eyes. "Six? Ten?"

"I didn't kill anybody."

". . . monster."

The knife in Reynolds' hand was the paper knife Gavin himself had wielded. He approached Gavin with it. There was no doubt: he had every intention of using it. Gavin flinched, and Reynolds seemed to take hope from his fear.

"Had you forgotten what it was like, being flesh and blood?"

The man had lost his marbles.

"Look . . . I just came here to talk."

"You came here to kill me. I could reveal you . . . so you came to kill me."

"Do you know who I am?" Gavin said.

Reynolds sneered: "You're not the queer boy. You look like him, but you're not."

"For pity's sake . . . I'm Gavin . . . Gavin—"

The words to explain, to prevent the knife pressing any closer, wouldn't come.

"Gavin, you remember?" was all he could say.

Reynolds faltered a moment, staring at Gavin's face.

"You're sweating," he said. The dangerous stare fading in his eyes.

Gavin's mouth had gone so dry he could only nod.

"I can see," said Reynolds, "you're sweating."

He dropped the point of the knife.

"It could never sweat," he said. "Never had, never would have, the knack of it. You're the boy . . . not it. The boy."

His face slackened, its flesh a sack which was almost emptied.

"I need help," said Gavin, his voice hoarse. "You've got to tell me what's going on."

"You want an explanation?" Reynolds replied. "You can have whatever you can find."

He led the way into the main room. The curtains were drawn, but even in the gloom Gavin could see that every antiquity it had contained had been smashed beyond repair. The pottery shards had been reduced to smaller shards, and those shards to dust. The stone reliefs were destroyed, the tombstone of Flavinus the Standard-Bearer was rubble.

"Who did this?"

"I did," said Reynolds.

"Why?"

Reynolds sluggishly picked his way through the destruction to the window, and peered through a slit in the velvet curtains.

"It'll come back, you see," he said, ignoring the question.

Gavin insisted: "Why destroy it all?"

"It's a sickness," Reynolds replied. "Needing to live in the past."

He turned from the window.

"I stole most of these pieces," he said, "over a period of many years. I was put in a position of trust, and I misused it."

He kicked over a sizeable chunk of rubble: dust rose.

"Flavinus lived and died. That's all there is to tell. Knowing his name means nothing, or next to nothing. It doesn't make Flavinus real again: he's dead and happy."

"The statue in the bath?"

Reynolds stopped breathing for a moment, his inner eye meeting the painted face.

"You thought I was it, didn't you? When I came to the door."

"Yes. I thought it had finished its business."

"It imitates."

Reynolds nodded. "As far as I understand its nature," he said, "yes, it imitates."

"Where did you find it?"

"Near Carlisle. I was in charge of the excavation there. We found it lying in the bathhouse, a statue curled up into a ball beside the remains of an adult male. It was a riddle. A dead man and a statue, lying together in a bathhouse. Don't ask me what drew me to the thing, I don't know. Perhaps it works its will through the mind as well as the physique. I stole it, brought it back here."

"And you fed it?"

Reynolds stiffened.

"Don't ask."

"I *am* asking. You fed it?"

"Yes."

"You intended to bleed me, didn't you? That's why you brought me here: to kill me, and let it wash itself—"

Gavin remembered the noise of the creature's fists on the sides of the bath, that angry demand for food, like a child beating on its cot. He'd been so close to being taken by it, lamb-like.

"Why didn't it attack me the way it did you? Why didn't it just jump out of the bath and feed on me?"

Reynolds wiped his mouth with the palm of his hand.

"It saw your face, of course."

Of course: it saw my face, and wanted it for itself, and it couldn't steal the face of a dead man, so it let me be. The rationale for its behaviour was fascinating, now it was revealed: Gavin felt a taste of Reynolds' passion, unveiling mysteries.

"The man in the bathhouse. The one you uncovered—"

"Yes . . . ?"

"He stopped it doing the same thing to him, is that right?"

"That's probably why his body was never moved, just sealed up. No-one understood that he'd died fighting a creature that was stealing his life."

The picture was near as damn it complete; just anger remaining to be answered.

This man had come close to murdering him to feed the effigy. Gavin's fury broke surface. He took hold of Reynolds by shirt and skin, and shook him. Was it his bones or teeth that rattled?

"It's almost got my face." He stared into Reynolds' bloodshot eyes. "What happens when it finally has the trick off pat?"

"I don't know."

"You tell me the worst—tell me!"

"It's all guesswork," Reynolds replied.

"Guess then!"

"When it's perfected its physical imitation, I think it'll steal the one thing it can't imitate: your soul."

Reynolds was past fearing Gavin. His voice had sweetened, as though he was talking to a condemned man. He even smiled.

"Fucker!"

Gavin hauled Reynolds' face yet closer to his. White spittle dotted the old man's cheek.

"You don't care! You don't give a shit, do you?"

He hit Reynolds across the face, once, twice, then again and again, until he was breathless.

The old man took the beating in absolute silence, turning his face up from one blow to receive another, brushing the blood out of his swelling eyes only to have them fill again.

Finally, the punches faltered.

Reynolds, on his knees, picked pieces of tooth off his tongue.

"I deserved that," he murmured.

"How do I stop it?" said Gavin.

Reynolds shook his head.

"Impossible," he whispered, plucking at Gavin's hand. "Please," he said, and taking the fist, opened it and kissed the lines.

Gavin left Reynolds in the ruins of Rome, and went into the street. The interview with Reynolds had told him little he hadn't guessed. The only thing he could do now was find this beast that had his beauty, and best it. If he failed, he failed attempting to secure his only certain attribute: a face that was wonderful. Talk of souls and humanity was for him so much wasted air. He wanted his face.

There was rare purpose in his step as he crossed Kensington. After years of being the victim of circumstance he saw circumstance embodied at last. He would shake sense from it, or die trying.

. . .

In his flat Reynolds drew aside the curtain to watch a picture of evening fall on a picture of a city.

No night he would live through, no city he'd walk in again. Out of sighs, he let the curtain drop, and picked up the short stabbing sword. The point he put to his chest.

"Come on," he told himself and the sword, and pressed the hilt. But the pain as the blade entered his body a mere half inch was enough to make his head reel: he knew he'd faint before the job was half-done. So he crossed to the wall, steadied the hilt against it, and let his own body-weight impale him. That did the trick. He wasn't sure if the sword had skewered him through entirely, but by the amount of blood he'd surely killed himself. Though he tried to arrange to turn, and so drive the blade all the way home as he fell on it, he fluffed the gesture, and instead fell on his side. The impact made him aware of the sword in his body, a stiff, uncharitable presence transfixing him utterly.

It took him well over ten minutes to die, but in that time, pain apart, he was content. Whatever the flaws of his fifty-seven years, and they were many, he felt he was perishing in a way his beloved Flavinus would not have been ashamed of.

Towards the end it began to rain, and the noise on the roof made him believe God was burying the house, sealing him up forever. And as the moment came, so did a splendid delusion: a hand, carrying a light, and escorted by voices, seemed to break through the wall, ghosts of the future come to excavate his history. He smiled to greet them, and was about to ask what year this was when he realised he was dead.

. . .

The creature was far better at avoiding Gavin than he'd been at avoiding it. Three days passed without its pursuer snatching sight of hide or hair of it.

But the fact of its presence, close, but never too close, was indisputable. In a bar someone would say: "Saw you last night on the Edgware Road" when he'd not been near the place, or "How'd you make out with that Arab then?" or "Don't you speak to your friends any longer?"

And God, he soon got to like the feeling. The distress gave way to a pleasure he'd not known since the age of two: ease.

So what if someone else was working his patch, dodging the law and the street-wise alike; so what if his friends (what friends? Leeches) were being cut by this supercilious copy; so what if his life had been taken from him and was being worn to its length and its breadth in lieu of him? He could sleep, and know that he, or something so like him it made no difference, was awake in the night and being adored. He began to see the creature not as a monster terrorising him, but as his tool, his public persona almost. It was substance: he shadow.

He woke, dreaming.

It was four-fifteen in the afternoon, and the whine of traffic was loud from the street below. A twilight room; the air breathed and rebreathed and breathed again so it smelt of his lungs. It was over a week since he'd left Reynolds to the ruins, and in that time he'd only ventured out from his new digs (one tiny bedroom, kitchen, bathroom) three times. Sleep was more important now than food or exercise. He had enough dope to keep him happy when sleep wouldn't come, which was seldom, and he'd grown to like the staleness of the air, the flux of light through the curtainless window, the sense of a world elsewhere which he had no part of or place in.

Today he'd told himself he ought to go out and get some fresh air, but he hadn't been able to raise the enthusiasm. Maybe later, much later, when the bars were emptying and he wouldn't be noticed, then he'd slip out of his cocoon and see what could be seen. For now, there were dreams—

Water.

He'd dreamt water; sitting beside a pool in Fort Lauderdale, a pool full of fish. And the splash of their leaps and dives was continuing, an overflow from sleep. Or was it the other way round? Yes; he had been hearing running water in his sleep and his dreaming mind had made an illustration to accompany the sound. Now awake, the sound continued.

It was coming from the adjacent bathroom, no longer running, but lapping. Somebody had obviously broken in while he was asleep, and was now taking a bath. He ran down the short list of possible intruders: the few who knew he was here. There was Paul: a nascent hustler who'd bedded down on the floor two nights before; there was Chink, the dope dealer; and a girl from downstairs he thought was called Michelle. Who was he kidding? None of these people would have broken the lock on the door to get in. He knew very well who it must be. He was just playing a game with himself, enjoying the process of elimination, before he narrowed the options to one.

Keen for reunion, he slid out from his skin of sheet and duvet. His body turned to a column of gooseflesh as the cold air encased him, his sleep-erection hid its head. As he crossed the room to where his dressing gown hung on the back of the door he caught sight of himself in the mirror, a freeze frame from an atrocity film, a wisp of a man, shrunk by cold, and lit by a rainwater light. His reflection almost flickered, he was so insubstantial.

Wrapping the dressing gown, his only freshly purchased garment, around him, he went to the bathroom door. There was no noise of water now. He pushed the door open.

The warped linoleum was icy beneath his feet; and all he wanted to do was to see his friend, then crawl back into bed. But he owed the tatters of his curiosity more than that: he had questions.

The light through the frosted glass had deteriorated rapidly in the three minutes since he'd woken: the onset of night and a rain-storm congealing the gloom. In front of him the bath was almost filled to overflowing, the water was oil-slick calm, and dark. As before, nothing broke surface. It was lying deep, hidden.

How long was it since he'd approached a lime-green bath in a lime-green bathroom, and peered into the water? It could have been yesterday: his life between then and now had become one long night. He looked down. It was there, tucked up, as before, and asleep, still wearing all its clothes as though it had had no time to undress before it hid itself. Where it had been bald it now sprouted a luxuriant head of hair, and its features were quite complete. No trace of a painted face remained: it had a plastic beauty that was his own absolutely, down to the last mole. Its perfectly finished hands were crossed on its chest.

The night deepened. There was nothing to do but watch it sleep, and he became bored with that. It had traced him here, it wasn't likely to run away again, he could go back to bed. Outside the rain had slowed the commuters' homeward journey to a crawl, there were accidents, some fatal; engines overheated, hearts too. He listened to the chase; sleep came and went. It was the middle of the evening when thirst woke him again: he was dreaming water, and there was the sound as it had been before. The creature was hauling itself out of the bath, was putting its hand to the door, opening it.

There it stood. The only light in the bedroom was coming from the street below; it barely began to illuminate the visitor.

"Gavin? Are you awake?"

"Yes," he said.

"Will you help me?" it asked. There was no trace of threat in its voice, it asked as a man might ask his brother, for kinship's sake.

"What do you want?"

"Time to heal."

"Heal?"

"Put on the light."

Gavin switched on the lamp beside the bed and looked at the figure at the door. It no longer had its arms crossed on its chest, and Gavin saw that the position had been covering an appalling shotgun wound. The flesh of its chest had been blown open, exposing its colourless innards. There was, of course, no blood: that it would never have. Nor, from this distance, could Gavin see anything in its interior that faintly resembled human anatomy.

"God Almighty," he said.

"Preetorius had friends," said the other, and its fingers touched the edge of the wound. The gesture recalled a picture on the wall of his mother's house. Christ in Glory—the Sacred Heart floating inside the Saviour—while his fingers, pointing to the agony he'd suffered, said: "This was for you."

"Why aren't you dead?"

"Because I'm not yet alive," it said.

Not yet: remember that, Gavin thought. It has intimations of mortality.

"Are you in pain?"

"No," it said sadly, as though it craved the experience, "I feel nothing. All the signs of life are cosmetic. But I'm learning." It smiled. "I've got the knack of the yawn, and the fart." The idea was both absurd and touching; that it would aspire to farting, that a farcical failure in the digestive system was for it a precious sign of humanity.

"And the wound?"

"—is healing. Will heal completely in time."

Gavin said nothing.

"Do I disgust you?" it asked, without inflection.

"No."

It was staring at Gavin with perfect eyes, his perfect eyes.

"What did Reynolds tell you?" it asked.

Gavin shrugged.

"Very little."

"That I'm a monster? That I suck out the human spirit?"

"Not exactly."

"More or less."

"More or less," Gavin conceded.

It nodded. "He's right," it said. "In his way, he's right. I need blood: that makes me monstrous. In my youth, a month ago, I bathed in it. Its touch gave wood the appearance of flesh. But I don't need it now: the process is almost finished. All I need now—"

It faltered; not, Gavin thought, because it intended to lie, but because the words to describe its condition wouldn't come.

"What do you need?" Gavin pressed it.

It shook its head, looking down at the carpet. "I've lived

several times, you know. Sometimes I've stolen lives and got away with it. Lived a natural span, then shrugged off that face and found another. Sometimes, like the last time, I've been challenged, and lost—"

"Are you some kind of machine?"

"No."

"What then?"

"I am what I am. I know of no others like me; though why should I be the only one? Perhaps there *are* others, many others: I simply don't know of them yet. So I live and die and live again, and learn nothing"—the word was bitterly pronounced—"of myself. Understand? You know what you are because you see others like you. If you were alone on earth, what would you know? What the mirror told you, that's all. The rest would be myth and conjecture."

The summary was made without sentiment.

"May I lie down?" it asked.

It began to walk towards him, and Gavin could see more clearly the fluttering in its chest-cavity, the restless, incoherent forms that were mushrooming there in place of the heart. Sighing, it sank face-down on the bed, its clothes sodden, and closed its eyes.

"We'll heal," it said. "Just give us time."

Gavin went to the door of the flat and bolted it. Then he dragged a table over and wedged it under the handle. Nobody could get in and attack it in sleep: they would stay here together in safety, he and it, he and himself. The fortress secured, he brewed some coffee and sat in the chair across the room from the bed and watched the creature sleep.

The rain rushed against the window heavily one hour, lightly the next. Wind threw sodden leaves against the glass and they clung there like inquisitive moths; he watched them sometimes, when he tired of watching himself, but before long he'd want to look again, and he'd be back staring at the casual beauty of his outstretched arm, the light flicking the wrist-bone, the lashes. He fell asleep in the chair about midnight, with an ambulance complaining in the street outside, and the rain coming again.

It wasn't comfortable in the chair, and he'd surface from sleep every few minutes, his eyes opening a fraction. The creature was up: it was standing by the window, now in front of the mirror, now in the kitchen. Water ran: he dreamt water. The creature undressed: he dreamt sex. It stood over him, its chest whole, and he was reassured by its presence: he dreamt, it was for a moment only, himself lifted out of a street through a window into Heaven. It dressed in his clothes: he murmured his assent to the theft in his sleep. It was whistling: and there was a threat of day through the window, but he was too dozy to stir just yet, and quite content to have the whistling young man in his clothes live for him.

At last it leaned over the chair and kissed him on the lips, a brother's kiss, and left. He heard the door close behind it.

After that there were days, he wasn't sure how many, when he stayed in the room, and did nothing but drink water. This thirst had become unquenchable. Drinking and sleeping, drinking and sleeping, twin moons.

The bed he slept on was damp at the beginning from where the creature had laid, and he had no wish to change the sheets. On the contrary he enjoyed the wet linen, which his body dried out too soon. When it did he took a bath himself in the water the thing had lain in and returned to the bed dripping wet, his skin crawling with cold, and the scent of mildew all around. Later, too indifferent to move, he allowed his bladder free rein while he lay on the bed, and that water in time became cold, until he dried it with his dwindling body-heat.

But for some reason, despite the icy room, his nakedness, his hunger, he couldn't die.

He got up in the middle of the night of the sixth or seventh day, and sat on the edge of the bed to find the flaw in his resolve. When the solution didn't come he began to shamble around the room much as the creature had a week earlier, standing in front of the mirror to survey his pitifully changed body, watching the snow shimmer down and melt on the sill.

Eventually, by chance, he found a picture of his parents he remembered the creature staring at. Or had he dreamt that? He thought not: he had a distinct idea that it had picked up this picture and looked at it.

That was, of course, the bar to his suicide: that picture. There were respects to be paid. Until then how could he hope to die?

He walked to the Cemetery through the slush wearing only a pair of slacks and a tee-shirt. The remarks of middle-aged women and school-children went unheard. Whose business but his own was it if going barefoot was the death of him? The rain came and went, sometimes thickening towards snow, but never quite achieving its ambition.

There was a service going on at the church itself, a line of brittle coloured cars parked at the front. He slipped down the side into the churchyard. It boasted a good view, much spoiled today by the smoky veil of sleet, but he could see the trains and the high-rise flats; the endless rows of roofs. He ambled amongst the headstones, by no means certain of where to find his father's grave. It had been sixteen years: and the day hadn't been that memorable. Nobody had said anything illuminating about death in general, or his father's death specifically, there wasn't even a social gaff or two to mark the day: no aunt broke wind at the buffet table, no cousin took him aside to expose herself.

He wondered if the rest of the family ever came here: whether indeed they were still in the country. His sister had always threatened to move out: go to New Zealand, begin again. His mother was probably getting through her fourth husband by now, poor sod, though perhaps she was the pitiable one, with her endless chatter barely concealing the panic.

Here was the stone. And yes, there were fresh flowers in the marble urn that rested amongst the green marble chips. The old bugger had not lain here enjoying the view unnoticed. Obviously somebody, he guessed his sister, had come here seeking a little comfort from Father. Gavin ran his fingers over the name, the date, the platitude. Nothing exceptional, which was only right and proper, because there'd been nothing exceptional about him.

Staring at the stone, words came spilling out, as though Father was sitting on the edge of the grave, dangling his feet, raking his hair across his gleaming scalp, pretending, as he always pretended, to care.

"What do you think, eh?"

Father wasn't impressed.

"Not much, am I?" Gavin confessed.

You said it, son.

"Well I was always careful, like you told me. There aren't any bastards out there, going to come looking for me."

Damn pleased.

"I wouldn't be much to find, would I?"

Father blew his nose, wiped it three times. Once from left to right, again left to right, finishing right to left. Never failed. Then he slipped away.

"Old shithouse."

A toy train let out a long blast on its horn as it passed and Gavin looked up. There he was—himself—standing absolutely still a few yards away. He was wearing the same clothes he'd put on a week ago when he'd left the flat. They looked creased and shabby from constant wear. But the flesh! Oh, the flesh was more radiant than his own had ever been. It almost shone in the drizzling light; and the tears on the doppelganger's cheeks only made the features more exquisite.

"What's wrong?" said Gavin.

"It always makes me cry, coming here." It stepped over the graves towards him, its feet crunching on gravel, soft on grass. So real.

"You've been here before?"

"Oh yes. Many times, over the years—"

Over the years? What did it mean, over the years? Had it mourned here for people it had killed?

As if in answer:

"—I come to visit Father. Twice, maybe three times a year."

"This isn't your father," said Gavin, almost amused by the delusion. "It's mine."

"I don't see any tears on your face," said the other.

"I feel . . ."

"Nothing," his face told him. "You feel nothing at all, if you're honest."

That was the truth.

"Whereas I . . ." The tears began to flow again, its nose ran. "I will miss him until I die."

It was surely playacting, but if so why was there such grief in its eyes: and why were its features crumpled into ugliness as it wept. Gavin had seldom given in to tears: they'd always made him feel weak and ridiculous. But this thing was proud of tears, it gloried in them. They were its triumph.

And even then, knowing it had overtaken him, Gavin could find nothing in him that approximated grief.

"Have it," he said. "Have the snots. You're welcome."

The creature was hardly listening.

"Why is it all so painful?" it asked, after a pause. "Why is it loss that makes me human?"

Gavin shrugged. What did he know or care about the fine art of being human? The creature wiped its nose with its sleeve, sniffed, and tried to smile through its unhappiness.

"I'm sorry," it said, "I'm making a damn fool of myself. Please forgive me."

It inhaled deeply, trying to compose itself.

"That's all right," said Gavin. The display embarrassed him, and he was glad to be leaving.

"Your flowers?" he asked as he turned from the grave.

It nodded.

"He hated flowers."

The thing flinched.

"Ah."

"Still, what does he know?"

He didn't even look at the effigy again; just turned and started up the path that ran beside the church. A few yards on, the thing called after him:

"Can you recommend a dentist?"

Gavin grinned, and kept walking.

It was almost the commuter hour. The arterial road that ran by the church was already thick with speeding traffic: perhaps it was Friday, early escapees hurrying home. Lights blazed brilliantly, horns blared.

Gavin stepped into the middle of the flow without looking to right or left, ignoring the squeals of brakes, and the curses, and began to walk amongst the traffic as if he were idling in an open field.

The wing of a speeding car grazed his leg as it passed, another almost collided with him. Their eagerness to get somewhere, to arrive at a place they would presently be itching to depart from again, was comical. Let them rage at him, loathe him, let them glimpse his featureless face and go home haunted. If the circumstances were right, maybe one of them would panic, swerve, and run him down. Whatever. From now on he belonged to chance, whose Standard-Bearer he would surely be.

THE STONE CHAMBER

♦♦♦

H. B. MARRIOTT WATSON

It was not until early summer that Warrington took possession of Marvyn Abbey. He had bought the property in the preceding autumn, but the place had so fallen into decay through the disorders of time that more than six months elapsed ere it was inhabitable. The delay, however, fell out conveniently for Warrington; for the Bosanquets spent the winter abroad, and nothing must suit but he must spend it with them. There was never a man who pursued his passion with such ardour. He was ever at Miss Bosanquet's skirts, and bade fair to make her as steadfast a husband as he was attached a lover. Thus it was not until after his return from that prolonged exile that he had the opportunity of inspecting the repairs discharged by his architect. He was nothing out of the common in character, but was full of kindly impulses and a fellow of impetuous blood. When he called upon me in my chambers he spoke with some excitement of his Abbey, as also of his approaching marriage; and finally, breaking into an exhibition of genuine affection, declared that we had been so long and so continuously intimate that I, and none other, must help him warm his house and marry his bride. It had indeed been always understood between us that I should serve him at the ceremony, but now it appeared that I must start my duties even earlier. The prospect of a summer holiday in Utterbourne pleased me. It was a charming village, set upon the slope of a wooded hill and within call of the sea. I had a slight knowledge of the district from a riding excursion taken through that part of Devonshire; and years before, and ere Warrington had come into his money, had viewed the Abbey ruins from a distance with the polite curiosity of a passing tourist.

I examined them now with new eyes as we drove up the avenue. The face which the ancient building presented to the valley was of magnificent design, but now much worn and battered. Part of it, the right wing, I judged to be long past the uses of a dwelling, for the walls had crumbled away, huge gaps opened in the foundations, and the roof was quite dismantled. Warrington had very wisely left this portion to its own sinister decay; it was the left wing which had been restored, and which we were to inhabit. The entrance, I will confess, was a little mean, for the large doorway had been bricked up and an ordinary modern door gave upon the spacious terrace and the winding gardens. But apart from this, the work of restoration had been undertaken with skill and piety, and the interior had retained its native dignity, while resuming an air of proper comfort. The old oak had been repaired congruous with the original designs, and the great rooms had been as little altered as was requisite to adapt them for daily use.

Warrington passed quickly from chamber to chamber in evident delight, directing my attention upon this and upon that, and eagerly requiring my congratulations and approval. My comments must have satisfied him, for the place attracted me vastly. The only criticism I ventured was to remark upon the size of the rooms and to question if they might dwarf the insignificant human figures they were to entertain.

He laughed. "Not a bit," said he. "Roaring fires in winter in those fine old fireplaces; and as for summer, the more space the better. We shall be jolly."

I followed him along the noble hall, and we stopped before a small door of very black oak.

"The bedrooms," he explained, as he turned the key, "are all upstairs, but mine is not ready yet. And besides, I am reserving it; I won't sleep in it till—you understand," he concluded, with a smiling suggestion of embarrassment.

I understood very well. He threw the door open.

"I am going to use this in the meantime," he continued. "Queer little room, isn't it? It used to be a sort of library. How do you think it looks?"

We had entered as he spoke, and stood, distributing our glances in that vague and general way in which a room is surveyed. It was a chamber of much smaller proportions than the rest, and was dimly lighted by two long narrow windows sunk in the great walls. The bed and the modern fittings looked strangely out of keeping with its ancient privacy. The walls were rudely distempered with barbaric frescoes dating, I conjectured, from the fourteenth century; and the floor was of stone, worn into grooves and hollows with the feet of many generations. As I was taking in these facts, there came over me a sudden curiosity as to those dead Marvyns who had held the Abbey for so long. This silent chamber seemed to suggest questions of their history; it spoke eloquently of past ages and past deeds, fallen now into oblivion. Here, within these thick walls, no echo from the outer world might carry, no sound would ring within its solitary seclusion. Even the silence seemed to confer with one upon the ancient transactions of that extinct House.

Warrington stirred, and turned suddenly to me. "I hope

it's not damp," said he, with a slight shiver. "It looks rather solemn. I thought furniture would brighten it up."

"I should think it would be very comfortable," said I. "You will never be disturbed by any sounds at any rate."

"No," he answered, hesitatingly; and then, quickly, on one of his impulses: "Hang it, Heywood, there's too much silence here for me." Then he laughed. "Oh, I shall do very well for a month or two." And with that appeared to return to his former placid cheerfulness.

The train of thought started in that sombre chamber served to entertain me several times that day. I questioned Warrington at dinner, which we took in one of the smaller rooms, commanding a lovely prospect of dale and sea. He shook his head. Archaeological lore, as indeed anything else out of the borders of actual life, held very little interest for him.

"The Marvyns died out in 1714, I believe," he said, indifferently. "Someone told me that—the man I bought it from, I think. They might just as well have kept the place up since; but I think it has been only occupied twice between then and now, and the last time was forty years ago. It would have rotted to pieces if I hadn't taken it. Perhaps Mrs. Batty could tell you. She's lived in these parts almost all her life."

To humour me, and affected, I doubt not, by a certain pride in his new possession, he put the query to his housekeeper upon her appearance subsequently; but it seemed that her knowledge was little fuller than his own, though she had gathered some vague traditions of the countryside. The Marvyns had not left a reputable name, if rumour spoke truly; theirs was a family to which black deeds had been credited. They were ill-starred also in their fortunes, and had become extinct suddenly; but for the rest, the events had fallen too many generations ago to be current now between the memories of the village.

Warrington, who was more eager to discuss the future than to recall the past, was vastly excited by his anticipations. St. Pharamond, Sir William Bosanquet's house, lay across the valley, barely five miles away; and as the family had now returned, it was easy to forgive Warrington's elation.

"What do you think?" he said, late that evening; and clapping me upon the shoulder. "You have seen Marion, here is the house. Am I not lucky? Damn it, Heywood, I'm not pious, but I am disposed to thank God! I'm not a bad fellow, but I'm no saint; it's fortunate that it's not only the virtuous that are rewarded. In fact, it's usually contrariwise. I owe this to—Lord, I don't know what I owe it to. Is it my money? Of course, Marion doesn't care a rap for that; but then, you see, I mightn't have known her without it. Of course, there's the house, too. I'm thankful I have money. At any rate, here's my new life. Just look about and take it in, old fellow. If you knew how a man may be ashamed of himself! But there, I've done. You know I'm decent at heart—you must count my life from today." And with this outbreak he lifted the glass between fingers that trembled with the warmth of his emotions, and tossed off his wine.

He did himself but justice when he claimed to be a good fellow; and, in truth, I was myself somewhat moved by his obvious feeling. I remember that we shook hands very affectionately, and my sympathy was the prelude to a long and confidential talk, which lasted until quite a late hour.

At the foot of the staircase, where we parted, he detained me.

"This is the last of my wayward days," he said, with a smile. "Late hours—liquor—all go. You shall see. Good-night. You know your room. I shall be up long before you." And with that he vanished briskly into the darkness that hung about the lower parts of the passage.

I watched him go, and it struck me quite vaguely what a slight impression his candle made upon that channel of opaque gloom. It seemed merely as a thread of light that illumined nothing. Warrington himself was rapt into the prevalent blackness; but long afterwards, and even when his footsteps had died away upon the heavy carpet, the tiny beam was visible, advancing and flickering in the distance.

My window, which was modern, opened upon a little balcony, where, as the night was warm and I was indisposed for sleep, I spent half an hour enjoying the air. I was in a sentimental mood, and my thoughts turned upon the suggestions which Warrington's conversation had induced. It was not until I was in bed, and had blown out the light, that they settled upon the square, dark chamber in which my host was to pass the night. As I have said, I was wakeful, owing, no doubt, to the high pitch of the emotions which we had encouraged; but presently my fancies became inarticulate and incoherent, and then I was overtaken by profound sleep.

Warrington was up before me, as he had predicted, and met me in the breakfast-room.

"What a beggar you are to sleep!" he said, with a smile. "I've hammered at your door for half an hour."

I apologized for myself, alleging the rich country air in my defence, and mentioned that I had had some difficulty in getting to sleep.

"So had I," he remarked, as we sat down to the table. "We got very excited, I suppose. Just see what you have there, Heywood. Eggs? Oh, damn it, one can have too much of eggs!" He frowned, and lifted a third cover. "Why in the name of common sense can't Mrs. Batty give us more variety?" he asked, impatiently.

I deprecated his displeasure, suggesting that we should do very well; indeed, his discontent seemed to me quite unnecessary. But I supposed Warrington had been rather spoiled by many years of club life.

He settled himself without replying, and began to pick over his plate in a gingerly manner.

"There's one thing I will have here, Heywood," he observed. "I will have things well appointed. I'm not going to let life in the country mean an uncomfortable life. A man can't change the habits of a lifetime."

In contrast with his exhilarated professions of the previous evening, this struck me with a sense of amusement at the moment; and the incongruity may have occurred to him, for he went on: "Marion's not over strong, you know, and must have things *comme il faut.* She shan't decline upon a lower level. The worst of these rustics is that they have no imagination." He held up a piece of bacon on his fork, and surveyed it with disgust. "Now, look at that! Why the devil don't they take tips from civilized people like the French?"

It was so unlike him to exhibit this petulance that I put it down to a bad night, and without discovering the connection of my thoughts, asked him how he liked his bedroom.

"Oh, pretty well, pretty well," he said, indifferently. "It's not so cold as I thought. But I slept badly. I always do in a strange bed," and pushing aside his plate, he lit a cigarette. "When you've finished that garbage, Heywood, we'll have a stroll round the Abbey," he said.

His good temper returned during our walk, and he

indicated to me various improvements which he contemplated, with something of his old ardour. The left wing of the house, as I have said, was entire, but a little apart were the ruins of a chapel. Surrounded by a low moss-grown wall, it was full of picturesque charm; the roofless chancel was spread with ivy, but the aisles were intact. Grass grew between the stones and the floor, and many creepers had strayed through chinks in the wall into those sacred precincts. The solemn quietude of the ruin, maintained under the spell of death, awed me a little, but upon Warrington apparently it made no impression. He was only zealous that I should properly appreciate the distinction of such a property. I stooped and drew the weeds away from one of the slabs in the aisle, and was able to trace upon it the relics of lettering, well-nigh obliterated under the corrosion of time.

"There are tombs," said I.

"Oh, yes," he answered, with a certain relish. "I understand the Marvyns used it as a mausoleum. They are all buried here. Some good brasses, I am told."

The associations of the place engaged me; the aspect of the Abbey faced the past; it seemed to refuse communion with the present; and somehow the thought of those two decent humdrum lives which should be spent within its shelter savoured of the incongruous. The white-capped maids and the emblazoned butlers that should tread these halls offered a ridiculous appearance beside my fancies of the ancient building. For all that, I envied Warrington his home, and so I told him, with a humorous hint that I was fitter to appreciate its glories than himself.

He laughed. "Oh, I don't know," said he. "I like the old-world look as much as you do. I have always had a notion of something venerable. It seems to serve you for ancestors." And he was undoubtedly delighted with my enthusiasm.

But at lunch again he chopped round to his previous irritation, only now quite another matter provoked his anger. He had received a letter by the second post from Miss Bosanquet, which, if I may judge from his perplexity, must have been unusually confused. He read and re-read it, his brow lowering.

"What the deuce does she mean?" he asked, testily. "She first makes an arrangement for us to ride over today, and now I can't make out whether we are to go to St. Pharamond, or they are coming to us. Just look at it, will you, Heywood?"

I glanced through the note, but could offer no final solution, whereupon he broke out again:

"That's just like women—they never can say anything straightforwardly. Why, in the name of goodness, couldn't she leave things as they were? You see," he observed, rather in answer, as I fancied, to my silence, "we don't know what to do now; if we stay here they mayn't come, and if we go probably we shall cross them." And he snapped his fingers in annoyance.

I was cheerful enough, perhaps because the responsibility was not mine, and ventured to suggest that we might ride over, and return if we missed them. But he dismissed the subject sharply by saying:

"No, I'll stay. I'm not going on a fool's errand," and drew my attention to some point in the decoration of the room.

The Bosanquets did not arrive during the afternoon, and Warrington's ill-humour increased. His love-sick state pleaded in excuse of him, but he was certainly not a pleasant companion. He was sour and snappish, and one could introduce no statement to which he would not find a contradiction. So unamiable did he grow that at last I discovered a pretext to leave him, and rambled to the back of the Abbey into the precincts of the old chapel. The day was falling, and the summer sun flared through the western windows upon the bare aisle. The creepers rustled upon the gaping walls, and the tall grasses waved in shadows over the bodies of the forgotten dead. As I stood contemplating the effect, and meditating greatly upon the anterior fortunes of the Abbey, my attention fell upon a huge slab of marble, upon which the yellow light struck sharply. The faded lettering rose into greater definition before my eyes and I read slowly:

"Here lyeth the body of Sir Rupert Marvyn."

Beyond a date, very difficult to decipher, there was nothing more; of eulogy, of style, of record, of pious considerations such as were usual to the period, not a word. I read the numerals variously as 1723 and 1745; but however they ran it was probable that the stone covered the resting-place of the last Marvyn. The history of this futile house interested me not a little, partly for Warrington's sake, and in part from a natural bent towards ancient records; and I made a mental note of the name and date.

When I returned Warrington's surliness had entirely vanished, and had given place to an effusion of boisterous spirits. He apologized jovially for his bad temper.

"It was the disappointment of not seeing Marion," he said. "You will understand that some day, old fellow. But, anyhow, we'll go over tomorrow," and forthwith proceeded to enliven the dinner with an ostentation of good-fellowship I had seldom witnessed in him. I began to suspect that he had heard again from St. Pharamond, though he chose to conceal the fact from me. The wine was admirable; though Warrington himself was no great judge, he had entrusted the selection to a good palate. We had a merry meal, drank a little more than was prudent, and smoked our cigars upon the terrace in the fresh air. Warrington was restless. He pushed his glass from him. "I'll tell you what, old chap," he broke out, "I'll give you a game of billiards. I've got a decent table."

I demurred. The air was too delicious, and I was in no humour for a sharp use of my wits. He laughed, though he seemed rather disappointed.

"It's almost sacrilege to play billiards in an Abbey," I said, whimsically. "What would the ghosts of the old Marvyns think?"

"Oh, hang the Marvyns!" he rejoined, crossly. "You're always talking of them."

He rose and entered the house, returning presently with a flagon of whisky and some glasses.

"Try this," he said. "We've had no liqueurs." And pouring out some spirit he swallowed it raw.

I stared, for Warrington rarely took spirits, being more of a wine drinker; moreover, he must have taken nearly the quarter of a tumbler. But he did not notice my surprise, and, seating himself, lit another cigar.

"I don't mean to have things quiet here," he observed, reflectively. "I don't believe in your stagnant rustic life. What I intend to do is to keep the place warm—plenty of house parties, things going on all the year. I shall expect you down for the shooting, Ned. The coverts promise well this year."

I assented willingly enough, and he rambled on again.

"I don't know that I shall use the Abbey so much. I think I'll live in town a good deal. It's brighter there. I don't know though. I like the place. Hang it, it's a rattling good shop, there's no mistake about it. Look here," he broke off, abruptly, "bring your glass in, and I'll show you something."

I was little inclined to move, but he was so peremptory that I followed him with a sigh. We entered one of the smaller rooms which overlooked the terrace, and had been diverted into a comfortable library. He flung back the windows.

"There's air for you," he cried. "Now, sit down," and walking to a cupboard produced a second flagon of whisky. "Irish!" he ejaculated, clumping it on the table. "Take your choice," and turning again to the cupboard, presently sat down with his hands under the table. "Now, then, Ned," he said, with a short laugh. "Fill up, and we'll have some fun," with which he suddenly threw a pack of cards upon the board.

I opened my eyes, for I do not suppose Warrington had touched cards since his college days; but, interpreting my look in his own way, he cried:

"Oh, I'm not married yet. Warrington's his own man still. Poker? Eh?"

"Anything you like," said I, with resignation.

A peculiar expression of delight gleamed in his eyes, and he shuffled the cards feverishly.

"Cut," said he, and helped himself to more whisky.

It was shameful to be playing there with that beautiful night without, but there seemed no help for it. Warrington had a run of luck, though he played with little skill; and his excitement grew as he won.

"Let us make it ten shillings," he suggested.

I shook my head. "You forget I'm not a millionaire," I replied.

"Bah!" he cried. "I like a game worth the victory. Well, fire away."

His eyes gloated upon the cards, and he fingered them with unctuous affection. The behaviour of the man amazed me. I began to win.

Warrington's face slowly assumed a dull, lowering expression; he played eagerly, avariciously; he disputed my points, and was querulous.

"Oh, we've had enough!" I cried in distaste.

"By Jove, you don't!" he exclaimed, jumping to his feet. "You're the winner, Heywood, and I'll see you damned before I let you off my revenge!"

The words startled me no less than the fury which rang in his accents. I gazed at him in stupefaction. The whites of his eyes showed wildly, and a sullen, angry look determined his face. Suddenly I was arrested by the suspicion of something upon his neck.

"What's that?" I asked. "You've cut yourself."

He put his hand to his face. "Nonsense," he replied, in a surly fashion.

I looked closer, and then I saw my mistake. It was a round, faint red mark, the size of a florin, upon the column of his throat, and I set it down to the accidental pressure of some button.

"Come on!" he insisted, impatiently.

"Bah! Warrington," I said, for I imagined that he had been over-excited by the whisky he had taken. "It's only a matter of a few pounds. Why make a fuss? Tomorrow will serve."

After a moment his eyes fell, and he gave an awkward laugh. "Oh, well, that'll do," said he. "But I got so infernally excited."

"Whisky," said I, sententiously.

He glanced at the bottle. "How many glasses have I had?" and he whistled. "By Jove, Ned, this won't do! I must turn over a new leaf. Come on; let's look at the night."

I was only too glad to get away from the table, and we were soon upon the terrace again. Warrington was silent, and his gaze went constantly across the valley, where the moon was rising, and in the direction in which, as he had indicated to me, St. Pharamond lay. When he said good-night he was still preoccupied.

"I hope you will sleep better," he said.

"And you, too," I added.

He smiled. "I don't suppose I shall wake the whole night through," he said; and then, as I was turning to go, he caught me quickly by the arm.

"Ned," he said, impulsively and very earnestly, "don't let me make a fool of myself again. I know it's the excitement of everything. But I want to be as good as I can for her."

I pressed his hand. "All right, old fellow," I said; and we parted.

I think I have never enjoyed sounder slumber than that night. The first thing I was aware of was the singing of thrushes outside my window. I rose and looked forth, and the sun was hanging high in the eastern sky, the grass and the young green of the trees were shining with dew. With an uncomfortable feeling that I was very late I hastily dressed and went downstairs. Warrington was waiting for me in the breakfast-room, as upon the previous morning, and when he turned from the window at my approach, the sight of his face startled me. It was drawn and haggard, and his eyes were shot with blood; it was a face broken and savage with dissipation. He made no answer to my questioning, but seated himself with a morose air.

"Now you have come," he said, sullenly, "we may as well begin. But it's not my fault if the coffee's cold."

I examined him critically, and passed some comment upon his appearance.

"You don't look up to much," I said. "Another bad night?"

"No; I slept well enough," he responded, ungraciously; and then, after a pause: "I'll tell you what, Heywood. You shall give me my revenge after breakfast."

"Nonsense," I said, after a momentary silence. "You're going over to St. Pharamond."

"Hang it!" was his retort. "One can't be always bothering about women. You seem mightily indisposed to meet me again."

"I certainly won't this morning," I answered, rather sharply, for the man's manner grated upon me. "This evening, if you like; and then the silly business shall end."

He said something in an undertone of grumble, and the rest of the meal passed in silence. But I entertained an uneasy suspicion of him, and after all he was my friend, with whom I was under obligations not to quarrel; and so when we rose, I approached him.

"Look here, Warrington," I said. "What's the matter with you? Have you been drinking? Remember what you asked me last night."

"Hold your damned row!" was all the answer he vouchsafed, as he whirled away from me, but with an embarrassed display of shame.

But I was not to be put off in that way, and I spoke somewhat more sharply.

"We're going to have this out, Warrington," I said. "If you are ill, let us understand that; but I'm not going to stay here with you in this cantankerous spirit."

"I'm not ill," he replied testily.

"Look at yourself," I cried, and turned him about to the mirror over the mantelpiece.

He started a little, and a frown of perplexity gathered on his forehead.

"Good Lord! I'm not like that, Ned," he said, in a different voice. "I must have been drunk last night." And with a sort of groan, he directed a piteous look at me.

"Come," I was constrained to answer, "pull yourself together. The ride will do you good. And no more whisky."

"No, by Heaven, no!" he cried vehemently, and seemed to shiver; but then, suddenly taking my arm, he walked out of the room.

The morning lay still and golden. Warrington's eyes went forth across the valley.

"Come round to the stables, Ned," he said, impulsively. "You shall choose your own nag."

I shook my head. "I'll choose yours," said I, "but I am not going with you." He looked surprised. "No, ride by yourself. You don't want a companion on such an errand. I'll stay here, and pursue my investigations into the Marvyns."

A scowl crossed his face, but only for an instant, and then he answered: "All right, old chap; do as you like. Anyway, I'm off at once." And presently, when his horse was brought, he was laughing merrily.

"You'll have a dull day, Ned; but it's your own fault, you duffer. You'll have to lunch by yourself, as I shan't be back till late." And, gaily flourishing his whip, trotted down the drive.

It was some relief for me to be rid of him, for, in truth, his moods had worn my nerves, and I had not looked for a holiday of this disquieting nature. When he returned, I had no doubt it would be with quite another face, and meanwhile I was excellent company for myself. After lunch I amused myself for half an hour with idle tricks upon the billiard-table, and, tiring of my pastime, fell upon the housekeeper as I returned along the corridor. She was a woman nearer to sixty than fifty, with a comfortable, portly figure, and an amiable expression. Her eyes invited me ever so respectfully to conversation, and stopping, I entered into talk. She inquired if I liked my room and how I slept.

" 'Tis a nice look-out you have, Sir," said she. "That was where old Lady Martin slept."

It appeared that she had served as kitchen-maid to the previous tenants of the Abbey, nearly fifty years before.

"Oh, I know the old house in and out," she asserted, "and I arranged the rooms with Mr. Warrington."

We were standing opposite the low doorway which gave entrance to Warrington's bedroom, and my eyes unconsciously shot in that direction. Mrs. Batty followed my glance.

"I didn't want him to have that," she said, "but he was set upon it. It's smallish for a bedroom, and in my opinion isn't fit for more than a lumber-room. That's what Sir William used it for."

I pushed open the door and stepped over the threshold, and the housekeeper followed me.

"No," she said, glancing round, "and it's in my mind that it's damp, Sir."

Again I had a curious feeling that the silence was speaking in my ear; the atmosphere was thick and heavy, and a musty smell, as of faded draperies, penetrated my nostrils. The whole room looked indescribably dingy, despite the new hangings. I went over to the narrow window and peered through the diamond panes. Outside, but seen dimly through that ancient and discoloured glass, the ruins of the chapel confronted me, bare and stark, in the yellow sunlight. I turned.

"There are no ghosts in the Abbey, I suppose, Mrs. Batty?" I asked, whimsically.

But she took my inquiry very gravely. "I have never

heard tell of one, Sir," she protested, "and if there was such a thing I should have known it."

As I was rejoining her a strange low whirring was audible, and looking up I saw in a corner of the high-arched roof a horrible face watching me out of black narrow eyes. I confess that I was very much startled at the apparition, but the next moment realized what it was. The creature hung with its ugly fleshy wings extended over a grotesque stone head that leered down upon me, its evil-looking snout projecting into the room; it lay perfectly still, returning me glance for glance, until moved by the repulsion of its presence I clapped my hands, and cried loudly; then, slowly flitting in a circle round the roof, it vanished with a flapping of wings into some darker corner of the rafters. Mrs. Batty was astounded, and expressed surprise that it had managed to conceal itself for so long.

"Oh, bats live in holes," I answered. "Probably there is some small access through the masonry." But the incident had sent an uncomfortable shiver through me all the same.

Later that day I began to recognize that, short of an abrupt return to town, my time was not likely to be spent very pleasantly. But it was the personal problem so far as it concerned Warrington himself that distressed me even more. He came back from St. Pharamond in a morose and ugly temper, quite alien to his kindly nature. It seems that he had quarrelled bitterly with Miss Bosanquet, but upon what I could not determine, nor did I press him for an explanation. But the fumes of his anger were still rising when we met, and our dinner was a most depressing meal. He was in a degree of irritation which rendered it impossible to address him, and I soon withdrew into my thoughts. I saw, however, that he was drinking far too much, as, indeed, was plain subsequently when he invited me into the library. Once more he produced the hateful cards, and I was compelled to play, as he reminded me somewhat churlishly that I had promised him his revenge.

"Understand, Warrington," I said, firmly, "I play tonight, but never again, whatever the result. In fact, I am in half the mind to return to town tomorrow."

He gave me a look as he sat down, but said nothing, and the game began. He lost heavily from the first, and as nothing would content him but we must constantly raise the stakes, in a short time I had won several hundred pounds. He bore the reverses very ill, breaking out from time to time into some angry exclamation, now petulantly questioning my playing, and muttering oaths under his breath. But I was resolved that he should have no cause of complaint against me for this one night, and disregarding his insane fits of temper, I played steadily and silently. As the tally of my gains mounted he changed colour slowly, his face assuming a ghastly expression, and his eyes suspiciously denoting my actions. At length he rose, and throwing himself quickly across the table, seized my hand ferociously as I dealt a couple of cards.

"Damn you! I see your tricks," he cried, in frenzied passion. "Drop that hand, do you hear? Drop that hand, or by—"

But he got no further, for, rising myself, I wrenched my hand from his grasp, and turned upon him, in almost as great a passion as himself. But suddenly, and even as I opened my mouth to speak, I stopped short with a cry of horror. His face was livid to the lips, his eyes were cast with blood, and upon the dirty white of his flesh, right in the centre of his throat, the round red scar, flaming and ugly as a wound, stared upon me.

"Warrington!" I cried. "What is this? What have you—" And pointed in alarm to the spot.

"Mind your own business," he said, with a sneer. "It is well to try and draw off attention from your knavery. But that trick won't answer with me."

Without another word I flung the IOU's upon the table, and turning on my heel, left the room. I was furious with him, and fully resolved to leave the Abbey in the morning. I made my way upstairs to my room, and then, seating myself upon the balcony, endeavoured to recover my self-possession.

The more I considered, the more unaccountable was Warrington's behaviour. He had always been a perfectly courteous man, with a great lump of kindness in his nature; whereas these last few days he had been nothing other than a savage. It seemed certain that he must be ill or going mad; and as I reflected upon this the conjecture struck me with a sense of pity. If it was that he was losing his senses, how horrible was the tragedy in face of the new and lovely prospects opening in his life. Stimulated by this growing conviction, I resolved to go down and see him, more particularly as I now recalled his pleading voice that I should help him, on the previous evening. Was it not possible that this pathetic appeal derived from the instinct of the insane to protect themselves?

I found him still in the library; his head had fallen upon the table, and the state of the whisky bottle by his arm showed only too clearly his condition. I shook him vigorously, and he opened his eyes.

"Warrington, you must go to bed," I said.

He smiled, and greeted me quite affectionately. Obviously he was not so drunk as I had supposed.

"What is the time, Ned?" he asked.

I told him it was one o'clock, at which he rose briskly.

"Lord, I've been asleep," he said. "Help me, Ned. I don't think I'm sober. Where have you been?"

I assisted him to his room, and he undressed slowly, and with an effort. Somehow, as I stood watching him, I yielded to an unknown impulse and said, suddenly:

"Warrington, don't sleep here. Come and share my room."

"My dear fellow," he replied, with a foolish laugh, "yours is not the only room in the house. I can use a half-a-dozen if I like."

"Well, use one of them," I answered.

He shook his head. "I'm going to sleep here," he returned, obstinately.

I made no further effort to influence him, for, after all, now that the words were out, I had absolutely no reason to give him or myself for my proposition. And so I left him. When I had closed the door, and was turning to go along the passage, I heard very clearly, as it seemed to me, a plaintive cry, muffled and faint, but very disturbing, which sounded from the room. Instantly I opened the door again. Warrington was in bed, and the heavy sound of his breathing told me that he was asleep. It was impossible that he could have uttered the cry. A night-light was burning by his bedside, shedding a strong illumination over the immediate vicinity, and throwing antic shadows on the walls. As I turned to go, there was a whirring of wings, a brief flap behind me, and the room was plunged in darkness. The obscene creature that lived in the recesses of the roof must have knocked out the tiny light with its wings. Then Warrington's breathing ceased, and there was no sound at all. And then once more the silence seemed to gather round me slowly and heavily, and whisper to me. I had a vague sense of being prevailed upon, of being enticed and lured by something in the surrounding air; a sort of horror circumscribed me, and I broke from the invisible ring and rushed from the room. The door clanged behind me, and as I hastened along the hall, once more there seemed to ring in my ears the faint and melancholy cry.

I awoke, in the sombre twilight that precedes the dawn, from a sleep troubled and encumbered with evil dreams. The birds had not yet begun their day, and a vast silence brooded over the Abbey gardens. Looking out of my window, I caught sight of a dark figure stealing cautiously round the corner of the ruined chapel. The furtive gait, as well as the appearance of a man at that early hour, struck me with surprise; and hastily throwing on some clothes, I ran downstairs, and, opening the hall-door, went out. When I reached the porch which gave entrance to the aisle I stopped suddenly, for there before me, with his head to the ground, and peering among the tall grasses, was the object of my pursuit. Then I stepped quickly forward and laid a hand upon his shoulder. It was Warrington.

"What are you doing here?" I asked.

He turned and looked at me in bewilderment. His eyes wore a dazed expression, and he blinked in perplexity before he replied.

"It's you, is it?" he said weakly. "I thought—" and then paused. "What is it?" he asked.

"I followed you here," I explained. "I only saw your figure, and thought it might be some intruder."

He avoided my eyes. "I thought I heard a cry out here," he answered.

"Warrington," I said, with some earnestness, "come back to bed."

He made no answer, and slipping my arm in his, I led

him away. On the doorstep he stopped, and lifted his face to me.

"Do you think it's possible—" he began, as if to inquire of me, and then again paused. With a slight shiver he proceeded to his room, while I followed him. He sat down upon his bed, and his eyes strayed to the barred window absently. The black shadow of the chapel was visible through the panes.

"Don't say anything about this," he said, suddenly. "Don't let Marion know."

I laughed, but it was an awkward laugh.

"Why, that you were alarmed by a cry for help, and went in search like a gentleman?" I asked, jestingly.

"You heard it, then?" he said, eagerly.

I shook my head, for I was not going to encourage his fancies. "You had better go to sleep," I replied, "and get rid of these nightmares."

He sighed and lay back upon his pillow, dressed as he was. Ere I left him he had fallen into a profound slumber.

If I had expected a surly mood in him at breakfast I was much mistaken. There was not a trace of his nocturnal dissipations; he did not seem even to remember them, and he made no allusion whatever to our adventure in the dawn. He perused a letter carefully, and threw it over to me with a grin.

"Lor', what queer sheep women are!" he exclaimed, with rather a coarse laugh.

I glanced at the letter without thinking, but ere I had read half of it I put it aside. It was certainly not meant for my eyes, and I marvelled at Warrington's indelicacy in making public, as it were, that very private matter. The note was from Miss Bosanquet, and was clearly designed for his own heart, couched as it was in the terms of warm and fond affection. No man should see such letters save he for whom they are written.

"You see, they're coming over to dine," he remarked, carelessly. "Trust a girl to make it up if you let her alone long enough."

I made no answer; but though Warrington's grossness irritated me, I reflected with satisfaction upon his return to good humour, which I attributed to the reconciliation.

When I moved out upon the terrace the maid had entered to remove the breakfast things. I was conscious of a slight exclamation behind me, and Warrington joined me presently, with a loud guffaw.

"That's a damned pretty girl!" he said, with unction. "I'm glad Mrs. Batty got her. I like to have good-looking servants."

I suddenly interpreted the incident, and shrugged my shoulders.

"You're a perfect boot this morning, Warrington," I exclaimed, irritably.

He only laughed. "You're a dull dog of a saint, Heywood," he retorted. "Come along," and dragged me out in no amiable spirit.

I had forgotten how perfect a host Warrington could be, but that evening he was displayed at his best. The Bosanquets arrived early. Sir William was an easy-going man, fond of books and of wine, and I now guessed at the taste which had decided Warrington's cellar. Miss Bosanquet was as charming as I remembered her to be; and if any objection might be taken to Warrington himself by my anxious eyes it was merely that he seemed a trifle excited, a fault which, in the circumstances, I was able to condone. Sir William hung about the table, sipping his wine. Warrington, who had been very abstemious, grew restless, and, finally apologizing in his graceful way, left me to keep the baronet company. I was the less disinclined to do so as I was anxious not to intrude upon the lovers, and Sir William was discussing the history of the Abbey. He had an old volume somewhere in his library which related to it, and, seeing that I was interested, invited me to look it up.

We sat long, and it was not until later that the horrible affair which I must narrate occurred. The evening was close and oppressive, owing to the thunder, which already rumbled far away in the south. When we rose we found that Warrington and Miss Bosanquet were in the garden, and thither we followed. As at first we did not find them, Sir William, who had noted the approaching storm with some uneasiness, left me to make arrangements for his return; and I strolled along the paths by myself, enjoying a cigarette. I had reached the shrubbery upon the further side of the chapel, when I heard the sound of voices—a man's rough and rasping, a woman's pleading and informed with fear. A sharp cry ensued, and without hesitation I plunged through the thicket in the direction of the speakers. The sight that met me appalled me for the moment. Darkness was falling, lit with ominous flashes; and the two figures stood out distinctly in the bushes, in an attitude of struggle. I could not mistake the voices now. I heard Warrington's, brusque with anger, and almost savage in its tones, crying, "You shall!" and there followed a murmur from the girl, a little sob, and then a piercing cry. I sprang forward and seized Warrington by the arm; when, to my horror, I perceived that he had taken her wrist in both hands and was roughly twisting it, after the cruel habit of schoolboys. The malevolent cruelty of the action so astounded me that for an instant I remained motionless; I almost heard the bones in the frail wrist cracking; and then, in a second, I had seized Warrington's hands in a grip of iron, and flung him violently to the ground. The girl fell with him, and as I picked her up he rose too, and, clenching his fists, made as though to come at me, but instead turned and went sullenly, and with a ferocious look of hate upon his face, out of the thicket.

Miss Bosanquet came to very shortly, and though the agony of the pain must have been considerable to a delicate girl, I believe it was rather the incredible horror of the act under which she swooned. For my part I had nothing to say: not one word relative to the incident dared pass my lips. I inquired if she was better, and then, putting her arm in mine, led her gently towards the house. Her heart beat hard against me, and she breathed heavily, leaning on me for support. At the chapel I stopped, feeling suddenly that I dare not let her be seen in this condition, and bewildered greatly by the whole atrocious business.

"Come and rest in here," I suggested, and we entered the chapel.

I set her on a slab of marble, and stood waiting by her side. I talked fluently about anything; for lack of a subject, upon the state of the chapel and the curious tomb I had discovered. Recovering a little, she joined presently in my remarks. It was plain that she was putting a severe restraint upon herself. I moved aside the grasses, and read aloud the inscription on Sir Rupert's grave-piece, and turning to the next, which was rankly overgrown, feigned to search further. As I was bending there, suddenly, and by what thread of thought I know not, I identified the spot with that upon which I had found Warrington stooping that morning. With a sweep of my hand I brushed back the weeds, uprooting some with my fingers, and kneeling in the twilight, pored over the monument. Suddenly a wild flare of light streamed down the sky, and a great crash of thunder followed. Miss Bosanquet started to her feet and

I to mine. The heaven was lit up, as it were, with sunlight, and, as I turned, my eyes fell upon the now uncovered stone. Plainly the lettering flashed in my eyes:

"Priscilla, Lady Marvyn."

Then the clouds opened, and the rain fell in spouts, shouting and dancing upon the ancient roof overhead.

We were under a very precarious shelter, and I was uneasy that Miss Bosanquet should run the risk of that flimsy, ravaged edifice; and so in a momentary lull I managed to get her to the house. I found Sir William in a restless state of nerves. He was a timorous man, and the thunder had upset him, more particularly as he and his daughter were now storm-bound for some time. There was no possibility of venturing into those rude elements for an hour or more. Warrington was not inside, and no one had seen him. In the light Miss Bosanquet's face frightened me; her eyes were large and scared, and her colour very dead white. Clearly she was very near a breakdown. I found Mrs. Batty, and told her that the young lady had been severely shaken by the storm, suggesting that she had better lie down for a little. Returning with me, the housekeeper led off the unfortunate girl, and Sir William and I were left together. He paced the room impatiently, and constantly inquired if there were any signs of improvement in the weather. He also asked for Warrington, irritably. The burden of the whole dreadful night seemed fallen upon me. Passing through the hall I met Mrs. Batty again. Her usually placid features were disturbed and aghast.

"What is the matter?" I asked. "Is Miss Bosanquet—"

"No, Sir; I think she's sleeping," she replied. "She's in—she is in Mr. Warrington's room."

I started. "Are there no other rooms?" I asked, abruptly.

"There are none ready, Sir, except yours," she answered, "and I thought—"

"You should have taken her there," I said, sharply. The woman looked at me and opened her mouth. "Good heavens!" I said, irritably. "What is the matter? Everyone is mad tonight."

"Alice is gone, Sir," she blurted forth.

Alice, I remembered, was the name of one of her maids.

"What do you mean?" I asked, for her air of panic betokened something graver than her words. The thunder broke over the house and drowned her voice.

"She can't be out in this storm—she must have taken refuge somewhere," I said.

At that the strings of her tongue loosened, and she burst forth with her tale. It was an abominable narrative.

"Where is Mr. Warrington?" I asked; but she shook her head.

There was a moment's silence between us, and we eyed each other aghast. "She will be all right," I said at last, as if dismissing the subject.

The housekeeper wrung her hands. "I never would have thought it!" She repeated dismally, "I never would have thought it!"

"There is some mistake," I said; but, somehow, I knew better. Indeed, I felt now that I had almost been prepared for it.

"She ran towards the village," whispered Mrs. Batty. "God knows where she was going! The river lies that way."

"Pooh!" I exclaimed. "Don't talk nonsense. It is all a mistake. Come, have you any brandy?"

Brought back to the material round of her duties she bustled away with a sort of briskness, and returned with a flagon and glasses. I took a strong nip, and went back to Sir William. He was feverish, and declaimed against the weather unceasingly. I had to listen to the string of misfortunes which he recounted in the season's crops. It seemed all so futile, with his daughter involved in her horrid tragedy in a neighbouring room. He was better after some brandy, and grew more cheerful, but assiduously wondered about Warrington.

"Oh, he's been caught in the storm and taken refuge somewhere," I explained, vainly. I wondered if the next day would ever dawn.

By degrees that thunder rolled slowly into the northern parts of the sky, and only fitful flashes seamed the heavens. It had lasted now more than two hours. Sir William declared his intention of starting, and asked for his daughter. I rang for Mrs. Batty, and sent her to rouse Miss Bosanquet. Almost immediately there was a knock upon the door, and the housekeeper was in the doorway, with an agitated expression, demanding to see me. Sir William was looking out of the window, and fortunately did not see her.

"Please come to Miss Bosanquet, Sir," she cried, very scared. "Please come at once."

In alarm I hastily ran down the corridor and entered Warrington's room. The girl was lying upon the bed, her hair flowing upon the pillow; her eyes, wide open and filled with terror, stared at the ceiling, and her hands clutched and twined in the coverlet as if in an agony of pain. A gasping sound issued from her, as though she were struggling for breath under suffocation. Her whole appearance was as of one in the murderous grasp of an assailant.

I bent over. "Throw the light, quick," I called to Mrs. Batty; and as I put my hand on her shoulder to lift her, the creature that lived in the chamber rose suddenly from the shadow upon the further side of the bed, and sailed with a flapping noise up to the cornice. With an exclamation of horror I pulled the girl's head forward, and the candlelight glowed on her pallid face. Upon the soft flesh of the slender throat was a round red mark, the size of a florin.

At the sight I almost let her fall upon the pillow again; but, commanding my nerves, I put my arms round her, and, lifting her bodily from the bed, carried her from the room. Mrs. Batty followed.

"What shall we do?" she asked, in a low voice.

"Take her away from this damned chamber!" I cried. "Anywhere—the hall, the kitchen rather."

I laid my burden upon a sofa in the dining-room, and despatching Mrs. Batty for the brandy, gave Miss Bosanquet a draught. Slowly the horror faded from her eyes; they closed, and then she looked at me.

"What have you—where am I?" she asked.

"You have been unwell," I said. "Pray don't disturb yourself yet."

She shuddered, and closed her eyes again.

Very little more was said. Sir William pressed for his horses, and as the sky was clearing I made no attempt to detain him, more particularly as the sooner Miss Bosanquet left the Abbey the better for herself. In half an hour she recovered sufficiently to go, and I helped her into the carriage. She never referred to her seizure, but thanked me for my kindness. That was all. No one asked after Warrington—not even Sir William. He had forgotten everything, save his anxiety to get back. As the carriage turned from the steps I saw the mark upon the girl's throat, now grown fainter.

I waited up till late into the morning, but there was no sign of Warrington when I went to bed. Nor had he made his appearance when I descended to breakfast. A letter in his handwriting, however, and with the London postmark, awaited me. It was a pitiful scrawl, in the very penmanship of which one might trace the desperate emotions by which he was torn. He implored my forgiveness. "*Am I a devil?*" he asked. "*Am I mad? It was not I! It was not I!*" he repeated, underlining the sentence with impetuous dashes. "*You know,*" he wrote, "*and you know, therefore, that everything is at an end for me. I am going abroad today. I shall never see the Abbey again.*"

It was well that he had gone, as I hardly think that I could have faced him; and yet I was loth myself to leave the matter in this horrible tangle. I felt that it was enjoined upon me to meet the problems, and I endeavoured to do so as best I might. Mrs. Batty gave me news of the girl Alice. It was bad enough, though not so bad as both of us had feared. I was able to make arrangements on the instant, which I hoped might bury that lamentable affair for the time. There remained Miss Bosanquet; but that difficulty seemed beyond me. I could see no avenue out of the tragedy. I heard nothing save that she was ill—an illness attributed upon all hands to the shock of exposure to the thunderstorm. Only I knew better, and a vague disinclination to fly from the responsibilities of the position kept me hanging on at Utterbourne.

It was in those days before my visit to St. Pharamond that I turned my attention more particularly to the thing which had forced itself relentlessly upon me. I was never a superstitious man; the gossip of old wives interested me merely as a curious and unsympathetic observer. And yet I was vaguely discomfited by the transaction in the Abbey, and it was with some reluctance that I decided to make a further test of Warrington's bedroom. Mrs. Batty received my determination to change my room easily enough, but with a protest as to the dampness of the Stone Chamber. It was plain that her suspicions had not marched with mine. On the second night after Warrington's departure I occupied the room for the first time.

I lay awake for a couple of hours, with a reading lamp by my bed, and a volume of travels in my hand, and then, feeling very tired, put out the light and went to sleep. Nothing distracted me that night; indeed, I slept more soundly and peaceably than before in that house. I rose, too, experiencing quite an exhilaration, and it was not until I was dressing before the glass that I remembered the circumstances of my mission; but then I was at once pulled up, startled swiftly out of my cheerful temper. Faintly visible upon my throat was the same round mark which I had already seen stamped upon Warrington and Miss Bosanquet. With that, all my former doubts returned in force, augmented and militant. My mind recurred to the bat, and tales of bloodsucking by those evil creatures revived in my memory. But when I had remembered that these were of foreign beasts, and that I was in England, I dismissed them lightly enough. Still, the impress of that mark remained, and alarmed me. It could not come by accident; to suppose so manifold a coincidence was absurd. The puzzle dwelt with me, unsolved, and the fingers of dread slowly crept over me.

Yet I slept again in the room. Having but myself for company, and being somewhat bored and dull, I fear I took more spirit than was my custom, and the result was that I again slept profoundly. I awoke about three in the morning, and was surprised to find the lamp still burning. I had forgotten it in my stupid state of somnolence. As I turned to put it out, the bat swept by me and circled for an instant above my head. So overpowered with torpor was I that I scarcely noticed it, and my head was no sooner at rest than I was once more unconscious. The red mark was stronger next morning, though, as on the previous day, it wore off with the fall of evening. But I merely observed the fact without any concern; indeed, now the matter of my investigation seemed to have drawn very remote. I was growing indifferent, I supposed, through familiarity. But the solitude was palling upon me, and I spent a very restless day. A sharp ride I took in the afternoon was the one agreeable experience of the day. I reflected that if this burden were to continue I must hasten up to town. I had no desire to tie myself to Warrington's apron, in his interest. So dreary was the evening, that after I had strolled round the grounds and into the chapel by moonlight, I returned to the library and endeavoured to pass the time with Warrington's cards. But it was poor fun with no antagonist to pit myself against; and I was throwing down the pack in disgust when one of the manservants entered with the whisky.

It was not until long afterwards that I fully realized the course of my action; but even at the time I was aware of a curious sub-feeling of shamefacedness. I am sure that the thing fell naturally, and that there was no awkwardness in my approaching him. Nor, after the first surprise, did he offer any objection. Later he was hardly expected to do so, seeing that he was winning very quickly. The reason of that I guessed afterwards, but during the play I was amazed to note at intervals how strangely my irritation was aroused. Finally, I swept the cards to the floor, and rose, the man, with a smile in which triumph blended with uneasiness, rose also.

"Damn you, get away!" I said, angrily.

True to his traditions to the close, he answered me with respect, and obeyed; and I sat staring at the table. With a sudden flush, the grotesque folly of the night's business came to me, and my eyes fell on the whisky bottle. It was nearly empty. Then I went to bed.

Voices cried all night in that chamber—soft, pleading voices. There was nothing to alarm in them; they seemed in a manner to coo me to sleep. But presently a sharper cry roused me from my semi-slumber; and getting up, I flung open the window. The wind rushed round the Abbey, sweeping with noises against the corners and gables. The black chapel lay still in the moonlight, and drew my eyes. But, resisting a strange, unaccountable impulse to go further, I went back to bed.

The events of the following day are better related without comment.

At breakfast I found a letter from Sir William Bosanquet, inviting me to come over to St. Pharamond. I was at once conscious of an eager desire to do so: it seemed somehow as though I had been waiting for this. The visit assumed preposterous proportions, and I was impatient for the afternoon.

Sir William was polite, but not, as I thought, cordial. He never alluded to Warrington, from which I guessed that he had been informed of the breach, and I conjectured also that the invitation extended to me was rather an act of courtesy to a solitary stranger than due to a desire for my company. Nevertheless, when he presently suggested that I should stay to dinner, I accepted promptly. For, to say the truth, I had not yet seen Miss Bosanquet, and I experienced a strange curiosity to do so. When at last she made her appearance, I was struck, almost for the first time, by her beauty. She was certainly a handsome girl, though she had a delicate air of ill-health.

After dinner Sir William remembered by accident the book on the Abbey which he had promised to show me, and after a brief hunt in the library we found it. Shortly afterwards he was called away, and with an apology left me. With a curious eagerness I turned the pages of the volume and settled down to read.

It was published early in the century, and purported to

relate the history of the Abbey and its owners. But it was one chapter which specially drew my interest—that which recounted the fate of the last Marvyn. The family had become extinct through a bloody tragedy; that fact held me. The bare narrative, long since passed from the memory of tradition, was here set forth in the baldest statements. The names of Sir Rupert Marvyn and Priscilla, Lady Marvyn, shook me strangely, but particularly the latter. Some links of connection with those gravestones lying in the Abbey chapel constrained me intimately. The history of that evil race was stained and discoloured with blood, and the end was in fitting harmony—a lurid holocaust of crime. There had been two brothers, but it was hard to choose between the foulness of their lives. If either, the younger, William, was the worse; so at least the narrative would have it. The details of his excesses had not survived, but it was abundantly plain that they were both notorious gamblers. The story of their deaths was wrapt in doubt, the theme of conjecture only, and probability; for none was by to observe save the three veritable actors—who were at once involved together in a bloody dissolution. Priscilla, the wife of Sir Rupert, was suspected of an intrigue with her brother-in-law. She would seem to have been tainted with the corruption of the family into which she had married. But according to a second rumour, chronicled by the author, there was some doubt if the woman were not the worst of the three. Nothing was known of her parentage; she had returned with the passionate Sir Rupert to the Abbey after one of his prolonged absences, and was accepted as his legal wife. This was the woman whose infamous beauty had brought a terrible sin between the brothers.

Upon the night which witnessed the extinction of this miserable family, the two brothers had been gambling together. It was known from the high voices that they had quarrelled, and it is supposed that, heated with wine and with the lust of play, the younger had thrown some taunt at Sir Rupert in respect to his wife. Whereupon—but this is all conjecture—the elder stabbed him to death. At least, it was understood that at this point the sounds of a struggle were heard, and a bitter cry. The report of the servants ran that upon this noise Lady Marvyn rushed into the room and locked the door behind her. Fright was busy with those servants, long used to the savage manners of the house. According to witnesses, no further sound was heard subsequently to Lady Marvyn's entrance; yet when the doors were at last broken open by the authorities, the three bodies were discovered upon the floor.

How Sir Rupert and his wife met their deaths there was no record. "This tragedy," proceeded the scribe, "took place in the Stone Chamber underneath the stairway."

I had got so far when the entrance of Miss Bosanquet disturbed me. I remember rising in a dazed condition—the room swung about me. A conviction, hitherto resisted and stealthily entertained upon compulsion, now overpowered me.

"I thought my father was here," explained Miss Bosanquet, with a quick glance round the room.

I explained the circumstances, and she hesitated in my neighbourhood with a slight air of embarrassment.

"I have not thanked you properly, Mr. Heywood," she said presently, in a low voice, scarcely articulate. "You have been very considerate and kind. Let me thank you now." And ended with a tiny spasmodic sob.

Somehow, an impulse overmastered my tongue. Fresh from the perusal of that chapter, queer possibilities crowded in my mind, odd considerations urged me.

"Miss Bosanquet," said I, abruptly, "let me speak of that a little. I will not touch on details."

"Please," she cried, with a shrinking notion as of one that would retreat in very alarm.

"Nay," said I, eagerly. "Hear me. It is no wantonness that would press the memory upon you. You have been a witness to distressful acts; you have seen a man under the influence of temporary madness. Nay, even yourself, you have been a victim to the same unaccountable phenomena."

"What do you mean?" she cried, tensely.

"I will say no more," said I. "I should incur your laughter. No, you would not laugh, but my dim suspicions would leave you still incredulous. But if this were so, and if these were the phenomena of a brief madness, surely you would make your memory a grave to bury the past."

"I cannot do that," she said, in low tones.

"What!" I asked. "Would you turn from your lover, aye, even from a friend, because he was smitten with disease? Consider; if your dearest upon earth tossed in a fever upon his bed, and denied you in his ravings, using you despitefully, it would not be he that entreated you so. When he was quit of his madness and returned to his proper person, would you not forget—would you not rather recall his insanity with the pity of affection?"

"I do not understand you," she whispered.

"You read your Bible," said I. "You have wondered at the evil spirits that possessed poor victims. Why should you decide that these things have ceased? We are too dogmatic in our modern world. Who can say under what malign influence a soul may pass, and out of its own custody?"

She looked at me earnestly, searching my eyes.

"You hint at strange things," said she, very low.

But somehow, even as I met her eyes, the spirit of my mission failed me. My gaze, I felt, devoured her ruthlessly. The light shone on her pale and comely features; they burned me with an irresistible attraction. I put forth my hand and took hers gently. It was passive to my touch, as though in acknowledgment of my kindly offices. All the while I experienced a sense of fierce elation. In my blood ran, as it had been fire, a horrible incentive, and I knew that I was holding her hand very tightly. She herself seemed to grow conscious of this, for she made an effort to withdraw her fingers, at which, the passion rushing through my body, I clutched them closer, laughing aloud. I saw a wondering look dawn in her eyes, and her bosom, thinly veiled, heaved with a tiny tremor. I was aware that I was drawing her steadily to me. Suddenly her bewildered eyes, dropping from my face, lit with a flare of terror, and, wrenching her hand away, she fell back with a cry, her gaze riveted upon my throat.

"That accursed mark! What is it? What is it?—" she cried, shivering from head to foot.

In an instant, the wild blood singing in my head, I sprang towards her. What would have followed I know not, but at that moment the door opened and Sir William returned. He regarded us with consternation; but Miss Bosanquet had fainted, and the next moment he was at her side. I stood near, watching her come to with a certain nameless fury, as of a beast cheated of its prey. Sir William turned to me, and in his most courteous manner begged me to excuse the untoward scene. His daughter, he said, was not at all strong, and he ended by suggesting that I should leave them for a time.

Reluctantly I obeyed, but when I was out of the house, I took a sudden panic. The demoniac possession lifted, and in a craven state of trembling I saddled my horse, and rode for the Abbey as if my life depended upon my speed.

I arrived at about ten o'clock, and immediately gave orders to have my bed prepared in my old room. In my shaken condition the sinister influences of that stone chamber terrified me, and it was not until I had drunk deeply that I regained my composure.

But I was destined to get little sleep. I had steadily resolved to keep my thoughts off the matter until the morning, but the spell of the chamber was strong upon me. I awoke after midnight with an irresistible feeling drawing me to the room. I was conscious of the impulse, and combated it, but in the end succumbed; and throwing on my clothes, took a light and went downstairs. I flung wide the door of the room and peered in, listening, as though for some voice of welcome. It was as silent as a sepulchre; but directly I crossed the threshold voices seemed to surround and coax me. I stood wavering, with a curious fascination upon me. I knew I could not return to my own room, and I now had no desire to do so. As I stood, my candle flaring solemnly against the darkness, I noticed upon the floor in an alcove bare of carpet, a large black mark, which appeared to be a stain. Bending down, I examined it, passing my fingers over the stone. It moved to my touch. Setting the candle upon the floor, I put my fingertips to the edges, and pulled hard. As I did so the sounds that were ringing in my ears died instantaneously; the next moment the slab turned with a crash, and I discovered a gaping hole of impenetrable blackness.

The patch of chasm thus opened to my eyes was near a yard square. The candle held to it shed a dim light upon a stone step a foot or two below, and it was clear to me that a stairway communicated with the depths. Whether it had been used as a cellar in times gone by I could not divine, but I was soon to determine this doubt; for, stirred by a strange eagerness, I slipped my legs through the hole, and let myself cautiously down with the light in my hand. There were a dozen steps to descend ere I reached the floor and what turned out to be a narrow passage. The vault ran forward straight as an arrow before my eyes, and slowly I moved on. Dank and chill was the air in those close confines, and the sound of my feet returned from those walls dull and sullen. But I kept on, and, with infinite care, must have penetrated quite a hundred yards along that musty corridor ere I came out upon an ampler chamber. Here the air was freer, and I could perceive with the aid of my light that the dimensions of the place were lofty. Above, a solitary ray of moonlight, sliding through a crack, informed me that I was not far from the level of the earth. It fell upon a block of stone which rose in the middle of the vault, and which I now inspected with interest. As the candle threw its flickering beams upon this I realized where I was. I scarcely needed the rude lettering upon the coffins to acquaint me that here was the family vault of the Marvyns. And now I began to perceive upon all sides whereon my feeble light fell the crumbling relics of the forgotten dead—coffins fallen into decay, bones and grinning skulls resting in corners, disposed by the hand of chance and time. This formidable array of the mortal remains of that poor family moved me to a shudder. I turned from those ugly memorials once more to the central altar where the two coffins rested in this sombre silence. The lid had fallen from the one, disclosing to my sight the grisly skeleton of a man, that mocked and leered at me. It seemed in a manner to my fascinated eyes to challenge my mortality, inviting me too to the rude and grotesque sleep of death. I knew, as by an instinct, that I was standing by the bones of Sir Rupert Marvyn, the protagonist in that terrible crime which had locked three souls in eternal ruin. The consideration of this miserable spectacle held me motionless for some moments, and then I moved a step closer and cast my light upon the second coffin.

As I did so I was aware of a change within myself. The grave and melancholy thoughts which I had entertained, the sober bent of my solemn reflections, gave place instantly to a strange exultation, an unholy sense of elation. My pulse swung feverishly, and, while my eyes were riveted upon the tarnished silver of the plate, I stretched forth a tremulously eager hand and touched the lid. It rattled gently under my fingers. Disturbed by the noise, I hastily withdrew them; but whether it was the impetus offered by my touch, or through some horrible and nameless circumstance—God knows—slowly and softly a gap opened between the lid and the body of the coffin! Before my startled eyes the awful thing happened, and yet I was conscious of no terror, merely of surprise and—it seems terrible to admit—of a feeling of eager expectancy. The lid rose slowly on the one side, and as it lifted the dark space between it and the coffin grew gently charged with light. At that moment my feeble candle, which had been gradually diminishing, guttered and flickered. I seemed to catch a glimpse of something, as it were, of white and shining raiment inside the coffin; and then came a rush of wings and a whirring sound within the vault. I gave a cry, and stepping back missed my foothold; the guttering candle was jerked from my grasp, and I fell prone to the floor in darkness. The next moment a sheet of flame flashed in the chamber and lit up the grotesque skeletons about me; and at the same time a piercing cry rang forth. Jumping to my feet, I gave a dazed glance at the conflagration. The whole vault was in flames. Dazed and horror-struck, I rushed blindly to the entrance; but as I did so the horrible cry pierced my ears again, and I saw the bat swoop round and circle swiftly into the flames. Then, finding the exit, I dashed with all the speed of terror down the passage, groping my way along the walls, and striking myself a dozen times in my terrified flight.

Arrived in my room, I pushed over the stone and listened. Not a sound was audible. With a white face and a body torn and bleeding I rushed from the room, and locking the door behind me, made my way upstairs to my bedroom. Here I poured myself out a stiff glass of brandy.

It was six months later ere Warrington returned. In the meantime he had sold the Abbey. It was inevitable that he should do so; and yet the new owner, I believe, has found no drawback in his property, and the Stone Chamber is still used for a bedroom upon occasions, being considered very old-fashioned. But there are some facts against which no appeal is possible, and so it was in his case. In my relation of the tragedy I have made no attempt at explanation, hardly even to myself; and it appears now for the first time in print, of course with suppositious names.

THE WEREWOLF AND THE VAMPIRE

♦♦♦

R. CHETWYND-HAYES

George Hardcastle's downfall undoubtedly originated in his love for dogs. He could not pass one without stopping and patting its head. A flea-bitten mongrel had only to turn the corner of the street and he was whistling, calling out: "Come on, boy. Come on then," and behaving in the altogether outrageous fashion that is peculiar to the devoted animal lover.

Tragedy may still have been averted had he not decided to spend a day in the Greensand Hills. Here in the region of Clandon Down, where dwarf oaks, pale birches, and dark firs spread up in a long sweep to the northern heights, was a vast hiding place where many forms of often invisible life lurked in the dense undergrowth. But George, like many before him, knew nothing about this, and tramped happily up the slope, aware only that the air was fresh, the silence absolute, and he was young.

The howl of what he supposed to be a dog brought him to an immediate standstill and for a while he listened, trying to determine from which direction the sound came. Afterwards he had reason to remember that none of the conditions laid down by legend and superstition prevailed. It was midafternoon and in consequence there was not, so far as he was aware, a full moon. The sun was sending golden spears of light through the thick foliage and all around was a warm, almost overpowering atmosphere, tainted with the aroma of decaying undergrowth. The setting was so commonplace and he was such an ordinary young man—not very bright perhaps, but gifted with good health and clean boyish good looks, the kind of Saxon comeliness that goes with clear skin and blond hair.

The howl rang out again, a long, drawn-out cry of canine anguish, and now it was easily located. Way over to his left, somewhere in the midst of, or just beyond a curtain of, saplings and low, thick bushes. Without thought of danger, George turned off the beaten track and plunged into the dim twilight that held perpetual domain during the summer months under the interlocked higher branches. Imagination supplied a mental picture of a gin-trap and a tortured animal that was lost in a maze of pain. Pity lent speed to his feet and made him ignore the stinging offshoots that whipped at his face and hands, while brambles tore his trousers and coiled round his ankles. The howl came again, now a little to his right, but this time it was followed by a deep-throated growl, and if George had not been the person he was, he might have paid heed to this warning note of danger.

For some fifteen minutes, he ran first in one direction, then another, finally coming to rest under a giant oak which stood in a small clearing. For the first time fear came to him in the surrounding gloom. It did not seem possible that one could get lost in an English wood, but here, in the semilight, he conceived the ridiculous notion that night left its guardians in the wood during the day, which would at any moment move in and smother him with shadows.

He moved away from the protection of the oak tree and began to walk in the direction he thought he had come, when the growl erupted from a few yards to his left. Pity fled like a leaf before a raging wind, and stark terror fired his brain with blind, unreasoning panic. He ran, fell, got up, and ran again, and from behind came the sound of a heavy body crashing through undergrowth, the rasp of laboured breathing, the bestial growl of some enraged being. Reason had gone, coherent thought had been replaced by an animal instinct for survival; he knew that whatever ran behind him was closing the gap.

Soon, and he dare not turn his head, it was but a few feet away. There was snuffling, whining, terribly eager growling, and suddenly he shrieked as a fierce, burning pain seared his right thigh. Then he was down on the ground and the agony rose up to become a scarlet flame, until it was blotted out by a merciful darkness.

An hour passed, perhaps more, before George Hardcastle returned to consciousness. He lay quite still and tried to remember why he should be lying on the ground in a dense wood, while a dull ache held mastery over his right leg. Then memory sent its first cold tentacles shuddering across his brain and he dared to sit up and face reality.

The light had faded: night was slowly reinforcing its advance guard, but he was still able to see the dead man who lay but a few feet away. He shrank back with a little muffled cry and tried to dispel this vision of a purple face and bulging eyes, by the simple act of closing his own. But this was not a wise action for the image of that awful countenance was etched upon his brain, and the memory was even more macabre than the reality. He opened his eyes again, and there it was: a man in late middle life, with grey, close-cropped hair, a long moustache, and yellow teeth, that were bared in a death grin. The purple face suggested he had died of a sudden heart attack.

The next hour was a dimly remembered nightmare.

George dragged himself through the undergrowth and by sheer good fortune emerged out on to one of the main paths.

He was found next morning by a team of boy scouts.

Police and an army of enthusiastic volunteers scoured the woods, but no trace of a ferocious wild beast was found. But they did find the dead man, and he proved to be a farm worker who had a reputation locally of being a person of solitary habits. An autopsy revealed he had died of a heart attack, and it was assumed that this had been the result of his efforts in trying to assist the injured boy.

The entire episode assumed the proportions of a nine-day wonder, and then was forgotten.

Mrs. Hardcastle prided herself on being a mother who, while combating illness, did not pamper it. She had George back on his feet within three weeks and despatched him on prolonged walks. Being an obedient youth he followed these instructions to the letter, and so, on one overcast day, found himself at Hampton Court. As the first drops of rain were caressing his face, he decided to make a long-desired tour of the staterooms. He wandered from room to room, examined pictures, admired four-poster beds, then listened to a guide who was explaining the finer points to a crowd of tourists. By the time he had reached the Queen's Audience Room, he felt tired, so seated himself on one of the convenient window-seats. For some while he sat looking out at the rain-drenched gardens, then with a yawn, he turned and gave a quick glance along the long corridor that ran through a series of open doorways.

Suddenly his attention was captured by a figure approaching over the long carpet. It was that of a girl in a black dress; she was a beautiful study in black and white. Black hair, white face and hands, black dress. Not that there was anything sinister about her, for as she drew nearer he could see the look of indescribable sadness in the large, black eyes, and the almost timid way she looked round each room. Her appearance was outstanding, so vivid, like a black-and-white photograph that had come to life.

She entered the Queen's Audience Room and now he could hear the light tread of her feet, the whisper of her dress, and even those small sounds seemed unreal. She walked round the room, looking earnestly at the pictures, then as though arrested by a sudden sound, she stopped. Suddenly the lovely eyes came round and stared straight at George.

They held an expression of alarmed surprise, that gradually changed to one of dawning wonderment. For a moment George could only suppose she recognised him, although how he had come to forget her, was beyond his comprehension. She glided towards him, and as she came a small smile parted her lips. She sank down on the far end of the seat and watched him with those dark, wondering eyes.

She said: "Hullo. I'm Carola."

No girl had made such an obvious advance towards George before, and shyness, not to mention shock, robbed him of speech. Carola seemed to be reassured by his reticence, for her smile deepened and when she spoke her voice held a gentle bantering tone.

"What's the matter? Cat got your tongue?"

This impertinent probe succeeded in freeing him from the chains of shyness and he ventured to make a similar retort.

"I can speak when I want to."

"That's better. I recognised the link at once. We have certain family connections, really. Don't you think so?"

This question was enough to dry up his powers of communication for some time, but presently he was able to breathe one word. "Family!"

"Yes." She nodded and her hair trembled like black silk in sunlight. "We must be at least distantly related in the allegorical sense. But don't let's talk about that. I am so pleased to be able to walk about in daylight. It is so dreary at night, and besides, I'm not really myself then."

George came to the conclusion that this beautiful creature was at least slightly mad, and therefore made a mundane, but what he thought must be a safe remark.

"Isn't it awful weather?"

She frowned slightly and he got the impression he had committed a breach of good taste.

"Don't be so silly. You know it's lovely weather. Lots of beautiful clouds."

He decided this must be a joke. There could be no other interpretation. He capped it by another.

"Yes, and soon the awful sun will come out."

She flinched as though he had hit her, and there was the threat of tears in the lovely eyes.

"You beast. How could you say a dreadful thing like that? There won't be any sun, the weather forecast said so. I thought you were nice, but all you want to do is frighten me."

And she dabbed her eyes with a black lace handkerchief, while George tried to find his way out of a mental labyrinth where every word seemed to have a double meaning.

"I am sorry. But I didn't mean . . ."

She stifled a tiny sob. "How would you like it if I said—silver bullets?"

He scratched his head, wrinkled his brow, and then made a wry grimace.

"I wouldn't know what you meant, but I wouldn't mind."

She replaced the lace handkerchief in a small handbag, then got up and walked quickly away. George watched her retreating figure until it disappeared round the corner in the direction of the long gallery. He muttered: "Potty. Stark raving potty."

On reflection he decided it was a great pity that her behaviour was so erratic, because he would have dearly liked to have known her better. In fact, when he remembered the black hair and white face, he was aware of a deep disappointment, a sense of loss, and he had to subdue an urge to run after her. He remained seated in the window bay and when he looked out on to the gardens, he saw the rain had ceased, but thick cloud banks were billowing across the sky. He smiled gently and murmured, "Lovely clouds—horrible sunshine."

George was half way across Anne Boleyn's courtyard when a light touch on his shoulder made him turn, and there was Carola of the white face and black hair, with a sad smile parting her lips.

"Look," she said, "I'm sorry I got into a huff back there, but I can't bear to be teased about—well, you know what. But you are one of us, and we mustn't quarrel. All forgiven?"

George said, "Yes, I'm sorry I offended you. But I didn't mean to." And at that moment he was so happy, so ridiculously elated, he was prepared to apologise for breathing.

"Good." She sighed and took hold of his arm as though

it were the most natural action in the world. "We'll forget all about it. But, please, don't joke about such things again."

"No. Absolutely not." George had not the slightest idea what it was he must not joke about, but made a mental note to avoid mention of the weather and silver bullets.

"You must come and meet my parents," Carola insisted, "they'll be awfully pleased to see you. I bet they won't believe their noses."

This remark was in the nature of a setback, but George's newly found happiness enabled him to ignore it—pretend it must be a slip of the tongue.

"That's very kind of you, but won't it be a bit sudden? I mean, are you sure it will be convenient?"

She laughed, a lovely little silver sound and, if possible, his happiness increased.

"You are a funny boy. They'll be tickled pink, and so they should be. For the first time for years, we won't have to be careful of what we say in front of a visitor."

George had a little mental conference and came to the conclusion that this was meant to be a compliment. So he said cheerfully, "I don't mind what people say. I like them to be natural."

Carola thought that was a very funny remark and tightened her grip on his arm, while laughing in a most enchanting fashion.

"You have a most wonderful sense of humour. Wait until I tell Daddy that one. 'I like them to be natural . . .' "

And she collapsed into a fit of helpless laughter in which George joined, although he was rather at a loss to know what he had said that was so funny. Suddenly the laugh was cut short, was killed by a gasp of alarm, and Carola was staring at the western sky where the clouds had taken on a brighter hue. The words came out as a strangled whisper.

"The sun! O Lucifer, the sun is coming out."

"Is it?" George looked up and examined the sky with assumed interest. "I wouldn't be surprised if you're not right . . ." Then he stopped and looked down at his lovely companion with concern. "I'm sorry, you . . . you don't like the sun, do you?"

Her face was a mask of terror and she gave a terrible little cry of anguish. George's former suspicion of insanity returned, but she was still appealing—still a flawless pearl on black velvet. He put his arm round the slim shoulders, and she hid her eyes against his coat. The muffled, tremulous whisper came to him.

"Please take me home. Quickly."

He felt great joy in the fact that he was able to bring comfort.

"There's no sign of sunlight. Look, it was only a temporary break in the clouds."

Slowly the dark head was raised, and the eyes, so bright with unshed tears, again looked up at the western sky. Now, George was rewarded, for her lips parted, the skin round her eyes crinkled, and her entire face was transformed by a wonderful, glorious smile.

"Oh, how beautiful! Lovely, lovely, *lovely* clouds. The wind is up there, you know. A big, fat wind-god, who blows out great bellows of mist, so that we may not be destroyed by demon-sun. And sometimes he shrieks his rage across the sky; at others he whispers soft comforting words and tells us to have faith. The bleak night of loneliness is not without end."

George was acutely embarrassed, not knowing what to make of this allegorical outburst. But the love and compassion he had so far extended to dogs was now enlarged and channelled towards the lovely, if strange, young girl by his side.

"Come," he said, "let me take you home."

George pulled open a trellis iron gate and allowed Carola to precede him up a crazy-paved path, which led to a house that gleamed with new paint and well-cleaned windows. Such a house could have been found in any one of a thousand streets in the London suburbs, and brashly proclaimed that here lived a woman who took pride in the crisp whiteness of her curtains, and a man who was no novice in the art of wielding a paint brush. They had barely entered the tiny porch, where the red tiles shone like a pool at sunset, when the door was flung open and a plump, grey-haired woman clasped Carola in her arms.

"Ee, love, me and yer dad were that worried. We thought you'd got caught in a sun-storm."

Carola kissed her mother gently, on what George noted was another dead-white cheek, then turned and looked back at him with shining eyes.

"Mummy, this . . ." She giggled and shook her head. "It's silly, but I don't know your name."

"George. George Hardcastle."

To say Carola's mother looked alarmed is a gross understatement. For a moment she appeared to be terrified, and clutched her daughter as though they were confronted by a man-eating tiger. Then Carola laughed softly and whispered into her mother's ear. George watched the elder woman's expression change to one of incredulity and dawning pleasure.

"You don't say so, love? Where on earth did you find him?"

"In the Palace," Carola announced proudly. "He was sitting in the Queen's Audience Room."

Mummy almost ran forward and, after clasping the startled George with both hands, kissed him soundly on either cheek. Then she stood back and examined him with obvious pleasure.

"I ought to have known," she said, nodding her head as though with sincere conviction. "Been out of touch for too long. But what will you think of me manners? Come in, love. Father will be that pleased. It's not much of a death for him, with just us two women around."

Again George was aware of a strange slip of the tongue, which he could only assume was a family failing. So he beamed with the affability that is expected from a stranger who is the recipient of sudden hospitality, and allowed himself to be pulled into a newly decorated hall, and relieved of his coat. Then Mummy opened a door and ordered in a shouted whisper: "Father, put yer tie on, we've got company." There was a startled snort, as though someone had been awakened from a fireside sleep, and Mummy turned a bright smile on George.

"Would you like to go upstairs and wash yer hands, like? Make yourself comfy, if you get my meaning."

"No, thank you. Very kind, I'm sure."

"Well then, you'd best come into the parlour."

The "parlour" had a very nice paper on the walls, bright pink lamps, a well stuffed sofa and matching armchairs, a large television set, a low, imitation walnut table, a record player, some awful coloured prints, and an artificial log electric fire. A stout man with thinning grey hair struggled up from the sofa, while he completed the adjustment of a tie that was more eye-catching than tasteful.

"Father," Mummy looked quickly round the room as though to seek reassurance that nothing was out of place, "this is George. A young man that Carola has brought home, like." Then she added in an undertone, "He's all right. No need to worry."

Father advanced with outstretched hand and announced in a loud, very hearty voice: "Ee, I'm pleased to meet ye, lad. I've always said it's about time the lass found herself a young spark. But the reet sort is 'ard to come by, and that's a fact."

Father's hand was unpleasantly cold and flabby, but he radiated such an air of goodwill, George was inclined to overlook it.

"Now, Father, you're embarrassing our Carola," Mummy said. And indeed the girl did appear to be somewhat disconcerted, only her cheeks, instead of blushing, had assumed a greyish tinge. "Now, George, don't stand around, lad. Sit yerself down and make yerself at 'ome. We don't stand on ceremony here."

George found himself on the sofa next to Father, who would insist on winking, whenever their glances met. In the meanwhile Mummy expressed solicitous anxiety regarding his well-being.

"Have you supped lately? I know you young doggies don't 'ave to watch yer diet like we do, so just say what you fancy. I've a nice piece of 'am in t' fridge, and I can fry that with eggs, in no time at all."

George knew that somewhere in that kindly invitation there had been another slip of the tongue, but he resolutely did not think about it.

"That's very kind of you, but really . . ."

"Let 'er do a bit of cooking, lad," Father pleaded. "She don't get much opportunity, if I can speak without dotting me *i*'s and crossing me *t*'s."

"If you are sure it will be no trouble."

Mummy made a strange neighing sound. "Trouble!

'Ow you carry on. It's time for us to have a glass of something rich, anyway."

Mother and daughter departed for the kitchen and George was left alone with Father, who was watching him with an embarrassing interest.

"Been on 'olidays yet, lad?" he enquired.

"No, it's a bit late now . . ."

Father sighed with the satisfaction of a man who is recalling a pleasant memory. "We 'ad smashing time in Clacton. Ee, the weather was summat greet. Two weeks of thick fog—couldn't see 'and in front of face."

George said, "Oh, dear," then lapsed into silence while he digested this piece of information. Presently he was aware of an elbow nudging his ribs.

"I know it's delicate question, lad, so don't answer if you'd rather not. But—'ow often do you change?"

George thought it was a very delicate question, and could only think of a very indelicate reason why it had been asked. But his conception of politeness demanded he answer.

"Well . . . every Friday actually. After I've had a bath."

Father gasped with astonishment. "As often as that! I'm surprised. The last lad I knew in your condition only changed when the moon was full."

George said, "Goodness gracious!" and then tried to ask a very pertinent question. "Why, do I . . ."

Father nodded. "There's a goodish pong. But don't let it worry you. We can smell it, because we've the reet kind of noses."

An extremely miserable, not to say self-conscious, young man was presently led across the hall and into the dining-room, where one place was set with knife, fork, and spoon, and three with glass and drinking straw. He was too dejected to pay particular heed to this strange and unequal arrangement, and neither was he able to really enjoy the plate of fried eggs and ham that Mummy put down before him, with the remark: "Here you are, lad, get wrapped round that, and you'll not starve."

The family shared the contents of a glass jug between them, and as this was thick and red, George could only suppose it to be tomato juice. They all sucked through straws; Carola, as was to be expected, daintily, Mummy with some anxiety, and Father greedily. When he had emptied his glass, he presented it for a refill and said: "You know, Mother, that's as fine a jug of AB as you've ever served up."

Mummy sighed. "It's not so bad. Mind you, youngsters don't get what I call top-grade nourishment, these days. There's nothing like getting yer teeth stuck into the real thing. This stuff 'as lost the natural goodness."

Father belched and made a disgusting noise with his straw.

"We must be thankful, Mother. There's many who 'asn't a drop to wet their lips, and be pleased to sup from tin."

George could not subdue a natural curiosity and the question slipped out before he had time to really think about it.

"Excuse me, but don't you ever eat anything?"

The shocked silence which followed told him he had committed a well nigh unforgivable sin. Father dropped his glass and Carola said, "Oh, George," in a very reproachful voice, while Mummy creased her brow into a very deep frown.

"George, haven't you ever been taught manners?"

It was easy to see she spoke more in sorrow than anger, and although the exact nature of his transgression was not quite clear to George, he instantly apologised.

"I am very sorry, but . . ."

"I should think so, indeed." Mummy continued to speak gently but firmly. "I never expected to hear a question like that at my table. After all, you wouldn't like it if I were to ask who or what you chewed up on one of your moonlight strolls. Well, I've said me piece, and now we'll forget that certain words were ever said. Have some chocolate pudding."

Even while George smarted under this rebuke, he was aware that once again, not so much a slip of the tongue, as a sentence that demanded thought had been inserted between an admonishment and a pardon. There was also a growing feeling of resentment. It seemed that whatever he said to this remarkable family gave offence, and his supply of apologies was running low. He waited until Mummy had served him with a generous helping of chocolate pudding, and then replenished the three glasses from the jug, before he relieved his mind.

"I don't chew anyone."

Mummy gave Father an eloquent glance, and he cleared his throat.

"Listen, lad, there are some things you don't mention in front of ladies. What you do in change period is between you and black man. So let's change subject."

Like all peace-loving people George sometimes reached a point where war, or to be more precise, attack seemed to be the only course of action. Father's little tirade brought him to such a point. He flung down his knife and fork and voiced his complaints.

"Look here, I'm fed up. If I mention the weather, I'm ticked off. If I ask why you never eat, I'm in trouble. I've been asked when I change, told that I stink. Now, after being accused of chewing people, I'm told I mustn't mention it. Now, I'll tell you something. I think you're all round the bend."

Carola burst into tears and ran from the room. Father swore, or rather he said, "Satan's necktie," which was presumably the same thing, and Mummy looked very concerned.

"Just a minute, son." She raised a white, rather wrinkled forefinger. "You're trying to tell us you don't know the score?"

"I haven't the slightest idea what you're talking about," George retorted.

Mummy and Father looked at each other for some little while, then as though prompted by a single thought, they both spoke in unison.

"He's a just bittener."

"Someone should tell 'im," Mummy stated, after she had watched the, by now, very frightened George for an entire minute. "It should come from a man."

"If 'e 'ad gumption he were born with, 'e'd know," Father said, his face becoming quite grey with embarrassment. "Hell's bells, my dad didn't 'ave to tell me I were vampire."

"Yes, but you can see he's none too bright," Mummy pointed out. "We can't all 'ave your brains. No doubt the lad has 'eart, and I say 'eart is better than brains any day. Been bitten lately, lad?"

George could only nod and look longingly at the door.

"Big long thing, with a wet snout, I wouldn't be surprised. It's a werewolf you are, son. You can't deceive the noses of we vamps: yer glands are beginning to play up—give out a bit of smell, see? I should think . . . What's the state of the moon, Father?"

"Seven eights."

Mummy nodded with grim relish. "I should think you're due for a change round about Friday night. Got any open space round your way?"

"There's . . ." George took a deep breath. "There's Clapham Common."

"Well, I should go for a run round there. Make sure you cover your face up. Normal people go all funny like when they first lays eyes on a werewolf. Start yelling their 'eads off, mostly."

George was on his feet and edging his way towards the door. He was praying for the priceless gift of disbelief. Mummy was again displaying signs of annoyance.

"Now there's no need to carry on like that. You must 'ave known we were all vampires—what did you think we were drinking? Raspberry juice? And let me tell you this. We're the best friends you've got. No one else will want to know you, once full moon is peeping over barn door. So don't get all lawn tennis with us . . ."

But George was gone. Running across the hall, out of the front door, down the crazy-paving path, and finally along the pavement. People turned their heads as he shouted: "They're mad . . . mad . . . mad . . ."

There came to George—as the moon waxed full—a strange restlessness. It began with insomnia, which rocketed him out of a deep sleep into a strange, instant wakefulness. He became aware of an urge to go for long moonlit walks; and when he had surrendered to this temptation, an overwhelming need to run, leap, roll over and over down a grassy bank, anything that would enable him to break down the hated walls of human convention—and express. A great joy—greater than he had ever known—came to him when he leaped and danced on the common, and could only be released by a shrill, doglike howl that rose up from the sleeping suburbs and went out, swift as a beam of light, to the face of mother-moon.

This joy had to be paid for. When the sun sent its first enquiring rays in through George's window, sanity returned and demanded a reckoning. He examined his face and hands with fearful expectancy. So far as he was aware there had been no terrible change, as yet. But these were early days—or was it nights? Sometimes he would fling himself down on his bed and cry out his great desire for disbelief.

"It can't happen. Mad people are sending me mad."

The growing strangeness of his behaviour could not go undetected. He was becoming withdrawn, apt to start at every sound, and betrayed a certain distrust of strangers by an eerie widening of his eyes, and later, the baring of his teeth in a mirthless grin. His mother commented on these peculiarities in forcible language.

"I think you're going up the pole. Honest I do. The milkman told me yesterday, he saw you snarling at Mrs. Redfern's dog."

"It jumped out at me," George explained. "You might have done the same."

Mrs. Hardcastle shook her head. "No. I can honestly say I've never snarled at a dog in my life. You never inherited snarling from me."

"I'm all right." George pleaded for reassurance. "I'm not turning into—anything."

"Well, you should know." George could not help thinking that his mother was regarding him with academic interest, rather than concern. "Do you go out at nights after I'm asleep?"

He found it impossible to lie convincingly, so he countered one question with another. "Why should I do that?"

"Don't ask me. But some nut has been seen prancing round the common at three o'clock in the morning. I just wondered."

The physical change came gradually. One night he woke with a severe pain in his right hand and lay still for a while, not daring to examine it. Then he switched on the bedside lamp with his left hand and, after further hesitation, brought its right counterpart out from the sheets. A thick down had spread over the entire palm and he found the fingers would not straighten. They had curved and the nails were thicker and longer than he remembered. After a while the fear—the loathing—went away, and it seemed most natural for him to have claws for fingers and hair-covered hands. Next morning his right hand was as normal as his left, and at that period he was still able to dismiss, even if with little conviction, the episode as a bad dream.

But one night there was a dream—a nightmare of the blackest kind, where fantasy blended with fact and George was unable to distinguish one from the other. He was running over the common, bounding with long, graceful leaps, and there was a wonderful joy in his heart and a limitless freedom in his head. He was in a black-and-white world. Black grass, white-tinted trees, grey sky, white moon. But with all the joy, all the freedom, there was a subtle, ever-present knowledge, that this was an unnatural experience, that he should be utilising all his senses to dispel. Once his brain—that part which was still unoccupied territory—screamed: "Wake up," but he was awake, for did not the black grass crunch beneath his feet, and the night breeze ruffle his fur? A large cat was running in front, trying to escape—up trees—across the roofs—round bushes—he finally trapped it in a hole. Shrieks—scratching claws—warm blood—tearing teeth . . . It was good. He was fulfilled.

Next morning when he awoke in his own bed, it could have been dismissed as a mad dream, were it not for the scratches on his face and hands and the blood in his hair.

He thought of psychiatrists, asylums, priests, religion, and at last came to the only possible conclusion. There was, so far as he knew, only one set of people on earth who could explain and understand.

Mummy let George in. Father shook him firmly by the hand. Carola kissed him gently and put an arm round his shoulders when he started to cry.

"We don't ask to be what we are," she whispered. "We keep more horror than we give away."

"We all 'ave our place in the great graveyard," Father said. "You hunt, we sup, ghouls tear, shaddies lick, mocks blow, and fortunately shadmocks can only whistle."

"Will I always be—what I am?" George asked.

They all nodded. Mummy grimly, Father knowingly, Carola sadly. "Until the moon leaves the sky," they all chanted.

"Or you are struck in the heart by a silver bullet," Carola whispered, "fired by one who has only thought about sin. Or maybe when you are very, very old, the heart may give out after a transformation . . ."

"Don't be morbid," Mummy ordered. "Poor lad's got enough on plate without you adding to it. Make him a nice cup of tea. And you can mix us a jug of something rich while you're about it. Don't be too 'eavy-handed on the O group."

They sat round the artificial log fire, drinking tea, absorbing nourishment, three giving, one receiving advice, and there was a measure of cosiness.

"All 'M's' should keep away from churches, parsons, and boy scouts," Father said.

"Run from a cross and fly from a prayer," intoned Mummy.

"Two can run better than one," Carola observed shyly.

Next day George told his mother he intended to leave home and set up house for himself. Mrs. Hardcastle did not argue as strongly as she might have had a few weeks earlier. What with one thing and another, there was a distinct feeling that the George, who was standing so grim and white-faced in the kitchen doorway, was not the one she had started out with. She said, "Right, then. I'd say it's about time," and helped him to pack.

Father, who knew someone in the building line, found George a four-roomed cottage that was situated on the edge of a churchyard, and this he furnished with a few odds and ends that the family were willing to part with. The end product was by no means as elegant or deceptive as the house at Hampton Court, but it was somewhere for George to come back to after his midnight run.

He found the old legends had been embellished, for he experienced no urge to rend or even bite. There was no reason why he should; the body was well fed and the animal kingdom only hunts when goaded by hunger. It was sufficient for him to run, leap, chase his tail by moonlight, and sometimes howl with the pure joy of living. And it is pleasant to record that his joy grew day by day.

For obvious reasons the wedding took place in a registry office, and it seemed that the dark gods smiled down upon the union, for there was a thick fog that lasted from dawn to sunset. The wedding-supper and the reception which followed were, of necessity, simple affairs. There was a wedding cake for those that could eat it: a beautiful, three-tier structure, covered with pink icing, and studded with what George hoped were glace cherries. He of course had invited no guests, for there was much that might have alarmed or embarrassed the uninitiated. Three ghouls in starched, white shrouds sat gnawing something that was best left undescribed. The bride and her family sipped a basic beverage from red goblets, and as the bridegroom was due for a turn, he snarled when asked to pass the salt. Then there was Uncle Deitmark, a vampire of the old school, who kept demanding a trussed-up victim, so that he could take his nourishment direct from the neck.

But finally the happy couple were allowed to depart, and Mummy and Father wept as they threw the traditional coffin nails after the departing hearse. "Ee, it were champion," Father exclaimed, wiping his eyes on the back of his hand. "Best blood-up I've seen for many a day. You did 'em proud, Mother."

"I believe in giving the young 'uns a good send-off," Mummy said. "Now they must open their own vein, as the saying goes."

Carola and George watched the moon come up over the church steeple, which was a little dangerous for it threw the cross into strong relief, but on that one night they would have defied the very Pope of Rome himself.

"We are no longer alone," Carola whispered. "We love and are loved, and that surely has transformed us from monsters into gods."

"If happiness can transform a tumbledown cottage into paradise," George said, running his as yet uncurved fingers through her hair, "then I guess we are gods."

But he forgot that every paradise must have its snake, and their particular serpent was disguised in the rotund shape of the Reverend John Cole. This worthy cleric had an allegorical nose for smelling out hypothetical evil, and it was not long before he was considering the inhabitants of the house by the churchyard with a speculative eye.

He called when George was out and invited Carola to join the young wives' altar dressing committee. She turned grey and begged to be excused. Mr. Cole then suggested she partake in a brief reading from holy scripture, and Carola shrank from the proffered Bible, even as a rabbit recoils from a hooded cobra. Then the Reverend John Cole accidentally dropped his crucifix on to her lap, and she screamed like one who is in great pain, before falling to the floor in a deathlike faint. And the holy minister departed with the great joy that comes to the sadist who knows he is only doing his duty.

Next day George met the Reverend Cole, who was hastening to the death bed of a sinful woman, and laid a not too gentle hand on the flabby arm.

"I understand you frightened my wife, when I was out yesterday."

The clergyman bared his teeth and, although George was now in the shape with which he had been born, they resembled two dogs preparing to fight.

"I'm wondering," the Reverend Cole said, "what kind of woman recoils from the good book and screams when the crucifix touches her."

"Well, it's like this," George tightened his grip on the black-clad arm, "we are both allergic to Bibles, crosses, and nosy parsons. I am apt to burn one, break two, and pulverise three. Am I getting through?"

"And I have a duty before God and man," John Cole said, looking at the retaining hand with marked distaste, "and that is to stamp evil whenever it be found. And may I add, with whatever means are at my disposal."

They parted in mutual hate, and George in his innocence decided to use fear as an offensive weapon, not realising that its wounds strengthen resistance more often than they weaken. One night, when the moon was full, turning the graveyard into a gothic wonderland, the Reverend John Cole met something that robbed him of speech for nigh on twelve hours. It walked on bent hindlegs, and had two very long arms which terminated in talons that seemed hungry for the ecclesiastical throat, and a nightmare face whose predominant feature was a long, slavering snout.

At the same time, Mrs. Cole, a very timid lady who had yet to learn of the protective virtues of two pieces of crossed wood, was trying so hard not to scream as a white-faced young woman advanced across the bedroom. The reaction of husband and wife was typical of their individual characters. The Reverend John Cole, after the initial cry, did not stop running until he was safely barricaded in the church with a processional cross jammed across the doorway. Mrs. Cole, being unable to scream, promptly fainted, and hence fared worse than her fleetfooted spouse. John Cole, after his run, was a little short of breath; Mary Cole, when she returned to consciousness, was a little short of blood.

Mr. Cole was an erratic man who often preached sermons guaranteed to raise the scalps of the most urbane congregation, if that is to say they took the trouble to listen. The tirade which was poured out from the pulpit on the Sunday after Mrs. Cole's loss and Mr. Cole's fright woke three slumbering worshippers, and caused a choirboy to swallow his chewing-gum.

"The devil has planted his emissaries in our midst," the vicar proclaimed. "Aye, do they dwell in the church precincts and do appear to the God-fearing in their bestial form."

The chewing-gum-bereft choirboy giggled, and Mr. Cole's wrath rose and erupted into admonishing words.

"Laugh not. I say to you of little faith, laugh not. For did I not come face to face—aye, but a few yards from where you now sit—with a fearsome beast that did drool and nuzzle, and I feared that my windpipe might soon lie upon my shirtfront. But, and this be the truth, which did turn my bowels to water, there was the certain knowledge that I was in the presence of a creature that is without precedence in Satan's hierarchy—the one—the only—the black angel of hell—the dreaded werewolf."

At least ten people in the congregation thought their vicar had at last turned the corner and become stark raving mad. Twenty more did not understand what he was talking about, and one old lady assumed she was listening to a brilliant interpretation of Revelation, chapter XIII, verses 1 to 3. The remainder of the congregation had not been listening, but noted the vicar was in fine fettle, roaring and pounding the pulpit with his customary gusto. His next disclosure suffered roughly the same reception.

"My dear wife—my helpmeet, who has walked by my side these past twenty years—was visited in her chamber by a female of the species . . ." Mr. Cole nodded bitterly. "A vampire, an unclean thing that has crept from its foul grave, and did take from my dear one, that which she could ill afford to lose . . ."

Ignorance, inattention, Mr. Cole's words fell on very stony ground and no one believed—save Willie Mitcham. Willie did believe in vampires, werewolves, and, in fact, also accepted the existence of banshees, demons, poltergeists, ghosts of every description, monsters of every shape and form, and the long wriggly thing, which, as everyone knows, has yet to be named. As Willie was only twelve years of age, he naturally revelled in his belief, and moreover made himself an expert on demonology. To his father's secret delectation and his mother's openly expressed horror, he had an entire cupboard filled with literature that dwelt on every aspect of the subject. He knew, for example, that the only sure way of getting a banshee off your back is to spit three times into an open grave, bow three times to the moon, then chant in a loud voice:

Go to the north, go to the south,
Go to the devil, but shut your mouth.
Scream not by day, or howl by night,
But gibber alone by candlelight.

He also knew, for had not the facts been advertised by printed page, television set, and cinema screen, that the only sure way of killing a vampire is to drive a sharp pointed object through its heart between the hours of sunrise and sunset. He was also joyfully aware of the fatal consequences that attend the arrival of a silver bullet in a werewolf's hairy chest. So it was that Willie listened to the Reverend John Cole with ears that heard and understood, and he wanted so desperately to shout out the simple and time-honoured cures, the withal, the ways and means, the full, glorious, and gory details. But his mother nudged him in the ribs and told him to stop fidgeting, so he could only sit and seethe with well-nigh uncontrollable impatience.

One bright morning in early March the total population of the graveyard cottage was increased by one. The newly risen sun peeped in through the neatly curtained windows and gazed down upon what, it is to be hoped, was the first baby werevamp. It was like all newly born infants, small, wrinkled, extremely ugly, and favoured its mother insofar as it had been born with two prominent eye-teeth. Instead of crying, it made a harsh hissing sound, not unlike that of an infant king-cobra, and was apt to bite anything that moved.

"Isn't he sweet?" Carola sighed, then waved a finger at her offspring, who promptly curled back an upper lip and made a hissing snarl. "Yes he is . . . he's a sweet 'ickle diddums . . . he's Mummy's 'ickle diddums . . ."

"I think he's going to be awfully clever," George stated after a while. "What with that broad forehead and those dark eyes, one can see there is a great potential for intelligence. He's got your mouth, darling."

"Not yet he hasn't," Carola retorted, "but he soon will have, if I'm not careful. I suppose he's in his humvamp period now; but when the moon is full, he'll have sweet little hairy talons, and a dinky-winky little tail."

Events proved her to be absolutely correct.

The Reverend John Cole allowed several weeks to pass before he made an official call on the young parents. During this time he reinforced his courage, of which it must be confessed he had an abundance; sought advice from his superiors, who were not at all helpful; and tried to convince anyone who would listen of the danger in their midst. His congregation shrank, people crossed the road whenever he came into view, and he was constantly badgered by a wretched little boy, who poured out a torrent of nauseating information. But at last the vicar was as ready for the fatal encounter as he ever would be, and so, armed with a crucifix, faith, and a small bottle of whisky, he went forth to do battle. From his bedroom window that overlooked the vicarage, Willie Mitcham watched the black figure as it trudged along the road. He flung the window open and shouted: "Yer daft coot. It's a full moon."

No one answered Mr. Cole's thunderous assault on the front door. This was not surprising, as Carola was paying

Mrs. Cole another visit, and George was chasing a very disturbed sheep across a stretch of open moorland. Baby had not yet reached the age when answering doors would be numbered among his accomplishments. At last the reverend gentleman opened the door and, after crossing himself with great fervour, entered the cottage.

He found himself in the living-room, a cosy little den with whitewashed walls, two ancient chairs, a folding table, and some very nice rugs on the floor. There was also a banked-up fire, and a beautiful old ceiling oil-lamp that George had cleverly adapted for electricity. Mr. Cole called out: "Anyone there?" and, receiving no answer, sank down into one of the chairs to wait. Presently, the chair being comfortable, the room warm, the clergyman felt his caution dissolve into a hazy atmosphere of well-being. His head nodded, his eyelids flickered, his mouth fell open and, in no time at all, a series of gentle snores filled the room with their even cadence.

It is right to say Mr. Cole fell asleep reluctantly, and while he slept he displayed a certain amount of dignity. But he awoke with a shriek and began to thresh about in a most undignified manner. There was a searing pain in his right ankle, and when he moved something soft and rather heavy flopped over his right foot and at the same time made a strange hissing sound. The vicar screamed again and kicked out with all his strength, and that which clung to his ankle went hurling across the room and landed on a rug near the window. It hissed, yelped; then turning over, began to crawl back towards the near prostrate clergyman. He tried to close his eyes, but they insisted on remaining open and so permitted him to see something that a person with a depraved sense of humour might have called a baby. A tiny, little white—oh, so white—face, which had two microscopic fangs jutting out over the lower lip. But for the rest it was very hairy; had two wee claws, and a proudly erect, minute tail, that was, at this particular moment in time lashing angrily from side to side. Its little hind legs acted as projectors and enabled the hair-covered torso to leap along at quite an amazing speed. There was also a smear of Mr. Cole's blood round the mouth; and the eyes held an expression that suggested the ecclesiastical fluid was appealing to the taste-buds, and their owner could hardly wait to get back to the fount of nourishment.

Mr. Cole released three long, drawn-out screams, then, remembering that legs have a decided and basic purpose, leaped for the door. It was truly an awe-inspiring sight to see a portly clergyman, who had more than reached the years of discretion, running between graves, leaping over tombstones, and sprinting along paths. Baby-werevamp sat on his hind legs and looked as wistfully as his visage permitted at the swiftly retreating cleric. After a while baby set up a prolonged howl, and thumped the floor with clenched claws. His distress was understandable. He had just seen a well-filled feeding bottle go running out of the door.

Willie Mitcham had at last got through. One of the stupid, blind, not to mention thick-headed adults had been finally shocked into seeing the light. When Willie found the Reverend John Cole entangled in a hawthorn bush, he also stumbled on a man who was willing to listen to advice from any source. He had also retreated from the frontiers of sanity, and was therefore in a position to be driven, rather than to command.

"I saw 'im." Willie was possibly the happiest boy in the world at that moment. "I saw 'im with his 'orrible fangs and he went leaping towards the moors."

Mr. Cole said, "Ah!" and began to count his fingers.

"And I saw 'er," Willie went on. "She went to your house and drifted up to the main bedroom window. Just like in the film *Mark of the Vampire.*"

"Destroy all evil," the Reverend Cole shouted. "Root it out. Cut into . . ."

"Its 'eart," Willie breathed. "The way to kill a vampire is drive a stake through its 'eart. And a werewolf must be shot with a silver bullet fired by 'im who had only thought about sin."

"From what authority do you quote this information?" the vicar demanded.

"Me 'orror comics," Willie explained. "They give all the details, and if you go and see the *Vampire of 'Ackney Wick,* you'll see a 'oly father cut off the vampire's 'ead and put a sprig of garlic in its mouth."

"Where are these documents?" the clergyman enquired.

Mr. and Mrs. Mitcham were surprised and perhaps a little alarmed when their small son conducted the vicar through the kitchen and, after a perfunctory "It's all right, Mum, parson wants to see me 'orror comics," led the frozen-faced clergyman upstairs to the attic.

It was there that Mr. Cole's education was completed. Assisted by lurid pictures and sensational text, he learned of the conception, habits, hobbies, and disposal procedures of vampires, werewolves, and other breathing or non-breathing creatures that had attended the same school.

"Where do we get . . . ?" he began.

"A tent peg and Mum's coal 'ammer will do fine." Willie was quick to give expert advice.

"But a silver bullet." The vicar shook his head. "I cannot believe there is a great demand . . ."

"Two of Grandad's silver collar studs melted down with a soldering iron, and a cartridge from Dad's old .22 rifle. Mr. Cole, please say we can do it. I promise never to miss Sunday school again, if you'll say we can do it."

The Reverend John Cole did not consider the problem very long. A bite from a baby werevamp is a great decision maker.

"Yes," he nodded, "we have been chosen. Let us gird up our loins, gather the sinews of battle, and go forth to destroy the evil ones."

"Cool."Willie nodded vigorously. "All that blood. Can I cut 'er 'ead off?"

If anyone had been taking the air at two o'clock next morning, they might have seen an interesting sight. A large clergyman, armed with a crucifix and a coal hammer, was creeping across the churchyard, followed by a small boy with a tent peg in one hand and a light hunting rifle in the other.

They came to the cottage and Mr. Cole first turned the handle, then pushed the door open with his crucifix. The room beyond was warm and cosy; firelight painted a dancing pattern on the ceiling, brass lamp twinkled and glittered like a suspended star, and it was as though a brightly designed nest had been carved out of the surrounding darkness. John Cole strode into the room like a black marble angel of doom and, raising his crucifix, bellowed, "I have come to drive out the iniquity, burn out the sin. For, thus saith the Lord, cursed be you who hanker after darkness."

There was a sigh, a whimper—maybe a hissing whimper. Carola was crouched in one corner, her face whiter than a slab of snow in moonlight, her eyes dark pools of terror, her lips deep, deep red, as they had been brought to life by a million blood-tinted kisses, and her hands were pale ghost-moths, beating out their life against the wall of intolerance. The vicar lowered his cross and the whimper grew up and became a cry of despair.

"Why?"

"Where is the foul babe that did bite my ankle?"

Carola's staring eyes never left the crucifix towering over her. "I took him . . . took him . . . to his grandmother."

"There is more of your kind? Are you legion? Has the devil's spawn been hatched?"

"We are on the verge of extinction."

The soul of the Reverend John Cole rejoiced when he saw the deep terror in the lovely eyes, and he tasted the fruits of true happiness when she shrieked. He bunched the front of her dress up between trembling fingers and jerked her first upright, then down across the table. She made a little hissing sound; an instinctive token of defiance, and for a moment the delicate ivory fangs were bared and nipped the clergyman's hand, but that was all. There was no savage fight for existence, no calling on the dark gods; just a token resistance, the shedding of a tiny dribble of blood, then complete surrender. She lay back across the table, her long, black hair brushing the floor, as though this were the inevitable conclusion from which she had been too long withheld. The vicar placed the tip of the tent peg over her heart, and taking the coal hammer from the overjoyed Willie, shouted the traditional words.

"Get thee to hell. Burn for ever and a day. May thy foul carcase be food for jackals, and thy blood drink for pariah dogs."

The first blow sent the tent peg in three or four inches, and the sound of a snapping rib grated on the clergyman's ear, so that for a moment he turned his head aside in revulsion. Then, as though alarmed lest his resolve weaken, he struck again, and the blood rose up in a scarlet fountain; a cascade of dancing rubies, each one reflecting the room with its starlike lamp, and the dripping, drenched face of a man with a raised coal hammer. The hammer, like the mailed hand of fate, fell again, and the ruby fountain sank low, then collapsed into a weakly gushing pool. Carola released her life in one long, drawn-out sigh, then became a black and white study in still life.

"You gotta cut 'er 'ead off," Willie screamed. "Ain't no good, unless you cut 'er 'ead off and put a sprig of garlic in 'er mouth."

But Mr. Cole had, at least temporarily, had a surfeit of blood. It matted his hair, clogged his eyes, salted his mouth, drenched his clothes from neck to waist, and transformed his hands into scarlet claws.

Willie was fumbling in his jacket pocket.

"I've got me mum's bread knife here, somewhere. Should go through 'er neck a treat."

The reverend gentleman wiped a film of red from his eyes and then daintily shook his fingers.

"Truly is it said a little child shall lead them. Had I been more mindful of the Lord's business, I would have brought me a tenon saw."

He was not more than half way through his appointed task, when the door was flung back and George entered. He was on the turn. He was either about to "become," or return to "as was." His silhouette filled the moonlit doorway, and he became still; a black menace that was no less dangerous because it did not move. Then he glided across the room, round the table and the Reverend John Cole retreated before him.

George gathered up the mutilated remains of his beloved, then raised agony-filled eyes.

"We loved—she and I. Surely, that should have forgiven us much. Death we would have welcomed—for what is death, but a glorious reward for having to live. But this . . ."

He pointed to the jutting tent peg, the half-severed head, then looked up questioningly at the clergyman. Then the Reverend John Cole took up his cross and, holding it before him, he called out in a voice that had been made harsh by the dust of centuries.

"I am Alpha and Omega, saith the Lord, and into the pit which is before the beginning and after the end shall ye be cast. For you and your kind are a stench and an abomination, and whatever evil is done unto you shall be deemed good in my sight."

The face of George Hardcastle became like an effigy carved from rock. Then it seemed to shimmer, the lines dissolved and ran one into the other; the hairline advanced, while the eyes retreated into deep sockets, and the jaw and nose merged and slithered into a long, pointed snout. The werewolf dropped the mangled remains of its mate and advanced upon her killer.

"Satanus Avaunt."

The Reverend Cole thrust his crucifix forward as though it were a weapon of offence, only to have it wrenched from his grasp and broken by a quick jerk of hair-covered wrists. The werewolf tossed the pieces to one side, then with a howl leaped forward and buried his long fangs into the vicar's shoulder.

The two locked figures—one representing good, the other evil—swayed back and forth in the lamplight, and there was no room in either hate-fear-filled brain for the image of one small boy, armed with a rifle. The sharp little cracking sound could barely be heard above the grunting, snarling battle that was being waged near the hanging brass lamp, but the result was soon apparent. The werewolf shrieked, before twisting round and staring at the exuberant Willie, as though in dumb reproach. Then it crashed to the floor. When the clergyman had recovered to look down, he saw the dead face of George Hardcastle, and had he been a little to the right of the sanity frontier, there might well have been terrible doubts.

"Are you going to finish cutting off 'er 'ead?" Willie enquired.

They put the Reverend John Cole in a quiet house surrounded by a beautiful garden. Willie Mitcham they placed in a home, as a juvenile court decided, in its wisdom, that he was in need of care and protection. The remains of George and Carola they buried in the churchyard and said some beautiful words over their graves.

It is a great pity they did not listen to Willie, who after all knew what he was talking about when it came to a certain subject.

One evening, when the moon was full, two gentlemen who were employed in the house surrounded by the beautiful garden, opened the door, behind which resided all that remained of the Reverend John Cole. They both entered the room and prepared to talk. They never did. One dropped dead from pure, cold terror, and the other achieved a state of insanity which had so far not been reached by one of his patients.

The Reverend John Cole had been bitten by a baby werevamp, nipped by a female vampire, and clawed and bitten by a full-blooded buck werewolf.

Only the good Lord above, and the bad one below, knew what he was.

AYLMER VANCE AND THE VAMPIRE

◆◆◆

ALICE AND CLAUDE ASKEW

Aylmer Vance had rooms in Dover Street, Piccadilly, and now that I had decided to follow in his footsteps and to accept him as my instructor in matters psychic, I found it convenient to lodge in the same house. Aylmer and I quickly became close friends, and he showed me how to develop that faculty of clairvoyance which I had possessed without being aware of it. And I may say at once that this particular faculty of mine proved of service on several important occasions.

At the same time I made myself useful to Vance in other ways, not the least of which was that of acting as recorder of his many strange adventures. For himself, he never cared much about publicity, and it was some time before I could persuade him, in the interests of science, to allow me to give any detailed account of his experiences to the world.

The incidents which I will now narrate occurred very soon after we had taken up our residence together, and while I was still, so to speak, a novice.

It was about ten o'clock in the morning that a visitor was announced. He sent up a card which bore upon it the name of Paul Davenant.

The name was familiar to me, and I wondered if this could be the same Mr. Davenant who was so well known for his polo playing and for his success as an amateur rider, especially over the hurdles. He was a young man of wealth and position, and I recollected that he had married, about a year ago, a girl who was reckoned the greatest beauty of the season. All the illustrated papers had given their portraits at the time, and I remember thinking what a remarkably handsome couple they made.

Mr. Davenant was ushered in, and at first I was uncertain as to whether this could be the individual whom I had in mind, so wan and pale and ill did he appear. A finely-built, upstanding man at the time of his marriage, he had now acquired a languid droop of the shoulders and a shuffling gait, while his face, especially about the lips, was bloodless to an alarming degree.

And yet it was the same man, for behind all this I could recognize the shadow of the good looks that had once distinguished Paul Davenant.

He took the chair which Aylmer offered him—after the usual preliminary civilities had been exchanged—and then glanced doubtfully in my direction. "I wish to consult you privately, Mr. Vance," he said. "The matter is of considerable importance to myself, and, if I may say so, of a somewhat delicate nature."

Of course I rose immediately to withdraw from the room, but Vance laid his hand upon my arm.

"If the matter is connected with research in my particular line, Mr. Davenant," he said, "if there is any investigation you wish me to take up on your behalf, I shall be glad if you will include Mr. Dexter in your confidence. Mr. Dexter assists me in my work. But, of course—"

"Oh, no," interrupted the other, "if that is the case, pray let Mr. Dexter remain. I think," he added, glancing at me with a friendly smile, "that you are an Oxford man, are you not, Mr. Dexter? It was before my time, but I have heard of your name in connection with the river. You rowed at Henley, unless I am very much mistaken."

I admitted the fact, with a pleasurable sensation of pride. I was very keen upon rowing in those days, and a man's prowess at school and college always remains dear to his heart.

After this we quickly became on friendly terms, and Paul Davenant proceeded to take Aylmer and myself into his confidence.

He began by calling attention to his personal appearance. "You would hardly recognize me for the same man I was a year ago," he said. "I've been losing flesh steadily for the last six months. I came up from Scotland about a week ago, to consult a London doctor. I've seen two—in fact, they've held a sort of consultation over me—but the result, I may say, is far from satisfactory. They don't seem to know what is really the matter with me."

"Anaemia—heart," suggested Vance. He was scrutinizing his visitor keenly, and yet without any particular appearance of doing so. "I believe it not infrequently happens that you athletes overdo yourselves—put too much strain upon the heart—"

"My heart is quite sound," responded Davenant. "Physically it is in perfect condition. The trouble seems to be that it hasn't enough blood to pump into my veins. The doctors wanted to know if I had met with an accident involving a great loss of blood—but I haven't. I've had no accident at all, and as for anaemia, well, I don't seem to show the ordinary symptoms of it. The inexplicable thing is that I've lost blood without knowing it, and apparently this has been going on for some time, for I've been getting steadily worse. It was almost imperceptible at first—not a sudden collapse, you understand, but a gradual failure of health."

"I wonder," remarked Vance slowly, "what induced you to consult me? For you know, of course, the direction in which I pursue my investigations. May I ask if you have reason to consider that your state of health is due to some cause which we may describe as super-physical?"

A slight colour came to Davenant's white cheeks.

"There are curious circumstances," he said in a low and earnest tone of voice. "I've been turning them over in my mind, trying to see light through them. I daresay it's all the sheerest folly—and I must tell you that I'm not in the least a superstitious sort of man. I don't mean to say that I'm absolutely incredulous, but I've never given thought to such things—I've led too active a life. But, as I have said, there are curious circumstances about my case, and that is why I decided upon consulting you."

"Will you tell me everything without reserve?" said Vance. I could see that he was interested. He was sitting up in his chair, his feet supported on a stool, his elbows on his knees, his chin in his hands—a favourite attitude of his. "Have you," he suggested, slowly, "any mark upon your body, anything that you might associate, however remotely, with your present weakness and ill-health?"

"It's a curious thing that you should ask me that question," returned Davenant, "because I have got a curious mark, a sort of scar, that I can't account for. But I showed it to the doctors, and they assured me that it could have nothing whatever to do with my condition. In any case, if it had, it was something altogether outside their experience. I think they imagined it to be nothing more than a birthmark, a sort of mole, for they asked me if I'd had it all my life. But that I can swear I haven't. I only noticed it for the first time about six months ago, when my health began to fail. But you can see for yourself."

He loosened his collar and bared his throat. Vance rose and made a careful scrutiny of the suspicious mark. It was situated a very little to the left of the central line, just above the clavicle, and, as Vance pointed out, directly over the big vessels of the throat. My friend called to me so that I might examine it, too. Whatever the opinion of the doctors may have been, Aylmer was obviously deeply interested.

And yet there was very little to show. The skin was quite intact, and there was no sign of inflammation. There were two red marks, about an inch apart, each of which was inclined to be crescent in shape. They were more visible than they might otherwise have been owing to the peculiar whiteness of Davenant's skin.

"It can't be anything of importance," said Davenant, with a slightly uneasy laugh. "I'm inclined to think the marks are dying away."

"Have you ever noticed them more inflamed than they are at present?" inquired Vance. "If so, was it at any special time?"

Davenant reflected. "Yes," he replied slowly, "there have been times, usually, I think perhaps invariably, when I wake up in the morning, that I've noticed them larger and more angry looking. And I've felt a slight sensation of pain—a tingling—oh, very slight, and I've never worried about it. Only now you suggest it to my mind, I believe that those same mornings I have felt particularly tired and done up—a sensation of lassitude absolutely unusual to me. And once, Mr. Vance, I remember quite distinctly that there was a stain of blood close to the mark. I didn't think anything of it at the time, and just wiped it away."

"I see." Aylmer Vance resumed his seat and invited his

visitor to do the same. "And now," he resumed, "you said, Mr. Davenant, that there are certain peculiar circumstances you wish to acquaint me with. Will you do so?"

And so Davenant readjusted his collar and proceeded to tell his story. I will tell it as far as I can, without any reference to the occasional interruptions of Vance and myself.

Paul Davenant, as I have said, was a man of wealth and position, and so, in every sense of the word, he was a suitable husband for Miss Jessica MacThane, the young lady who eventually became his wife. Before coming to the incidents attending his loss of health, he had a great deal to recount about Miss MacThane and her family history.

She was of Scottish descent, and although she had certain characteristic features of her race, she was not really Scotch in appearance. Hers was the beauty of the far South rather than that of the Highlands from which she had her origin. Names are not always suited to their owners, and Miss MacThane's was peculiarly inappropriate. She had, in fact, been christened Jessica in a sort of pathetic effort to counteract her obvious departure from normal type. There was a reason for this which we were soon to learn.

Miss MacThane was especially remarkable for her wonderful red hair, hair such as one hardly ever sees outside of Italy—not the Celtic red—and it was so long that it reached to her feet, and it had an extraordinary gloss upon it so that it seemed almost to have individual life of its own. Then she had just the complexion that one would expect with such hair, the purest ivory white, and not in the least marred by freckles, as is so often the case with red-haired girls. Her beauty was derived from an ancestress who had been brought to Scotland from some foreign shore—no one knew exactly whence.

Davenant fell in love with her almost at once and he had every reason to believe, in spite of her many admirers, that his love was returned. At this time he knew very little about her personal history. He was aware only that she was very wealthy in her own right, an orphan, and the last representative of a race that had once been famous in the annals of history—or rather infamous, for the MacThanes had distinguished themselves more by cruelty and lust of blood than by deeds of chivalry. A clan of turbulent robbers in the past, they had helped to add many a blood-stained page to the history of their country.

Jessica had lived with her father, who owned a house in London, until his death when she was about fifteen years of age. Her mother had died in Scotland when Jessica was still a tiny child. Mr. MacThane had been so affected by his wife's death that, with his little daughter, he had abandoned his Scotch estate altogether—or so it was believed—leaving it to the management of a bailiff—though, indeed, there was but little work for the bailiff to do, since there were practically no tenants left. Blackwick Castle had borne for many years a most unenviable reputation.

After the death of her father, Miss MacThane had gone to live with a certain Mrs. Meredith, who was a connection of her mother's—on her father's side she had not a single relation left. Jessica was absolutely the last of a clan once so extensive that intermarriage had been a tradition of the family, but for which the last two hundred years had been gradually dwindling to extinction.

Mrs. Meredith took Jessica into Society—which would never have been her privilege had Mr. MacThane lived, for he was a moody, self-absorbed man, and prematurely old—one who seemed worn down by the weight of a great grief.

Well, I have said that Paul Davenant quickly fell in love

with Jessica, and it was not long before he proposed for her hand. To his great surprise, for he had good reason to believe that she cared for him, he met with a refusal; nor would she give any explanation, though she burst into a flood of pitiful tears.

Bewildered and bitterly disappointed, he consulted Mrs. Meredith, with whom he happened to be on friendly terms, and from her he learnt that Jessica had already had several proposals, all from quite desirable men, but that one after another had been rejected.

Paul consoled himself with the reflection that perhaps Jessica did not love them, whereas he was quite sure that she cared for himself. Under these circumstances he determined to try again.

He did so, and with better result. Jessica admitted her love, but at the same time she repeated that she would not marry him. Love and marriage were not for her. Then, to his utter amazement, she declared that she had been born under a curse—a curse which, sooner or later, was bound to show itself in her, and which, moreover, must react cruelly, perhaps fatally, upon anyone with whom she linked her life. How could she allow a man she loved to take such a risk? Above all, since the evil was hereditary, there was one point upon which she had quite made up her mind: no child should ever call her mother—she must be the last of her race indeed.

Of course, Davenant was amazed and inclined to think that Jessica had got some absurd idea into her head which a little reasoning on his part would dispel. There was only one other possible explanation. Was it lunacy she was afraid of?

But Jessica shook her head. She did not know of any lunacy in her family. The ill was deeper, more subtle than that. And then she told him all that she knew.

The curse—she made use of that word for want of a better—was attached to the ancient race from which she had her origin. Her father had suffered from it, and his father and grandfather before him. All three had taken to themselves young wives who had died mysteriously, of some wasting disease, within a few years. Had they observed the ancient family tradition of intermarriage this might possibly not have happened, but in their case, since the family was so near extinction, this had not been possible.

For the curse—or whatever it was—did not kill those who bore the name of MacThane. It only rendered them a danger to others. It was as if they absorbed from the blood-soaked walls of their fatal castle a deadly taint which reacted terribly upon those with whom they were brought into contact, especially their nearest and dearest.

"Do you know what my father said we have it in us to become?" said Jessica with a shudder. "He used the word vampires. Paul, think of it—vampires—preying upon the life blood of others."

And then, when Davenant was inclined to laugh, she checked him. "No," she cried out, "it is not impossible. Think. We are a decadent race. From the earliest times our history has been marked by bloodshed and cruelty. The walls of Blackwick Castle are impregnated with evil—every stone could tell its tale of violence, pain, lust, and murder. What can one expect of those who have spent their lifetime between its walls?"

"But you have not done so," exclaimed Paul. "You have been spared that, Jessica. You were taken away after your mother died, and you have no recollection of Blackwick Castle, none at all. And you need never set foot in it again."

"I'm afraid the evil is in my blood," she replied sadly,

"although I am unconscious of it now. And as for not returning to Blackwick—I'm not sure I can help myself. At least, that is what my father warned me of. He said there is something there, some compelling force, that will call me to it in spite of myself. But, oh, I don't know—I don't know, and that is what makes it so difficult. If I could only believe that all this is nothing but an idle superstition, I might be happy again, for I have it in me to enjoy life, and I'm young, very young, but my father told me these things when he was on his death-bed." She added the last words in a low, awe-stricken tone.

Paul pressed her to tell him all that she knew, and eventually she revealed another fragment of family history which seemed to have some bearing upon the case. It dealt with her own astonishing likeness to that ancestress of a couple of hundred years ago, whose existence seemed to have presaged the gradual downfall of the clan of the MacThanes.

A certain Robert MacThane, departing from the traditions of his family, which demanded that he should not marry outside his clan, brought home a wife from foreign shores, a woman of wonderful beauty, who was possessed of glowing masses of red hair and a complexion of ivory whiteness—such as had more or less distinguished since then every female of the race born in the direct line.

It was not long before this woman came to be regarded in the neighbourhood as a witch. Queer stories were circulated abroad as to her doings, and the reputation of Blackwick Castle became worse than ever before.

And then one day she disappeared. Robert MacThane had been absent upon some business for twenty-four hours, and it was upon his return that he found her gone. The neighbourhood was searched, but without avail, and then Robert, who was a violent man and who had adored his foreign wife, called together certain of his tenants whom he suspected, rightly or wrongly, of foul play, and had them murdered in cold blood. Murder was easy in those days, yet such an outcry was raised that Robert had to take to flight, leaving his two children in the care of their nurse, and for a long while Blackwick Castle was without a master.

But its evil reputation persisted. It was said that Zaida, the witch, though dead, still made her presence felt. Many children of the tenantry and young people of the neighbourhood sickened and died—possibly of quite natural causes; but this did not prevent a mantle of terror settling upon the countryside, for it was said that Zaida had been seen—a pale woman clad in white—flitting about the cottages at night, and where she passed sickness and death were sure to supervene.

And from that time the fortune of the family gradually declined. Heir succeeded heir, but no sooner was he installed at Blackwick Castle than his nature, whatever it may previously have been, seemed to undergo a change. It was as if he absorbed into himself all the weight of evil that had stained his family name—as if he did, indeed, become a vampire, bringing blight upon any not directly connected with his own house.

And so, by degrees, Blackwick was deserted of its tenantry. The land around it was left uncultivated—the farms stood empty. This had persisted to the present day, for the superstitious peasantry still told their tales of the mysterious white woman who hovered about the neighbourhood, and whose appearance betokened death—and possibly worse than death.

And yet it seemed that the last representatives of the MacThanes could not desert their ancestral home. Riches they had, sufficient to live happily upon elsewhere, but, drawn by some power they could not contend against, they had preferred to spend their lives in the solitude of the now half-ruined castle, shunned by their neighbours, feared and execrated by the few tenants that still clung to their soil.

So it had been with Jessica's grandfather and great-grandfather. Each of them had married a young wife, and in each case their love story had been all too brief. The vampire spirit was still abroad, expressing itself—or so it seemed—through the living representatives of bygone generations of evil, and young blood had been demanded as the sacrifice.

And to them had succeeded Jessica's father. He had not profited by their example, but had followed directly in their footsteps. And the same fate had befallen the wife whom he passionately adored. She had died of pernicious anaemia—so the doctors said—but he had regarded himself as her murderer.

But, unlike his predecessors, he had torn himself away from Blackwick—and this for the sake of his child. Unknown to her, however, he had returned year after year, for there were times when the passionate longing for the gloomy, mysterious halls and corridors of the old castle, for the wild stretches of moorland, and the dark pine-woods, would come upon him too strongly to be resisted. And so he knew that for his daughter, as for himself, there was no escape, and he warned her, when the relief of death was at last granted to him, of what her fate must be.

This was the tale that Jessica told the man who wished to make her his wife, and he made light of it, as such a man would, regarding it all as foolish superstition, the delusion of a mind overwrought. And at last—perhaps it was not very difficult, for she loved him with all her heart and soul—he succeeded in inducing Jessica to think as he did, to banish morbid ideas, as he called them, from her brain, and to consent to marry him at an early date.

"I'll take any risk you like," he declared. "I'll even go and live at Blackwick if you should desire it. To think of you, my lovely Jessica, a vampire! Why, I never heard such nonsense in my life."

"Father said I'm very like Zaida, the witch," she protested, but he silenced her with a kiss.

And so they were married and spent their honeymoon abroad, and in the autumn Paul accepted an invitation to a house party in Scotland for the grouse shooting, a sport to which he was absolutely devoted, and Jessica agreed with him that there was no reason why he should forgo his pleasure.

Perhaps it was an unwise thing to do, to venture to Scotland, but by this time the young couple, more deeply in love with each other than ever, had got quite over their fears. Jessica was redolent with health and spirits, and more than once she declared that if they should be anywhere in the neighbourhood of Blackwick she would like to see the old castle out of curiosity, and just to show how absolutely she had got over the foolish terrors that used to assail her.

This seemed to Paul to be quite a wise plan, and so one day, since they were actually staying at no great distance, they motored over to Blackwick, and finding the bailiff, got him to show them over the castle.

It was a great castellated pile, grey with age, and in places falling into ruin. It stood on a steep hillside, with the rock of which it seemed to form part, and on one side of it there was a precipitous drop to a mountain stream a hundred feet below. The robber MacThanes of the old days could not have desired a better stronghold.

At the back, climbing up the mountainside were dark

pinewoods, from which, here and there, rugged crags protruded, and these were fantastically shaped, some like gigantic and misshapen human forms, which stood up as if they mounted guard over the castle and the narrow gorge, by which alone it could be approached.

This gorge was always full of weird, uncanny sounds. It might have been a storehouse for the wind, which, even on calm days, rushed up and down as if seeking an escape, and it moaned among the pines and whistled in the crags and shouted derisive laughter as it was tossed from side to side of the rocky heights. It was like the plaint of lost souls—that is the expression Davenant made use of—the plaint of lost souls.

The road, little more than a track now, passed through this gorge, and then, after skirting a small but deep lake, which hardly knew the light of the sun so shut in was it by overhanging trees, climbed the hill to the castle.

And the castle! Davenant used but a few words to describe it, yet somehow I could see the gloomy edifice in my mind's eye, and something of the lurking horror that it contained communicated itself to my brain. Perhaps my clairvoyant sense assisted me, for when he spoke of them I seemed already acquainted with the great stone halls, the long corridors, gloomy and cold even on the brightest and warmest of days, the dark, oak-panelled rooms, and the broad central staircase up which one of the early MacThanes had once led a dozen men on horseback in pursuit of a stag which had taken refuge within the precincts of the castle. There was the keep, too, its walls so thick that the ravages of time had made no impression upon them, and beneath the keep were dungeons which could tell terrible tales of ancient wrong and lingering pain.

Well, Mr. and Mrs. Davenant visited as much as the

bailiff could show them of this ill-omened edifice, and Paul, for his part, thought pleasantly of his own Derbyshire home, the fine Georgian mansion, replete with every modern comfort, where he proposed to settle with his wife. And so he received something of a shock when, as they drove away, she slipped her hand into his and whispered:

"Paul, you promised, didn't you, that you would refuse me nothing?"

She had been strangely silent till she spoke those words. Paul, slightly apprehensive, assured her that she only had to ask—but the speech did not come from his heart, for he guessed vaguely what she desired.

She wanted to go and live at the castle—oh, only for a little while, for she was sure she would soon tire of it. But the bailiff had told her that there were papers, documents, which she ought to examine, since the property was now hers—and, besides, she was interested in this home of her ancestors, and wanted to explore it more thoroughly. Oh, no, she wasn't in the least influenced by the old superstition—that wasn't the attraction—she had quite got over those silly ideas. Paul had cured her, and since he himself was so convinced that they were without foundation he ought not to mind granting her her whim.

This was a plausible argument, not easy to controvert. In the end Paul yielded, though it was not without a struggle. He suggested amendments. Let him at least have the place done up for her—that would take time; or let them postpone their visit till next year—in the summer—not move in just as the winter was upon them.

But Jessica did not want to delay longer than she could help, and she hated the idea of redecoration. Why, it would spoil the illusion of the old place, and, besides, it would be a waste of money since she only wished to remain there for a week or two. The Derbyshire house was not quite ready yet; they must allow time for the paper to dry on the walls.

And so, a week later, when their stay with their friends was concluded, they went to Blackwick, the bailiff having engaged a few raw servants and generally made things as comfortable for them as possible. Paul was worried and apprehensive, but he could not admit this to his wife after having so loudly proclaimed his theories on the subject of superstition.

They had been married three months at this time—nine had passed since then, and they had never left Blackwick for more than a few hours—till now Paul had come to London—alone.

"Over and over again," he declared, "my wife has begged me to go. With tears in her eyes, almost upon her knees, she has entreated me to leave her, but I have steadily refused unless she will accompany me. But that is the trouble, Mr. Vance, she cannot; there is something, some mysterious horror, that holds her there as surely as if she were bound with fetters. It holds her more strongly even than it held her father—we found out that he used to spend six months at least of every year at Blackwick—months when he pretended that he was travelling abroad. You see the spell—or whatever the accursed thing may be—never really relaxed its grip of him."

"Did you never attempt to take your wife away?" asked Vance.

"Yes, several times; but it was hopeless. She would become so ill as soon as we were beyond the limit of the estate that I invariably had to take her back. Once we got as far as Dorekirk—that is the nearest town, you know—and I thought I should be successful if only I could get through the night. But she escaped me; she climbed out of a window—she meant to go back on foot, at night, all those long miles. Then I have had doctors down; but it is I who wanted the doctors, not she. They have ordered me away, but I have refused to obey them till now."

"Is your wife changed at all—physically?" interrupted Vance.

Davenant reflected. "Changed," he said, "yes, but so subtly that I hardly know how to describe it. She is more beautiful than ever—and yet it isn't the same beauty, if you can understand me. I have spoken of her white complexion, well, one is more than ever conscious of it now, because her lips have become so red—they are almost like a splash of blood upon her face. And the upper one has a peculiar curve that I don't think it had before, and when she laughs she doesn't smile—do you know what I mean? Then her hair—it has lost its wonderful gloss. Of course, I know she is fretting about me; but that is so peculiar, too, for at times, as I have told you, she will implore me to go and leave her, and then perhaps only a few minutes later, she will wreathe her arms round my neck and say she cannot live without me. And I feel that there is a struggle going on within her, that she is only yielding slowly to the horrible influence—whatever it is—that she is herself when she begs me to go, but when she entreats me to stay—and it is then that her fascination is most intense—oh, I can't help remembering what she told me before we were married, and that word"—he lowered his voice—"the word 'vampire'—"

He passed his hand over his brow that was wet with perspiration. "But that's absurd, ridiculous," he muttered. "These fantastic beliefs have been exploded years ago. We live in the twentieth century."

A pause ensued, then Vance said quietly, "Mr.

Davenant, since you have taken me into your confidence, since you have found doctors of no avail, will you let me try to help you? I think I may be of some use—if it is not already too late. Should you agree, Mr. Dexter and I will accompany you, as you have suggested, to Blackwick Castle as early as possible—by tonight's mail North. Under ordinary circumstances I should tell you as you value your life, not to return—"

Davenant shook his head. "That is advice which I should never take," he declared. "I had already decided, under any circumstances, to travel North tonight. I am glad that you both will accompany me."

And so it was decided. We settled to meet at the station, and presently Paul Davenant took his departure. Any other details that remained to be told he would put us in possession of during the course of the journey.

"A curious and most interesting case," remarked Vance when we were alone. "What do you make of it, Dexter?"

"I suppose," I replied cautiously, "that there is such a thing as vampirism even in these days of advanced civilization? I can understand the evil influence that a very old person may have upon a young one if they happen to be in constant intercourse—the worn-out tissue sapping healthy vitality for their own support. And there are certain people—I could think of several myself—who seem to depress one and undermine one's energies, quite unconsciously, of course, but one feels somehow that vitality has passed from oneself to them. And in this case, when the force is centuries old, expressing itself, in some mysterious way, through Davenant's wife, is it not feasible to believe that he may be physically affected by it, even though the whole thing is sheerly mental?"

"You think, then," demanded Vance, "that it is sheerly

mental? Tell me, if that is so, how do you account for the marks on Davenant's throat?"

This was a question to which I found no reply, and though I pressed him for his views, Vance would not commit himself further just then.

Of our long journey to Scotland I need say nothing. We did not reach Blackwick Castle till late in the afternoon of the following day. The place was just as I had conceived it—as I have already described it. And a sense of gloom settled upon me as our car jolted us over the rough road that led through the Gorge of the Winds—a gloom that deepened when we penetrated into the vast cold hall of the castle.

Mrs. Davenant, who had been informed by telegram of our arrival, received us cordially. She knew nothing of our actual mission, regarding us merely as friends of her husband's. She was most solicitous on his behalf, but there was something strained about her tone, and it made me feel vaguely uneasy. The impression that I got was that the woman was impelled to everything that she said or did by some force outside herself—but, of course, this was a conclusion that the circumstances I was aware of might easily have conduced to. In every other aspect she was charming, and she had an extraordinary fascination of appearance and manner that made me readily understand the force of a remark made by Davenant during our journey.

"I want to live for Jessica's sake. Get her away from Blackwick, Vance, and I feel that all will be well. I'd go through hell to have her restored to me—as she was."

And now that I had seen Mrs. Davenant I realized what he meant by those last words. Her fascination was stronger than ever, but it was not a natural fascination—not that of a normal woman, such as she had been. It was the fascination of a Circe, of a witch, of an enchantress—and as such was irresistible.

We had a strong proof of the evil within her soon after our arrival. It was a test that Vance had quietly prepared. Davenant had mentioned that no flowers grew at Blackwick, and Vance declared that we must take some with us as a present for the lady of the house. He purchased a bouquet of pure white roses at the little town where we left the train, for the motorcar had been sent to meet us.

Soon after our arrival he presented these to Mrs. Davenant. She took them it seemed to me nervously, and hardly had her hand touched them before they fell to pieces, in a shower of crumpled petals, to the floor.

"We must act at once," said Vance to me when we were descending to dinner that night. "There must be no delay."

"What are you afraid of?" I whispered.

"Davenant has been absent a week," he replied grimly. "He is stronger than when he went away, but not strong enough to survive the loss of more blood. He must be protected. There is danger tonight."

"You mean from his wife?" I shuddered at the ghastliness of the suggestion.

"That is what time will show." Vance turned to me and added a few words with intense earnestness. "Mrs. Davenant, Dexter, is at present hovering between two conditions. The evil thing has not yet completely mastered her—you remember what Davenant said, how she would beg him to go away and the next moment entreat him to stay? She has made a struggle, but she is gradually succumbing, and this last week, spent here alone, has strengthened the evil. And that is what I have got to fight, Dexter—it is to be a contest of will, a contest that will go on silently till one or the other obtains the mastery. If you watch, you may see. Should a change show itself in Mrs. Davenant you will know that I have won."

Thus I knew the direction in which my friend proposed to act. It was to be a war of his will against the mysterious power that had laid its curse upon the house of MacThane. Mrs. Davenant must be released from the fatal charm that held her.

And I, knowing what was going on, was able to watch and understand. I realized that the silent contest had begun even while we ate dinner. Mrs. Davenant ate practically nothing and seemed ill at ease; she fidgeted in her chair, talked a great deal, and laughed—it was the laugh without a smile, as Davenant had described it. And as soon as she was able to she withdrew.

Later, as we sat in the drawing-room, I could feel the clash of wills. The air in the room felt electric and heavy, charged with tremendous but invisible forces. And outside, round the castle, the wind whistled and shrieked and moaned—it was as if all the dead and gone MacThanes, a grim army, had collected to fight the battle of their race.

And all this while we four in the drawing-room were sitting and talking the ordinary commonplaces of after-dinner conversation! That was the extraordinary part of it—Paul Davenant suspected nothing, and I, who knew, had to play my part. But I hardly took my eyes from Jessica's face. When would the change come, or was it, indeed, too late!

At last Davenant rose and remarked that he was tired and would go to bed. There was no need for Jessica to hurry. He would sleep that night in his dressing-room and did not want to be disturbed.

And it was at that moment, as his lips met hers in a goodnight kiss, as she wreathed her enchantress arms about him, careless of our presence, her eyes gleaming hungrily, that the change came.

It came with a fierce and threatening shriek of wind, and a rattling of the casement, as if the horde of ghosts without was about to break in upon us. A long, quivering sigh escaped from Jessica's lips, her arms fell from her husband's shoulders, and she drew back, swaying a little from side to side.

"Paul," she cried, and somehow the whole timbre of her voice was changed, "what a wretch I've been to bring you back to Blackwick, ill as you are! But we'll go away, dear; yes, I'll go, too. Oh, will you take me away—take me away tomorrow?" She spoke with an intense earnestness—unconscious all the time of what had been happening to her. Long shudders were convulsing her frame. "I don't know why I've wanted to stay here," she kept repeating. "I hate the place, really—it's evil—evil."

Having heard these words I exulted, for surely Vance's success was assured. But I was to learn that the danger was not yet past.

Husband and wife separated, each going to their own room. I noticed the grateful, if mystified glance that Davenant threw at Vance, vaguely aware, as he must have been, that my friend was somehow responsible for what had happened. It was settled that plans for departure were to be discussed on the morrow.

"I have succeeded," Vance said hurriedly, when we were alone, "but the change may be a transitory one. I must keep watch tonight. Go you to bed, Dexter, there is nothing that you can do."

I obeyed—though I would sooner have kept watch, too—watch against a danger of which I had no understanding. I went to my room, a gloomy and sparsely furnished apartment, but I knew that it was quite impossible for me to think of sleeping. And so, dressed as I was, I went and sat by the open window, for now the wind that had raged round the castle had died down to a low moaning in the pine trees—a whimpering of time-worn agony.

And it was as I sat thus that I became aware of a white figure that stole out from the castle by a door that I could not see, and, with hands clasped, ran swiftly across the terrace to the wood. I had but a momentary glance, but I felt convinced that the figure was that of Jessica Davenant.

And instinctively I knew that some great danger was imminent. It was, I think, the suggestion of despair conveyed by those clasped hands. At any rate, I did not hesitate. My window was some height from the ground, but the wall below was ivy-clad and afforded good foothold. The descent was quite easy. I achieved it, and was just in time to take up the pursuit in the right direction, which was into the thickness of the wood that clung to the slope of the hill.

I shall never forget that wild chase. There was just sufficient room to enable me to follow the rough path, which, luckily, since I had now lost sight of my quarry, was the only possible way that she could have taken; there were no intersecting tracks, and the wood was too thick on either side to permit of deviation.

And the wood seemed full of dreadful sounds—moaning and wailing and hideous laughter. The wind, of course, and the screaming of night birds—once I felt the fluttering of wings in close proximity to my face. But I could not rid myself of the thought that I, in my turn, was being pursued, that the forces of hell were combined against me.

The path came to an abrupt end on the border of the sombre lake that I have already mentioned. And now I realized that I was indeed only just in time, for before me, plunging knee deep in the water, I recognized the white-clad figure of the woman I had been pursuing. Hearing my footsteps, she turned her head, and then threw up her arms and screamed. Her red hair fell in heavy masses about her shoulders, and her face, as I saw it in that moment, was hardly human for the agony of remorse that it depicted.

"Go!" she screamed. "For God's sake let me die!"

But I was by her side almost as she spoke. She struggled with me—sought vainly to tear herself from my clasp—implored me, with panting breath, to let her drown.

"It's the only way to save him!" she gasped. "Don't you understand that I am a thing accursed? For it is I—I—who have sapped his life blood! I know it now, the truth has been revealed to me tonight! I am a vampire, without hope in this world or the next, so for his sake—for the sake of his unborn child—let me die—let me die!"

Was ever so terrible an appeal made? Yet I—what could I do? Gently I overcame her resistance and drew her back to shore. By the time I reached it she was lying a dead weight upon my arm. I laid her down upon a mossy bank, and, kneeling by her side, gazed intently into her face.

And then I knew that I had done well. For the face I looked upon was not that of Jessica the vampire, as I had seen it that afternoon, it was the face of Jessica, the woman whom Paul Davenant had loved.

And later Aylmer Vance had his tale to tell.

"I waited," he said, "until I knew that Davenant was asleep, and then I stole into his room to watch by his bedside. And presently she came, as I guessed she would, the vampire, the accursed thing that has preyed upon the souls of her kin, making them like to herself when they too have passed into Shadowland, and gathering sustenance for her horrid task from the blood of those who are alien to her race. Paul's body and Jessica's soul—it is for one and the other, Dexter, that we have fought."

"You mean," I hesitated, "Zaida the witch?"

"Even so," he agreed. "Hers is the evil spirit that has fallen like a blight upon the house of MacThane. But now I think she may be exorcized for ever."

"Tell me."

"She came to Paul Davenant last night, as she must have done before, in the guise of his wife. You know that Jessica bears a strong resemblance to her ancestress. He opened his arms, but she was foiled of her prey, for I had taken my precautions; I had placed that upon Davenant's breast while he slept which robbed the vampire of her power of ill. She sped wailing from the room—a shadow—she who a minute before had looked at him with Jessica's eyes and spoken to him with Jessica's voice. Her red lips were Jessica's lips, and they were close to his when his eyes were opened and he saw her as she was—a hideous phantom of the corruption of the ages. And so the spell was removed, and she fled away to the place whence she had come—"

He paused. "And now?" I inquired.

"Blackwick Castle must be razed to the ground," he replied. "That is the only way. Every stone of it, every brick, must be ground to powder and burnt with fire, for therein is the cause of all the evil. Davenant has consented."

"And Mrs. Davenant?"

"I think," Vance answered cautiously, "that all may be well with her. The curse will be removed with the destruction of the castle. She has not—thanks to you—

perished under its influence. She was less guilty than she imagined—herself preyed upon rather than preying. But can't you understand her remorse when she realized, as she was bound to realize, the part she had played? And the knowledge of the child to come—its fatal inheritance—"

"I understand," I muttered with a shudder. And then, under my breath, I whispered, "Thank God!"

THE DRIFTING SNOW

♦♦♦

AUGUST DERLETH

Aunt Mary's advancing footsteps halted suddenly, short of the table, and Clodetta turned to see what was keeping her. She was standing very rigidly, her eyes fixed upon the French windows just opposite the door through which she had entered, her cane held stiffly before her.

Clodetta shot a quick glance across the table toward her husband, whose attention had also been drawn to his aunt; his face vouchsafed her nothing. She turned again to find that the old lady had transferred her gaze to her, regarding her stonily and in silence. Clodetta felt uncomfortable.

"Who withdrew the curtains from the west windows?"

Clodetta flushed, remembering. "I did, Aunt. I'm sorry. I forgot about your not wanting them drawn away."

The old lady made an odd, grunting sound, shifting her gaze once again to the French windows. She made a barely perceptible movement, and Lisa ran forward from the shadow of the hall, where she had been regarding the two at table with stern disapproval. The servant went directly to the west windows and drew the curtains.

Aunt Mary came slowly to the table and took her place at its head. She put her cane against the side of her chair, pulled at the chain around her neck so that her lorgnette lay in her lap, and looked from Clodetta to her nephew, Ernest.

Then she fixed her gaze on the empty chair at the foot of the table, and spoke without seeming to see the two beside her.

"I told both of you that none of the curtains over the west windows was to be withdrawn after sundown, and you must have noticed that none of those windows has been for one instant uncovered at night. I took especial carc to put you in rooms facing east, and the sitting room is also in the east."

"I'm sure Clodetta didn't mean to go against your wishes, Aunt Mary," said Ernest abruptly.

"No, of course not, Aunt."

The old lady raised her eyebrows, and went on impassively. "I didn't think it wise to explain why I made such a request. I'm not going to explain. But I do want to say that there is a very definite danger in drawing away the curtains. Ernest has heard that before, but you, Clodetta, have not."

Clodetta shot a startled glance at her husband. The old lady caught it, and said, "It's all very well to believe that my mind's wandering or that I'm getting eccentric, but I shouldn't advise you to be satisfied with that."

A young man came suddenly into the room and made for the seat at the foot of the table, into which he flung himself with an almost inaudible greeting to the other three.

"Late again, Henry," said the old lady.

Henry mumbled something and began hurriedly to eat. The old lady sighed, and began presently to eat also, whereupon Clodetta and Ernest did likewise. The old servant, who had continued to linger behind Aunt Mary's chair, now withdrew, not without a scornful glance at Henry.

Clodetta looked up after a while and ventured to speak.

"You aren't as isolated as I thought you might be up here, Aunt Mary."

"We aren't, my dear, what with telephones and cars and all. But only twenty years ago it was quite a different thing, I can tell you." She smiled reminiscently and looked at Ernest. "Your grandfather was living then, and many's the time he was snowbound with no way to let anybody know."

"Down in Chicago, when they speak of 'up north' or the 'Wisconsin woods' it seems very far away," said Clodetta.

"Well, it *is* far away," put in Henry, abruptly. "And, Aunt, I hope you've made some provision in case we're locked in here for a day or two. It looks like snow outside, and the radio says a blizzard's coming."

The old lady grunted and looked at him. "Ha, Henry—you're overly concerned, it seems to me. I'm afraid you've been regretting this trip ever since you set foot in my house. If you're worrying about a snowstorm, I can have Sam drive you down to Wausau, and you can be in Chicago tomorrow."

"Of course not."

Silence fell, and presently the old lady called gently, "Lisa," and the servant came into the room to help her from her chair, though, as Clodetta had previously said to her husband, "She didn't need help."

From the doorway, Aunt Mary bade them all goodnight, looking impressively formidable with her cane in one hand and her unopened lorgnette in the other, and vanished into the dusk of the hall, from which her receding footsteps sounded together with those of the servant, who was seldom seen away from her. These two were alone in the house most of the time, and only very brief periods when the old lady had up her nephew Ernest, "dear John's boy," or Henry, of whose father the old lady never spoke, helped to relieve the pleasant somnolence of their quiet lives. Sam, who usually slept in the garage, did not count.

Clodetta looked nervously at her husband, but it was Henry who said what was uppermost in their thoughts.

"I think she's losing her mind," he declared matter-of-factly. Cutting off Clodetta's protest on her lips, he got up and went into the sitting room, from which came presently the strains of music from the radio.

Clodetta fingered her spoon idly and finally said, "I do think she is a little queer, Ernest."

Ernest smiled tolerantly. "No, I don't think so. I've an idea why she keeps the west windows covered. My grandfather died out there—he was overcome by the cold one night, and froze on the slope of the hill. I don't rightly know how it happened—I was away at the time. I suppose she doesn't like to be reminded of it."

"But where's the danger she spoke of, then?"

He shrugged. "Perhaps it lies in her—she might be affected and affect us in turn." He paused for an instant, and finally added, "I suppose she *does* seem a little strange to you—but she was like that as long as I can remember; next time you come, you'll be used to it."

Clodetta looked at her husband for a moment before replying. At last she said, "I don't think I like the house, Ernest."

"Oh, nonsense, darling." He started to get up, but Clodetta stopped him.

"Listen, Ernest. I remembered perfectly well Aunt Mary's not wanting those curtains drawn away—but I just felt I had to do it. I didn't want to, but—*something made me do it.*" Her voice was unsteady.

"Why, Clodetta," he said, faintly alarmed. "Why didn't you tell me before?"

She shrugged. "Aunt Mary might have thought I'd gone wool-gathering."

"Well, it's nothing serious, but you've let it bother you a little and that isn't good for you. Forget it; think of something else. Come and listen to the radio."

They rose and moved toward the sitting room together. At the door Henry met them. He stepped aside a little, saying, "I might have known we'd be marooned up here," and adding, as Clodetta began to protest, "We're going to be all right. There's a wind coming up and it's beginning to snow, and I know what that means." He passed them and went into the deserted dining room, where he stood a moment looking at the too-long table. Then he turned aside and went over to the French windows, from which he drew away the curtains and stood there peering out into the darkness. Ernest saw him standing at the window, and protested from the sitting room.

"Aunt Mary doesn't like those windows uncovered, Henry."

Henry half turned and replied, "Well, *she* may think it's dangerous, but I can risk it."

Clodetta, who had been staring beyond Henry into the night through the French windows, said suddenly, "Why, there's someone out there!"

Henry looked quickly through the glass and replied, "No, that's the snow; it's coming down heavily, and the wind's drifting it this way and that." He dropped the curtains and came away from the windows.

Clodetta said uncertainly, "Why, I could have sworn I saw someone out there, walking past the window."

"I suppose it does look that way from here," offered Henry, who had come back into the sitting room. "But personally, I think you've let Aunt Mary's eccentricities impress you too much."

Ernest made an impatient gesture at this, and Clodetta did not answer. Henry sat down before the radio and began to move the dial slowly. Ernest had found himself a book, and was becoming interested, but Clodetta continued to sit with her eyes fixed upon the still slowly-moving curtains cutting off the French windows. Presently she got up and left the room, going down the long hall into the east wing, where she tapped gently upon Aunt Mary's door.

"Come in," called the old lady.

Clodetta opened the door and stepped into the room where Aunt Mary sat in her dressing robe, her dignity, in the shape of her lorgnette and cane, resting respectively on her bureau and in the corner. She looked surprisingly benign, as Clodetta at once confessed.

"Ha, thought I was an ogre in disguise, did you?" said the old lady, smiling in spite of herself. "I'm really not, you see, but I am a sort of bogey about the west windows, as you have seen."

"I wanted to tell you something about those windows, Aunt Mary," said Clodetta. She stopped suddenly. The expression on the old lady's face had given way to a curiously dismaying one. It was not anger, not distaste—it was a lurking suspense. Why, the old lady was afraid!

"What?" she asked Clodetta shortly.

"I was looking out—just for a moment or so—and I thought I saw someone out there."

"Of course, you didn't, Clodetta. Your imagination, perhaps, or the drifting snow."

"My imagination? Maybe. But there was no wind to drift the snow, though one has come up since."

"I've often been fooled that way, my dear. Sometimes I've gone out in the morning to look for footprints—there weren't any, ever. We're pretty far away from civilization in a snowstorm, despite our telephones and radios. Our nearest neighbor is at the foot of the long, sloping rise—over three miles away—and all wooded land between. There's no highway nearer than that."

"It was so clear, I could have sworn to it."

"Do you want to go out in the morning and look?" asked the old lady shortly.

"Of course not."

"Then you didn't see anything."

It was half-question, half-demand. Clodetta said, "Oh, Aunt Mary, you're making an issue of it now."

"Did you or didn't you in your own mind see anything, Clodetta?"

"I guess I didn't, Aunt Mary."

"Very well. And now do you think we might talk about something more pleasant?"

"Why, I'm sure—I'm sorry, Aunt. I didn't know that Ernest's grandfather had died out there."

"Ha, he's told you that, has he? Well?"

"Yes, he said that was why you didn't like the slope after sunset—that you didn't like to be reminded of his death."

The old lady looked at Clodetta impassively.

"Perhaps he'll never know how nearly right he was."

"What do you mean, Aunt Mary?"

"Nothing for you to know, my dear." She smiled again, her sternness dropping from her. "And now I think you'd better go, Clodetta; I'm tired."

Clodetta rose obediently and made for the door, where the old lady stopped her. "How's the weather?"

"It's snowing—hard, Henry says—and blowing."

The old lady's face showed her distaste at the news. "I don't like to hear that, not at all. Suppose someone should look down that slope tonight?" She was speaking to herself, having forgotten Clodetta at the door. Seeing her again abruptly, she said, "But you don't know, Clodetta. Goodnight."

Clodetta stood with her back against the closed door, wondering what the old lady could have meant. *But you don't know, Clodetta.* That was curious. For a moment or two the old lady had completely forgotten her.

She moved away from the door, and came upon Ernest just turning into the east wing.

"Oh, there you are," he said. "I wondered where you had gone."

"I was talking a bit with Aunt Mary."

"Henry's been at the west windows again—and now *he* thinks there's someone out there."

Clodetta stopped short. "Does he really think so?"

Ernest nodded gravely. "But the snow's drifting frightfully, and I can imagine how that suggestion of yours worked on his mind."

Clodetta turned and went back along the hall. "I'm going to tell Aunt Mary."

He started to protest, but to no avail, for she was already tapping on the old lady's door, and indeed opening the door and entering the room before he could frame an adequate protest.

"Aunt Mary," she said, "I didn't want to disturb you again, but Henry's been at the French windows in the dining room, and he says he's seen someone out there."

The effect on the old lady was magical. "He's seen them!" she exclaimed. Then she was on her feet, coming rapidly over to Clodetta. "How long ago?" she demanded, seizing her almost roughly by the arms. "Tell me, quickly. How long ago did he see them?"

Clodetta's amazement kept her silent for a moment,

but at last she spoke, feeling the old lady's keen eyes staring at her. "It was some time ago, Aunt Mary, after supper."

The old lady's hands relaxed, and with it her tension. "Oh," she said, and turned and went back slowly to her chair, taking her cane from the corner where she had put it for the night.

"Then there *is* someone out there?" challenged Clodetta, when the old lady had reached her chair.

For a long time, it seemed to Clodetta, there was no answer. Then presently, the old lady began to nod gently, and a barely audible "yes" escaped her lips.

"Then we had better take them in, Aunt Mary."

The old lady looked at Clodetta earnestly for a moment; then she replied, her voice firm and low, her eyes fixed upon the wall beyond. "We can't take them in, Clodetta—because they're not alive."

At once Henry's words came flashing into Clodetta's memory—"She's losing her mind"—and her involuntary start betrayed her thought.

"I'm afraid I'm not mad, my dear—I hoped at first I might be, but I wasn't. I'm not, now. There was only one of them out there at first—the girl; Father is the other. Quite long ago, when I was young, my father did something which he regretted all his days. He had a too strong temper, and it maddened him. One night, he found out that one of my brothers—Henry's father—had been very familiar with one of the servants, a very pretty girl, older than I was. He thought she was to blame, though she wasn't, and he didn't find it out until too late. He drove her from the house, then and there. Winter had not yet set in, but it was quite cold, and she had some five miles to go to her home. We begged Father not to send her away—

though we didn't know what was wrong then—but he paid no attention to us. The girl had to go.

"Not long after she had gone, a biting wind came up, and close upon it a fierce storm. Father had already repented his hasty action, and sent some of the men to look for the girl. They didn't find her, but in the morning she was found frozen to death on the long slope of the hill to the west."

The old lady sighed, paused a moment, and went on. "Years later—she came back. She came in a snowstorm, as she went; but she had become a vampire. We all saw her. We were at the supper table, and Father saw her first. The boys had already gone upstairs, and Father and the two of us girls, my sister and I, did not recognize her. She was just a dim shape floundering around in the drifting snow beyond the French windows. Father ran out to her, calling to us to send the boys after him. We never saw him alive again. In the morning we found him in the same spot where years before the girl had been found. He, too, had died of exposure.

"Then, a few years after—she returned with the snow, and she brought him along; he, too, had become a vampire. They stayed until the last snow, always trying to lure someone out there. After that, I knew, and had the windows covered during the winter nights, from sunset to dawn, because they never went beyond the west slope.

"Now you know, Clodetta."

Whatever Clodetta was going to say was cut short by running footsteps in the hall, a hasty rap, and Ernest's head appearing suddenly in the open doorway.

"Come on, you two," he said, almost gaily, "there *are* people out on the west slope—a girl and an old man—and Henry's gone out to fetch them in!"

Then, triumphant, he was off. Clodetta came to her feet, but the old lady was before her, passing her and almost running down the hall, calling loudly for Lisa, who presently appeared in nightcap and gown from her room.

"Call Sam, Lisa," said the old lady, "and send him to me in the dining room."

She ran on into the dining room, Clodetta close on her heels. The French windows were open, and Ernest stood on the snow-covered terrace beyond, calling his cousin. The old lady went directly over to him, even striding into the snow to his side, though the wind drove the snow against her with great force. The wooded western slope was lost in a snow-fog; the nearest trees were barely discernible.

"Where could they have gone?" Ernest said, turning to the old lady, whom he had thought to be Clodetta. Then, seeing that it was the old lady, he said, "Why, Aunt Mary—and so little on, too! You'll catch your death of cold."

"Never mind, Ernest," said the old lady. "I'm all right. I've had Sam get up to help you look for Henry—but I'm afraid you won't find him."

"He can't be far; he just now went out."

"He went before you saw where; he's far enough gone."

Sam came running into the blowing snow from the dining room, muffled in a greatcoat. He was considerably older than Ernest, almost the old lady's age. He shot a questioning glance at her and asked, "Have they come again?"

Aunt Mary nodded. "You'll have to look for Henry. Ernest will help you. And remember, don't separate. And don't go far from the house."

Clodetta came with Ernest's overcoat, and together the two women stood there, watching them until they were swallowed up in the wall of driven snow. Then they turned slowly, and went back into the house.

The old lady sank into a chair facing the windows. She was pale and drawn, and looked, as Clodetta said afterward, "as if she'd fallen together." For a long time she said nothing. Then, with a gentle little sigh, she turned to Clodetta and spoke.

"Now there'll be three of them out there."

Then, so suddenly that no one knew how it happened, Ernest and Sam appeared beyond the windows, and between them they dragged Henry. The old lady flew to open the windows, and the three of them, cloaked in snow, came into the room.

"We found him—but the cold's hit him pretty hard, I'm afraid," said Ernest.

The old lady sent Lisa for cold water, and Ernest ran to get himself other clothes. Clodetta went with him, and in their rooms told him what the old lady had related to her.

Ernest laughed. "I think you believed that, didn't you, Clodetta? Sam and Lisa do, I know, because Sam told me the story long ago. I think the shock of Grandfather's death was too much for all three of them."

"But the story of the girl, and then—"

"That part's true, I'm afraid. A nasty story, but it did happen."

"But those people Henry and I saw!" protested Clodetta weakly.

Ernest stood without movement. "That's so," he said, "I saw them, too. Then they're out there yet, and we'll have to find them!" He took up his overcoat again, and went from the room, Clodetta protesting in a shrill unnatural voice. The old lady met him at the door of the dining room, having overheard Clodetta pleading with him.

"No, Ernest—you can't go out there again," she said. "There's no one there."

He pushed gently into the room and called to Sam. "Coming, Sam? There's still two of them out there—we almost forgot them."

Sam looked at him strangely. "What do you mean?" he demanded roughly. He looked challengingly at the old lady, who shook her head.

"The girl and the old man, Sam. We've got to get them, too."

"Oh, *them*," said Sam. "They're dead!"

"Then I'll go out alone," said Ernest.

Henry came to his feet suddenly, looking dazed. He walked forward a few steps, his eyes travelling from one to the other of them, yet apparently not seeing them. He began to speak abruptly, in an unnatural, childlike voice.

"The snow," he murmured, *"the snow—the beautiful hands, so little, so lovely—her beautiful hands—and the snow, the beautiful, lovely snow, drifting and falling around her . . ."*

He turned slowly and looked toward the French windows, the others following his gaze. Beyond was a wall of white, where the snow was drifting against the house. For a moment Henry stood quietly watching, then suddenly a white figure came forward from the snow—a young girl, cloaked in long snow-whips, her glistening eyes strangely fascinating.

The old lady flung herself forward, her arms outstretched to cling to Henry, but she was too late. Henry had run toward the windows, had opened them, and even as Clodetta cried out, had vanished into the wall of snow beyond.

Then Ernest ran forward, but the old lady threw her

arms around him and held him tightly, murmuring, "You shall not go! Henry is gone beyond our help!"

Clodetta came to help her, and Sam stood menacingly at the French windows, now closed against the wind and the sinister snow. So they held him, and would not let him go.

"And tomorrow," said the old lady in a harsh whisper, "we must go to their graves and stake them down. We should have gone before."

In the morning they found Henry's body crouched against the bole of an ancient oak, where the two others had been found years before. There were almost obliterated marks of where something had dragged him, a long, uneven swath in the snow, and yet no footprints, only strange, hollowed places along the way, as if the wind had whirled the snow away, and only the wind.

But on his skin were signs of the snow vampire—the delicate small prints of a young girl's hands.

Permissions Acknowledgments

◆◆◆

Clive Barker: "Human Remains" by Clive Barker, copyright © 1984 by Clive Barker. Originally published in *Books of Blood, Vol. 3* (London: Sphere, 1984). Reprinted by permission of the author.

R. Chetwynd-Hayes: "The Werewolf and the Vampire" by R. Chetwynd-Hayes, copyright © 1975 by R. Chetwynd-Hayes. Originally published in *The Monster Club* (New English Library, 1975). Reprinted by permission of the Dorian Literary Agency, acting on behalf of the author's estate, Linda Smith.

Frederick Cowles: "Princess of Darkness" by Frederick Cowles, copyright © 1993 by Michael W. Cowles. Originally published in *Fear Walks the Night* (London: Ghost Story Press, 1993). Reprinted by permission of Michael W. Cowles.

August Derleth: "The Drifting Snow" by August Derleth, copyright © 1948 by August Derleth, copyright renewed 1976 by April R. Derleth and Walden W. Derleth. Originally published in *Weird Tales*, February 1939. Reprinted by permission of April R. Derleth for Arkham House Publishers Inc.

Gardner Dozois and Jack Dann: "Down Among the Dead Men" by Gardner Dozois with Jack Dann. Copyright © 1982 by Gardner Dozois and Jack Dann. Originally published in *Oui*, July 1982. Reprinted by permission of Gardner Dozois.

Richard Laymon: "Special" by Richard Laymon, copyright © 1991 by Richard Laymon. Originally published in *Under the Fang*, edited by Robert R. McCammon (New York: Pocket Books, 1991). Reprinted by permission of Ann Laymon.

Fritz Leiber: "The Girl with the Hungry Eyes" by Fritz Leiber, copyright © 1949 by Fritz Leiber, copyright renewed. Originally published in *The Girl with the Hungry Eyes*, edited by Donald Wollheim (New York: Avon, 1949). Reprinted by permission of the Estate of Fritz Leiber.

Brian Lumley: "Necros" by Brian Lumley, copyright © 1998 by Brian Lumley. Originally published in *The Second Book of After Midnight Stories*, edited by Amy Myers (William Kimber, 1986). Reprinted by permission of Brian Lumley.

Richard Matheson: "Drink My Red Blood" by Richard Matheson, copyright © 1951, copyright renewed 1979 by Richard Matheson. Originally published in *Imagination*, April 1951. Reprinted by permission of Don Congdon Associates, Inc.

Anne Rice: "The Master of Rampling Gate" by Anne Rice, copyright © 1984 by Anne O'Brien Rice. Originally published in *Redbook*, February 1984. Reprinted by permission of Anne Rice.

David J. Schow: "A Week in the Unlife" by David J. Schow, copyright © 1991 by David J. Schow. Originally published in *A Whisper of Blood*, edited by Ellen Datlow (New York: William Morrow & Co., 1991). Reprinted by permission of David J. Schow.

ALSO EDITED BY
OTTO PENZLER

THE VAMPIRE ARCHIVES

The Most Complete Volume of Vampire Tales Ever Published

The Vampire Archives is the biggest, hungriest, undeadliest collection of vampire stories, as well as the most comprehensive bibliography of vampire fiction ever assembled. Whether imagined by Bram Stoker or Anne Rice, vampires are part of the human lexicon and as old as blood itself. They are your neighbors, your friends, and they are always lurking. Now Otto Penzler has compiled the darkest, the scariest, and by far the most evil collection of vampire stories ever. With over eighty stories, including the works of Stephen King and D. H. Lawrence, alongside Lord Byron and Tanith Lee, not to mention Edgar Allan Poe and Harlan Ellison, it will drive a stake through the heart of any other collection out there.

Fiction/978-0-307-47389-9

ALSO AVAILABLE IN MASS-MARKET VOLUMES:

BLOODSUCKERS

The Vampire Archives, Volume 1

Including stories by Stephen King, Dan Simmons, and Bram Stoker

Fiction/978-0-307-74184-4

COFFINS

The Vampire Archives, Volume 3

Including stories by Harlan Ellison, Robert Bloch, and Edgar Allan Poe

Fiction/978-0-307-74223-0

Forthcoming from Vintage Books in Fall 2010 . . .

THE BLACK LIZARD BIG BOOK OF PULPS

The Best Crime Stories from the Pulps During Their Golden Age—The '20s, '30s & '40s

Weighing in at over a thousand pages, containing more than fifty stories and two novels, this book is big baby, bigger and more powerful than a freight train—a bullet couldn't pass through it. Here are the best stories and every major writer who ever appeared in celebrated pulps like *Black Mask*, *Dime Detective*, *Detective Fiction Weekly*, and more. These are the classic tales that created the genre and gave birth to hard-hitting detectives who smoke criminals like cheap cigars; sultry dames whose looks are as lethal as a dagger to the chest; and gin-soaked hideouts where conversations are just preludes to murder. This is crime fiction at its gritty best.

Crime Fiction/978-0-307-28048-0

THE BLACK LIZARD BIG BOOK OF *BLACK MASK* STORIES

An unstoppable anthology of crime stories culled from *Black Mask*, the magazine where the first hardboiled detective story, which was written by Carroll John Daly, appeared. It was the slum in which Dashiell Hammett, Raymond Chandler, Horace McCoy, Cornell Woolrich, John D. MacDonald all got their start. It was the home of stories with titles like "Murder *Is* Bad Luck," "Ten Carats of Lead," "Diamonds Mean Death," and "Drop Dead Twice." Also here is *The Maltese Falcon* as it originally appeared in the magazine. Delivered in the same trademark package as the New York Times bestselling *The Black Lizard Big Book of Pulps*, crime writing gets no better than this.

Crime Fiction/978-0-307-45543-7

Forthcoming from Vintage Books in Fall 2010 . . .

AGENTS OF TREACHERY

Never Before Published Spy Fiction from Today's Most Exciting Writers

For the first time ever, legendary editor Otto Penzler has handpicked some of the most respected and best-selling thriller writers working today for a riveting collection of spy fiction. From first to last, this stellar collection signals mission accomplished. Featuring: Lee Child with an incredible look at the formation of a special ops team; James Grady writing about an Arab undercover FBI agent with an active cell; Joseph Finder riffing on a Boston architect who's convinced that his Persian neighbors are up to no good; John Lawton concocting a Len Deighton-esque story about British intelligence; Stephen Hunter thrilling us with a tale about a WWII brigade; and much more.

Spy Fiction/978-0-307-47751-4